A LITTLE COMPLICATED

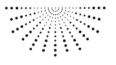

KELSIE RAE

TWISTY PINES PUBLISHING, LLC

A Little Complicated
Cover Art by Cover My Wagon Dragon Art
Editing by Wickedcoolflight Editing Services
Proofreading by Marjorie Lord
Published by Twisty Pines Publishing, LLC
November 2023 Edition
Published in the United States of America

To all the girls who love a good cry and the founders of Kleenex.
You're welcome.

DISCLAIMER

This book contains heavy themes.
For a specific list, go to
https://authorkelsierae.com/alc-trigger-warning/

Family Connections

Colt & Ashlyn
(Don't Let Me Fall)
Jaxon
Griffin
Dylan

Biological Siblings
Colt & Blakely
Theo & Macklin

Theo & Blakely
(Don't Let Me Go)
Ophelia
Tatum

Macklin & Kate
(Don't Let Me Break)
Everett
Finley

Henry & Mia
(Don't Let Me Down)
Archer & Maverick (twins)
Rory

PROLOGUE

OPHELIA

"You know, the only reason I'm going to prom tonight is so I can meet Mystery Man and make sure he isn't a dick, right?" Dylan asks. She's my cousin as well as my best friend, and it's been killing her how she's yet to meet the infamous Mystery Man I've been dating. Her determination to ensure he measures up to her standards is the *only* reason she agreed to go to prom tonight. By the look of things, I think she might regret her decision as she stands in front of the floor-length mirror in my bedroom, examining her outfit and fiddling with the skirt. Her dusty blue dress makes her aquamarine eyes pop even brighter, and the sweetheart neckline and tulle fabric make her look straight out of a Cinderella movie despite the skirt not being too full or fluffy. But even the fairytale-esque dress does shit to hide the anxious energy radiating off her.

"Dylan, you look gorgeous," I tell her.

She forces herself to stop fidgeting with her skirt, turns to me, and shamelessly checks me out. "Ditto. We almost look like we know how to dress up for these things."

"Almost," I repeat with a grin while smoothing the black

1

satin fabric along my stomach in front of the bathroom mirror. My bedroom is connected to a private bathroom, leaving us plenty of room to chat while getting ready without feeling squished or running into each other.

"Are you nervous?" she asks. "To introduce the family to your infamous Mystery Man?"

Mystery Man.

I roll my eyes, but the butterflies in my stomach continue flapping away despite my laid-back facade. Nervous doesn't even begin to cover everything I'm feeling. Anxious. Excited. Terrified. The list goes on and on.

I've never had a boyfriend. Even the title gives me anxiety. But I've been dating Mystery Man for a few months, and it's been...kind of awesome.

Okay, the term *dating* is sort of a stretch. It's more like stolen kisses, sexy rendezvous, and late-night phone calls, but I think those still count. After all, he's taking me to prom tonight, which is insane on so many levels, especially considering he'll be a senior in college in the fall. Prom was his idea, not mine. Which, in my opinion, gives it even more weight.

So yeah. We're dating... I *think*.

"Yeah, you're totally nervous to introduce him to me," Dylan decides. A wry grin plays on her full lips.

I give her the side-eye in the mirror. "It depends. Are you going to be a brat when you meet him?"

"Hey, I'm the nice one," she argues, lifting her hands in defense. "If you want to worry about anyone being a brat when meeting the man who stole your heart, it's Finley."

With a laugh, I pull the mascara wand from its pink tube and lacquer my lashes. "Then I guess it's a good thing Finley's across the country, isn't it?"

"Yup. Pretty sure you dodged a bullet until Mystery Man's forced to face her at LAU in a few months."

LAU is the university we're all attending in the fall, but

2

Dylan's right. Mystery Man is in for a rude awakening once we all move in, that's for sure.

"But for tonight," Dylan continues, "he'll only have to deal with your family and me. As long as he isn't a dick, we should be good to go."

"Mm-hmm," I hum. "And you're most likely going to be too busy attempting to make conversation with your own date to interrogate mine, so I call it a win-win."

She groans and collapses onto my bed. "Don't remind me. Why are boys the worst?"

"Boys aren't the worst."

"Uh, yes, they are," she argues. "Every time I'm in the same room with one, I get all tongue-tied and awkward."

"Technically, you only get tongue-tied around the hot ones."

Her nose wrinkles, and she tosses a pillow at me. As I dodge the lump of feathers, she adds, "You're not helping!"

I laugh a little harder. "No offense, but with two older brothers who both play hockey and have hot friends who *also* play hockey, you'd think you'd be used to hanging out around good-looking guys by now."

"Well, yeah, but—"

My phone rings, cutting her off.

Seeing Mystery Man's name flash across the screen, I grin.

"Let me guess," Dylan murmurs as she climbs to her feet. "Mystery Man?"

My smile widens as I answer the call. "Hello?"

"Hey," his low voice rumbles.

"Hey," I repeat.

Silence.

My brows pinch. "Everything okay?"

"I'm, uh, I'm not going to make it tonight."

"What's going on?" I turn away from Dylan's concerned

stare and face the empty shower instead. "We talked an hour ago, and you told me you'd be coming right after your doctor's appointment."

"I know what I said," he mutters, his concession laced with defeat. "Look." He hesitates. "This is a bad idea."

"What? *Prom?*"

Silence.

"Okay, so we won't go," I offer. "It was your idea anyway."

"You know what I mean, Goose." The stupid pet name doesn't give me any warm fuzzies, and I close my eyes.

Is this really happening?

My bedroom door closes with a quiet click, ringing louder than a siren, pulling me back to our conversation. With a quick look over my shoulder, I find the room empty. Dylan must've slipped out, sensing my need for privacy.

The girl's a saint.

Who would've thought I'd need it right now.

Shifting my cell to my other ear, I let out a slow breath and walk into my now-empty bedroom. A chill falls over my skin. My body is on full alert, my muscles poised for fight or flight despite not being in any danger. It's like my body already knows what I don't want to accept, and a tremor races along my spine.

"Seriously, what's going on, Mav?" I ask. "Where are you? Are you close yet? Maybe we can talk about this in person."

"Ophelia…"

The silence following my full name sears me, and I collapse onto the edge of my bed. I don't like it. The quiet. The heaviness. The way my skin feels tight and cold, then hot and uncomfortable. "Are you breaking up with me?"

Another beat of silence passes, and nausea churns in my stomach.

"Are you breaking up with me?" I repeat. My voice is stronger this time, but even I can hear the twinge of desperation. It makes me sound so immature. So stupid. Of course, it does. I might be a senior in high school, but Mystery Man? He's in college. The fact he even gave me the time of day is a miracle. I mean, to be fair, I kind of jumped his bones and didn't exactly expect it to turn into anything in the beginning, but now that it has? Well, he got my hopes up, dammit.

The silence continues stretching, and my nerves get the best of me, so I push, "Just answer the question."

"We were never together," he rasps. "Not officially."

"Says the guy who told me I'm his, right? Yeah, it makes this so much better." I mock. "You're ending things over the phone and bailing on me an hour before my senior prom after twisting my arm to let you take me in the first place. Gee, thanks. You're a real peach."

"You don't think I already feel like shit?"

"Then don't bail on me," I beg. "My parents, and my sister, and Dylan? They're all dying to officially—"

"Don't make this harder than it has to be," he interrupts.

"Harder than it has to be?" I look down at my dress. "I'm literally sitting on my bed in my prom dress. My makeup is done. I curled my hair. None of which would've happened if you hadn't asked me in the first place."

"Look, I know how fucked-up this is. I know what I said when I asked you, and...I'm sorry. I know it isn't enough, but...I'm sure you can find someone else to take you."

"You're right," I say with a laugh. "A whole slew of seniors are waiting at my door, praying my date will fall through. And what do you know? That's exactly what happened." A scoff slips out of me. "Ya know, you were the one who wanted to take this to the next level."

"Yeah, and I was wrong," he mutters. "Like I said, I'm sorry, but...I'm trying to do what's best for you. It is what it is."

"It is what it is?" I repeat, convinced I'm hallucinating

because this guy? He's cold and indifferent and...a fucking asshole.

"I don't know what else you want me to say, Ophelia." The same heavy dose of resignation taints his sigh as he adds, "I'm sorry."

"Can we talk—"

"I gotta go."

He hangs up the phone, and I touch my lips with my fingers, willing the burn behind my eyes to go away, when a light knock echoes from the opposite side of my bedroom door.

Dropping my phone onto the mattress, I blink my unfallen tears away. "Come in."

The door opens with a soft squeak, and my mom, Blakely, rests her shoulder against the doorjamb, her expression pinched. "Hey. Everything okay?"

"Dylan already told you?" I ask.

She grimaces. "She may have voiced her concern."

"Of course she did," I mutter as my mom walks into my room and sits beside me on the edge of the bed.

"What can I do?" she asks.

"Nothing. Actually, scratch that. I want ice cream," I decide. "Lots and lots of ice cream."

"Your Aunt Ashlyn would be so proud," she muses, mentioning Dylan's mom. "She's a big believer in ice cream fixing everything, but I have another idea for this particular situation."

I frown. "What is it?"

"Well, Mia mentioned the twins are coming back from LAU tonight. They're staying for the weekend. What if Archer takes you?"

Archer.

He's my best friend. Well, other than Dylan and Finley. We text daily and talk about everything with each other.

Everything except dating. The idea of actually *going* on a date with him? It feels like I'm crossing a line, one we've both drawn without ever discussing it. And after everything with Mystery Man? I'm pretty sure the timing couldn't be worse.

"That's a bad idea," I murmur.

"Why? He's your best friend."

"It just is." After the phone call, I'm feeling on edge. Like a shaken-up can of soda ready to explode at any second, and it's a real possibility if I can't get my emotions under control.

Breathe, I remind myself.

I shove my feelings deep down inside my chest cavity like a garbage compactor on steroids, adding, "Archer's probably busy tonight, anyway, and Dylan's date will be here in less than an hour. It's not like Archer can be ready in time. Speaking of which, I've gotta tell Dylan her date needs to drive since we were all planning on riding in Mystery Man's car. Shit."

I start to stand, but my mom stops me. "Don't worry about the driving arrangements yet. We'll figure it out. As for Archer being ready in time, I'm pretty sure he can steal one of his dad's tuxedos. Actually, I'm almost sure he already owns one. Those boys have attended events fancier than this since they were babies."

My lips press together, knowing she's right. Their parents are freaking billionaires. Literally. Those boys have been attending fancy soirees since before they could walk, so of course, Archer has a tux. But it doesn't mean it's a good idea to go with him.

"What if I mention it to his mom?" she suggests. "Let her feel him out and see if he'd be okay taking you?"

"And make me the pity-party prom girl who can't keep a date?" I stick out my bottom lip. "No, thank you."

"Too late!" Dylan chimes in from the doorway. "I already texted Archer."

My adrenaline kicks into full gear, and my eyes cut to hers. "You did what?"

"I texted Archer."

"Why would you do that?"

"Because you're not allowed to miss prom because your Mystery Man is a dick."

"Who is he, anyway?" my mom asks. "I want to know what name I should be cursing."

"It doesn't matter." I fist my hands in my lap and shake my head, my emotions threatening to ruin my makeup. "*He* doesn't matter."

"Lia," my mom murmurs.

"Clearly, it's over, and…" I sniff. "I don't want to talk about him. I need to figure out tonight, and—"

"We've already figured out tonight," Dylan says. "Like I said, Archer's gonna take you."

"It isn't Archer's responsibility—"

"He already said he'll be here in thirty," Dylan interrupts, tapping the edge of her cell against her chin. "So there's nothing you can do about it."

There's a lump in my throat, but I swallow it back, willing away the stupid burn in my eyes–again–and lick my lips. "He said he'd take me?"

"Duh. Archer loves you," Dylan reminds me.

It'll be fine. Everything. Will. Be. Fine.

"See?" my mom offers. "I knew he'd be happy to take you. What do you say? Are you ready to dance the night away?"

I sniffle and stand, pulling on my proverbial big girl panties and letting out a slow breath. "Okay. I'll go."

IT'S QUIET AND AWKWARD AS ARCHER DRIVES US TO THE DANCE. When we pull up to the curb, Dylan's date opens her door and offers his hand to help her out of the car. She reaches for it, her baby blues glued to the ground. As she unfolds herself from the backseat, she steps on the hem of her dress and rolls her ankle. Her knees hit the pavement with a crash, and she curses under her breath while I watch the chaos in the passenger side mirror.

Oh, shit.

My knee-jerk reaction is to rush out of the car and help her up, but I have a feeling it would only embarrass her more, so I stay seated. Heat floods Dylan's cheeks as she pushes herself up, her date standing helplessly beside her with his hands raised in the air. Once her feet are back on the ground, she smooths out the front of her dress and slams the door behind her, marching toward the entrance without waiting for her date to catch up.

I cover my laugh behind my hand and stare at my lap.

Apparently, I'm not the only one having a rough night.

Poor girl.

Pulling the car away from the front of the building, Archer notes, "There she is."

My eyes meet his as my brows pinch. "What do you mean?"

"Despite your Oscar-worthy acting skills, you've seemed down since the moment I picked you up." He turns the steering wheel and checks his blind spot like a seasoned pro, but I don't miss the slight tension in his muscles as he fights for nonchalance, adding, "You okay?"

Ah, so that's why he's acting funny.

He's worried about me.

I guess it makes sense. I've hardly looked at him tonight. I haven't been able to. Not without seeing his twin brother instead. I never thought they looked alike. Have never struggled to recognize their differences. I still don't. But my mind is such a muddled clusterfuck of all things Maverick it's hard for me to focus on anything else. Hell, I'm pretty sure a stranger could walk up to me, and even they would remind me of the boy who broke my heart tonight.

He isn't here right now, I remind myself. *Archer is.*

With a nod, I reach over and grab Archer's hand resting on his knee while the other guides the car with the steering wheel. "Yeah, I'm okay." I gulp, unsure what else to say.

"You sure?"

No.

"Yeah, of course. Thanks for driving. And for taking me tonight. You didn't have to."

"Are you kidding me?" He chuckles, squeezes my hand, and lets me go so he can pull into a parking spot near the back of the lot. It's crowded with limos and high schoolers dressed like they're about to step onto a fashion runway in Milan. A girl from my English class spots me in the passenger seat and waves as she loops her arm through her boyfriend's.

Archer slides his car into park and murmurs, "I wouldn't wanna be anywhere else, Lia."

"Because you're a saint." I turn to him again and lean my head back against the black leather seat, focusing on the physical traits that make Archer *Archer* and not his identical twin. My exhaustion already threatens to pull me under, and we haven't even stepped out of the car yet.

"I'm not a saint. I'm your best friend." He turns the ignition off but doesn't reach for the door handle. Instead, he wipes his palms along his dark slacks. "You wanna talk about it?"

"Talk about what?"

"About the guy I'm replacing tonight. I believe Dylan called him...*Mystery Man?*" He tilts his head as the nickname rolls off his tongue.

I smile despite myself. Archer's cute when he's curious.

When he's trying to bring up a subject he doesn't know how to broach. Then again, he's Archer. The guy's cute all the time, and I'm not the only one who thinks so. Archer Buchanan is basically the equivalent of the boy next door with a side of Prince Charming all rolled into one.

It would annoy me if he wasn't so genuine.

How he isn't already tied down is a mystery to literally everyone who's ever seen him, let alone had an actual conversation with the dude.

He's *that* perfect.

"Not gonna tell me about Mystery Man, huh?" he prods when I've been silent too long.

Other than the fact he's your twin brother, and I hate myself for opening up to him? Yeah, no. No, thank you.

Pushing aside how fucked-up this entire situation is, I give him a half-assed shrug and lie, "There isn't much to tell."

"You sure?"

I nod, then shake my head. "Honestly, I don't even know anymore."

"Was it serious?"

"I mean, we weren't official, but…"

"But you wanted to be," he concludes.

"I knew what I was getting into when we started seeing each other."

"Doesn't make it better, though."

I pick at my cuticles in my lap as my entire non-relationship with Mystery Man circles through my head like water swirling down a drain. "I guess not."

Scratching his jaw, Archer turns to me fully and rests his wrist on the steering wheel. "How come I never heard about him, Lia?"

"Mystery Man?" I hesitate, well-aware of the *exact* reason Archer never heard of him until tonight, and why I need to

11

keep it this way. "Uh, I don't know? We've never really been friends who talk about our dating lives."

"Is there a reason we don't talk about it?" he questions.

I lift a shoulder again and repeat, "I don't know? What do you think?"

"I think I'm happy to be here, Ophelia."

Another smile touches my lips as I take in the man beside me. He's dressed to the nines in a dark tuxedo with his brown hair combed away from his face and his chiseled jaw on full display, looking every bit the drool-worthy, perfect prom date I asked him to be. Honestly, I'm still not sure how he pulled it off so quickly. That's a lie. Even in sweats and a T-shirt, I'm pretty sure he'd pull off the perfect prom date title with ease. Yet here he is, with me. "Surprisingly, I'm happy you're here too," I tell him. And it's the truth. I didn't think it would even be possible to smile tonight, and Archer's helped me accomplish it more than once already.

His brows lift. "Yeah?"

With a laugh, I repeat, "Yeah. I wasn't really looking forward to tonight, and honestly, I'm still kind of on the fence. But if I have any hope of enjoying my prom after everything with Mystery Man, I think you're the only guy who could actually help me pull it off."

The laugh lines around his eyes soften, tugging at the duct tape I'd wrapped around my shattered heart in preparation for surviving tonight. No one wants to be around a sad girl, especially at a party. But I have a feeling Archer sees right through it, leaving me exposed and way more vulnerable than I want to be for the evening.

"I'm sorry he hurt you," he murmurs. His words hang in the quiet cab of the car.

"It isn't a big deal."

"Yeah, it is. It's okay to be sad."

"Thank you," I whisper as my eyes fall to my lap again.

I hate it. How crappy I feel. How crappy the whole situation is. How much it hurts. How confusing it is. How lost I seem. I want to be at home in bed, eating a shit-ton of ice cream. But I also want to be here with Archer. Making memories and being young and carefree. It's conflicting. And confusing. And draining.

Maybe I really should go home.

"Come on," Archer urges as if he can see the wheels turning in my head. "Let's go inside, dance the night away, and help you forget about everything, even if it's only for a little while."

He doesn't wait for me to answer. He exits the car, rounds the front, and opens my door. When he offers his hand, I take it, willing my legs to move.

"Help me forget," I plead.

His smile is soft as he rubs his thumb along the back of my hand. "I've got you, Lia."

~

My feet are killing me, and so are my cheeks. I've been smiling so hard tonight I'll be surprised if they aren't sore for a week.

Archer dropped Dylan and her date off—both agreeing it was best to go their separate ways. And now, we're on my parents' front lawn with the stars twinkling above us as we make our way toward the porch.

It's beautiful and peaceful and exactly what I needed.

I peek at Archer beside me, crossing my arms and rubbing my hands up and down my bare skin. "Thanks again for tonight. I don't know what I would've done without you."

"Anytime, Lia," Archer replies. "You know, I've been thinking."

I look over my shoulder at my best friend. His pace has

slowed, so he's behind me instead of by my side. "About what?" I ask.

"Seeing you like this…" His gaze follows the curves of my dress. When he looks at my face again, it's brief. So quick, I'm surprised I notice. But it's there. Interest. Reverence almost. And I don't know how I feel about it.

Archer clears his throat and squeezes the back of his neck as if realizing he's been caught. It's boyish and innocent, and so adorable I kind of want to tease him for it.

"You were saying?" I quip.

"Well, I mean…spending time with you like this. Where we're dancing and laughing and looking at the stars. It's been nice, don't you think?"

"Yeah, it's been really nice," I agree.

"Good." He smiles at me again. "Really good. 'Cause I, uh, I like you, Lia. I like you as more than a friend."

Caught off guard, my pace slows, and Archer catches up with me at the base of my front steps.

"I've liked you as more than a friend for a long time now," he continues, "but I didn't want to ruin what we've always had. Then tonight happened, and I feel like we just kinda… fit. Don't you?"

I bite the inside of my cheek, unsure what to say. "I had a good time."

"Yeah, me too." His smile stretches and softens, tapping into the boy next door vibe the man wears like one of his fitted suits. Reaching for me, he rubs his thumbs along the backs of my hands. "I know the timing is shitty because you just broke up with your Mystery Man, but…I dunno. Like I said, I had fun tonight. I had fun being with you. I always have fun being with you," he clarifies. "But tonight felt different. It felt like we could be more than friends."

He's right. It did. It's like we accidentally stumbled into relationship territory without either of us meaning to. But it doesn't change who I've been seeing. It doesn't change how I had my heart broken earlier tonight or how differently it all would've gone if Mystery Man hadn't bailed on me at the last second.

I look down at our entwined hands. They fit. They shouldn't, but they do. Or maybe they should fit. Maybe they've always fit, and—

"I see you're debating something," he notes.

My eyes snap to his, and I blurt out, "I'm a mess, Archer."

With a smirk, he nods. "Yeah, I know."

"I'm being serious."

"I know you are." He steps closer to me until we're nearly chest-to-chest. "But I'm okay with it."

Lifting my head, I hold his gaze. "Archer, I'm still hung up—"

The heat from his lips against mine swallows my rebuttal as he kisses me, angling my face to his. I'm so surprised, I just stand there, motionless. He tastes like mint. It's a silly real-ization, but it's true. Gently, he cradles my cheeks, pouring every ounce of pent-up attraction and restraint he's carried for me into the kiss until I can feel it from the top of my head to the tips of my toes. It's nice. Comforting almost. Even familiar, though we've never kissed before. Not like this. Part of me wants to curl up against his chest and cry. The other part wants to lean into the kiss. To accept it. To let it mend my broken heart and erase every touch before his. Because if it did, maybe I wouldn't hurt so much. Maybe I wouldn't miss *him*.

I feel guilty. Guilty for kissing someone who isn't my stupid Mystery Man, despite the knowledge he's the one who pushed me away. He's the one who didn't want me anymore. The one who bailed on us. On *me*.

And Archer? His hand snakes around my waist, and he tugs me into him.

He wants me.

Pulling away from the kiss, Archer catches his breath and rests his forehead against mine. "Tell me you felt nothing."

My eyes stay closed as his challenge brushes against my cheeks. Forcing a smirk, I answer, "We both know you're hot, Archer. I'd have to be an iceberg not to feel anything after a kiss like that."

He smiles against my lips. "Give me a chance."

Blinking my eyes open, I repeat, "I'm a mess."

"And I'm a patient asshole who doesn't mind putting you back together again."

A light laugh slips out of me, and I shake my head. "Archer…"

"Please, Lia?" he begs. "You like me, I know you do—"

"I do," I interrupt. "You're right, okay? Yes, I felt something two seconds ago when you kissed me, and in another world, I would do anything to be in this position, to witness you giving me the time of day when you are so far out of my league, it's not even funny." I laugh softly and run my fingers along the lapel of his tuxedo jacket. Indecision and resignation tear at me like a vulture picking apart the corpse of my previous relationship.

"I feel like there's a but coming," he muses.

Another quiet laugh slips out of me. "*But* I literally just broke up with my…whatever…a few hours ago. I'm…" I let go of his lapel and slide my hand along his chest. "I'm not ready, and I'm confused, and I'm a mess."

"Then let me make this easier for you." He rubs his thumb along my cheek, tilting my head up, his gaze practically brimming with awe. "Give me a chance, and I'll give you whatever you need."

"Whatever I need?"

"*Whatever* you need," he emphasizes. "Time. Distractions. Space. Ice cream. Orgasms."

"Archer!" I smack his chest as my cheeks pinch with amusement.

He pulls me into him again. "I'm kidding. Kind of," he teases. "I like you for you. Always have. Always will. And even if this doesn't work out, that won't change. But the idea of not giving this a shot after the amazing night we had... I'd regret it for the rest of my life."

We did have an amazing night. And Archer's my best friend. Archer would never bail on me or hurt me. Not like Mystery Man did—er, Mystery *Boy*. It's probably a more fitting term, now that I think about it.

He sounded so...detached on the phone. It's a sound I'll never forget. It makes me want to scrub my brain and erase every single memory from the past few months. If only I could.

"Give me a chance," Archer begs. "We can take things as slow as you want."

I do love Archer. I've always loved him.

Would it be so bad to be with someone I *know* would never break my heart?

Nibbling my bottom lip, I mumble, "I can't promise you anything."

"All I need is a chance, Lia. A chance to convince you I'm worth your time."

And even though I'm as confused as before, it's nice. Seeing his resolution. His determination. His adoration.

"Let me think about it," I whisper.

"Like I said, whatever you need."

Leaning into his touch, I push aside the betrayal filtering through me. "We'll see."

1
OPHELIA

A few weeks later

"You really think this is a good idea, Blake?" my dad asks as he sets the final cardboard box down in the center of the cluttered family room of my new home for the next four years.

"Come on, Teddy," my mom urges, using my dad's nickname. "When the girls decided to attend LAU, we agreed it was best to have the boys stay close and keep an eye on them."

"That was before my oldest daughter started dating one of them." My dad gives me a pointed look from beneath the brim of his worn baseball hat. Placing his hands on his lower back, he arches it, probably hoping it'll ease the ache he's been complaining about ever since he tweaked it a few years ago while playing hockey. I doubt it helps much.

Maverick ghosted me after prom. I texted him fourteen times—I counted—and the asshole didn't bother to respond even once. I called him too—seventeen times, to be exact—but he ignored those too.

And since he clearly didn't care enough about me to give me the time of day, I decided to try and move on, too, even if it's with his brother.

Maybe it's stupid—okay, it probably is—but I was best friends with Archer long before Maverick and I started hooking up. I've known each of them individually for so long it doesn't feel strange or wrong. Then again, I've never really compared Archer with Maverick, even when we were all kids, so...I don't know.

Why should Maverick have any control over what I do or don't do anymore, anyway?

He shouldn't.

I won't let him.

With that in mind, I started hanging out with Archer in a less platonic way. It's easier than I thought it would be. Effortless almost. I shouldn't be surprised. We were used to talking every day. Now, a few kisses are thrown in here and there when we hang out, and we cuddle when watching movies. Otherwise? It's pretty much the same. Our parents have taken a little while to get used to it, despite their constant joking about us getting married once we're older. When I pointed out it was kind of my mom's fault because she's the one who suggested Archer take me to prom in the first place, she accepted my new relationship with open arms, grateful I wasn't wallowing in self-pity or heartbreak. Thankfully, Archer's parents did the same.

It's kind of funny in an *I-want-to-claw-my-eyes-out* sort of way. How much I dreaded telling my parents and their friends about a relationship between me and one of their kids and how supportive they've been.

If I'd only known.

"Just because Lia's dating one of the twins doesn't mean all of our plans should implode," my mom scolds from across the family room.

"Yeah," I pipe in. "It wasn't my idea for you and your friends to build a massive house for all of your kids to stay in. Pretty sure if you wanna blame anyone, you should look in the mirror, old man."

"Har, har," he grumbles. "The decision was made before I remembered what it was like to attend LAU while living at the Taylor House when I was your age. You can't blame an old man for wanting to keep his baby safe."

Ah, the Taylor House.

I've heard stories. Lots of them. I wondered when he would bring up his college shenanigans with his friends. The original Taylor House was owned by my grandparents, and my dad took full advantage by offering housing to the entire LAU hockey team under the guise of building camaraderie. I'm pretty sure it was more along the lines of making things easier for puck bunnies to warm the players' beds, but what do I know?

The Taylor House must not have been all bad since my parents and their friends agreed to invest in a massive duplex near LAU's campus as soon as their kids started reaching college age. One side is for the girls, the other for the boys. It was either a clever decision or a ludicrous one, though it's too early to tell.

Jaxon, my oldest cousin, was the first to enroll at LAU after receiving a full-ride hockey scholarship. Next, my cousin, Everett, joined him, then Jaxon's little brother, and the twins were accepted on the roster. Now, here I am, attending LAU like the rest of them.

One. After. Another.

Dylan and Finley will move in with me soon. But, I was recruited to play for the new girls' hockey team this year, so I was asked to come early to train with the rest of my teammates to prepare for the new season.

It's crazy. How LAU is kicking off an all-girl hockey team.

Then again, I guess it makes sense, considering the men's team's fanbase. Who knows? Maybe the concept will even spread.

It's a well-known fact that girls' sports are rarely taken as seriously as men's. Things are slowly changing, though. My parents have been nothing but supportive since I was a little girl and chose to play hockey with the rest of the boys despite the odds stacked against me in terms of it becoming a career.

That being said, I'm not completely delusional. The odds of making a living playing hockey professionally are slim to none, which means I need to pick a major at some point. But that's a problem for future Ophelia. And I have no issue passing the puck to her and enjoying today's moments while I have them.

Like right now. In the middle of a family room right down the hall from a bedroom I get to call home for the next four years. I could leap for joy right here, right now.

"Look at the bright side," my mom offers. "At least there's a wall separating the girls from the boys."

"Like that makes it any better," my dad mutters under his breath. "You sure you'll be okay here by yourself, Lia?"

Stealing my dad's hat from his head, I slap the worn black material on top of my strawberry blonde waves and smile at him. "I'm a big girl. Trust me, I'll be fine. Besides, it's like you said. The guys are only a wall away."

He scrubs his hand over his face. "Knowing your boyfriend's one of them doesn't exactly make me feel better."

"And now this conversation is going in circles." I laugh and kiss his cheek. "Have a little faith in me, Dad."

"What about the motorcycle out front?" he questions.

My forehead wrinkles. "What about it?"

"Well, who does it belong to?"

"How would I know?"

His bushy brows dip, and he peeks out the front window, taking in the sleek, black motorcycle parked in the driveway.

"It probably belongs to Reeves," my mom suggests. "It's not like any of our friends would let their kids buy a motorcycle."

"No offense, but all of the guys are twenty-one or over, which means they're officially adults," I remind them. "I doubt they need their parents' permission to buy a motorcycle."

"Are you saying you're gonna do whatever you want since you're now a big girl living all alone at college?" Dad demands.

I pat his chest. "I'm saying it doesn't matter who owns the bike because it's none of our business. And it sure as hell doesn't mean I'm going to be riding on it, so what's the problem?"

"You don't own a car," my dad points out.

"And who's fault is that?" I volley back at him without bothering to hide my amusement.

My parents might be awesome, but they're also the anti-hand-your-daughter-free-stuff type, so I'm saving money to buy a car on my own. And since I've been so focused on graduating high school and preparing for the upcoming hockey season, I've been a bit preoccupied. Thankfully, the duplex is right next to campus, so it's not like I need a car to get to and from my classes or anything. If I do need a ride anywhere, I have three cousins and a boyfriend who would be happy to drive me somewhere. I'll be fine.

"Don't remind me," Dad mutters, glancing at my mom. "You know I wanted to—"

"Don't you dare throw me under the bus, Teddy." Mom points her finger at him and steps closer, jabbing it into his chest. "We both agreed raising strong, independent girls included being the bad guys every once in a while."

"But does she have to figure out how to be strong and independent while living next to her boyfriend without a car?" he whines.

"Give her a break, will you?" my mom interjects. "She'll be fine. And it's not like you don't love Archer and how he treats your baby girl anyway."

She's not wrong.

Our relationship might still be relatively new, but Archer and I have been best friends since puberty. Until then, he had a stick up his ass like his twin brother. But as soon as Archer's balls dropped, he decided the opposite sex wasn't so bad, and we became really close. Then, prom happened. We danced all night, and he kissed me in my front yard, and the rest, as they say, is history. The guy has never let me down and clearly has the patience of a saint since I've been hesitant to jump into our relationship with both feet, proving his sainthood all over again.

Which reminds me... I kind of want to go see my boyfriend before he leaves for his internship.

My mom scans the boxes littering the family room and orders, "Theo, why don't you go pick up some breakfast for us while I help Lia—"

"Nope," I interrupt. "I love you guys, but I think it's time you got out of here." I push my parents toward the door, adding, "I can unpack on my own like the strong, independent woman you raised me to be, and if you don't leave now, you'll be late for Tatum's piano recital."

"Your little sister would kill us if we missed it," my mom agrees. "Although, we were hoping to stop by to say hello to the boys."

"You really think the boys want to be woken up this early on a Saturday?" I challenge.

"Good point." Mom follows my lead and pushes my dad

toward the door, but he half-heartedly resists before giving in like a great, big teddy bear.

"Fine." He slaps the brim of the hat I stole from him. "You can keep the hat."

I bat my lashes and give him a syrupy-sweet smile. "Aw. It's cute you thought I'd give it back in the first place."

With a grunt, he hugs me goodbye, and my mom does the same, giving me one final squeeze as we all head outside. The sun is shining brightly in the sky despite it being relatively early. I lift my head, basking in its warmth as my parents walk to the midnight blue truck in the driveway.

"See you soon!" I call.

"Love you!" My mom waves as they climb into the truck, pull onto the street, and leave me in blissful silence.

Well, other than the birds.

Yup. They're chirping in the trees lining the sidewalk and acting like the cherry on top of a pretty picturesque morning. It makes me feel like I'm Snow White, and if I didn't have neighbors, I might start whistling. Basking in my excitement, I stretch my arms out and lift my head toward the sky again.

Hello, freedom.

Hello, future.

Hello, college life.

2

MAVERICK

Scrubbing my hand over my tired face, I kick a stray red Solo cup littering the floor and make my way down the hall.

I shouldn't have partied last night.

I'm hungover and feel like shit.

My head throbs. The party is a blur, but at least I woke up alone. Or maybe it would've been better if I hadn't. Then again, the idea of hooking up with someone makes the tequila in my stomach churn, so I shove the thought aside.

When I reach the family room, I catch my buddy, Reeves, looking out the front window with a coffee cup clutched to his chest. The guy appears as hungover as I feel. His body is slumped, bags are under his eyes, and his lids are hooded as he takes a sip of coffee.

With my shoulder pressed against the doorjamb, I grunt my greeting to him. "Fuck tequila."

"Dude, come here," he orders.

"What is it?"

He tilts his head toward the window but doesn't stop staring at whatever is outside. "Just come look."

26

Pushing away from the doorjamb, I stride toward him and glance out the crack between the dusty, white blinds. There's a girl in jean shorts with toned legs and a white cropped top. Strawberry blonde curls spill beneath a black hat and hang down her back as she looks up at the sky. My mouth goes dry in an instant.

"Fuck," Reeves breathes out. "Am I right?"

Slapping his hand away from the blinds, I force the view of my front yard to disappear. "Don't waste your time."

"Why not?'

"She's already taken."

His eyes widen. "You know her?"

"Yeah."

"Who is she?"

"Archer's girlfriend."

He lifts the blind with his index finger again and whistles. "Fuck."

Yeah.

"Come on," I mutter. "You look like a perv."

"Dude, she's coming this way."

My spine pricks, but I keep my feet planted where they are.

I knew she was coming.

Knew she was moving in.

Knew I'd be around her again after avoiding her for so long.

It's why I had to get shit-faced last night.

Archer gave me some bullshit lecture about how I needed to play nice when she arrived. How I had to make her feel welcome. It only left me more on edge.

He's gone for the day despite attempting to shift shit around at his internship so he could be here to greet her. Go figure. Now, it's my job.

A loud knock echoes from the solid door, and Reeves rubs his hands together with a mischievous grin.

"Don't do it," I warn.

"Do what?" he asks innocently.

"Whatever you're thinking."

"Why not? It's not like she's *your* girlfriend," he reminds me.

Reeves is kind of an ass. He's also one of my roommates and best friends, despite that. Although, at times like this, I'm not entirely sure why I put up with him. Having Ophelia on my radar is one thing. Having her on Reeves'? It's a disaster waiting to happen.

The house belongs to more than just me. I live with Jaxon and Griffin, who are brothers, along with Everett, Reeves, and my twin. It's a full house on a good day, but Jaxon graduated this spring, so we should have more space soon if we're lucky.

Speak of the devil.

Jaxon's heavy footsteps echo down the stairs as he heads to the front door and answers it, ignoring us in the main room.

"Jax!" Ophelia gushes when she comes into view. She throws her arms around him.

"Hey, baby cousin," he returns.

"I'm hardly a baby, old man," she quips, letting him go. "Congrats on graduating and the new coaching position, by the way. I still can't believe you turned down signing with the Lions to coach a bunch of girls."

"Yeah, neither can I. Are you ready for me to kick your ass during conditioning?"

"Yes, *Coach*," she replies. "I'm excited to get the girls' team off to a good start."

"Me too. I've been brainstorming with Sanderson, and we thought it would be cool to do a fundraiser or something with the men's team to hype up the season and hopefully sell some tickets."

Sanderson is the men's coach. He's been mentoring Jaxon on how to handle the girls' team and start them out on the right foot. Apparently, it includes a fundraiser or some shit I'll likely be dragged to.

Can't fucking wait.

"What a great idea!" Ophelia raves. "Let me know what you need from me, and I'm there."

"Sounds good."

"So, are you still living here, or...?" She peeks around Jax in the doorway and takes in the family room, the set of stairs, and the garbage littering the floor from last night's party. When her eyes fall on me, she forces a smile and looks up at Jaxon again like he's the most interesting person in the world.

Yeah, Opie. I know. It's good to see you too.

"Nah. I'm still looking for a new place," Jaxon answers her. "Uncle Henry offered to let me use his penthouse, but we'll see."

Technically, my dad isn't Jaxon's uncle by blood, but since we were raised together, all of our parents are more like aunts and uncles to us than simply our parents' *friends*. Not recognizing the difference was fine until we hit middle school and realized we could play Spin the Bottle and Truth or Dare whenever we hung out at family barbecues and shit. Yeah, then the differentiation was something we zeroed in on.

I'm not surprised my dad offered the penthouse to Jaxon, but I'll be shocked if Jaxon takes him up on it. The guy's been adamant about paving his own path since he was a kid. Part of me thinks it's one of the reasons he decided to turn down the NHL offer since my dad's the owner of the Lions team, but he'd never admit it out loud. No, Jaxon's too much of a recluse to open up to anyone or tell them what he thinks and wants out of life.

Then again, I guess we have that in common.

"It's probably a good idea, though," Ophelia replies, bringing me back to the conversation. "Ya know, stay close so you can keep an eye on these boys. Or maybe not," she adds dryly. "You're not their team captain anymore. No need to babysit, right?"

"Yeah, but if I don't do it, who will?" Jaxon questions with a grin. He opens the door a little wider. "Come in."

"It's early," she starts. "I don't want to intrude. I saw someone peeking through the blinds, so I figured I'd stop by and say hi."

"I'm Reeves," my buddy interjects. He steps toward her with an outstretched hand. "Nice to meet you."

"Nice to meet you too. I'm Ophelia, but you can call me Lia." She takes his hand and shakes it.

"Lia," Reeves repeats as if he's tasting it. "Pretty name."

Her mouth lifts. "Thanks."

"I gotta get going," Jaxon announces. "Griffin and Everett are at the rink getting in some skate time, and Archer's at B-Tech until tonight."

"I know," Lia replies. "I was hoping to say hi before he left, but apparently, he had to be at the office at the ass-crack of dawn to prepare for a meeting or something."

"Yeah, the guy's got goals," Jaxon agrees. "But if you need anything, let Maverick know. He'll be around. Won't you, Mav?"

Ophelia's eyes slide to mine, and her tongue peeks out of her mouth, wetting her bottom lip. "Mav."

I keep my feet planted where they are and fold my arms. "Hey."

"Hey." She tucks her thumbs into her back pockets, looking anywhere but at me despite my face matching her boyfriend's. I doubt she knows her stance accentuates her breasts, but I don't call her out for it. *Yet.* If Reeves keeps staring at her, I might have to.

"Do you need any help moving in?" Jaxon prods.

She shakes her head. "I'm good, thanks."

"Okay," Jaxon replies. "I'll see you later. Maybe we can all hang out tonight or something."

"I'm sure Archer already has plans with Opie," I interrupt.

Her caramel-colored eyes heat as they meet mine again. "Pretty sure I've told you not to call me Opie."

"Only a thousand times," I reply, knowing how much it gets under her skin.

Those pouty lips purse before she runs her tongue along her teeth and turns to Jaxon. "Unfortunately, Mav's right. Archer said he wants to take me out tonight, but maybe tomorrow or something?"

My chest puffs out as a spur-of-the-moment idea hits me, and I voice it aloud. "There's a party tomorrow."

"We had a party last night," Jaxon notes as if my hangover isn't enough of a reminder already.

"And we're having another one tomorrow," I reply.

His eyes thin. "Captain's rules…"

"Yeah, but you're not captain anymore," I remind him dryly. "Griffin is."

Griffin is Jaxon's little brother. And since Jaxon graduated, he's also a shoo-in for the captain spot, and we both know it. Which means I don't have to listen to Jax. Not any longer. And Griff? The guy might be demanding on occasion, but he's a hell of a lot less controlling than Jax, so I'll take it.

"A party sounds fun," Ophelia quips, probably in an attempt to diffuse the situation like she always does.

Ever the people pleaser, Opie.

Why am I not surprised?

With a Cheshire grin, Reeves replies, "Yeah, they're

awesome. Just wait 'til you come to one of the game nights or costume parties—"

"Costume parties?" she asks.

"Yeah." Reeves laughs. "Sometimes we—"

"You'll have to ask Arch," I interrupt. "And since he isn't here…" My shoulders lift. "Guess you'll have to be patient until he's around."

"We won't do a costume party tomorrow night, anyway," Reeves says. "But since I won last week's game, it's my turn to pick what we play. I say we—"

"We'll figure out logistics later," I interrupt.

Ophelia's gaze holds mine, and she tilts her head, studying me for a solid three seconds, then she looks at the ground. "And on that note, I should probably finish unpacking." Her eyes find Jaxon's again. "Good to see you, Jax."

"You too."

"Nice to meet you, Reeves," she adds.

"Same."

Her gaze cuts to mine. "Mav."

"Opie," I return.

Annoyance flashes in her caramel-colored eyes, and she turns on her heel and leaves.

3
OPHELIA

ARCHER

You have no idea how sorry I am I didn't get to see you this morning.

ME

Stop apologizing. Seriously. :)

ARCHER

Still sorry. I'll see you tonight, right?

ME

Duh. You really think you can get rid of me so easily?

ARCHER

I hope not. What are you doing until then?

ME

The sun's out, so I'll probably lay out in the backyard or something. I also still need to finish unpacking. So we'll see.

ARCHER

Wish I was there to help you unpack. Maybe Mav can help?

> **ME**
> I'm good. Thanks, though.

> **ARCHER**
> I'm sure he wouldn't mind.

> **ME**
> And I'm sure you're smoking something. :)
> Regardless, I'm a big girl. Pretty sure I can
> handle emptying a few boxes by myself. I'll
> see you later.

> **ARCHER**
> See you at 7.

> **ME**
> See you.

Sometimes it feels weird. Dating Archer. Okay, weird isn't the right word. It's…nice. He's a great kisser, and I know I'm attracted to him. It's just different. Figuring out how to connect friendship Archer with boyfriend Archer.

Both are good. Great, actually. But it still takes some getting used to. It helps that he's more than willing to take things at my pace. But it still feels strange. Part of me wonders if this is what it's like for everyone. Learning how to let go of certain relationships so you can move on to future ones. It *has* to be normal, doesn't it?

I push the thought aside and get back to work unpacking all my things. Thankfully, the place is already furnished, so I don't have to deal with any big items, mainly clothes, hockey gear, makeup, and other toiletries. I should hit up the grocery store, too, but since I don't have a car, I'll probably have to bum a ride off Archer or one of the other boys sometime soon.

That's another problem for future Ophelia, I decide as I bend down and get to work.

Sweat dribbles down my back as I unload another box. This one is filled with dishes for the kitchen. The glasses are tinted with pink and have little dots indented in the clear crystal glass. With a breath of laughter, I slide one into the cabinet, knowing how much it'll piss Dylan off when she sees them. The girl hates pink with a vengeance. Each of my roommates donated items to the house, and since Finley and Dylan love getting under each other's skin, they took full advantage. Sure, Finley might've chosen these glasses because she knows Dylan hates pink, but Dylan picked the shower curtain in the bathroom covered in Finley's greatest fear. Finley's going to pee her pants when she sees all the cartoon frogs decorating the bathroom. So, a little splash of pink here and there? Yeah. Pretty sure it's an even trade-off.

I dig another glass from the cardboard box when the rumble of an engine at the front of the house grabs my attention. I pause, setting the glass onto the counter and heading to the window overlooking the driveway. I peek through the blinds in time to witness the motorcycle pulling onto the street and disappearing down the road. The driver was wearing a dark helmet, keeping the bike's owner a mystery while only piquing my curiosity more.

Okay, then.

ARCHER WAS LATE. HE DIDN'T MEAN TO BE, BUT APPARENTLY, he's the cat's pajamas at his internship and was wrangled into helping one of the principals with another presentation or something. Once he was finished, he raced to my place and took me out to dinner. Now, here we are, catching up on lost time on his front porch. Technically, it's kind of *our* front porch since they're connected, our front doors sitting side by side.

Weird.

He wraps his arms around my waist and squeezes tightly, stealing the breath from my lungs.

Squirming against him, I pull in a lungful of air. "Careful. If you keep squeezing me like this, I might lose my dinner."

His grip loosens instantly, and he brushes my hair away from my face. "Shit, sorry."

With a light laugh, I tilt my head up, kissing his full lips. It's warm. Comfortable. He reminds me of hot chocolate or a nice bath after sledding, like when we were kids.

I like it.

I like *him*.

The thought flutters around my mind and envelops my constant reluctance whenever I get lost in my head. I lean into his touch a little more, enjoying the moment. The summer air around us is still warm, and the twinkling stars hang high in the sky. It's beautiful and peaceful and perfect. Honestly? I've been building up my expectations for life after high school in my head for so long, it's nice to finally be here. On campus. With Archer and an awesome college experience here for the taking.

"Can't believe you're finally here," he murmurs, reading my mind.

I sigh against his lips. "Me too."

"And this time, you aren't going anywhere." He squeezes me again like he can't help himself. "I'm so glad you decided to come to LAU."

I pull away slightly. "You really think I would've chosen somewhere else?"

"Good point." He kisses me again. "How was moving in? I'm sorry I couldn't be here."

"It was fine. I blasted some music, rolled up my sleeves, and got to work."

"That's my girl."

"Your girl, huh?" I cock my head as the words roll off my tongue.

"Is that a problem?"

I bite my bottom lip, considering his question.

I don't know. Is it?

I should be happy he's so casual about claiming me.

Wanting me.

But there's a twinge of tightness in my stomach, and I can't pinpoint why. Is it excitement? Anticipation? *Fear?* Of losing my best friend if we continue down this road and decide dating is a bad idea. Fear of us moving too fast. Fear of rocking the boat and pissing his family off if things don't work out. Honestly, I'm not sure, but I'm not delusional enough to think it has nothing to do with my still-mending heart.

"Did I say something wrong?" Archer asks. He dips low and puts himself in my line of sight in hopes of bringing me back to the present.

It works.

"No, you definitely didn't say anything wrong," I promise. "I guess I was so used to being Mystery Man's dirty little secret, it's kind of strange having a guy openly call me his."

"Well, I'll shout it from the rooftops if I have to."

"No need," I interrupt with a laugh, adding, "Seriously, don't. Although you should be jealous because Jaxon asked if I wanted to hang out tonight with everyone, and I told him you already had plans of stealing me."

"Damn right, I had plans with you." He squeezes me against his chest again before letting me go. "But I'm glad you have everyone else to hang out with too. I actually feel kind of bad. My mentor wants me to travel with him quite a bit this summer, so it will be busy for me."

"Dude, same." I smooth out the starched dress shirt against his strong chest as it expands beneath my touch. "Not about the traveling part, but between hockey practice and the fundraiser Jaxon mentioned, I'm afraid I might be so busy I won't even notice you're gone."

He grimaces. "Well, I hope you'll *kind of* notice."

I roll my eyes. "You know what I mean."

"Yeah." He pushes my hair away from my face. "I still feel bad, though."

"Don't. Seriously. Especially about the travel part. I think it's awesome. Did Coach Sanderson say anything about how many practices you'll miss?"

"Since the internship will be over by the end of August, I won't miss any games, so as long as I condition on my own, he's okay with it."

"That's good."

"Yeah, it is. And knowing you're okay with it too…" He dips down and kisses my nose.

"You can breathe easier?" I offer.

"Exactly." His eyes search my face. "Can I be honest with you?"

"Always."

"I'm sorry if I'm acting weird. I'm still trying to figure out how to treat girlfriend Ophelia compared to how I would treat friend Ophelia."

"Dude, I've literally had the same thought more times than I can count since we started dating. Meshing the two together is…" I hesitate. "Good. But it's strange sometimes too."

"Yeah." He brings my fingers to his lips and kisses them softly. "We'll figure it out though, right?"

With a smile, I nod. "Yeah, of course. Speaking of figuring things out, Mav mentioned you guys throw costume parties sometimes? But he made it sound like it was a code word or something, and I can't figure out what it means."

"It's not necessarily a code word, but it's hard to explain

what they're like unless you've been to one." He chuckles as if reliving a memory, adding, "Why was he talking about costume parties?"

"Apparently, Mav's throwing a party tomorrow and—"

"One of Reeves' parties?"

"Uh, I'm not sure." I hesitate, lifting a shoulder. "Yes?"

"I'm out of town tomorrow."

"Oh." I frown. "That sucks."

"Yeah." His expression is tight as he stares down at me. "So..."

"So...," I mimic, rising onto my tiptoes and giving him a quick peck.

"So, I'm debating on whether or not I should encourage girlfriend Ophelia to attend one of those parties while I'm away."

"You think I shouldn't go?"

"I've never been naive enough to think I can control what you do," he counters, tugging me closer.

"Girlfriend Lia or Friend Lia?" I ask.

"Both," he answers. "But if you're here to get the full college experience, I guess attending Reeves' parties is part of the deal."

"To be fair, it's only logical since we agreed if I came to LAU, I was allowed to be a regular girl, remember? And that was before girlfriend Ophelia even became a thing." I play with the collar of his shirt, grazing my fingers against the nape of his neck.

"Well then, I hope you have fun at your first college party," he offers, bending closer.

My teeth graze my bottom lip as I grin up at him. "Why, thank you."

His gaze cuts to my lips, and he leans closer when the front door opens with a squeak. I yank away from Archer, finding his brother on the opposite side of the door. Maverick's expression tightens as soon as he sees us. His jaw squeezes, and his asshole persona takes over. Hell, I watch it happen. Like front-row seats on a movie set. The way he buries his real emotions under a blanket of sarcasm and cynicism.

Maverick's always been this way. Genuine. Kind. Then cold. Indifferent. Then, full of over-the-top snark you want to choke on. It's dizzying.

I straighten my spine and prepare myself for the inevitable as he steps onto the porch and closes the door behind him. He flashes his brother a smile, but it doesn't reach his eyes. "How come you started without me? I thought we were going to woo her together, brother."

Archer chuckles. "I think I can handle Lia on my own, but thanks."

Maverick clicks his tongue against the roof of his mouth, shamelessly checking me out and lifting one shoulder. "What a shame." He squeezes past us. "Well, don't let me interrupt your fuckfest."

"We're only kissing," I inform him. "I'd hardly call it fucking, but if you want to stick around, by all means, please do."

"Don't tempt me, Opie." His eyes darken. "I might surprise you."

"I was just telling Lia I'm going out of town tomorrow," Archer interrupts. "Any chance you can keep an eye on her?"

"I don't need anyone keeping an eye on me," I announce.

"See?" Mav waves his hand toward me as a car pulls up to the curb. "Our little Opie's a big girl. She'll be fine. Although, I'll be sure to play her pseudo-boyfriend at the party while you're away. You know, take one for the team and all." With a smirk, he skips the last two porch stairs, jogs toward the car parked out front, and climbs into the passenger seat.

"See ya, Lia!" Reeves calls from the driver's side.

I give him a small wave as he backs out of the driveway, disappearing down the road with Maverick beside him.

"Sorry." Archer looks sheepish as he grabs the back of his neck and offers a smile. "But at least he likes you, right?"

"No, he's being completely over the top and fake because you told him to be nice to me," I counter. "Didn't you?"

"I might've made a suggestion or two. How'd you know?"

"Because I might be girlfriend Ophelia, but I was friend Ophelia long before that," I remind him. "And I've also known Maverick my entire life." Hooking my thumb over my shoulder, I add, "The stranger who propositioned me is hardly your brother."

"It's better than him ignoring you, isn't it?"

"Honestly, I can't decide," I mutter. "Sometimes I wonder how you two share the same DNA."

"Pretty sure you aren't the only one."

"You guys couldn't be more opposite if you tried. Well, other than hockey and good looks," I clarify, tugging on the edge of his lapel in hopes of bringing him closer.

"Ah, so, my talent on the ice and my good looks are what's keeping me in your good graces?"

"Obviously," I say with a grin, kissing him.

When I pull away, I notice a slight dip in his brows as he studies me. "You okay?" he murmurs.

"With what?" I ask. "You mean with Maverick?" I snort. "Archer, I'm not a delicate flower."

"I know. But I hate how you two don't get along. And even when I ask him to play nice, he still manages to piss you off."

"It's Maverick," I remind him. "Does he get along with anyone?"

"Seems good with every other woman on the planet."

"Only when he's trying to get in their pants," I argue. "And since it's not an option where I'm concerned, he'll resort to...

41

whatever that was, which is fine, by the way," I add. "I can handle his sarcasm. I'll ignore him like I usually do."

"You won't be able to ignore him forever."

"That's a problem for future Lia," I quip.

"Mm-hmm." His hands tighten around my waist. "You still going to his party?"

I nod. "I'm here to experience college, remember? Even if it includes sarcastic buttheads like Maverick. So, yeah. I think I will."

"I'm almost sad I'll miss it."

"Ditto."

4

MAVERICK

F ucking hell.

I can hear them. It makes sense. We share a wall. Maybe they're watching a movie, or maybe they're fucking each other's brains out, but if I have to keep listening to this shit, I'll wind up putting a bullet in my skull if I'm not careful.

Fucking Opie. The woman knows how to get under my skin more than anyone else in the world, and she just had to wind up with my brother.

Shoving my pillow over my head, I wait for them to shut up and fall into a restless sleep.

AFTER PISSING IN THE BATHROOM, I HEAD TO THE KITCHEN BUT stop short when I find Lia leaning against the island in one of Archer's T-shirts. A coffee cup is pressed to her lips, and her hair is piled on top of her head, leaving curls of chaos framing her slender face. When she sees me, her eyes narrow over the rim of her cup, but she doesn't comment, taking another sip of coffee as she waits for something.

"Ever heard of pants?" I ask.

She looks down at her bare legs and quirks her brow. "Do you ever make your conquests wear pants?"

"You're not one of my conquests." My eyes slide down her bare legs. "Not recently, anyway."

"Keep dreaming, Maverick."

I bite my bottom lip. "You can fucking count on it."

She lets out a soft scoff and presses her pouty lips into a thin line.

"What? Is there a problem with me imagining myself between your pretty little thighs?" I bounce my brows up and down.

"Cut the bullshit," she snaps. "Archer isn't here to witness your charade or...whatever the hell this is, so give it a rest."

My facade falls, and I fold my arms. "Where is he?"

"Already left."

"Yet you're still here," I mutter, searching the cabinets and finding a mug of my own.

I fill it with coffee, ignoring the lethal gaze burning the side of my face.

"So, what's the problem?" she prods.

"You don't live here."

"So?"

"So, why are you here?" I ask. "If Archer already left, why are you standing in my kitchen in nothing but a thong and a borrowed T-shirt like you own the place?"

She lifts the shirt, showcasing a pair of boy shorts. They hug her ass and *almost* outline her pussy. She quirks her brow. "Not wearing a thong. And I'm not going anywhere. Although I *am* impressed with how you've set aside the snarky persona for a solid two minutes so we can potentially have an actual conversation. Bravo, Maverick."

"The question is, what do we do without it?" I move closer, crowding her space. "Do I put you on the counter and—"

"Stop," she orders.

"What? You don't want to hear me tell you all the ways I can make you come? I'd say it's hardly fair, considering the front-row seats I had to Archer being inside you last night."

Her flinch cuts me off, bringing a wave of guilt with it, but I hold back my apology and glare down at her, daring her to deny it. To tell me she didn't sleep with my brother. That she hasn't been sleeping with my brother.

"Mav," she whispers. And fuck me, the sound shoots straight to my groin.

"Say your peace so you can make yourself feel better, Opie," I snap, too fucking impatient for my own good. "Then you can be on your way since that's what you want, right?"

She shakes her head and keeps her voice quiet. "You're not allowed to be mad at me, Mav."

"Thank you for telling me how I'm allowed to feel," I return.

"I think it's time we—"

"I'm leaving." Frustration burns in my chest, and I step toward the exit.

Her grasp on my hand halts me as she wrenches me back. Well, tries to. The girl might be strong, but we both know she could never physically make me stay if I didn't want to.

So why am I still fucking standing here?

Glaring down at her, I take in her small, dainty hand encasing part of my wrist. The way her chest heaves as she stares up at me. The glint of hurt in her brown sugar irises. The way they make me want to crumble, right here, right now.

Been there. Done that. Didn't exactly get me far.

My upper lip curls at the reminder. "Get your hand off me."

"I'm sorry," she snaps. "I'm sorry my"—she scans the hallway, confirming we're alone—"*date* bailed on me an hour before prom, and I'm sorry I let your brother take me instead. I'm sorry I'm dating your brother and you have to hear us hanging out in his room at night. But it's not like you actually care. If you did, you wouldn't have—" Her mouth snaps closed, and she shakes her head. "Look, it doesn't even matter. Can we please move on and pretend like it never happened?"

"What do you think I've been doing?"

"Other than being an ass?" she quips. "Beats me."

"I'm always an ass," I remind her. "If you want the upstanding citizen, I suggest you talk to Archer."

"Archer isn't here."

"Exactly." I step forward, crowding her against the counter until her pert ass hits the edge of the granite. "So the question is, why are you?"

"Because I want to talk. I want to…make amends or something."

"Why?"

"Because you hate me, and I'm sick of you hating me."

"Fine. We're square. My pride is intact. You're fucking my brother. Everything's great."

Again, she flinches at the sharpness in my words but doesn't call me out for being a dick as she looks up at me. "Great."

"Great," I repeat.

"Great." She lets me go, grabs her keys from the counter and slips past me, storming out of the house. A moment later, I hear the familiar sound of another door banging closed.

She went home.

She's out of my hair.

For now, anyway.

If only she'd keep it that way so I could breathe.

Fucking great.

5

OPHELIA

I miss Dylan. And Finley. But especially Dylan since we grew closer after Finley's family moved across the country a few years ago. Not that it matters. Once they move in, Dylan will catch Finley up on all the drama in my life, and they can both laugh at me together. Regardless, I could really use a wingwoman to help me get through tonight. I'm still not sure why I'm here. Why I decided this was a good idea, especially after my conversation with Mav this morning. But I can't help it. I'm curious. What the Buchanan twins' lives are like when the veil is stripped away, and I can see what the *real* LAU college life is like instead of the glimpses I caught while visiting. The life they've kept separate from me until tonight. Until this moment.

Puffing out my cheeks, I stare at the boys' side of the duplex and try not to puke as I wipe my sweaty palms on my frayed jean shorts. There are so many people. Even the front lawn is packed with strangers holding cups of alcohol while laughing with each other. The front door is wedged open, allowing the glow from the entryway to spill onto the porch, highlighting a couple who are currently swallowing each other's tongues.

Wow.

Keeping my focus glued to the ground, I head to the front door and step inside, avoiding the tongue hockey competition on my right. The bass is thumping and all the furniture lines the walls, leaving a makeshift dance floor in the center of the family room. The open floor plan leaves the kitchen in sight from the front door. Different glass bottles, liters of soda, and plastic cups cover the kitchen table and granite countertops. Of course, there's free booze, and truth be told, I kind of want some. The lights are dim, and the scent of sweaty bodies, cheap cologne, and too-sweet perfume clings to the air as I head toward the kitchen. My nose wrinkles from the smell, but I don't retreat to my side of the duplex. I'm here to experience college, and if this is how some people experience it, then dammit, so will I.

I grew up absorbing my parents' stories of their experiences at LAU. How it was the best time of their lives. How it changed them forever. They only fed my curiosity more. Now, here I am. It's surreal.

And kind of terrifying.

"Lia, you're here!" a gruff voice greets me. It's Griffin, one of Dylan's older brothers. He pulls me into a bear hug.

"Hey, Griff!" I squeeze him back, and he lets me go. "Long time, no see."

"Yeah, it's been way too long," he agrees. "I didn't know you'd be coming to Game Night."

"You got a problem with me being here?"

His eyes thin as if he's caught in a silent debate with himself. "You sure you're ready for Game Night?"

"Why does everyone make Game Night sound so ominous?" I challenge.

"Because it's Reeves' turn to pick," he jokes. "Speaking of which, I'm going to make you a two."

"A two?"

"Reeves chose a game involving partners. Half the people here are ones, and the other half are twos." He grabs my hand, writes a big number two on the back of it with a permanent marker, and motions to the side table beside him. There's a massive glass bowl, a Sharpie, and a small stack of papers on the entry table. Griffin picks a slip of cardstock up and hands it to me. "Write your name on this."

"What's it for?"

"It's for the game." He motions to the half-full bowl. "This is how we make it random. People with a one on their hands will pick a name in a few minutes, and people with a two on their hands put their names in the pot."

"Okay, then." I uncap the black marker with my mouth, and after scrawling my name along the paper, I fold it in half and shove it into the bowl with the others.

Satisfied, Griffin presses his hand to my back. "All right, let me introduce you to a few people before the game begins. But first, you need a drink."

"You have no idea," I mutter.

Weaving between people, we make our way along the least crowded path to the kitchen, and I pour myself a rum and Coke while Griffin catches up with a few of his classmates. The carbonation bubbles tickle my nostrils as I take a sip, letting the soothing warmth spread down my throat.

Within minutes, Griffin's introductions blur together, and I have no idea if I could regurgitate a single name or fun fact, even if my life depended on it. Regardless, I appreciate his friendliness. His attempt to welcome me into the fold. There's a difference between being friendly at a family function and being friendly at a college party. Being friendly *here*?

When I feel like I'm on a different planet? It means more than I want to admit.

If only it would erase the niggling in the back of my mind. It's like a woodpecker is inside my skull. A baby wood-pecker. One without the strength to give me a full-blown headache, but it's still annoyingly persistent and keeps me scanning the main floor in search of a certain twin I want nothing to do with despite my best attempts to ignore him.

"Archer's not here," Griffin says as if he can read my mind.

I look up at him and smile in an attempt to seem like he didn't catch me doing something I shouldn't be. "I know. I was looking for your bathroom."

"Ah." He nods, gesturing toward the hallway. "Same place as yours. The layouts are just flipped."

"Got it," I reply. "I'll see you in a bit."

"Sounds good, but don't be late." He checks the time on his phone. "Game starts in five."

"Okay."

The bathroom door closes with a quiet click and mutes the chaos from the main area. After using the restroom, I wash my hands and take a deep breath, the incessant ques-tion of why I'm here rolling through my brain like a pinball.

I shouldn't have come.

Not when Archer isn't here.

But going home sounds pretty terrible too. Especially since I've been dreaming about my life at LAU long before prom. Long before my world was flipped upside down. Long before I had my heart broken by one person, only for their twin to be the one to put the pieces back together again. Or at least...most of them.

A loud bell rings throughout the main floor, and I jerk at the sound. Hands begin pounding on the walls outside the bathroom and down the hallway, followed by whistling and shouting. It shakes the picture frames on the wall and rattles my insides, piquing my curiosity. After drying my hands on the dark blue towel hanging from its hook, I open the bathroom door and freeze. The door on the opposite side of the hall opens at the same time. Maverick stops short when he sees me. His wavy hair is damp from a recent shower and looks like he's been running his fingers through it.

Surprised I actually came, Maverick? I want to ask. *Yeah, me too.*

The crooked smirk I've grown accustomed to plays at the edge of his lips as he slips his sarcastic mask into place. But it isn't meant for me. It's meant for everyone else. Everyone who might see us talking. Who might see us interact. Who might see Maverick chatting with his brother's girlfriend and playing nice despite our past no one knows about.

It's strange. The way it draws me to him yet pushes me away. Because I know it's fake. It's *all* fake. But even *I* have to admit he's convincing. With a look like that, you'd never know I was on his shit list. Too bad for me, my name is written on it in thick, bold Sharpie like the one I used to enter whatever game we're playing tonight, and there isn't anything on this planet strong enough to erase it. Then again, it isn't my problem. He's the asshole who broke my heart, not the other way around. It seems he's forgotten that little tidbit.

So what if his brother is the one offering to piece it back together again?

"You ready to play a game, Opie?" Maverick challenges.

I lift my chin and fold my arms. "Only if you stop calling me Opie."

He grins even bigger, but it doesn't reach his navy blue eyes as they flick over my body and return to my gaze. He holds my attention for another beat, then he heads down the hall and into the family room. My footsteps are hesitant as I follow behind him. Flurries of unease and curiosity flutter beneath my skin. The place is somehow even more packed than when I'd escaped to the bathroom. Reeves is standing on the coffee table in the family room, making himself an extra eighteen inches taller than everyone else in the space. There's a thick gold chain around his neck, along with a three-inch gaudy medallion, though I can't see what it says. When he sees me, Reeves smirks, and I give him a tiny wave as he stands on the small platform. Maverick witnesses the interaction and pushes me behind his back, placing himself between us while also cutting off my line of sight.

"Hey!" I grab his shirt at the base of his spine, attempting to step around him, but he mirrors my movements.

Barely casting me a glance, Maverick says, "Just trying to keep my friend from getting his ass kicked, Opie."

"By who? Archer isn't here, remember?" I shift from one foot to the other, attempting to move around him, but he meets my movements with his own.

Turning to face me, Maverick grunts, "Archer's not the one he'll have to deal with if Reeves doesn't get his head out of his ass." He grabs my shoulders to keep me from squirming. "Now stay."

"Am I a dog?" I question, but before he has a chance to reply, Reeves' voice booms off the walls and Maverick lets me go, turning to face his friend on the coffee table again. I peek around him, watching the night unfold.

"Ladies and gentlemen," Reeves announces. He does a slow turn on the table, confirming he has everyone's attention. "As you know, I was the victor at the last Game Night and won bragging rights, along with this bad boy right here." He lifts the oversized medallion and kisses it, pulling laughs from everyone around me. "Now, we have a few more people here tonight, so I'm gonna give you a quick run-through of the rules for Game Night. If you came here with a date, give them a kiss and step aside. Jealousy stays at the door. If you don't have enough faith in your relationship to last an evening at Game Night, you probably shouldn't be together in the first place. And remember, everything that happens at Game Night *stays* at Game Night. If you walked in here tonight, you agreed to play whatever game is announced, which is what I'll be doing as soon as every person is paired. Ones, pick a name, any name." Reeves' grin widens as the giant glass bowl is passed around the room from one pair of hands to the next. Sure enough, every person with a one scrawled on their skin sticks their hands into the bowl, pulls a piece of paper out, and scans the area for their partner. Once Everett has plucked a piece of paper from the mass, he hands Maverick the bowl. Mav takes a slip of paper and opens it, letting out a low, bitter laugh.

"Is there a problem?" I ask. I rise onto my tiptoes and peek over Maverick's shoulder to see who he's paired with, but he crumples the notecard and stuffs it in his back pocket.

The same low laugh greets me as he turns around, his expression unreadable. "Looks like you're with me, Opie."

My heels hit the ground, and I pull back. "Should I be worried?"

His mouth lifts, but it's tainted somehow. Like he's holding back a sneer. "Probably."

Great.

6
OPHELIA

"And now, for the game." Reeves spreads his arms wide as he stands on the coffee table in the center of the room like an announcer for the Hunger Games. "Tonight, we'll be playing The Floor is Lava!"

Cheering erupts.

Eating up the chaos, Reeves rubs his hands together and does another slow spin, confirming he still has everyone's attention. "Rules are simple. You touch the ground, your judge—which is me—decides whether your team takes a shot or loses an item of clothing. When I shout earthquake, you must move to a different piece of furniture without touching the ground. When I yell, *freeze*, you stop moving. If you don't, your judge again decides if you and your teammate take a shot or lose an item of clothing. You're out when you're puking or naked. The last team standing wins bragging rights, the medallion, and game choice at the next Game Night. Any questions?"

A beat of silence passes, and a kid who looks like he can't be much older than me approaches.

"You guys partners?" he asks, eyeing me and Mav, while he twirls a set of handcuffs around his forefinger.

With a nod, Maverick offers his wrist. The kid snaps a handcuff around it, giving me a look that says, "You too."

My brows crinkle, but I raise my arm, mimicking Maverick's offer. The metal is cold against my skin as the guy snaps it into place and moves on to the next team, leaving me alone —and literally chained—to the man beside me.

If only I didn't know he'd prefer to be teamed up with literally anyone else in the world. And the silence? The way he's avoiding me? It's not exactly comfortable. I wipe my hands against my shorts, but Maverick's arm follows. The back of his hand almost brushes against my crotch until I realize what's happening. My body locks up for a split second, and I straight-arm us both until our hands hang in front of us like we're starring in a zombie movie.

"Shit, sorry," I rush out. My cheeks flame as I stare at the ground in front of me, willing it to open up and swallow me entirely.

"Just...don't move," Mav mutters, slowly urging me to drop our hands to our sides.

"Got it." I click my tongue against the roof of my mouth.

The awkward silence is deafening, but at least he isn't being a sarcastic dickhead, so I guess it's a win, right? Then again, I'm not sure I'm a fan of him ignoring me, either. He can't even look at me, and I'm a foot away from him.

Rocking back on my heels, I peek up at Mav and ask, "So...who was that?"

"Who?"

I tilt my head toward the guy with the handcuffs.

When he realizes who I'm talking about, he challenges, "Why? Do you want his number too?"

"Wow." I ignore the sharp twinge in my chest and start to fold my arms, belatedly remembering we're still cuffed together. Fisting my hands at my sides, I mutter, "And here I thought you were giving asshole Maverick a night off."

"And here I thought you knew me better than that."

"Okay, fine," I huff. "We won't talk. We'll just silently stand next to each other until the game starts."

"Good."

"Yeah, not awkward at all, and it definitely won't raise any red flags to all your friends, now will it?" I glare up at him, daring him to tell me I'm wrong when we both know I'm not.

"Fine." His nostrils flare as he looks over my head. "I don't know his name. He's a freshman."

"And he's on handcuff duty?"

"The younger class helps with the shit work until they prove themselves and we let them participate in the games."

"But not me?" I prod. "I'm a freshman, and I haven't proven myself—"

"You're a girl."

"So?"

"The guys give free passes to the girls," he clarifies while *still* avoiding my gaze like I was diagnosed with syphilis or something.

I'd be offended if the reminder of which head guys like to think with didn't amuse me. "Of course they—"

Someone runs into Maverick, and like a stack of dominos, he bumps into me, bringing us chest-to-chest. My breath catches as his familiar scent washes over me, the memories of all our late nights together crashing into me all at once. Every inch of his body presses against mine. My hands are splayed against his pecs, the steady thump-thump of his heart beating against my palm. His warmth. His scent. His arms.

Snap the hell out of it, Lia!

I step back and tuck my hair behind my ear with my uncuffed hand. "So...are you still competitive?" I ask.

"You could say so." He clears his throat. "You?"

My mouth lifts, and I look up at him. "You could say so."

"Well, at least we have a chance of winning," he grumbles. His eyes fall to our connected hands, his jaw tightening as he looks away, not saying another word.

"I guess we do," I murmur, ignoring the zing of our hands brushing against each other. It's stupid. And juvenile. But then again, so is this game.

To be fair, I get it. The odds of me being hooked with Maverick freaking Buchanan is just my luck. Or *our* luck, apparently, since neither of us can seem to catch a break.

I don't bother filling the silence anymore. I'm not sure I can convince my tongue to form words anyway. Not when he's standing this close. Not when I can feel every single emotion radiating off him. Resentment. Annoyance. Frustration.

Like I'm a fly in his soup or an eyelash in his eye.

I nibble on my thumbnail of our non-connected hands while everyone finishes being cuffed to their partners. After a satisfied Reeves says something to one of the freshmen a minute later, he cups his hands around his mouth and yells, "Earthquake!"

Let the game begin.

7

OPHELIA

Like mice, everyone scurries for a surface above ground. Cushions are already spread out on the floor, and most of the tables have been cleared off, leaving a decent amount of room for people to stand, but the spots are filling up fast. Maverick pulls me toward a side table, and we climb onto it as a pair of *very* drunk girls race toward the same cushion on the ground with their men trailing behind. Clearly, they're already plastered, thanks to the free refreshments from earlier. They clash together like cymbals, landing on their asses as a bout of giggles overtakes them while their partners stare dumbfounded at each other, their feet still touching the ground, er, *lava*.

"Freeze!" Reeves yells. He stares down at the drunk girls from his perch on the coffee table and orders, "Tops."

Neither girl bats an eye as they reach for the hems of their shirts and pull them over their heads, leaving them in their bras while they succumb to another fit of giggles. The guys do the same, but thanks to the chain linking them to their partners, their clothes hang in the center, dangling next to the girls' already discarded shirts like a makeshift clothesline.

It isn't sexual. Honestly, it's kind of funny.

A few more girls stumble onto the ground, and Reeves orders them and their partners to take shots, all of which more freshmen deliver. When everyone has finished the shots, he yells, "Earthquake!" another time.

I jump off the side table onto a pillow, hopscotching it to the cushion-free couch. Maverick follows my movements when a few more people hit the ground with a thud.

"Freeze!" Reeves calls.

Another couple loses their shirts, and a few more take shots presented by the freshman who cuffed me to Maverick earlier.

Gotta give the kid an A-plus for his service.

Once they've downed their tequila, Reeves gives a satisfied nod and calls, "Earthquake!"—again—from the coffee table.

My mind races for a new place to stand. I jump from the couch to a discarded cushion on the floor to the coffee table in the center of the room. It brings me up close and personal with the judge himself. *Oops.* Maverick slides in behind me, his warmth hitting my back and pushing my front even closer to Reeves.

I'm sandwiched between them. Two hot bodies. Both literally *and* metaphorically.

Yeah. They're not exactly hard on the eyes. I'll give them that much.

Reeves grins down at me and cocks his head.

"Is this against the rules?" I murmur. "Like a no-go zone, or—"

"Freeze!" he booms, but he doesn't tear his attention from me as he points to a few more people who touched the ground. "Shot. Shot. Shot. Bottoms. Shot. Top." He rattles off the orders but doesn't shout earthquake again like I expect. He simply looks at me. Waiting. But I don't know what he's waiting for.

"Reeves?" I quirk my brow.

"I'm seriously regretting letting Mav talk me into The Floor is Lava."

"You and me both," Maverick grits out from behind me. The words caress the back of my head, causing a ripple of awareness to skate along my spine.

Attempting to ignore it, I ask Reeves, "And what would you have chosen?"

"I dunno." He shrugs, his eyes finding Maverick's and returning to me. "Spin the Bottle. Chase. Truth or Dare."

"Reeves," Maverick warns. His fingers brush mine, but Reeves continues rattling off game ideas, leaning closer to me. "Strip Poker. Seven Minutes in—"

"Are you gonna call earthquake yet?" Griffin interrupts from a few feet away. He's currently on his tiptoes, balancing between a couple of coasters tossed haphazardly on the floor with his partner clinging to him like a human backpack.

He's right. We're playing a game. And now is *not* the time to be sandwiched between two guys—especially when neither is my boyfriend—let alone discussing Spin the Bottle, Truth or Dare, or Seven Minutes in Heaven.

My tongue darts between my lips, pulling another smirk from Reeves, and I call out, "Earthquake!"

Reeves grabs my wrist to keep me in place, preventing my escape—*our* escape—as the rest of the teams scramble around us.

"Reeves," Maverick grits out from behind me.

Reeves ignores him, chuckling, "That was a foul, Lia."

"Oh, it was?"

"Mm-hmm." He nods. "Freeze!" The hustle and bustle

around us ceases almost instantly. "I'm gonna need you to lose some clothes," he adds.

"Reeves," Maverick grinds out.

"Two fouls?" I ask.

"You called earthquake when it wasn't your job, *and* you didn't move when you were supposed to after it was called," Reeves clarifies.

"You were holding my wrist," I point out.

"Happy coincidence. You need to take off your shirt and pants now." He locks eyes with Mav over the top of my head. "You, too, man. I don't make the rules."

"Pretty sure you're the only person who makes the rules," I muse.

Reeves smirks but doesn't deny it as his eyes fall on me again. "Chop, chop, Ophelia."

Rustling sounds behind me, followed by a light weight pressing against the chain connecting me to Maverick. Cotton skates against the back of my hand, and I look down. It's Maverick's T-shirt.

Apparently, Reeves wasn't kidding about the fouls.

Maverick bends down but is careful to stay planted on the coffee table as he shoves his jeans down his thighs and kicks them onto the ground, creating another option for us to stand on.

Smart.

If he wasn't so insane to oblige Reeves' bullshit rules in the first place.

Looking over my shoulder at Mav, I ask, "We're really doing this?"

"Mav's a competitive fucker, isn't he?" Reeves chimes in.

My lips bunch, knowing he isn't wrong, while I attempt to come to terms with the fact that I'm standing six inches from an almost naked Maverick covered in fresh tattoos.

What the hell?

Those are new.

Like, really new.

My fingers itch to reach out and touch them to see if they're real. To see if he's really had countless tattoos added in a matter of weeks. It's...strange.

Isn't it?

Once Maverick finishes stripping, Reeves grins down at me. "It's your turn, Opie."

"Don't call me Opie," I warn him.

"Why not?"

"Might wanna tread lightly," Maverick suggests, interrupting my rebuttal. "Our girl might look like an innocent fawn, but she isn't afraid to stab people in the back when she's been slighted." My jaw drops, and he adds, "Besides, she only likes it when I call her Opie."

I'm careful as I turn around so I don't bump any of us off the table and hold his stare with a quirked brow. "Pretty sure I don't like it when *anyone* calls me Opie."

"I could always call you Goose instead."

The name feels like a knife to the chest as an oblivious Reeves coos, "Aw, like *Top Gun*."

"We're adorable, I know," Maverick tells him as his eyes find mine again. "Now, hurry up and take your clothes off so we can finish this game, yeah?"

I roll my eyes but give in, tossing my pants onto the ground and leaving my shirt hanging on the chain between us until I'm in nothing but a pair of boy shorts and a gray cotton bra. It's nothing too crazy—hell, it covers more than some of my swimsuits—but I make a mental note to follow the rest of Reeves' orders until the end of the game because there's no way I'm getting naked in front of these fools no matter how competitive I can be.

No, thank you.

"Not too shabby," Reeves compliments behind me. I peek

over my shoulder for the hundredth time since we started this game, finding him shamelessly checking me out with the same boyish smile.

Maverick spins me around and covers my half-naked body with his, placing himself between me and his best friend. "Are we gonna keep the game going, or am I gonna have to beat your ass on behalf of my brother?"

"Your brother. *Right.*" Reeves jumps off the table and picks up a few of the pillows, along with Maverick's jeans and a bunch of coasters from the ground.

"What are you doing?" I ask Reeves.

Maverick answers for him. "The game never ends unless he makes it...*harder.*"

A few of the girls close by laugh at the innuendo, and Maverick winks at them while Griffin argues, "Ah, come on!" from across the room, thanks to Reeves grabbing the edge of the pillow from beneath Griffin's feet. Griff jumps onto the couch beside his partner so he doesn't wind up on his ass, taking the last patch of empty space. The sofa is packed now. So much so I'm kind of surprised Griff was able to fit his broad shoulders on the thing in the first place. There are at least seven people piled on there, each of them standing toe to toe. It's actually pretty comical. Seeing how tipsy everyone is while playing a childish game like this. One of the girls starts twerking against him playfully but loses her balance and lands on the carpet with a thump, dragging her partner with her. She's the same girl from the beginning who ran into a friend and landed on her ass.

Reeves shakes his head, telling her she and her partner are out. The girl sticks her bottom lip out but doesn't argue as Reeves shouts, "Earthquake!"

"Follow my lead this time," Maverick orders. My pants are still bunched by our feet, and he kicks them onto the floor. He uses them as a stepping stone and jumps to a large pillow about five feet away. He's careful not to drag me with him, but I bend at the waist anyway, giving him some more slack. Once he's situated, he motions for me to follow.

"Where do you expect me to land?" I ask.

"Just jump!" he urges. His attention slides to our pseudo-judge for the evening as if he's counting down the seconds until the inevitable order for us to freeze will ring through the air.

The pillow is barely big enough for Maverick's feet, let alone mine, but I leap onto it anyway, knowing how little time we have. When my feet hit the edge of the pillow, I lose my balance, but his hands find my waist, keeping me steady. Maverick wraps his free arm around my waist and pulls me closer until I'm plastered against him. I press my palm against his very naked, very tattooed chest while our chained hands hang at our sides. My breathing is chaotic and unsteady as I try to catch my breath, keep my balance, and *not* lose my shit, thanks to how close I am to a certain twin I want nothing to do with. This is a precarious position at best. Or maybe it isn't, and I'm overthinking things. Most of the teams have been in positions like this all night. So why should I care if our fronts are practically glued together? But even with that knowledge, my adrenaline from the jump mixes with fear and anticipation. Anticipation I definitely shouldn't be feeling right now. Not like this. Not when I'm only in my bra and underwear and I'm squished against my ex's bare chest.

Reeves must've yelled freeze because he's doling out punishments to anyone touching the ground while Maverick and I stay frozen in place, pressed together from head to freaking toe. I can hear his heart racing in my ear. Or maybe it's my own.

Okay, it's definitely my own.

The question is, can he hear it?

Pasting on a fake smile, I peek up at him, desperate to diffuse the tension swirling around me, even if I'm the only one feeling it.

"And you really thought this was better than Spin the Bottle or Truth or Dare?" I ask.

"Count on Reeves to spill all my secrets," he mutters, staring at the wall behind me.

"Not all of them," I whisper.

The words hit harder than I anticipate, and his eyes snap to mine before his attention falls to my mouth. I swear I can feel the air crackle around us. The way his arm flexes ever-so-slightly around my waist. The way his eyes heat a fraction. The way his full lips part as if he wants to say something, but he swallows it back.

Shit.

I shouldn't have said that.

I shouldn't have hinted…hinted about our secrets and how I was his.

It's always been this way with Maverick. He's unpredictable. Charged. Like a storm. Archer's the calm. And one is *so* much more dangerous than the other.

Pulling my free hand from his very hot, very naked chest, I shy away from him and ask, "So…any idea how we're going to be able to get off this pillow without losing?"

He blinks away the heat in his eyes and looks over my shoulder, scanning the ground for a safe haven. "I might have one idea."

"Oh?"

"Depends on if I'm feeling generous or not."

"You haven't decided?" I question, forcing a laugh.

"I mean, I'm *always* generous." He smirks. "Give me a sec."

He studies our options, and I do the same.

There's exactly one path to the barstool leading to the kitchen table and granite island. All the drinks have been set on the ground. Which is great unless you fall on them. Yeah, that would hurt. But still. There's a lot of open counter space in the kitchen. If we want to win, we need to get there.

"We're gonna need a truce if we wanna win this," he mutters.

"Okay?" I lift one shoulder. "Truce."

With a soft bob of his head, he prods, "Do you trust me?"

It's a dangerous question, especially considering everything we've gone through, and I find myself shaking my head. "Not in the slightest, but in this circumstance? Sure, why not?"

Amusement tugs at the corners of his full lips as he stares down at me, noting, "Someone's feeling sassy."

"I learned from the best."

"Mm-hmm." He leans closer, his breath kissing the shell of my ear. "I'd say I should smack your ass, but since it isn't my job anymore..." I gulp, and he pulls away from me. "Be a good little monkey and climb on my back."

My brows bunch. "What?"

"I'm gonna turn around, and you're gonna climb on my back." He shifts slightly from left to right, attempting to change position.

Friction sparks from his movements and burns my bare skin, but I ignore it as I try not to fall on my ass and lose the game. "Stop moving," I order. "You'll knock me off."

He stops almost instantly and scrubs his hand over his face. "Fine. Do you have any suggestions?"

"Uh, what if I..." I swallow, the words getting lost on my tongue.

"What if you what?"

"Here." I grab onto his shoulder with my good hand, preparing to wrap my legs around his waist when his hand finds my thigh, and he squeezes.

"Don't get me wrong, I love it when a girl wraps her legs

around my waist, but when it's my brother's girlfriend?" He tsks. "I gotta draw the line somewhere, right?"

My eyes narrow. "Don't flatter yourself."

"Aw, come on, Goose. You think I don't notice the way your cheeks are flushed? I bet if I slipped my hand—"

"Will you shut up?" I seethe. "If we want to win, this is the way to do it."

He scoffs and looks at the barstool a few feet away. "You really think I can make the jump while carrying you?"

"Well, for starters, I'm pretty sure you were the one who suggested you carry me in the first place. And second, is the infamous Maverick Buchanan questioning himself?" I shake my head and shove him *just* hard enough so he doesn't lose his footing but still feels my amusement. "Come on. You can do anything."

"Fine. But only because Griff and Everett are dicks when they win these things." With a deep breath, he grabs my thighs and lifts me up. I use my free hand to hold onto his shoulder and jump. Once my legs are wrapped around his waist, I burrow my head into his neck, holding on tight and attempting to help meld our centers of gravity into one so it's easier for him to stick the landing. His arms are like a vice as he holds me close, readying himself for the inevitable order from Reeves to start the next round.

"Earthquake!" Reeves calls.

Squeezing my eyes shut, I hold on for dear life and squeal when Maverick's feet leave the ground. As his feet land on the edge of the barstool, Mav bends forward to keep the stool from tipping over, and when I realize we've made it, I laugh, slowly untucking my head from the crook of his neck. Caught between triumph and disbelief, I peek up at him. When our eyes meet, his cock twitches against my core, and my mouth falls open, my lungs seizing as I recognize the familiar swell of his erection nestled between my thighs.

Shit.

His eyes hold mine hostage, and my heart rate goes haywire, my clit pulsing against him as my hips shift subtly like they have a mind of their own. The familiar word "Freeze" echoes off the wall. I barely register it. I'm too distracted. Too turned on. And apparently, I'm not the only one because Maverick doesn't move.

It doesn't matter how competitive he is. It doesn't matter how much he hates losing and showing weakness. I've thrown him off his game. And right now—with a single look and a subtle shift of my hips—we both know it.

He jumps off the barstool, marching us toward the freshman with the keys while I cling to him like the stupid little monkey I am.

"Off. Now." When he smacks my ass, *hard,* my feet hit the ground in an instant as I slide off him, but my thoughts and libido and heart are still ten seconds behind while I replay what just happened. The freshman finds the key and unlocks the cuffs around our wrists, though I'm too dazed to notice.

Once he's free, Maverick heads back to his room and closes the door behind him without a single glance in my direction while Reeves calls him a pussy for quitting. I know he's kidding. I know he has no clue what transpired between Maverick and me.

But one thing's for sure.

Wrapping your legs around your ex's waist under the guise of an innocent game is a bad idea.

A really bad idea.

I won't let it happen again.

8

OPHELIA

I took a month off. One. Freaking. Month. Thirty-two days, to be exact. I was a little busy with prom, and having my heart broken, and dating my best friend, and surviving high school graduation, and moving, and signing up for fall classes, and the list goes on and on and on. Unfortunately, my body is yelling at me for it.

I feel like I'm being asphyxiated as I sprint from one end of the rink to the other, decked out in my pads, gloves, chest protector, neck guard, and helmet. It's as if my body weighs an extra hundred pounds, and all things considered, I'm probably not too far off. My first practice with the girls' team starts next week, and I want to be ready. Or at least as ready as I can be. Thankfully, Jaxon informed me the guys haven't started their official practices yet either, so as long as the reservation form for the rink is blank, I can practice here as often as I want. And if my screaming lungs are anything to go by, I'll probably eat, breathe, and sleep here for the foreseeable future. It's probably for the best, considering last night's Game Night. I still can't believe I felt him against

70

me. I can't believe he still affects me like that. That I still affect him.

Get a grip, girl.

He broke *your* heart, remember?

I don't affect him.

It was nothing more than a physical response. That's it.

Purely. Physical.

Just like the rest of our relationship.

Sweat drips down my spine, but I don't surrender to my desire for rest. Instead, I push myself harder, racing past the red line and stopping short in an instant. Slush sprays against the opposing net, and I catch my breath when applause sounds behind me.

Curious, I turn around. Six guys are lined up near LAU's bench wearing their skates, leggings, and gloves like I am, but their pads and helmets are missing, leaving their amused expressions on full display. I recognize a few of them from the party, but remembering their names is a lost cause, so instead, I call out, "Hey, guys."

"Hey," one of them replies. "Impressive."

Forcing a smile as I slide off my helmet, I rest it against my hip and continue catching my breath. "Thanks."

"You finished yet?" another one asks.

"With what?"

"*Playing* hockey."

He says the words like I'm a little girl. Like I'm *pretending* to play hockey the same way I would pretend to play house when I was younger.

"I'm sorry, am I not allowed to use the rink?" I ask. "From what I understood, no one had it scheduled—"

"Hey, Lia!" a familiar voice calls.

I lift my chin in greeting when I recognize who it belongs to. "Hey, Reeves."

"You know her?" the original asshole asks. He's blonde

and tan and basically a live-action Ken doll with a side of misogyny as he glances at me again, his eyes dancing with... what? Condescension? Amusement? Interest?

Not in this lifetime, asshole.

"Yeah, this is Lia, Archer's girl," Reeves clarifies.

The asshole's brows jump. "The freshman?"

"Yeah," Reeves confirms, then addresses me again. "Did you have fun at the party last night?"

"Uh..." I gulp. "Sure, it was great. Thanks again for including me."

"Hey, I'll *include* you in whatever you want," he quips. "Sorry Mav bailed before you had a chance to win, though."

"Hey, when you gotta pee, you gotta pee, right?" I lie.

Another chuckle rumbles through his chest. "Yeah, I guess so." His gaze skims over me, but it isn't laced with interest like his teammate's, only simple curiosity as he takes in my gear. "Mav didn't mention you play hockey."

"'Cause Mav's ashamed I'm better at it than him," I point out dryly.

"Is that right?" a low voice questions. Maverick appears from the tunnel with Griffin and Everett beside him.

Whoops.

We haven't spoken since last night. Technically, we haven't really spoken since he broke my heart, but hey. What else is new? Shifting my attention from how attractive the bastard looks in his gear, I focus on the boys beside him instead.

My smile spreads. "Hey, my two favorite hockey boys!"

"Hey, Lia," Griffin returns.

Mav clutches at his chest. "I'm offended."

"Sure you are," I mutter.

His friends ignore him and skate toward me, pulling me into a hug.

"Hey. Missed you," Everett says.

"Ditto." I squeeze him back.

"You've been here for a while now?" Everett's attention flicks to the hair clinging to my sweaty forehead, and I wipe it away with my glove.

"Yeah. A couple hours now. Gotta brush up on my skills before my first practice with the Lady Hawks."

"You're gonna kill it," Griff says beside us.

"I hope so. Especially since the blonde over there thinks I can only *play* hockey and not actually *play* hockey. Ya know what I mean?"

Griffin glances over his shoulder at the slew of their teammates behind us. "Yeah, that's Trevor Cameron. You'll have to excuse him."

"He's almost as much of a dick as Reeves is," Everett adds.

"Reeves is nice," I argue.

"Only because he doesn't want to get his ass kicked by Mav or Archer," Griffin returns.

"And why would they kick Reeves' ass?" I ask.

Griffin squeezes the back of his neck. "Because you're dating Archer, and Maverick is…"

"Maverick," Everett finishes for him.

My brows bunch. "What's that supposed to mean?"

"It means he isn't going to let anyone come near you when you've already been claimed by his brother."

"We're dating, but it doesn't mean I'm claimed or"—I wave my glove around—"whatever the hell it means."

"That's exactly what it means," Griffin argues.

"Nuh-uh."

"Uh-huh," he returns.

Reeves interrupts us, calling out, "Since when does Lia play? And why didn't anyone tell me?"

"Because it isn't any of your business," Everett replies. He tucks me behind him like he's my personal bodyguard.

"Someone's overprotective," Reeves mutters from the bench.

I lean around Everett's back and quip, "You should see him with his little sister."

The guys exchange glances as whispered, "Everett has a little sister?" comments echo around the arena.

I grimace, peeking up at a very unamused Everett in front of me. "Oops."

With a quick glare over his shoulder at me, Everett turns back to the rest of his team. "Ophelia's the Lady Hawks' goalie."

The blonde asshole laughs. "Hope you like playing in an empty arena, Ophelia."

My nostrils flare, but before I can defend myself, an almost-amused Maverick tsks, "Careful, Cameron, or you might get your ass handed to you."

"By who?" Cameron challenges. "You?"

"We both know that's a given, but…" Maverick doesn't bother looking at me as he tilts his head in my direction. "I actually meant her."

My heart flutters to life, and I gnash my lips together while another scoff erupts from Cameron's throat as he checks me out from skates to helmet. "This little thing? Doubtful."

Griffin smirks beneath his glove and offers, "We *are* here to play a friendly game. Lia, you in?"

"I mean…only if Trevor says it's okay." I bat my lashes back at Cameron, giving him my best doe-eyed impression.

"I like it when my women ask permission," he muses, pushing off from the bench and skating toward me.

Maverick skates into his path, folding his arms. "Don't get me wrong. I can see the appeal. Opie's cute in a girl-next-door kind of way, but she's Archer's girl. Something you might want to remember."

"Archer isn't here right now."

"Yeah, but I am," Maverick replies.

"What? Is she your girl too?" Cameron approaches Maverick now, only stopping when the toes of their skates are practically touching. "It's kind of fucked-up if you share with your brother, Buchanan."

Maverick chuckles darkly and scratches the scruff along his jaw. "Don't I know it."

A rope of guilt tightens around my chest, and it's impossible to shake off, but I skate toward the chaos. Once I'm practically wedged between them, I shove at their chests hoping to create another foot of distance. Maverick barely budges, but I press forward, announcing, "This is fun and all, but I thought we were going to play hockey not chitchat about your teammates' sex lives. I mean, unless you're all about a sausage fest, Trevor, then hey. Take your time. I don't judge."

Cameron glares down at me, his molars grinding. "You're right. I think it's time someone shows you what it's like to play with the big boys." He heads toward the red line while Maverick stays behind me.

Turning around, I lift my head and hold his stare. Stupid Cameron and his stupid asshole comment. Mav looks pissed again. Like Cameron has doused his thoughts in gasoline and tossed a match onto them, leaving him blazing.

"You okay?" I whisper. I don't want to draw attention to us, but I also don't want Maverick to be mad or for him to feel dirty or feel like he's second to his brother or—

"Why wouldn't I be okay?" he questions. "It's not like I'm sharing you with my brother, right?"

"Mav…"

"Get between the pipes, Opie."

"Maverick…"

He skates closer, and his eyes darken. "Get. Between. The pipes."

"Fine." I grab my blocker and catcher from the bench, then head to the goal as the rest of the guys take to the ice. I should probably be a little more on edge since these men are insanely good, but I've played with Everett, Griffin, Maverick, Jaxon, and Archer for as long as I can remember. A buffoon like Cameron with an ego the size of Texas? Yeah, I think I can handle him.

"Mav, you're with Cameron," Griffin says as he splits the players into teams.

"Why?" Maverick demands.

"Because if I put you against him, I'm pretty sure you'll wind up killing each other," Griffin mutters. "You cool playing center?"

"He's a defender," I remind Griff from the crease, not even bothering to hide how I was most definitely eavesdropping.

Griffin barely casts me a glance, answering, "We like to switch things up during practice."

"Well, yeah, but—"

"Afraid I'll score on you, Opie?" Maverick calls.

I press my lips together, and he smirks, turning back to Griffin. "Might be good to knock her down a few pegs," he adds. "I think the whole scholarship thing might've gone to her head."

Ah, sarcastic Maverick's back. Grrrreat.

Not giving Griff a chance to respond, I say, "Fine. Play center. Let's see if you can knock me down a few pegs, shall we?"

"Careful," Everett warns me. He's closer than the others, but I don't miss the way he's giving me a look saying I'd be an idiot not to listen to him.

"Careful of what? A *defender* scoring on me?" I laugh, watching Maverick palm his stick, his hot gaze burning a hole through my eye sockets. I'm not sure why. It's not like he wasn't defending me against Cameron two minutes ago, but hey. Once on his shit list, always on his shit list, apparently.

"Fine," Griffin gives in.

"Don't say I didn't warn you," Everett mutters to me and skates off to the center of the rink.

Griffin finishes splitting the teams in two, and we take our sides. Everett and Maverick meet at the center line. In a flash, they're off. Maverick passes the puck to Cameron, who slaps it toward my net, but I catch it with ease, letting it fall between my skates and arching my brow.

"Is this all you got, boo?"

His upper lip curls, and I pass the puck to one of the players on my team, who chips it off the board and toward the opposite side of the rink. Griffin catches it, cycling it with another random player near the boards. Everett moves into the slot, and Griff passes to him. In an instant, he shoots the puck past LAU's goalie, and I cheer from the opposite goal crease.

"Yes!"

A few minutes later, Cameron tries to score on me again, but I block the shot with my stick at the last second.

Okay, that was a close one.

A surge of adrenaline pulses through me when the asshole curses my name as he darts back to the blue line, and my team takes control of the puck once more.

Back and forth, we play the game when Mav catches me grinning from ear to ear near the net. "You like this?"

"Winning?" I chirp. "Why, yes. Yes, I do. You should try it sometime."

His mouth twitches, but I can't decide if it's in amusement or derision.

"Something funny?" I ask.

"Nah. Although I gotta say, you look kind of cute in your gear. Bet it gets Archer all hot and bothered."

He just *had* to mention Archer, didn't he? Here. In front of everyone. I don't think any of the guys heard him. They're all busy at the other end of the rink. It doesn't really matter, anyway. Because even if they did overhear his comment, to everyone else, it isn't a dig. It isn't a problem or an odd remark. I *am* with Archer. As far as everyone else is concerned, he's my one and only.

If only they knew.

I swallow back the acid on my tongue and hum, "Mm-hmm."

Mav skates around my goal, making me feel like an owl as my head swivels to follow his movements while my blood begins to boil.

So calloused. So...indifferent. I hate it.

Sensing how close he is to getting under my skin, he prods, "What? Is your sex life off-limits, Opie? Because if it is, you probably shouldn't have chosen my brother to fuck in the first place."

My gloved fingers tighten around my stick as he continues circling me.

"You're right," I reply. "I don't know what I'm shielding you from. It's not like you actually care."

"Exactly."

"You're right about the gear too," I continue. "Archer's quite the fan. You should see us role-play when I'm in it."

"As long as he doesn't slip one past the goalie, Opie." He winks, but I don't miss the slight shift in his tone or the way his jaw tics.

"Mav," Everett yells. "You playin' or what?"

Maverick skates off to the center of the rink. One of the defenders on Maverick's team steals the puck from Everett, chipping it off the board. Maverick catches it, crosses our blue line, and charges straight toward me. I squat low, keeping my elbows spread wide, trying to cover as much of the goal as my small frame can handle when he lifts back his stick and shoots. Whooshing hits my ear, followed by the familiar clash of the puck against ice. I look down at my skates, finding the round disc in the goal cage behind me.

Fuck.

"You do look cute, though," Maverick muses.

Slapping the puck at him, I grit out, "Again."

Cameron and Griffin head to the center line, and in an instant, Cameron steals the puck and passes it to Maverick, who slaps the puck into my net. My face grows hot with anger, and I slam my stick against the edge of the goal as Griffin skates toward me, keeping his voice low. "You okay?"

"What the fuck is Maverick doing? He's a defender—"

"You've been playing with Mav forever, Lia," Griffin mutters. "You really think he doesn't know your weak spots?"

My nostrils flare, but I don't argue with him. He's right. Of course, Mav knows exactly where my weak spot is. Both on and off the ice. And he just showed it to half of LAU's starting line.

At least none of my opponents are in the room.

Look at the bright side, right?

Even so, annoyance simmers beneath my skin. Scratch that. It's licking at my core, leaving me hot and bothered and way more pissed off than I have any right to be. It's only a stupid game. And you know what? I'm done playing for today. Without a backward glance, I rip off my helmet, tuck it under my arm, and head into the locker room.

"Aw, come on, Opie!" Maverick calls. "We were just having fun!"

Fuck that.

9

OPHELIA

The sun is setting in the sky, painting the horizon in different shades of oranges, pinks, and purples as I march down the winding path from the arena on campus. It's lined with green grass and flows all throughout LAU's property like its own little subway system. If I stay right, I can make it from the arena to home without ever having to leave the black pavement. One of the main roads is on my right, but the streets are quiet this time of day, and I soak up the ambiance while cursing under my breath as my gym bag swings by my side.

Stupid.

Stupid, stupid, stupid.

I can't believe I let Maverick get to me. Can't believe I stormed out of there like a freaking baby. I should've stayed. Should've finished the game. And I definitely shouldn't have let Maverick see how he affects me.

But motherfucker, his smirk and the way it reaches his eyes? It's like it has a direct line to my freaking libido, which is the last thing I need. Especially when he's so freaking arrogant and has no issue throwing my relationship with his brother in my face any chance he can.

Asshole.

I still don't understand why he does it. Why he feels like he has any right to paint me as the bad guy when he's the one who broke my heart in the first place.

You wanna blame someone for this mess, Maverick? Blame yourself.

I let out a huff, but it's cut off by the rumble of an engine on the otherwise silent street.

Glancing over my shoulder, I spot a motorcycle coming up the road and heading straight toward me. I step a little further away from the asphalt, giving the motorcycle idiot plenty of space in case he decides to run over the curb and hit me with the beast. Instead of passing me, the motorcycle slows. Hair prickles along the back of my neck, and I squeeze my gym bag strap while sneaking another peek over my shoulder.

Black leather. Black bike. Black helmet. Chrome accents.

Who the hell is this person?

It's clearly a guy, thanks to the broad shoulders hidden beneath the leather jacket and the thick thighs wrapped in dark denim. He pulls to a complete stop beside me, his boots hitting the ground as he reaches for his helmet. Fear races down my spine, and I tear my attention from the stranger, quickening my pace down the sidewalk when a low voice calls, "Opie!"

My muscles freeze, and I turn around to face the stranger again.

Maverick?

The name lodges in my throat. I fold my arms, watching as the stranger slips his helmet off, confirming my suspicion.

Sure enough. I'd recognize those rogue waves anywhere. They're a mess of coffee and caramel and look damp from the shower he probably took after I threw a fit and left the game. I should feel better knowing it's Maverick and not some stranger stalking me. Instead, I'm even more amped up than I was.

My eyes trail down his body one more time, and my lips pull to one side as I cross my arms. "You're joking."

"About what?"

"This is yours?"

He looks down at the motorcycle still nestled between his thighs and pats the engine. "Sure is."

"I'm sorry. Do you have a death wish?"

With a dark chuckle, he lifts his shoulder. "You only live once, right?"

"Do your parents know you bought one of these?"

"Over twenty-one, babe. I don't need their permission."

I scoff and step closer. "Yeah, because you know you wouldn't get it if you asked. These things are seriously dangerous—"

"I'm a big boy, Opie. Although I appreciate your concern." He rests his helmet in front of him. "It's hot as fuck."

"I see we're back to your *let's-make-Ophelia-as-uncomfortable-as-possible* game," I point out. "Which means I'm leaving." I give him my back and continue heading down the path.

"Aw, come on, Opie!"

"My name isn't Opie!" I call over my shoulder.

"Come on, Lia," he yells back. "Stop pouting. It was only a game."

My heels dig into the ground, and I face him again. "Since when do you play offense? And did you really have to make me look a complete newbie in front of everyone after telling them I could hand them their asses?" I throw my hands in the air and march closer to him. "Like seriously. At least pick a side. Do you hate me or not? Because this back-and-forth bullshit is driving me insane."

His chin drops to his chest, and he swings his leg over the motorcycle and leans his hip against it. "Trust me, no one thinks you're a newbie. And you *did* hand Cameron his ass. The guy didn't score on you once."

"Yeah, but you did," I remind him.

"So?"

"So?" My voice cracks, and my muscles vibrate with frustration. I turn on my heel and keep walking.

"Come on, Lia," he begs. "Let me take you home."

I twist around again and give his death trap a pointed glare. "On that thing? No, thank you."

"The sun is setting," he pushes. "You shouldn't be walking home by yourself in the dark."

"Why not?"

"It isn't safe."

"It's safer than climbing onto the back of your Harley or" —I wave my hand at his motorcycle—"whatever."

His mouth lifts. "It's a Ducati, and I think that's debatable. Come on."

"No."

"Why not?"

"Because."

"Because...?" His voice trails off while his eyes dare me to give him a legitimate excuse.

"Because my parents wouldn't want me on the back of a motorcycle," I tell him.

"Pretty sure they'd prefer it to you walking home alone in the dark and winding up on the news. This is a prime location for creepers, Lia, especially during the off-season."

I look around the shadowed, rolling hills and rub my hands up and down my arms. Whether I want to admit it or not, the guy has a point. Kind of. But even so, I'd rather take my chances on the sidewalk than spend five minutes pressed against Maverick's back. It's a bad idea on a good day. After last night, then him acting like an asshole during practice? No, thank you. For so many reasons. No. Thank. You.

"Look, I'm sorry I was a dick," he continues, pinching the bridge of his nose. "And for the things I said. It was wrong. I shouldn't stick my nose in your sex life. I should've gone easy on you—"

"I don't want you going easy on me," I snap.

Exasperated, he drops his hand. "Then what do you want?"

"I want to walk home by myself, in peace."

"Can't let you do it, Lia."

"What about Archer?" I press. "What would he think of me riding on your motorcycle?"

"Pretty sure he'd prefer it to you walking home alone, Opie."

Annoyance flares in my gut, and my jaw sets. "Oh, so you think he'd be cool with me on the back of it with you?"

"My brother trusts me."

I laugh dryly. "Jokes on him, right?"

His gaze darkens. "Just get on the motorcycle, Lia."

"No."

"Fine." He marches toward me and tosses me over his shoulder like a sack of potatoes until his ass is a few inches from my nose. My gym bag hangs awkwardly on my back and nearly reaches the ground, swaying back and forth with every footstep.

"Are you serious right now?" I smack his butt over and over again. "Let me go, Maverick!"

A loud slap reverberates through the air, instantly followed by a sharp sting against my ass, and I squeal. "Hey!"

"Don't dish it out if you can't take it. Now, are you gonna behave, or do I need to smack your ass again?"

My nostrils flare as I hang limply, waiting for him to set me down so I can make a run for it.

"You contemplating all the ways you can kill me?" he asks, and I swear I can hear the smile in his voice. It only pisses me off more.

"You know me too well," I say through gritted teeth.

"Damn right, I do," he agrees but sobers slightly. "You know me too, Lia. Do you really think I'm gonna let you walk home by yourself tonight?"

He's right. He won't. But it doesn't mean I want to give in to him.

The blood rushes to my head, and I smack his butt one more time. "I'll call Griffin or—"

"Will you stop being so damn stubborn?"

My body sags against him. "Fine."

"Thank you." He sets me back down beside his motorcycle and offers his helmet to me. "Here."

"That's yours," I point out.

"I don't have my spare. Take it."

"I don't want it."

"You can be mad at me all you want, but I need you safe, Ophelia." He slips the helmet over my messy waves, tilting my chin up and slipping the buckle into place. Satisfied, his mouth lifts with the barest of smiles but disappears as he steps away, putting a breath of distance between us.

If only it was enough to ease the pull in my stomach.

I stand beside the bike, feeling like a fish out of water as he tosses his leg over the motorcycle and pats the space behind him.

"Come on," he orders.

Tongue in cheek, I climb onto the behemoth and grab the back of the seat right behind my butt.

He starts the motorcycle but doesn't pull away from the curb. Instead, he glances back at me and waits, a glint of amusement and annoyance shining in his dark depths.

Glowering at him, I shift slightly in my seat. "You, uh, you can go now."

"Gonna need you to hold on, Opie."

"I *am* holding on."

He hesitates but doesn't argue. Grasping the handlebar, he twists his wrist. The motorcycle jerks forward then screeches to a halt, and I fly with it, my chest slamming into Maverick's back.

"You were saying?" he quips.

With a huff, I wrap my arms around him, and he slaps my thigh playfully.

"Fine, you win!" I yell over the rumbling engine.

He looks over his shoulder at me and smirks, but doesn't comment.

Then, we're off.

And it's loud. The wind. The engine. It cuts through the quiet ambiance like a hot knife through butter.

But I kind of like it.

The power of the engine between my thighs. The heat of Maverick's back against my chest.

He glances to the left, checking his blind spot and making a turn while giving me a glimpse of the boy I used to know. The one I fell for before I even knew what a real crush was. My heart tightens in my chest, and I start to let go of his waist, but his left hand encompasses mine, keeping me in place.

Giving in, I settle against him even more and close my eyes.

Because a girl can pretend, can't she? How things could've been different. Even if it's only for a moment. Even when she knows it's fleeting and reality will catch up to her soon. She can still pretend.

Just for a minute.

10

OPHELIA

rcher and I order pizza. Archer gets barbecue chicken and I opt for supreme. He's a sucker for a good routine, but so am I, so it works. With the boxes laid open on the coffee table in his family room along with some spiked lemonade, we catch up, and he tells me about his trip, though I'm too distracted to pay much attention to him. I'm still pissed about how I had my ass handed to me on the ice by a freaking defender.

Archer snaps his finger an inch from my nose, and I jerk back.

"Sorry," I mutter, playing with the edge of crust from my second slice of pizza.

He shifts his body on the couch until all I can see is him. "Rough day?"

Tossing the crust in the box, I brush the excess crumbs off and puff out my cheeks. "You could say that."

"What happened?"

"Nothing."

He smiles and lifts my chin. "We've been friends forever, Lia. You really think I don't know when you're lying to me?"

"Your brother's…" I sigh and pull away from Archer's innocent touch. "He's an ass, sometimes is all."

"Yeah, I'm aware." His scrutiny is palpable as he adds, "What did he do this time?"

This time.

I'd laugh if Archer weren't so spot-on.

Maverick's always gotten on my nerves. Even when we were little, he had a habit of driving me crazy. Later, he'd push my buttons so he could get us alone in the same room and shut me up by shoving his tongue down my throat.

It worked all too well.

"Not gonna tell me?" Archer prods.

"Fiiiine." I give in and tuck my feet under my butt. "This afternoon, I was at the rink doing some drills and wound up playing in an impromptu scrimmage with the guys, and…" I fold my lips between my teeth, unable to voice the ending to my pathetic sob story.

Without even bothering to be sneaky, he openly stares at me, waiting for me to finish as he chews the last bit of crust from his pizza. When I don't expand, he swallows his bite and asks, "And? How'd it go?"

I glance at the empty hallway leading to Maverick's bedroom. After driving me home, he disappeared into his room and hasn't left it since. I shouldn't notice. I shouldn't care. Where he is or what he's doing.

So stop caring.

I tear my attention from the hall and answer, "The scrimmage was going really well, actually."

"Yeah?"

"Mm-hmm…until Maverick—who was playing center at the time—scored on me twice in under two minutes."

Archer's eyes widen. "Shit."

"Yeah. It was bad."

"Sorry I wasn't there to tell him to fuck off."

With a snort, I lean further back on the couch, unfold my legs, scoot the pizza box over with one foot, and prop both of them on the coffee table in front of us. "You know I'm not afraid to tell Maverick to fuck off. Not that it would change anything," I mutter under my breath. "But Maverick does what he wants. He *always* does what he wants. And today, he wanted to put me in my place, which he succeeded in doing in front of most of the hockey team, so..." My voice trails off, and I pick at a few crumbs on the hoodie I'd stolen from Archer's room as shame and annoyance battle inside of me.

"Shit," Archer repeats.

Picking up the string of the hoodie, I run it along my bottom lip and sigh. "Yeah."

"Well, look at the bright side. Now you know your weak spot, so maybe he can help you."

I drop the string and quirk my brow. "Help me?"

"Yeah." With a shrug, Archer takes another piece of pizza from his box. "Help you."

I shake my head, way more confused than I should be, considering the unopened spiked lemonade next to the card-board box on the coffee table. Yeah, I'm sober as a saint, but the man in front of me is talking gibberish. "I'm sorry, what?"

"Maybe he can help you."

Sitting up, I tuck my feet beneath my ass again and clarify, "Help me with what? Hockey?"

Archer nods. "Yeah, why not?"

"I don't know, maybe because he's...busy or has better things to do and doesn't want to take time out of his day?"

Oh, and did I mention we hate each other's guts?

"He's not that busy," Archer argues. "And even if he is, you're a family friend *and* his brother's girlfriend. I'm pretty sure he'd be happy to help."

"I think you're assuming Maverick's a lot more sentimental than he actually is. The guy's never been attached to anything or anyone."

Archer grimaces, proving I'm right. "He's a fan of groveling, though," he points out.

"And you think if I kiss his ass enough, he'll throw me a bone and help me with a few things on the ice?"

Archer shrugs. "Couldn't hurt, right?"

Other than my pride, sure.

Nibbling the corner of my thumb, I consider Archer's suggestion. I love hockey more than almost anything, and Maverick is good. Extremely good. There's a reason the Lions drafted him during his senior year of high school, and it isn't because his dad owns the team. This is Mav's last season with the Hawks. Next year, he'll be living the dream of playing professional hockey, and I'm not arrogant enough to think there isn't anything I can learn from him. But being alone on the ice with my boyfriend's brother is already precarious enough. Considering our past, it feels like a recipe for disaster on way too many levels. And that's without taking into account we're talking about Mav. Maverick Buchanan. The guy's an asshole and already has a big head. I'm pretty sure asking for his help would inflate his ego to the size of a hot air balloon, not to mention the hit my pride would take if I gave him another minute of my time he doesn't deserve.

"What do you think?" Archer prods.

"I think he's good," I mutter. "But asking Maverick for help sounds about as pleasant as getting a pap smear."

"You've had a pap smear?"

"I had to get one when I got on birth control for my shitty periods in high school."

His eyes dance with mirth. "Hot."

Smacking him in the chest, I argue, "You have no idea how easy guys have it."

"Trust me." He grins ruefully. "We know."

"Aw, you bought me pizza?" Maverick asks as he heads into the family room from the hallway. My head snaps in his direction. With narrowed eyes, I watch him approach. Sure enough, the asshole reaches for a slice of supreme pizza and shoves it into his mouth without waiting for me to offer it.

"That's mine," I inform him.

"Ah, Opie, you shouldn't have. And my favorite flavor, too? You're a real peach."

"It's *my* favorite flavor," I argue.

Lifting the slice in a cheers motion, he counters, "Who knew you had such good taste?"

He did.

We've been the only two in the families who like supreme pizza for as long as I can remember. The fact he doesn't remember stings way more than I'd like to admit. Or maybe he did know, and he's hiding it. Hiding how he knows me the same way I know him. Or knew him, considering how he broke my heart and has kept me at arm's length ever since.

"Hey, so we were thinking," Archer announces.

Regret lines my insides, and I sit up straighter, fighting the urge to slap my hand over Archer's mouth to keep him from talking. I bite the inside of my cheek as my attention cuts to his twin brother. I'm caught between curiosity and terror as to how this will turn out.

Maverick's chewing stops mid-bite. He swallows the bite of pizza whole and wipes his mouth with the back of his hand. "Yeah?"

Archer nudges my shoulder, and Maverick's eyes fall to me. "Spit it out, Opie."

"Don't be a dick," Archer warns. "I'm going to the bathroom. I'll be back in a minute." He stands and looks at me as if to say *the floor's all yours.*

Perfect.

It's rare when I want to smack Archer, but as I watch him round the corner, throwing me to the wolves—er, *wolf*, since there's only one Maverick Buchanan—my hand feels twitchy. I tuck it under my thigh and let out a slow breath. Once we're officially alone, I run my tongue along my teeth, unsure what to say or how to get out of this mess.

"Are we gonna stand here all day? Or…?" Maverick folds his arms and cocks his head. Like he's waiting for me to get to the point.

"I'm surprised you're so anxious to hear me out," I note. "I figured pissing me off is the highlight of your day, and you'd want to bask in it for as long as possible."

"Can you blame me?" He bends down and grabs another slice of pizza from the box but stops when he's close to me, his eyes practically drinking me in as he drops his voice to a husky whisper. "Watching my ex snuggle with my brother in my family room, only to see her squirm as soon as she sees me, is *exactly* how I enjoy spending my time, don't you think?"

I glance from his mouth to his dark blue eyes. "You're a dick."

"Never claimed to be the knight." He stands up straight again, making me feel tiny in comparison. "Now spit it out, Opie."

Fine.

"I told Archer about how you kicked my ass on the ice today."

"And?" he prods. He's on edge. I can see it. Feel it. Practically taste it.

"And Archer thinks I could learn a thing or two from you."

"Archer thinks you could learn a thing or two from me, or *you* think you could learn a thing or two from me?" His eyes gleam knowingly.

I was right. He wants me to beg. To kiss his stupidly muscular ass and inflate his ego until it almost bursts and the clock's ticking. Archer will be back any minute. If I back out now, he'll wonder why I have a problem receiving a few tips and tricks from his other half. I could always ask Jaxon for help. Or Griff or Everett. I could ask any of them. But whether or not I want to admit it, Maverick knows me better than any of them. On *and* off the ice. Which makes this entire situation that much less palatable.

"You think you could learn a thing or two from me, Opie?" Mav prods.

"You know, now that I think about it, I've already learned plenty from you," I decide. "I think I'll pass on learning how to defend against your magic voodoo stick handling."

His mouth quirks, and he grabs his junk through his sweats. Not going to lie. It's quite the handful, and my eyes fall to his package without me even realizing it.

"You don't want to learn how to defend yourself against my magic voodoo stick, Opie?" he jokes.

My eyes snap from his crotch to his knowing smirk. "Ew."

"Aw, come on," he pouts, "Girls love my magic voodoo stick."

"I'm sure they do." I scan the empty hallway. "Now, please get your hand off your junk before your brother gets back out here."

"And why would we care about whether or not my brother sees you staring at my junk, Ophelia?" he questions thoughtfully, but the bastard's nice enough to give in despite his sarcasm. He lets himself go and reaches for the last slice of my pizza, ripping his teeth into it. His Adam's apple bobs up and down his throat when he swallows, leaving my mouth dry while his eyes pin me in place. The guy's so infuriating it's nauseating on a good day. But after the shitty one I've endured thanks to him, I'm two seconds from slapping the cocky smirk off his stupidly handsome face with my own two hands.

"Thanks for confirming my decision," I murmur. "Tell Archer I went home." I stand up and head to the door, but Maverick grabs my bicep, stopping my retreat. Cotton fills my mouth from the heat of his palm. And I hate how I know them. His hands. What they feel like on my body. In my hair. Against my cheeks.

"You really want my help, Opie?" Mav asks.

I tear my attention from his hand wrapped around my arm and slide it up to his blue eyes. They're darker than Archer's. Harder too. Especially when he's frustrated. Like right now. Tiny flecks of navy surround his pupils as he waits for my response. For my groveling.

Shoving the memories assaulting me aside, I murmur, "If I were talking to the old Mav, I'd say yes. You know how much hockey means to me, and I could really use your help. But asshole Maverick? I think I'll pass."

He stays quiet, his grip as firm as ever, while I squirm beneath his scrutiny, sucking my bottom lip into my mouth.

His attention flicks to my lips before meeting my hesitant gaze again. "Fine." He lets me go and steps back, giving me room to breathe. "Meet me out front tomorrow morning at seven. I'll drive you to the rink."

Drive. Rink.

Right.

I snap out of the stupid haze from our close proximity and shake my head. "On your death trap motorcycle? I think not."

His mouth lifts on one side. "I thought you liked my motorcycle."

"You've been on his motorcycle?" Archer questions from the hallway.

Shit, I almost forgot he was coming back.

My lips smash together as my attention shifts from Maverick to his brother. "It's a long story."

"Not that long," Maverick chimes in. "She's got quite the grip, brother."

A flicker of jealousy flashes in Archer's eyes, but he tilts his head and slides in behind me, wrapping his arms around my waist and pulling me into him. "You being a dick again, Mav?"

"Would you expect anything less?" Maverick volleys back. He turns, giving me a half-bow. "I'll meet you at the rink at eight."

"I thought you said seven?" I counter.

"Pretty sure my brother wouldn't want his girlfriend walking in the dark." Mav leans closer and shoves the last bite of crust into his mouth. "You're welcome."

He saunters back to his bedroom and closes the door.

11

MAVERICK

It's early. The sun has barely begun to rise above the horizon as I stretch my legs out on the back patio. I like it like this. The quiet. The dew clinging to the grass. The birds chirping in the trees. I couldn't sleep. The silence in my room was too much. But out here? It's nice. The good kind of quiet. I've been coming out here more lately. It's the only time I've found peace. In the mornings when I'm by myself or late at night on the roof with no one to bother me but my thoughts. I need to meet Ophelia at the rink in a couple of hours. Part of me still wishes I'd said no. Said I was too busy.

But it's Ophelia.

Despite being an ass sometimes, I've never been able to tell her no.

Bringing my lukewarm coffee to my lips, I take a sip, noting the grass needs trimming. It's Reeves' turn, which means he'll put it off for another week or so until he finally caves and mows it.

Ass.

A soft creak sounds behind me, cutting through the

comfortable silence, and I turn around. Archer's standing in the doorway with two mugs in his hands. Steam swirls through the air, bringing the scent of fresh-brewed coffee with it.

"That for me?" I ask.

"It was." His eyes cut to the mug in my hand. "Since when do you wake up early?"

Since I couldn't sleep, too lost in my thoughts of you and Opie fucking in the room beside mine.

"Thought I'd take a play out my brother's book and wake up at the ass-crack of dawn," I reply. "Now, gimme some coffee. Mine's shit." I set my subpar caffeine on the ground beside my feet and reach for one of Archer's offerings. He chuckles, hands me a mug, and sits beside me on the top stair of the patio leading to the grassy backyard in front of us.

"Listen," Archer says, but I lift my hand.

"Don't start."

"Come on, Mav. You're my brother and best friend."

"Seriously?" I scan the mountains in the distance and let out a long, slow breath. "That's the shit you're going to pull?"

"We talked about this before she got here. You promised you were going to be nice."

"I've been nice."

"You've been a sarcastic asshole," he points out.

My mouth lifts as I bring the fresh coffee to my lips and sip, taking my time as I taste the hot liquid.

Fuck, he even makes coffee better than I do.

"She's probably my future wife, man," Archer continues. "And I'm going to need my future wife to get along with my twin brother, don't you think?"

Wife.

The knife in my chest twists, making it hard to breathe, but I stop myself from wincing and shift on the stairs. "Look,

I agreed to help her on the ice while you're busy with your internship. I don't know what else you're looking for."

"I'm not going to be able to be there today."

"Yeah, which means I'm going to be even more miserable—"

"Don't piss her off," he snaps. "It's all I'm asking. Do you think you can do that for me?"

"I'll be nothing but a gentleman," I offer dryly, lifting my mug into the air in a silent salute and drinking it down. If only he'd spiked it with some whiskey. Or hell, even some bleach would work if it'd put me out of my misery.

His eyes narrow as he watches me from his periphery, but I don't look at him. I stare straight ahead, caught between hatred and guilt. Both of which are directed at me.

"Why do you hate her?" he demands.

I pull back, surprised by the accusation in his tone, along with his desire to address the elephant in the room we've both been avoiding for as long as I can remember. "I don't hate her."

"I'm serious," he pushes as I stare into my mug. "You've always been this way with her. And yeah, I was the same when we were kids. Following you around and pulling her pigtails because she was always trying to tag along and shit. But we aren't kids anymore, Mav. It's not funny when you're a dick to her, and you need to stop."

The last remnants of cream have finally dissipated into the dark liquid, turning the coffee a rich caramel color. It reminds me of Ophelia's eyes, and a humorless chuckle grates my throat. "Does it ever bother you? How our parents planned everything out for us? Our futures. Our friends. Our living arrangements." I motion to the house behind us, bought and paid for by our parents and their college friends. "Everything is mapped out. All of it. Do you ever wonder if it was even our choice to be friends with Everett, Griffin, and

Jaxon? To play hockey? To attend LAU? To sign with the Lions when we graduate?"

Archer shakes his head. "What are you talking about?"

"Mom and Dad have a picture of us at six weeks old, Arch. Six weeks. And we're at the Lions' arena, watching Uncle Theo and Uncle Colt play together. Fast forward to when we were ten, and we're playing on the same ice with everyone's kids, decked out in matching LAU jerseys. And here we are, almost twelve years later, living the life they mapped out for us."

He scrubs his hand over his face. "Let me get this straight. You're pissed at our parents for sharing their love of hockey with their kids?"

I shake my head. "It's not that."

"Then, what is it?"

"It's everything. It's our friend group. It's where we spend our holidays. It's the custom duplex all our parents built together, so we could watch out for the girls when they finally graduated high school and could attend LAU—the same school our parents attended. Doesn't it feel manipulative?"

"We chose to go here, you and me."

"Did you even look at any other schools?" I counter.

"I didn't need to. This is where I wanted to be. This is where *you* wanted to be."

"Yeah." I scratch at the scruff on my jaw, lost in thought. "I guess."

"Where is this coming from?"

"I don't know." I rest my elbows on my knees, letting my coffee hang between them. "Life is short. Sometimes, I look back and wonder where the time goes and how I got here. Part of me wonders if they even have spouses mapped out for us or some shit."

"Spouses?"

"You said so yourself, man. Ophelia's your potential wife, right?" The words taste sour, so I sip more coffee, hoping it'll wash away the remnants. It doesn't do shit, but I swallow the foul taste anyway and turn back to my brother. "Tell me something. Would you have asked her to prom and saved the day if Mom hadn't told you to?"

His frown deepens, and he sets his untouched coffee beside him. "She didn't tell me to ask Ophelia out."

"She told you Ophelia's date bailed at the last second," I argue.

"Technically, Dylan reached out to me."

"We both know Lia's mom would've reached out to ours and asked you to take her," I grit out as my frustration finally gets the best of me.

Sensing it, Archer nods and gives in. "Okay, you're right," he concedes. "She probably would've, so Ophelia's night wasn't ruined by some dick who bailed on her."

The irony that he's talking to the dick who bailed on Ophelia isn't lost on me. I smile sardonically against the rim of my cup, muttering, "Exactly," as I take another sip.

"But I was glad I could take her," Archer continues. "You know I've had a thing for Ophelia for a couple of years. She's been my best friend since middle school, and not long after sophomore year here, I wanted her."

"Yeah, I know." I scrub my hand over my face, ignoring how I wanted her long before then, as the guilt settles in my gut. It was never Mav and Ophelia, though. Not to our families. And I was too young to think I could change their perspective, so why try? I shove aside my resentment and continue, "But you proved my point. You were chosen to be hers from the beginning."

"Bullshit," he snaps. "Yeah, Mom and Dad always joked about me winding up with Lia, but no one ever took it seriously until I went to prom with Ophelia and kissed her.

Besides, even if they didn't joke about it, I would still want her, she'd still want me, and everyone would *still* be okay with it. Mom and Dad have been nothing but supportive. Hell, everyone's been supportive." He pins me with a stare that burns the side of my face as I look out at the trees and overgrown grass stretched in front of us. "Everyone but you," he adds.

Yeah. Because I'm the one with the stick up my ass. The one standing in the way of his future and his happiness. The one who had her first and let her go, only so my brother could be the one to pick up the fucking pieces.

And he has no idea.

It's been weeks. Weeks of torture. Of knowing what she tastes like without being able to savor her. Of knowing she's moved on and left me in the past. Of knowing I want to hate her new boyfriend while also knowing my brother is the *only* person on this planet with the power to treat her the way she deserves. But the worst part is knowing I can't even be bitter about it or blame her for choosing him. Because he's the better choice. For so many reasons. He's better than me. He's always been better. It only took Ophelia's heart breaking to see it. How good they could be together. And yeah, we might be young, and their intimate relationship might still be new, but the prospect of marriage when they've known each other for as long as they have? It isn't so crazy. Not really.

"I need your support, Mav," Archer tells me.

"I'm your brother," I mutter into the mug. "I'll do whatever you need me to."

"Thank you." He stands and slaps his hand against my shoulder. "Because I can't do this without you. I'm sick of playing referee between you two, so do it for me, yeah?" He squeezes my trapezius muscles. "Play nice?"

The coffee tastes like shit on my tongue, but I drink it away.

"And don't say you've been playing nice," he adds. "Because we both know you're full of shit. You've been pissing her off, which is starting to piss me off. You know what I mean?"

"Yeah," I grunt. "I hear you loud and clear."

"Good. And who knows? Maybe you'll even learn to like her." He chuckles and walks back inside, leaving me alone with my thoughts.

That's the problem.

I already do.

12

MAVERICK

"**K**eep your eye on the puck," I order. My patience is practically non-existent after my conversation with Archer this morning, but keeping it in check feels impossible as I skate toward another puck a few feet away. There are at least a dozen sprawled out along the red line and a few surrounding the crease where Ophelia stands. She's throttling the stick in her hands as if pretending it's my throat.

"I *am* keeping my eye on the puck," Lia snaps. Sweat trickles down her forehead behind her mask, but she doesn't bother wiping it away. She wouldn't be able to if she tried. The cage protecting her face is in the way, and it looks like it's *almost* blocking her line of sight.

I slap the puck into the top right, barely missing her glove and landing in the net behind her. Her head snaps toward it and she seethes, "Fuck!"

"Watch. The. Puck."

"How do you do it?" she demands. Her upper lip curls behind her mask. "How do you always know where to shoot it? And if you're really this good, why aren't you playing offense?"

She's sexy when she's fired up. Annoying. But her passion for the game makes up for it. The fire in her eyes. The steel in her jaw. It's like a player's wet dream. The things someone could do to her when she gets like this. The things she could do to them.

It's why I didn't want to bring her here. Not ever. But especially not when we're alone in my home away from home. And after my chat with Archer? My mind's even more fucked-up.

"Tell me," she pushes, snapping me back to the present.

"You're not going to like my answer." I skate closer to the crease.

Lia's chin inclines, and she holds my gaze until we're chest-to-chest.

"Tell me," she repeats.

"You're easy to read, Opie. Maybe not for everyone, which is why you've gotten as far as you have. But for me?" I laugh, skating around the net, attempting to work off some of my pent-up energy. "It's a walk in the park. I'm not this good against everyone. Just you."

Her gaze hardens as she watches me move around her. "Tell me how. How do I make it easy for you to read me?"

I stop short in front of her again and tilt her head up with my gloved knuckle against her chin. "Your eyes, Opie. They follow where you *think* the puck is going to be, not where it actually winds up. Don't get me wrong. Your gut is usually right, especially when you're facing off against an average player. It's the most logical move. The most logical shot from the opposing team. But if you wanna play against the best, you gotta understand some people aren't logical. They won't be predictable. Sometimes, they're going to do the exact opposite of what you expect."

"They're going to be impulsive," she concludes.

"Yeah. And for a girl who likes to plan things out ten moves ahead and run off logic alone, it throws you off to consider someone doing the opposite."

She nods, unoffended. "Okay. Let's do it again."

She moves back into the goal zone and spreads her arms wide, shifting her weight from one skate to the other, attempting to block as much of the net as possible with her tiny frame. The pads help, don't get me wrong, but she's still small. Still delicate. Bet she hates that part of her. How her petite body holds her back despite the hours she spends in the gym building muscle.

"Come on," she pushes.

I head to the red line and slowly charge toward her, dribbling the puck back and forth from left to right. When I get close, I flex the stick, watching Opie's eyes as she braces her body to push right, preparing for the puck to go in that direction since, generally speaking, a shot low and to her stick side is usually a more challenging one to stop. Instead, I hit the puck to her left.

The puck hits her glove at the last instant, and she cheers. "Yes!"

"Good job," I tell her. "Let's go again."

We continue practicing for another thirty minutes until sweat soaks my jersey and black dots spot my vision. I shouldn't be tired yet—or at least not *this* tired—but exhaustion burrows deep in my chest, leaving me craving rest like I've run a marathon. At least I worked off my pent-up energy. She's getting better. Or at least, I think she is. She's lagging a little now, her reflexes slower and less polished than when we first started, though she'd never admit it aloud the same way I won't. We've been at this for hours.

Checking the time on my phone lying on the bench, I wave her toward me. "Let's call it a day."

Her hair is a mess of strawberry blonde curls as she slides off her helmet. A few strands stick to the side of her face, and she shoves it away, cradling her helmet on her hip. "I want to keep going."

"No."

"Come on, you've been taking it easy on me."

"I haven't—"

"Yes, you have. You can tell I'm tired, and you're going easy on me." It isn't a question, but I answer it anyway. Or, at least partially.

"You look exhausted, Opie."

"So? Stop holding back. Let's do it again."

I want to laugh. To tell her I can't because *I'm* the one who's exhausted. I'm the one who needs to go home and sleep. The one who can barely hold himself up. But I swallow it back. Scrubbing my glove over my face, I mutter, "I've got shit to do."

"The sooner you stop holding back, the sooner I'll let you get to whatever shit you need to be doing," she offers.

Letting my hand fall to my side, I stare at her. "Opie…"

She slides her helmet back into place and heads to the goal, spreading her padded legs wide as she moves into position. "Come on, Mav. One more shot with all your strength. Let's see it."

All my strength.

If only.

"It's a bad idea," I start.

"I'm not weak."

"Never said you were weak," I argue. "Only stubborn."

"Then I guess it's time you give in and actually try," she quips.

"I've been trying."

"In the beginning, sure. For the last ten minutes or so?"

Her padded shoulders lift. "Not so much. Come on. Hit me with your best shot."

She shifts her weight back and forth, egging me on. I leave the bench and skate to the red line again. My muscles feel fucking flaccid, and I'd laugh at the correlation if it wasn't so pathetic. But seriously. I feel like I'm fucking eighty. Digging deep, I tap into the last of my strength and rush toward her, her eyes following the puck as I handle it with my stick. When I'm a few feet in front of her, I dart left, snapping the puck toward the right side of the net, but it ricochets off the post and nails the side of her helmet, causing her to stumble onto her ass.

Shit.

I round the back of the goal and race toward her, sliding onto my knees and unbuckling her chin strap as fast as my fumbling fingers can manage. Once it's free, I slip her helmet off, and she blinks slowly back at me, dazed.

"You okay?" I rasp, cradling her cheeks in my hands while willing away the dots lining my vision as I attempt to inspect her for any damage, but I'm lightheaded as shit.

Don't pass out, asshole.

With a laugh, she pushes my hands away from her. "Yeah, I'm good." Her smile widens. "Damn, Mav. There was a lot of power in your shot."

"I'm so sorry."

"Don't be." She peeks up at me. "Thank you."

My brows dip. "For what?"

"For not treating me with kid gloves." Her smile softens. "Honestly, it's one of my favorite things about you," she continues. When I frown, she clarifies, "Everyone treats me with kid gloves. My parents. Archer. Everyone but you."

She pushes to her feet and skates toward the bench, peeking over her shoulder at me. "You coming?"

I nod, forcing my legs to hold my weight as I grab the goalpost and stand. "Yeah. I'll be right there."

"You sure you're okay?" she asks.

I chuckle dryly. "You're not the only one who took a break the last few weeks, Opie."

With an understanding nod, she continues toward the bench. "Coach Sanderon's gonna love that."

"Yeah, he's gonna kick my ass if I can't get back into shape by the time the season starts," I grunt.

"But it's a problem for future Maverick, right?" She bats her lashes and skates backward, keeping her eyes on me as I make my way toward her.

"Sure, it is," I mutter. "Come on, let's get out of here."

"Okay."

MAVERICK

My gym bag lands with a thud on the granite countertop beside Reeves. We just finished at the gym, and my body is screaming at me. It's been a few days since I've seen Ophelia, thanks to Archer being home. The distance has been for the best despite me missing the shit out of her. It reminds me of the weeks following prom, only this time, she hasn't texted. Hasn't thought of me the way I've been thinking about her. I've been attempting to distract myself with the gym, a doctor's appointment, and a few long rides up the canyon on my bike. But they've done shit to quiet the voices in my head.

Reaching for a glass in the cabinet, I fill it with water from the fridge.

"Dude, those deadlifts kicked my ass today," Reeves says, bending at the waist and touching his toes, stretching out his lower back and hamstrings. "I dunno how I'm gonna mow the lawn now."

I gulp down the ice-cold water and set it on the counter, stretching my arms over my head and rolling my shoulders.

"Maybe if you hadn't procrastinated for the past two weeks, the grass wouldn't be such a bitch to mow today."

"Yeah, whatever," Reeves mutters. He glances out the half-open blinds and looks at the overgrown grass in the back-yard, but his glower lifts. Spreading the blinds wider, his attention catches on something, and he smirks. With a low whistle, he looks at me and back through the window. "Have you seen this yet?" he asks.

I walk over to him and look outside, and my pulse stalls. Right there, in the middle of the backyard, is a half-naked Ophelia. She's lying on a checkered blanket, probably attempting to tan the creamy skin on full display in spandex shorts and a sports bra. Both of which leave little to the imagination. Lying on her stomach with a book in front of her, she flips the page, oblivious to us checking her out. Then again, she's always oblivious when it comes to guys watching her. The girl has no idea how fucking tempting she is. Like right now. Looking all innocent and shit. Her elbows are bent as she rests her chin in her hands, smiling at whatever she's reading.

"Looks like I found a reason to mow the lawn sooner rather than later." Reeves lets out another whistle. "Fuck, man. That girl's ass is fine."

I slap his hands away from the blinds and step in front of the window, crossing my arms. "You've been putting mowing the lawn off for a week and a half."

His brows bounce up and down. "Guess it's time I get busy, right?"

"Trade weeks with me."

"Nah, I'm good."

He starts to step around me, but I block his way. "Trade. Weeks. With me," I repeat.

"And miss out on the view?" He laughs. "Why would I?"

"Archer wouldn't want you out there with her."

"And he'd want you to be?" Reeves laughs again. "No offense, but I'm not an idiot. What's going on with you two?"

"Nothing."

He tilts his head. "You sure?"

"She's dating my brother," I remind him. "You really think I'm that much of a dick?"

His mouth twitches. "Depends on the day."

I scoff and shake my head. "Fine, you don't even need to trade with me. I'll take both weeks so your pansy ass can recover from deadlifts."

"All right." He lifts his hands in surrender and heads down the hall toward his bedroom, calling over his shoulder, "Tell Lia hi for me!"

Dick.

I laugh under my breath but glance out the window one more time, unable to help it.

The girl's gorgeous with her father's hat on her head and her curls cascading down her back. She's still smiling at whatever she's reading, though I can't see the book's title. I tell myself I don't really care. The girl's a pain in my ass on a good day, even finding a way to ruin my Saturday, despite my best attempts at keeping my distance from her. Yet here I am, putting myself in her vicinity. I shouldn't. But the idea of Reeves being this close to her when she looks fucking edible is more than I can handle.

Tearing my attention from the swell of her ass, I head to the garage and pull the lawn mower out, wheeling it around the side of the house until I reach the backyard.

She must be listening to music because she doesn't flinch or look my way as I round the corner. I should get started, but her blanket is sprawled in the middle of the grass, making it impossible to do my job until she moves out of the way.

Someone else should be doing this. Not me. Not when she isn't mine.

So, why am I out here wasting my time?

Annoyed with myself, I scratch my jaw, watching Ophelia. Still lying on her stomach, she lifts her feet into the air, crossing one ankle over the other as she flips the page of her book.

Oblivious.

Fucking oblivious.

There's some bark around one of the flower beds my mom and Aunt Kate planted a while back. I pick a couple of pieces up and toss them at her. When one hits her upper thigh, she peeks over her shoulder.

Her brows crease, and she pulls one of her AirPods out of her ear. "Can I help you?"

"What are you doing out here?"

"Uh, what does it look like I'm doing?" she returns. "I'm soaking in some Vitamin D."

"Ah, so my brother didn't give you what you needed before he left this morning?"

"Some what?" Her nose scrunches. "Wait, I get it. Vitamin D, as in *dick*." She rolls her eyes, clearly unimpressed, adding, "And, ew. Gross."

"Sex is gross?"

"Discussing it with my boyfriend's brother is," she quips.

"Hey, there's nothing wrong with a little Vitamin D, Opie. Nothing to be ashamed of."

"Mm-hmm," she hums. "Of course not. Glad to see sarcastic Maverick's back."

With a smirk, I reply, "Baby, he never left."

"Sure, he didn't." Her lips bunch on one side. "Now, how can I help you?"

I bite the inside of my cheek to keep my sarcasm in check,

motioning to the lawn mower in front of me. "I need to mow the lawn."

"Okay." She motions toward the grass surrounding her the same way I had the lawn mower. "Mow away. When you get close, I'll lay the blanket on the part you've already cut."

Well, damn, if that isn't a logical resolution. It still doesn't keep her away from me.

"You should go inside," I suggest.

"Why?"

"Because Reeves has been checking you out from the window."

She looks at the windows and turns back to me. "Well, it looks like he's had his fill because he isn't there anymore, so what's the problem?"

What's the problem? She's lying half-naked in my back-yard. That's the problem. I'm trying to keep my distance. Trying to fucking respect how she's moved on after I pushed her away and I can't have her anymore. But this? This is fucking torture, and I've never been the strong one.

"Just go inside, Opie," I order.

"Why? I'm kind of at a good part." Lifting her book, she wiggles it back and forth as if to prove her point, but I don't budge.

"You really think Archer would be okay with you out here looking like this?"

"Like what?"

Like a fucking snack.

"Half-naked and shit," I clarify.

Pushing herself to a sitting position, she looks down at her outfit choice and tilts her head at me. "What's wrong with what I'm wearing?"

"Nothing. I'm just saying...if you're looking for Vitamin D, you might get more than you bargain for while wearing shit like that."

Again, she looks down at her sports bra and spandex shorts. "From who?"

I look toward the bright blue sky and pray for patience, knowing my mom would murder me if she knew I was acting like this, but I can't help it. Ophelia's killing me right now. "Look, I'm trying to be nice, okay? Go get some clothes on. Do it for Archer."

"Archer already saw me out here."

My eyes bulge. "And he didn't care if you look like this?"

"Like what?" she repeats.

"I already told you, half-naked and shit."

"He doesn't care how I dress. And he doesn't care if Reeves checks me out, either."

Another dose of annoyance floods my system, and I throttle the lawn mower's handle, caught between wanting to smack some fucking sense into my brother and wanting to rip off my own shirt so I can cover all the bare skin in front of me. But I stay still, my jaw set tight.

"You okay over there?" Ophelia questions. "You look like you're about to blow a gasket."

"Do you think my brother would care if he knew your mystery man could see you out here dressed like this?" I demand.

"Oh, so we're finally acknowledging you're the guy who ditched me before prom?" she tosses back at me. "Sorry, but I'm a bit surprised since you refused to answer any of my texts or calls afterward. For all I knew, I was secretly dating a ghost until now."

Regret spreads in my gut, and I squeeze the back of my neck, muttering, "I was a little preoccupied."

"Preoccupied?" She laughs, but it sounds squeaky and sharp. "Glad to know how little I meant to you."

"Guess I could say the same thing since you wound up

dating my brother afterward. You couldn't even wait twenty-four hours, could you."

One of her tan, freckled shoulders lifts into the air. "I guess not."

The dejection in her voice twists my self-loathing into something even less palatable, but I choke it back. "Good to know."

I bend down and turn the lawn mower on so my mouth doesn't get the best of me, and I say something I shouldn't. Still, it doesn't stop the words from filtering through my mind.

Too bad I'll never be able to move on from you.

14

OPHELIA

It's strange. Being here. Next to Archer. With his arm wrapped around my shoulders, we're snuggled on the couch in the middle of his family room, surrounded by his friends. *Our* friends. Griffin and Everett asked if we wanted to hang out tonight, and after Archer texted me privately to see how I felt, we said yes. In a way, it kind of feels like a coming-out party. Like we've officially crossed into actual relationship territory instead of *just* friends. It's stupid because we've been together for a little while now, but being together one-on-one versus front and center and surrounded by friends is...weird. Like it's official now, and there's no going back.

Maverick and I never made it to this point. Hell, as soon as we were even close, he ended things. I guess it's for the best. If he hadn't, there's no way I would've wound up with Archer.

So why do I feel guilty?

Archer laughs at Griffin and pulls me closer to him. I force my muscles to relax, attempting to focus on the conversation instead of the front door across the room. I haven't seen Maverick since he mowed the lawn while I was outside. It was awkward, and I barely lasted two minutes until I was packing up my things and disappearing into my side of the house.

It's normal, though.

Isn't it?

To think about your ex sometimes. To feel awkward around them. To remember what it was like to be with them while doing your best to get over them and move on with someone new.

It'd be easier if I had some semblance of closure. If I knew why he broke up with me. If he wasn't always around, reminding me of our past.

Then again, maybe not. He isn't around right now, and I can't stop wondering where he is or if he'll show up as soon as I let my guard down and relax with Archer, which is messed up on so many levels. Maybe it's a damned if you do and damned if you don't scenario, and there is no winning.

Probably.

Because if there was a solution, I'm pretty sure my over-thinking, overanalyzing brain would've figured it out by now.

"What do you think, Lia?" Griffin asks from one of the recliners across from the couch where I'm snuggling with Archer. A coffee table separates us, and Everett takes up the last chair beside Griffin, making a cozy little circle in the center of the family room.

I blink slowly and turn to him. "I'm sorry, what?"

"What do you think about next year?" Griffin repeats. "You think Archer's dad will trade anyone so we can all play together?"

Griffin signed with the Tornados, and Everett will play for the Rockets next year. Or at least, that's the plan. Archer passed on any contracts, telling everyone he planned to take a different route than the rest of his friends. He's choosing to focus on a career outside of hockey. Well, kind of. I have a hunch he'll wind up owning the Lions in the long run, but what do I know?

"Don't get me wrong. You guys would be awesome playing with anyone, but Uncle Henry isn't an idiot," I point out. "He knows how much stronger you are when you all play together. I bet he's messing with some things behind the scenes, seeing what he can do to get all of you to play for the Lions next year, but that's just me."

"Guess we'll have to wait and see," Everett says, looking unconvinced. "Mav's lucky his dad owns the team, and he's a shoo-in."

"You're lucky he plays defense," Archer says. "Try competing with him for everything."

"Is that why you decided not to sign with the Lions when they tried to recruit you?" Griff asks. "Because you both play the same position?"

Honestly, it's a good question. One I've been way too hesitant to ask, despite the years that've passed since contracts were sent out during their senior year of high school.

"Didn't make it easier," Archer mutters. "Mav's always been the better player."

"Bullshit," I untuck myself from his side and stare back at him. "You guys are even, and we all know it. Take a look at your stats—"

"No need to defend me, Lia," Archer interrupts. His eyes shine with amusement. "I know I'm good and everything. But we're used to being pitted against each other. I think both of us hope if I switch my focus to other shit, everyone will stop comparing us."

"So you did it for Mav?" I ask.

"I did it for both of us. Now, as long as Maverick doesn't squander his chance with the Lions, it'd be great."

"Squander it?" I pull away from Archer's side even more, my spine straightening. "What do you mean?"

"I don't know, I think he's been off," Everett explains. "Distracted, maybe?"

"Or maybe he's peaked," Griffin jokes, but the rest of the guys simply laugh.

Maverick? Peaked? Not possible. The guy was born to play on the ice, and we all know it. Even Archer does. And it isn't because Maverick's better. It's because Maverick eats, sleeps, and breathes hockey. The idea of him doing anything else or not giving it a hundred and ten percent every single day is laughable.

Literally.

"Should I leave so you can finish talking shit, or are you douchebags finished?" a low voice questions from behind the couch.

My breath stalls as I turn around and find Mav. He's in a pair of basketball shorts with his T-shirt tucked in the back. His glistening chest is on full display, and a smile plays at the edge of his lips as he crosses his arms after catching us talking about him, though he doesn't look offended. He looks amused. My eyes fall to his biceps. I gulp, turn back around, and face the blank television.

Peaked, my ass.

The guy's a Greek god. It's honestly kind of a problem.

It's funny. How Maverick and Archer are technically identical twins, but I could tell them apart in a lineup of clones while blindfolded. I'm not sure if it's a me thing or a them thing, but I've always been able to tell the differences, even when we were younger. There's something about both of them that sets them apart. Soft. Hard. Sweet. Sarcastic. Respectful. Jealous. The list goes on and on. Adding the tattoos along Maverick's bare chest is simply icing on the cake of differences between the Buchanan twins.

I wonder if it's why he did it. Why he got the tattoos after I started dating Archer. If it was his way to prove they aren't interchangeable.

Duh.

Trust me. I'm well aware of how different they are, both inside and out.

"Ah, the man of the hour," Griffin says, snapping me out of my funk. "Help us out, will you? Have you peaked, or are you just distracted?"

"Dude, I peaked in elementary when Madisyn Montgomery asked me to be her boyfriend for a week," Mav jokes as he rounds the arm of the couch. "Been going downhill ever since."

"So you're not distracted?" Everett prods.

Maverick's eyes hold mine for a long second until he looks at Everett again. "What would I be distracted by?" He rocks back on his heel and takes a backward step toward the hall. "I'm gonna shower. See you guys."

My lungs constrict as he turns around and leaves me with way more questions than answers. Then again, it's Maverick. Why would I expect anything less?

15

MAVERICK

A soft creak grabs my attention from the window, and I glance toward it, finding Lia. I should've known she'd find me up here. We used to escape to one of our roofs after everyone went to bed more times than I can count. At first, it was so we could argue more about how I cheated during Monopoly or why the Bruins would be idiots to trade Tukani to the Grizzlies. I shake off the memories as she climbs through the window and heads toward me on the roof. Her eyes are glued to her feet, making sure she doesn't slip as she approaches me with careful footsteps.

The window's connected to the study, and it's jammed with desks and old textbooks. It's where we go when we need to focus on homework, and let's be honest, it isn't used half as much as our parents hope it is. I'm okay with it, though. It gives me more opportunities to come out here without anyone noticing. This is one of the flattest spots on the roof, but it's surrounded by high peaks on both sides, shielding the area from view. Archer knows I come up here sometimes, but he also knows it's where I come when I need to be alone. When I need to think. When I need the chaos to quiet, even if it's only for a little while.

Apparently, Lia doesn't feel like granting me the same space.

Of course, she doesn't.

It's been a couple of hours since I walked in on Ophelia and Archer snuggled up on the couch like a cute as fuck couple. I've seen them together here and there since she moved in next door, but other than the one time on the front porch, they've never acted super lovey-dovey or anything. They've been their usual selves. Lia and Archer. The inseparable duo like always. Honestly, I wouldn't even know they're hooking up if I didn't swear I heard her soft moans or my brother's low groans through the wall since she moved in. Thankfully, they've started spending most of their nights at her place, but it hasn't made me feel any better.

This is on you, not her, I remind myself for the thousandth time as I rest my forearms on bent knees and stare up at the big dipper in the sky, wishing she'd go away so I wouldn't want to pull her closer.

"Can I ask you something?" Opie takes a seat beside me without waiting for an invitation.

I keep my eyes glued to the sky as I grunt, "Shouldn't you be with Archer?"

"He knows I'm out here."

"That isn't what I asked."

"I'm with Archer all the time," she clarifies, stretching her legs out beside mine on the roof. "And when you didn't come back out after your shower, I think he's afraid he or one of the other guys offended you."

My eyes slice to hers. "So he sent you to do his dirty work?"

"I asked to come see you," she clarifies.

"Now you need his permission?"

She scoffs. "Seriously, is there no winning with you?"

"Guess not."

She licks her lips. "I didn't come out here to fight."

"Then why are you here, Opie?"

Fuck, I sound like a dick, but I don't back down, pinning her with my glare.

With a huff, she asks, "Where's Reeves?"

"Probably working or on a date. Then again, those are one and the same," I grunt.

"What do you mean?"

"You'll have to ask Reeves."

Her brows bunch, but she doesn't push me. "Okay, then."

Annoyed by her curiosity, I ask, "Why do you want to know where Reeves is?"

"Because you're not usually a loner," she points out, running her hands along her bare thighs as she brushes something off them. "Are you out here because you're hiding from me?"

"Give me a little more credit, Opie," I grumble. "Maybe I simply wanted some peace and quiet tonight."

"Hmm." She tears her gaze from mine and turns to the skyline, looking less than convinced. She's beautiful like this. With the moonlight kissing her freckled cheeks, her wavy hair hanging down her back, and her father's worn baseball hat flipped backward, showcasing just how fucking perfect she really is.

"Wanna tell me what's on your mind?" she asks.

I blink slowly and scrub my hand over my face. "Nothing."

"The guys didn't mean anything by it. Just so you know."

It.

As in, my friends talking shit behind my back. They really think I'm this much of a pansy ass and am hiding away all because of a few comments? Hardly. Besides, I've been wondering the same thing for months. They're not the only ones wondering if I've peaked. Or maybe I *am* distracted, and I'll get my shit together before the season starts.

Yeah, and maybe pigs will fly.

"Seriously," she continues. "We were just talking, and—"

"I'm a big boy, Opie. Don't worry. My ego's fine."

Her lips incline. "Good. So, since we both know you haven't peaked, was the other theory more accurate? Are you distracted?"

By her? Fuck, yes. But she isn't the only thing plaguing my mind lately. I clench and unclench my fist, watching the way my veins pop in the moonlight.

"You ever wish you did something other than hockey?" I ask her.

She hesitates, her brows bunching, but only for a second. She answers my question despite the lack of relevance to the conversation.

"Not really," she replies. "Call me crazy, but I'm pretty sure it's in my blood." A smile teases her lips but disappears quickly. "Why?"

"I don't know. Sometimes, I wonder if we all would've turned out the way we did without our parents' influence."

"You mean like hockey and college and how close all of us are?"

"Yeah."

She shrugs. "I think all parents do it. They share something that brings them joy, hoping it'll bring their kids joy too. You know, like pizza and birthday cake and nostalgic movies. It doesn't mean they won't accept us if we decide it isn't our thing, though."

"You sure?"

She rests her chin in her hands and gives me her full attention. "You really think Finley could care any less about hockey?"

I scoff, thinking of Everett's sister and how much she despises sports in general. "Good point."

"Exactly." Lia laughs. "We share what we love, ya know?"

"I guess so."

"Why do you ask?" she prods. "Is there something bothering you? Something making you feel like it's out of your control?"

With a humorless laugh, I shake my head. "Everything's out of my control, Lia."

"Such as?"

A hundred different answers rise to the surface, but I push them back, choosing the simplest.

"Such as my Lions contract," I offer.

"What do you mean?"

"My dad owns the team, Opie."

"Well, yeah. But your dad isn't stupid. He isn't going to sign a bad player."

"A bad player, no. But an average player?" I run my tongue along the back of my teeth. "Someone who doesn't deserve—"

"I'm going to stop you right there," she interrupts. "Because if you finish your sentence by comparing yourself to an average player, I will slap you silly. And do you want to know why?"

Amusement almost beats out my morose thoughts as I reply, "Why?"

"Because I haven't had a player score on me consistently like you do in I don't know how long, and I'm one of the best goalies in the female league, so don't you dare make a fool out of me by saying it isn't a big deal or you aren't an amazing player." She gives me a pointed look, daring me to contradict her.

Instead, I scratch my jaw, feeling lighter. "Thanks, Opie."

"Of course. Besides, this is the future you've been

125

dreaming about, right? You'd better believe I'm not gonna let you shit on it simply because you're feeling a little down."

She has no idea.

"Speaking of the future," I reply. "Is college life everything you dreamed it would be?"

"I mean, technically, the school part hasn't started yet, but…" She hesitates. "I dunno. I think so? It's kind of weird. It's like you said. I've been dreaming about it for so long. Actually being here? Experiencing things? It's…surreal."

"Good surreal?" I prod.

"Mostly. It's also different than I expected, so…"

With a slow nod, I glance at her again, this time holding her gaze no matter how much it hurts to see her like this—basking in the moonlight like so many other nights. When things were different. When things were easy. Her warm eyes are darker than usual, but they're still shining with interest. An innocent interest. A genuine interest. But interest, none-theless.

And fuck me, it hurts.

"How is LAU different than you expected?" I ask.

I shouldn't. I already know her answer. She planned to be with me when she moved out here. We both were. Instead, she's with Archer. Spending her nights with him. Texting him. Talking to him. *Being* with him.

Me? I'm an unpleasant reality who knows how to score against her on the ice.

With a slow breath, Ophelia dodges my question and asks, "How 'bout you? We used to spend hours talking about what we wanted our futures to be like. It's your senior year. Are you excited? Do you have all your ducks in a row for after graduation?"

I'd laugh if the truth weren't so pathetic, choosing to look up at the starry sky above us instead of the gorgeous girl who will never be mine again. "Not really."

"Why not?"

With a shrug, I lie, "I dunno."

"Come on, tell me," she pushes. "Or do you reserve those kinds of conversations for secret girlfriends?"

"We were never officially dating," I remind her.

Fuck.

I don't mean to say it. To hint she meant anything less than my everything while we were together. But if I take the words back, what does it prove? That I care, even when I shouldn't?

Her eyes widen, her defenses snapping back into place as if only now realizing we aren't hiding on her roof at home anymore. We aren't friends anymore. We aren't anything. Not anymore.

"You're right," she says. "I was nothing more than your fuck buddy, er, *secret* fuck buddy. Of course, how could I forget?" A bitterness laces her words, and she shakes her head. When she attempts to stand, I stop her, preventing her escape as I grab hold of her hand, keeping her in place.

I shouldn't touch her. Not like this. Not like anything. She isn't mine to touch. But I can't help it. Letting her think I never cared about her when she has no fucking clue how wrong she is.

"You weren't my secret fuck buddy, Opie," I rasp.

"What was I, Mav?" She stares at my grasp on her arm, her breathing soft and shallow, and her words barely a whisper as she looks at me.

My everything.

The truth hurts, but I swallow it back, murmuring, "Important." My eyes hold hers. "You were important, Goose."

"And now?" she whispers, and fuck me, I swear I can taste her question on my lips. We're too close. Too caught up in the memory of a different rooftop we used to escape to. One

127

where I would strip her bare and kiss every inch of her perfect body. Where we would discuss our hopes and dreams and future. A future we don't have anymore. A future we *can't* have anymore.

"Now, you're my brother's girlfriend," I murmur, shining a black light on the truth, no matter how harsh it sounds. I let go of her arm and stand, the reality of our situation making it hard to breathe as she stays crouched beside me. It'd be so easy. To steal her from him. To make her mine again. To beg for forgiveness and promise to never hurt her again.

There's only one problem.

Hurting her is inevitable, and there's nothing I can do to stop it.

"'Night, Opie," I tell her as I climb back inside.

16

OPHELIA

I left my house early this morning, walking around campus and soaking up the atmosphere like a dry sponge. After my conversation with Maverick last night, I realized he's right. Well, about one thing. He's also an ass, but I'm too annoyed to dissect that particular tidbit, so I choose to focus on the positive I took away from our little chitchat.

This is my future. The future I've been dreaming about. It's here. And it might not be exactly what I anticipated, but I still want to grab hold of it with both hands. I've been so busy preparing for my first practice with the girls' team I feel like I've missed out on exploring my new stomping grounds, and since I worked so freaking hard to get here in the first place, I figure I deserve a morning off. A morning where I can just...be. Even if it's only for a little while.

I've been to LAU a hundred times, hell, maybe a thousand, but it's different now. Because I'm not visiting. I'm not here tagging along with my parents to a game or dropping by to hang out with Archer. This is my home now. Mine. At least for the next few years. And I'm not going to squander it.

There's a coffee shop called The Bean Scene close by. It's one of my favorites and serves the best pumpkin spice lattes in the fall, though their iced mocha is pretty awesome too. And their lattes? *Chef's. Kiss.*

I pull the Bean Scene's heavy glass door open, and my mouth waters when the scent of coffee hits me before I freeze in place. A Buchanan is at the front of the line. I'd recognize those broad shoulders anywhere. Unfortunately, I can't tell whether the fine backside belongs to Archer or Mav, so I stay by the entrance and wait. The twin laughs at the barista and slides his credit card across the counter. She smiles back and bats her lashes at him. She's flirting. The question is, is she flirting with my secret ex or my current boyfriend? And why does neither option make me feel any better?

The muscles in my stomach coil with jealousy, but I keep my feet planted, waiting to see who's in front of me while dreading it at the same time.

The barista giggles, waiving the payment off, telling him it's on the house. She grabs his cup from the stack beside the register and writes her number on the white material with a Sharpie, chatting with him as she fills it with black coffee and adds a splash of cream.

If only the boys had different coffee orders.

Flicking her long, dark hair over her shoulder, she hands him the cup and smirks as he runs his thumb across the phone number. His voice is too low for me to make out his response, giving me zero clues as to who I may or may not be kind of, sort of stalking.

The twin turns around, ready to exit the building, stopping short when he sees me hanging out near the entrance.

Aaaand, I've been spotted.

Heat builds in my chest, and I rub my lips together, unable to move even if I wanted to.

"Opie," Maverick greets me with a hint of annoyance on the tip of his tongue.

"My name isn't Opie," I remind him.

"What are you doing here?"

"I'm not stalking you, in case you're wondering. I was craving an iced latte, and—"

"I didn't think you were stalking me."

"Good," I snap. "Because I wasn't. I'm sorry if I interrupted your…"—my gaze flicks to the barista staring at us, and I tuck my hair behind my ear—"*conversation?*"

The corner of his mouth lifts, but he doesn't bother looking at the barista as he closes a bit of the distance between us. "Are you jealous, Opie?"

"Hardly," I lie. "Although, if you plan on hooking up with her tonight, you might want to let the guys know. I'd hate for you to bail on them."

"You keeping track of me, Lia?"

"Reeves got me a fake ID and invited me to your little night out at SeaBird," I mutter.

"Is my brother busy again?"

"He has a work thing tonight."

"So it's me, you, and the guys, huh?" he questions.

"And your date, who's busy staring at us." My attention slices to the barista behind him, but he doesn't bother to look.

"Not my date."

"*Yet.*" I step around him, heading toward the counter while pretending I'm unaffected by his presence. I doubt he buys it. That's what you get when you grow up with a person. They see through the bullshit, making it impossible to hide things you'd rather keep hidden. Honestly, it's annoying. I can feel him at my back as I place my order, but I do my best to ignore him despite the barista's pinball gaze bouncing between us. Her unspoken question grows louder and louder with every passing second.

Trust me, girlie. If I knew why he was still standing there, I'd tell you.

She makes my iced latte and hands it to me with a forced smile. After thanking her, I turn around and demand, "Why are you still here?" My phone vibrates in my pocket, and I lift a finger. "Just a second." Digging it out with my free hand, I see Archer's name flash across the screen as I slide my thumb to answer the call. "Hello?"

"Hey, what're you doing?" Archer asks.

"I'm at the Bean Scene. You?"

"Just finished a meeting," Archer answers. "I have some great news."

"Really? What kind of great news?" I shift my phone to my opposite ear, glancing at Maverick in front of me. Clearly, he knows who I'm talking to, and clearly, he refuses to give me any privacy, which makes zero sense since he ditched me on the rooftop last night after basically professing his love.

Okay, he didn't profess his love, but he did admit he cared about me while we were together.

It's for the best, and I'm not complaining. But am I in the wrong for feeling a bit whiplashed? I'm gonna go with *no.*

"You know the event I'm attending tonight? The one I was telling you about?" Archer asks, completely oblivious to my inner dialogue, thank goodness, and continues, "Well, I was able to grab you a seat."

"A seat?"

"Yeah. It's actually a pretty big deal. I know you're not usually a fan of events like this, but a lot of really incredible people will be there."

"That's…amazing, Archer," I answer, too distracted by the man in front of me to give my boyfriend my full attention.

He's staring at me. Shamelessly eavesdropping without giving a damn how uncomfortable it makes me.

"You're going to love it," Archer adds. "It's a black-tie event, though."

That grabs my attention, making my nose scrunch. "As in...*fancy?*"

"Yeah, and I know it's short notice, but I'd love it if you could come. Do you have any appropriate dresses?"

"Um...," I gulp. "I don't exactly own a lot of dresses, *period*, and I'm pretty sure none of them are considered black-tie worthy."

"Any chance you can go shopping today? I know you don't have a car, but I can see if I can ditch my next meeting or ask my mom to send over a dress."

"It's fine," I mutter. "I'll, uh, I'll figure it out."

"You sure? Maybe I can call Mav and see if—"

"I'm actually here with your brother now," I announce, because if I don't, I'll feel like I'm hiding something from him. Which is ridiculous. I have nothing to hide.

"You're with Maverick?" Archer asks.

"Yeah, I ran into him at the coffee shop, but, uh, he has a date, so he's a little busy and can't babysit me today. Bummer, right?"

"I don't have a date," Maverick growls. Thankfully, his brother doesn't hear him.

I turn around and face the barista again, desperate for privacy, as I check the time on the clock hanging on the wall behind her. "Besides, even if he wasn't busy, I'm a big girl, remember? I can figure out how to get a dress. What time do you need me to be ready?"

"Seven?" Archer offers.

I nod again. "Okay. Sure. I'll be ready at seven."

A pause follows, along with his sigh. "Are you sure you're okay going? I don't want to pressure you."

"It'll be fun," I argue, but I'm not sure who I'm trying to convince.

"Okay," he murmurs. "I'll see you then."

"Yup." I hang up the phone, reeling as my laid-back Saturday was just taken hostage.

"I'm too busy for what, exactly?" Maverick asks behind me. "And what's happening tonight?"

Twisting around, I take a sip of my latte, downing half of it as I shove my phone into my back pocket. "There's a dinner or something. Apparently, Archer found me a seat at his table? I don't really know how it works, but is there any chance you know a store where I can find a fancy dress?"

He frowns. "You hate dresses."

"How do you know I hate dresses?" I counter.

"When was the last time you wore a dress?"

"Prom," I offer, belatedly realizing the can of worms I accidentally opened.

Oops.

Instead of running from the awkward silence like usual, I let it wash over us, holding Maverick's unreadable stare as if daring him to ask me about it. About the night he bailed on me. About the night he broke my heart and refused to talk to me. The night he proved how little he cares.

Yeah. You fucked up, Buchanan. What are you gonna do about it?

The cords in his neck tighten. "You can't wear your prom dress tonight."

"Duh," I reply. "I might not be suited for black-tie events, but I'm not stupid. The question is, what *do* I wear?"

Tucking one of his thumbs into the front pocket of his jeans while sipping his coffee, he smacks his lips together and lifts his shoulders. "I don't know."

"Why not? Weren't you raised attending black-tie events, thanks to your parents?"

"Yeah, but I haven't been to one in forever. I stopped going as soon as I was old enough to realize they're full of boring people who like to show how much money they have."

"And then there's Archer," I quip.

"He got my grandpa's genes," Maverick informs me, mentioning his politician grandfather who practically basks in all the media's attention. It's nice. Seeing Maverick with his guard down. I hate how I notice.

"A hundred bucks says Archer winds up being a politician in the future," Mav adds.

"To be fair, he'd probably be really good at it since he actually has his head on straight."

"He'd have my vote," Maverick agrees with a dry laugh, rubbing his hand along the top of his head and squeezing the back of his neck. "As long as he doesn't make me attend any of his political rallies and shit." He shivers.

With a laugh, I admit, "I get it. I'm not one for the spotlight, either."

"Then why are you going tonight?" he asks.

"Because—"

"Don't answer that," he mutters. "Where do you want me to take you?"

His offer leaves me speechless, and I shake my head. "You don't have to take me anywhere."

"You don't have a car, remember?"

"Yeah, but it doesn't mean I need your help picking a dress. I'll hire an Uber or—"

"I'll wait outside, and you can pick your own shit. It's the least I can do, isn't it?" he offers. "Since I fucked up your prom and everything."

My expression falls, but my stupid heart? It flutters with...*something*. It's the first time he's apologized. I mean, technically, he said he was sorry when he broke my heart over the phone, but after that, he ghosted me. He ghosted me *hard*. He pretended like nothing happened between us while making me feel like the bad guy for winding up with his brother. And I know it isn't fair. I know I'm in the wrong, too, or at least made things a hell of a lot more complicated. But acknowledging he ruined my prom, leaving his brother to salvage it for me?

I don't know. It feels good. Like we're finally making a little progress. *Maybe.*

"Mav," I murmur, "you didn't—"

"Tell me I did," he orders, surprising me with the malice in his voice. The toes of his shoes hit mine as he steps closer and towers over me. "Tell me I fucked up your prom. Tell me the entire night was ruined. Lie if you have to."

It's his eyes that do me in. The stubbornness. The need. The way they narrow slightly while pleading with me at the same time.

"Why?" My voice is barely above a whisper as I battle the confusion tugging at me.

His breath touches my cheeks, the navy in his eyes swirling with different shades of blue. The combination pulls at my insides and makes it hard to breathe.

"Because the alternative's a bitch to accept," he rasps.

I open my mouth to ask what he means, but he tilts his head toward the exit. "Come on."

He turns on his heel and leads me outside to the parking lot. His sleek, black Ducati is parked beneath a tree at the far corner. I hesitate, remembering the last time I was on the stupid thing and how good it felt to wrap my arms around him.

"Is there a problem, Opie?" he asks as his long, strong legs carry him toward the dangerous beast.

So many I can barely think straight.

I lift my half-finished iced latte into the air. "What about my drink?"

He digs through one of the leather pouches attached to his motorcycle, pulling an olive green travel mug out. Twisting the cap off, he pours the water out of it onto some nearby grass and offers it to me. "Here. Washed it this morning."

Instead of reaching for it, I take a small step back. "I don't need you going out of your way for me."

"I'll be your chauffeur and nothing more."

My brows dip. "Why?"

He shrugs as if the answer's simple. As if he's known it all along. "Because I've been an ass, and you deserve happiness. Even if it isn't with me."

Fuck.

The words leave me aching, but so does his sincerity. And his acceptance. It makes me want to hit him and hug him at the same time. My eyes burn, but I will the sting to go away while standing numbly in the middle of a parking lot as question after question—the same ones plaguing me since his stupid phone call—flash through me.

Why? Why did you bail before prom? Why did you break up with me? Why didn't you want me anymore? What did I do wrong? Why do you care one minute and act like I don't matter the next? Why do you root for me and Archer only to make me crave you late at night?

I drop my gaze to the asphalt beneath our feet. The crunch of his shoes against the black pavement grates on my ears as he moves toward me, but still, I don't move a muscle.

Without a word, Mav takes my iced coffee from my hand and pours the rest of it into his mug, twisting the spill-proof lid into place. Then, he grabs his helmet, slips it on my head, buckles the stupid thing under my chin, and climbs onto his bike, staring straight in front of him.

In a daze, I slip behind him and grab onto his waist without any prodding. My movements are slow. Forced. Controlled. And I think he can feel it, too, but he doesn't comment on it as he cranks the engine.

And we're off.

1 7

MAVERICK

S hopping was torture. I waited outside like I promised. But the regret? The reminder of prom and how I bailed on her? It was fucked-up. I knew it then, and I know it now. But she doesn't get it. She doesn't understand. She never will. I thought I had come to terms with it, but the hurt in her eyes at the coffee shop? It was more than I could stomach, and it's becoming harder and harder to keep my resolve in check. To remember the why behind the phone call an hour before prom and the why behind every single fucking decision following it.

A soft knock on the door echoes through the house, snapping me from my self-loathing, and someone answers it as I grab a protein shake from the kitchen.

"Damn, Lia," Griffin compliments from the entryway. "You look awesome!"

"Why, thank you!" her soft, feminine voice replies.

I glance into the family room, giving me a full view of the couches, television, and the entryway where Griff is grasping the edge of the door and talking to Lia.

My mouth goes dry.

Long legs. Black dress. Straight, strawberry blonde hair. Smokey eyes.

Fuck.

When she catches me staring, Ophelia smiles big and bright, but it falls quickly, and she shakes her head, her cheeks heating. "Sorry, I thought you were Archer for a split second."

Like a punch to the gut, my lungs deflate. I lean against the counter to keep from landing on my ass. I'm used to it. Being mistaken for Archer. It's par for the course when you're an identical twin. But rarely by Ophelia. And not once since we started hooking up, and I gave her a glimpse of the real me. The reminder stings more than it should.

Are we so interchangeable, Opie?

Oblivious, Ophelia peeks down the hallway leading to the bedrooms and looks back at Griff. "Where is he?"

"I'll grab him for you," Griffin answers, disappearing down the hall. He knocks on Archer's door, tells my brother Ophelia has arrived, and heads into his own room while I stand motionless in the kitchen.

Everyone's getting ready to go to SeaBird tonight. It's a bar next to campus. The alcohol is cheap. The bands are good. And the women are plenty. But I don't care about any of them. Not when Ophelia's standing twenty feet in front of me. Fuck, she could be on another planet, and I still wouldn't care about the women at SeaBird.

None of them matter.

They never have and never will.

"So?" she prods, looking down at her dress. "What do you think?"

I set the protein shake on the counter and walk toward her, my movements slow and controlled when I'm anything but.

My mind's a mess. Like I'm caught in some fucked-up

deja vu loop. Is this what she looked like before prom? Before I broke up with her? Before I let her go?

I'm a fool.

I said I wanted her to be happy, even when it wasn't with me. But why him? Why my brother? Why do I have to put up with front-row seats to the girl of my dreams moving on without me? But even if I could choose someone different, would I? He treats her better than I ever could. He fucking worships her the way she deserves. And it's what I want. For Ophelia to be worshipped.

This dress, though? She's even more stunning than I imagined. And fuck me, I spent a lot of time imagining how pretty she must look when she was trying on her dresses in the store earlier today. She's gorgeous.

"You're hesitating," she notes, "which isn't exactly a good sign in case you're wondering."

When I reach her, I keep my voice low and lick my lips, reminding myself she isn't mine. Not anymore.

"You don't wear dresses," I remind her.

She tilts her head. "Is that a nice way of saying I look like shit?"

"Are you fishing for compliments?"

"I wasn't…" Her voice trails off, and she sighs, sucking her pouty lips into her mouth and gracing me with a glimpse of her eyes. The warm brown sugar is lined with a smokey brown and shoots straight to my groin.

Fuck, she's beautiful.

"It's like you said," she murmurs. "I don't usually wear dresses, and I have no idea if I'm pulling this off or not, but… thank you for deflecting? It's giving me a *great* confidence boost exactly when I need it, so you're a real peach." She gives me a thumbs up and tries to move past me, but I step in front of her, slowly dragging my hand from her fingers and up her forearm. Her skin feels like silk in my palm as I tug her closer, looking over the top of her head to confirm we're alone.

"You want the truth?" I rasp. "You look like a wet dream, Ophelia."

Her breath hitches, and she peeks up at me through her thick lashes. They're darker than usual, accentuating her caramel-colored eyes. Heat licks along my erection, and I nearly groan.

"And that's a...good thing?" she whispers.

"For my brother, yeah. The rest of us?" I press my tongue against my cheek and let her go. "Fucking torture. Have a good night."

I storm out the front door, pull my phone from my pocket, and shoot the group a text, letting them know I'll meet them at the bar because if I spend one more minute in Opie's presence, I'll lose my mind.

OPHELIA

As I watch a show on my laptop, a soft knock hits my bedroom window, and my brows dip. The same sound comes from the glass another time, and a muffled "Opie, it's me" filters in from outside.

It's almost midnight, and I have school tomorrow. I should be sleeping. The rest of my family is. So what's Maverick doing outside? It has to be him. No one else calls me Opie. Or at least, no one who lived to tell the tale. But he's supposed to be at LAU, so...

Curious, I toss my legs over the edge of my bed and push the white curtains aside. Sure enough, there he is.

Maverick Buchanan.

I unlock my window and push it open, coming face to face with the most attractive guy I've ever been lucky enough to know. I'm on the first floor, so it's not like it's hard for Maverick to sneak in through my window, but coming over unannounced?

This is new.

"What are you doing here?" I whisper, glancing at my closed bedroom door. If anyone catches us together, I'll have to answer some questions I'm not sure I'm ready to answer. Like how long I've been hooking up with Maverick Buchanan and if I'm sure it's a good idea.

"You gonna let me in or what?" he prods.

I roll my eyes but step aside when a small bag of something flies through the window and hits my comforter with a soft pfft.

"What was that?" I ask.

"Cinnamon bears."

"What for?"

"In case your mom catches me sneaking into your bedroom," he grunts. With his hands pressed against my window sill, Mav pushes himself up and climbs through the window. His biceps flex with the movement, his corded forearms on full display in his Broken Vows T-shirt. Not gonna lie. The sight toys with my libido, and I fold my arms, hiding my nipples from giving Maverick a full-blown salute as his feet hit the carpet in my bedroom and he slides my window shut again.

"So you bring my mom a present, but not me?" I quip, keeping my voice low. Not bothering to answer me, he slowly stalks toward me, and I take a step back, enjoying the chase. "What are you doing here?"

When my back hits my bedroom door with a quiet thud, he grabs my waist, pressing himself against me. "I came to see you."

"Duh," I reply with a smile. "The question is, why? Don't you have school tomorrow?"

"First class doesn't start 'til noon. I can make it back in time. I missed you," he adds, bending closer. His navy blue eyes skim my face as if I'm the most fascinating thing in the world.

"You missed me so much you had to sneak into my room on a school night?"

"Mm-hmm."

"If my parents catch you in here, they'll kill us."

"That's why I brought the cinnamon bears," he murmurs.

With a quiet laugh, I lift my chin, and he kisses me, making me melt in a matter of seconds. My fingers find the edge of his shirt. I twist the soft, gray fabric in my hand and attempt to memorize this. The feel of Maverick Buchanan's mouth on mine. His weight holding me to the door. His hot, cinnamon breath proving he stole a gummy or two before showing up at my window.

He's right. They're my mom's favorite. They've always been her favorite.

When he ends the kiss, I lick my bottom lip, tasting the cinnamon flavor one more time. "And how would you bribe my dad if he caught you in here with me?"

Maverick shivers. "There's no bribing the man. If he catches us, I'm diving back through the window and booking it to my car parked around the corner. Don't worry. I'll text you to let you know I made it out alive."

"Classy," I note.

"Never claimed to be the classy twin," he jokes. "Although..." Giving me a bit of space, he boops my nose, threads his fingers with mine, and tugs me toward my bed. "Rory's been on a 2000's chick-flick kick lately, and—"

"A chick-flick kick?" I repeat with a laugh. "Try saying that three times fast."

"Will you focus?" he demands, but I don't miss the crinkles of amusement around his eyes, and they only make my heart flutter more. "I'm trying to prove I can be classy."

I clear my throat. "Sorry, go on. Rory's been on a 2000's chick-flick kick lately, and..."

"My mom's been showing her a bunch of them," he explains, sitting on my bed. "And it reminded me of something."

"What something?"

He tugs me closer. "Prom."

With a laugh, I collapse on the edge of the mattress beside Mav. "What about prom?"

"Yours is coming up."

"And?"

"And I wanna take you," he clarifies.

145

A heady concoction of exhilaration and anticipation and excitement and...wariness hits me in an instant. Maverick's never asked anyone to a dance, especially not one two months away. And the fact that he's here contradicts the boy I've known since we were little and the charismatic guy I've been secretly hooking up with since Thanksgiving.

It's just a school dance, and saying yes should be simple, but since we haven't told anyone we've been hooking up, and Mav doesn't seem like a guy who would normally be interested in settling down, it isn't.

By some miracle, no one knows about us, and I've been hesitant to tell anyone. I don't want to look stupid if things don't work out. I don't want to hear, "I told you so," or, "You've known Mav forever. You really thought he'd settle down with you?" The thought alone makes me want to curl up in my blankets and cry. I know I was the one to suggest we keep things under wraps, and I know he's been pushing me to make us official for a while now, but I'm really not sure I can stomach losing him publicly.

Is it so wrong of me?

"You gonna answer me?" he prods. "You're making me sweat."

"Mav, I know we've been hooking up for a while, but that doesn't mean you have to—"

"I want to." He cups the side of my face and tilts my head toward him. "Want," he repeats. "No, I take it back. This isn't a want. It's a need.*"*

A smile plays at the edge of my lips. "Oh, it's a need, now?"

"School dances are a big deal in every movie my mom and Rory have made me and Archer sit through. Now, I might not be able to swing making you prom queen and shit,"—I snort—"but giving you a night you'll always remember is definitely within my power."

"And that's why you're here," I conclude. "To ask me to prom."

"Yeah." He nods, the same sweet smile turning my insides to mush as he rubs his thumb along the back of my hand. "Honestly,

I'm embarrassed it took me so long to remember it's coming up for you."

"It's two months away," I remind him.

"Perfect. You can mark your calendar."

My lips scrunch to one side while my doubt threatens to ruin his thoughtfulness. And he is being thoughtful. And sweet. And charismatic. And the fact he didn't ask me over text or didn't wait until the next time we were supposed to see each other is...kind of adorable.

"You still haven't answered me yet." Maverick lifts our entwined hands to his lips and kisses my knuckles.

"Are you sure you won't change your mind in two months?"

"Come on, Opie," he pushes. "Stop coming up with excuses to keep hiding our relationship from the family, and let me take you to prom."

"Speaking of our families, what happens when my mom asks who's taking me?" I question. "She already gives me enough crap for not telling her who my Mystery Man is. You really think she'll let me sneak out the back door in my prom dress without giving her an introduction?"

"So give her one," he offers.

Aaaand, there's the heart flutter again.

Pushing the feeling aside, I force myself to focus on our reality instead.

"Mav," I start.

"I'm serious." He pecks the tip of my nose and drops his hand to his lap. "Introduce me."

"If I introduce you to my parents, then..."

"Then what?"

"Then it makes"—I wiggle my finger between us—"this official. Are you sure you're ready?"

Gently, he pushes me back onto the mattress and rolls on top of me, pinning me to it. "You're my ride or die, Goose. And I know you've been putting off announcing our relationship to our families

147

because you're scared I'll change my mind, but I won't. The things you want? The future you want? I wanna give those to you. Like I said, I'm not gonna change my mind."

I search his expression for sincerity and find it in spades. The softness in his eyes. The affection shining in them. The way it warms me from the outside in, making me feel beautiful and special and delicate and so many more emotions I want to wrap myself up in him and never leave.

"How do you know you won't change your mind?" I whisper.

"I just do," he replies, simply. "I'm tired of keeping this casual when what I feel for you is so much more. I want the rest of the world—including our families—to know you're mine."

Mine.

He's never claimed me. I mean, he has. But not like this. Not so pointedly. We've talked about the future. About what we'll do at LAU, and how it's only a matter of time until we tell our families we've been seeing each other. But I always figured it was nothing more than talk. He'd grow bored or have cold feet by the time my graduation actually rolled around, and he'd back out. He'd change his mind. He'd break my heart.

Seeing him like this? Hearing him say the words I desperately want to hear?

I like it.

A lot.

"Say something, Goose," he prods.

Peeking up at him, I whisper. "I'm yours?"

"Every"—he kisses my nose—"fucking"—he dips lower, kissing my throat—"inch."

∽

"HEY," ARCHER MURMURS BESIDE ME, AND I FLINCH AT THE sound.

The dashboard highlights his handsome features, sharp jaw, sharp eyes, and kind smile as I peek over at him. "Hey."

"Where'd you go?"

"What do you mean?"

"I know you," he reminds me, reaching over the center console and squeezing my knee. "Your body's here, but your mind is somewhere else."

I look down at his hand on my thigh and place my palm over it. "Sorry."

"Don't apologize. What's going on?"

"Just…distracted, I guess. Thanks for bringing me tonight."

"Thanks for coming," he returns. "I know events like this aren't usually your thing."

"It was fun watching you in your element," I tell him. "You're quite the schmoozer, Arch."

He chuckles. "I had to be to win you over."

"Mm-hmm," I hum, turning back to the darkened windshield. It's late, and I'm tired. I can't tell if it's because I've been making small talk for the past three hours or because my feet hurt in my heels, but I'm ready to take my makeup off and call it a night. And if I don't run into a certain Mystery Man who called me a wet dream and stormed out of his house like a just-kicked puppy, even better.

"Are you going to tell me what's on your mind?" Archer prods.

My expression falls as I glance at my boyfriend beside me. "Arch…"

"Is it your Mystery Man again?"

My head dips forward, and so does my hair, shielding me from his view.

"I'll take it as a yes," he concludes. "He really fucked you up, didn't he."

It isn't said with any malice. It's more of an observation

than anything else. And it isn't a question, either. It doesn't need to be. Archer knows me better than almost anyone.

"I saw him earlier today, and it…it messed with me a little."

He nods knowingly. "What can I do to help?"

"Trust me, you're doing plenty."

"I hate seeing you like this." He glances at me. "Seeing you hurting."

He's always been this way. Putting everyone else first. It's one of the things I love most about him.

It also makes me hate myself.

I tuck my hair behind my ear and slouch a little further into the passenger seat. "I don't deserve you. You know that, right? Here we are, talking about another guy, and—"

"You want to know the greatest thing about me and you?" he offers. "I'm your best friend *first*, boyfriend *second*. I love how you can talk to me, even when the topic is shitty."

I grimace. "Like your girlfriend being hung up on another guy?"

"Like my best friend needing time for her heart to heal," he clarifies. "And I'm okay, Lia. Even a piece of you is enough until you're ready to let him go fully."

A sharp pressure hits my sternum because I don't know if I *can*.

"Don't say things like that." I press my finger against the corner of my eye, but he grabs my wrist and tangles our fingers together.

"We were friends before this, Ophelia. And if I gotta be patient. If I gotta let you heal. If I gotta glue the pieces back together by my fucking self until you feel whole again, I'll do it. You know that, right?"

My throat catches on the baseball-sized lump, but I swallow it back, nodding, as he pulls up to our connecting houses.

"Come inside with me," he suggests. "Let me hold you tonight."

"You hold me every night," I remind him.

"And I don't take a single one for granted." He brings our entwined fingers to his lips and kisses the back of my hand. Letting me go, he helps me out of the car and escorts me inside his place. My heart aches with every step. But the worst part? I can't tell if it's because I feel guilty for being here with Archer when I know his brother's hurting or if I feel guilty for thinking of his brother in the first place when I'm with him.

19
OPHELIA

I wake up to the sound of puking. It's violent and makes my stomach churn as I slip out of Archer's bed. Tiptoeing down the hallway, I find the bathroom light slipping through the crack beneath the closed door. It highlights the dark wood floors and the shadows along the walls, giving a forbidden, almost eerie vibe, causing my steps to slow. The sound of muffled heaving hits my ears again, and I bite the inside of my cheek. Indecision surges through me. I could always go back to bed. Pretend to sleep. Pretend I don't know who's on the opposite side of the door. But I can't convince my feet to move. Not when he sounds so miserable. Before I can talk myself out of it, I carefully push the bathroom door open and peek inside.

Maverick is wrapped around the toilet with his head pressed against the seat, looking sicker than a dog.

I rush forward and push his long, shaggy hair away from his forehead, checking his temperature. He doesn't feel warm, but his skin is cold and clammy, and his eyes are closed as he leans into my touch.

"You okay?" I murmur.

"Fucking hell."

I laugh lightly. "I take that as a no?"

He peels his eyes open and looks at me. "What are you doin' here, Opie?"

"I heard you puking."

"Tequila's a bitch."

Another laugh slips out of me as I reach for the toilet paper roll, rip a couple squares off, and wipe the corner of his mouth with them. "Are you done puking? Can I get you a cold compress or—"

"I'm fine."

"Then come on," I urge. "Let's get you to bed."

Keeping his ass where it's planted, he mutters, "You shouldn't be helping me."

"I think we've all been on the wrong side of alcohol, don't you?" I flush the toilet and grab his bicep, helping Mav to his feet. The dude's built like a brick wall, and I almost crumble beneath his massive body but steady myself with my hand against the dark granite countertop as I take his weight. His shirt is soaked in sweat, and he's still wearing his jeans. They hug his ass and his thighs, and the combination kind of makes me want to take a bite out of his backside. Scratch that. Even wasted and delirious, his entire body, face, and mussed-up hair make him look effortlessly gorgeous. Like he can't even help it. Like it simply comes naturally to the guy. Realizing I'm most definitely checking out my boyfriend's twin brother, I tear my gaze from our reflection and guide Maverick back to his room.

I keep the light off. I shouldn't. It's a bad idea. As if the darkness will hide the fact I'm in my boyfriend's brother's room instead of asleep in his bed. But I can't turn back now. I'm here. And so is Maverick. A very drunk Maverick who's leaning on my shoulders like his legs might give out at any second.

Guiding him to the bed, I make sure he's seated and order, "Arms up."

Maverick raises them into the air and waits. I slip the dark T-shirt over his head, revealing muscles stacked on muscles.

My mouth dries instantly. It's been three months, maybe more since I saw him up close and personal without his shirt? Since he let me touch him? Let me run my hands—my tongue—along every inch of tan skin on his Adonis body?

But it never looked like this. He's been working harder than ever. Probably preparing for the NHL next year, but what do I know? And the tattoos? It's the first time I've ever been able to get a close look at them. Dark ink takes up most of his chest now. Intricate lines and bold drawings cover every inch, turning the man I used to know into nothing but a stranger.

My fingers itch to reach out and run my hands along the V leading to his jeans, but I stop myself and breathe out, "Damn."

Mav's lips lift with amusement. "Like what you see, Goose?"

Tearing my attention from his shadowed torso, I tuck my messy hair behind my ear. "Don't call me Goose."

"But I'm your Maverick, right? Just like *Top Gun*. Except Goose is the one who dies." His forehead wrinkles. "Probably should've been the other way around."

"What?" Confusion taints my words as my attention bounces from his stupid chest to his stupid comment.

"Nothing." He licks his chapped lips and drops his chin to his chest, clearly still drunk out of his mind despite spilling most of the alcohol he consumed earlier tonight in the toilet.

"Since when do you have tattoos?" I ask.

"Ah, you noticed, did you?" He smacks his hand against his pec, right above his heart.

"They're kind of hard to miss," I muse.

"Yeah. Gotta deal with the pain somehow, right?"

"What pain?"

"I don't know? Hockey and shit," he deflects.

I stand in front of him. Unsure what to do or say or… anything. Because it's annoying. The way he talks to me. So hot and cold. Sometimes, it makes me believe we're almost friends again. Other times, it reminds me of what we used to do together. When it was dark and late, and he treated me like I was more than a friend. When we would kiss and touch and talk about our hopes and dreams. Our future. One we'd build together.

Frustration hits between my ribs, and I press my hand to his chest. "Lay down."

He doesn't budge. "Why? So you can climb on?"

"Very funny, Maverick. Come on." I push my hand against his chest with more force, and he rolls onto his back, tugging me with him.

Shit.

Yeah, laying on top of your ex while being half-naked is not a great position to be in. My long hair pools around us. My hands are pressed against his pecs, and my hip is pressed against his—yup. That's a hard-on.

He forces his eyes open. They stay hooded and dark as he stares up at me, drinking in our precarious position. A devilish smirk greets me. "Now *this* is a wet dream."

"No, this is a ticking time bomb." I push myself away from him and stand, ignoring the way my hands shake from the feel of his skin against my palms.

Snap out of it, Lia, I remind myself.

His sheets are nothing but a lump at the foot of the bed, so I reach for the hem and tug them up, covering Maverick's half-naked body. "Have you had any water or Gatorade yet?"

He shakes his head.

"Any painkillers?"

Another shake.

"I'll be right back." I start to step away, but he grabs my wrist, keeping me in place.

"There isn't any in the bathroom or in my room. You'll have to get it from the kitchen."

"Okay." I slip out of his grasp and pat his thigh, making my way to his door and peeking over my shoulder. It's like my eyes have a mind of their own. Then again, they might. They have a habit of finding Maverick whenever he's in the room despite my best efforts. Like right now. When I'm desperate to get out of here. To put some much-needed distance between us. I hoped spending more time with Mav these last couple of weeks would be like exposure therapy, and he wouldn't affect me anymore. Or his effect would at least be less overwhelming. Less consuming. But it's only made things worse, and still, I can't help but look at him. His arm rests above his head, showcasing his strong bicep as he closes his eyes. He seems so at ease. So comfortable. So freaking drool-worthy, and he isn't even trying.

Seriously, it isn't fair.

I hate how quickly he disarms me. How a simple look can bring me to my knees. How he can share the same face as my boyfriend, but I couldn't have a more drastic physical response, even if I tried. Things might be easier with Archer on paper, but no matter how hard I try to focus on said ease, I can't find the spark with him. The pull. The completely illogical *need* I have with Maverick.

It isn't fair.

And it's turning me into a crazy person.

Giving Mav my back, I tiptoe down the hall and into the kitchen. After finding some medicine in the cabinets and grabbing some Gatorade from the fridge, I head back to Maverick's room, careful of my footsteps in case he's already asleep. It's still dark, but the light from a lamppost outside filters in through the window, casting shadows along the walls and bed. There's a lined garbage can beneath his desk, and I pick it up, setting it beside the nightstand and adding the painkillers and hydration to the small table.

Satisfied I have everything in order, I start to tiptoe backward when his low voice rasps, "How was the party?"

I freeze. "It was fine."

"Did he fuck you in it?"

My lips part on a gasp, my mind spinning. "What?"

"The dress," he clarifies. "Did he fuck you in it?"

"That isn't fair, Mav."

"Life isn't fair," he counters.

"You said you only wanted me to be happy."

"Answer the question, Goose. I gotta know."

It isn't fair. The bitterness in his voice. The way he feels like he has any right to know if I've been with anyone else, when he was my first before breaking my heart.

Steeling my shoulders, I face him again and keep my head held high as I lie, "Technically, he took it off me first."

With a nod, Mav covers his eyes with his forearm and lets out a sigh. "I would've fucked you in it. Bent you over and slid it up your thighs. I would've palmed your round ass, and my cock would've been dripping to be inside you."

His words are so crass, so descriptive, I'm left speechless as my thighs press together.

"Would've fucked you so good, Lia. Would've made you feel so good."

"Mav," I breathe out. It's a plea. A desperate attempt to help him recognize the pain he's putting us both through and how much it's tearing me up inside.

"Should've had whiskey," he mutters.

My brows crease. "What?"

"Should've had whiskey," he repeats.

157

"Why?"

"Then I'd have *whiskey dick* instead of this." He keeps his eyes closed but blindly waves at his very apparent erection beneath the thin cotton sheets. "This is fucking torture."

My teeth dig into the inside of my cheek until I taste blood. And it hurts. All of this. Him. Me. The darkness surrounding us and all it hides. Our past. The way he broke my heart. My relationship with his brother.

I'm in a relationship with his *brother.*

The words hit me like a bucket of ice water, and I fold my arms, swallowing thickly and stepping away from the edge of his bed. "Painkillers and Gatorade are on the nightstand. Get some sleep."

I walk back to Archer's bedroom and slip beneath the covers. But I don't snuggle against Archer's bare chest, too ashamed and afraid I'll start wishing it was someone else's. I should go home. But if I do…is it admitting defeat? Does it prove I'm wasting Archer's time when—on paper—he couldn't be more perfect for me?

If I could only stop caring about Maverick. If I could only stop thinking about him. If I could let him go… Would I be happy?

Honestly, I don't know.

And I freaking hate it.

20

MAVERICK

I fucked up.

The three words circle in my brain like a carousel, making my stomach churn as I stare at the white ceiling in my bedroom.

It's still hazy. A blur. Only snippets rise to the surface, but they're jumbled and out of order. Something about whiskey dick, wet dreams, and feeling Ophelia's hands on my naked torso as she took off my shirt.

Otherwise, I'm clueless.

And filled with shame.

I shouldn't have gone to SeaBird. Shouldn't have gotten wasted. If I hadn't, I wouldn't be second-guessing what I said to my brother's girlfriend in the middle of the night when he was asleep in the next room.

Tossing my forearm over my eyes, I try to block out the memory. Nausea rolls up my throat, and I bend over the side of the bed, puking into the garbage can Ophelia set aside for me.

I'm not sure why she helped me in the bathroom. Not sure why she took me to bed and tucked me in. Not sure why she grabbed me some medicine or if she looked at my hard-on when I pointed it out to her. I'm not sure if she mentioned it to Archer, either. He would kick my ass if she did, but I'd deserve it.

Sometimes I wanna kick my own ass. For the things I think about. The things I want. The woman I want. Even after everything that's happened.

After cleaning up my mess in the garbage can, I slowly make my way down the hall.

The scent of coffee wafts from the kitchen, along with low voices. My stomach finally feels like it's settling since I've finished cleaning its contents out. Good. At least something's going my way.

I step into the kitchen and stop short.

Ophelia's ass is on the counter, and her legs are spread. Archer stands between them. The same shirt she wore last night is bunched around her waist. Tiny black shorts play peek-a-boo with my restraint as she leans back on her elbows, smiling up at him.

Archer.

My twin.

My best friend.

My fucking nemesis if he keeps looking at her like this. Like she's his world when she's always been mine.

Throwing her head back, she laughs as Reeves steps around me into the kitchen. When she catches the movement, her head snaps in my direction, and she freezes.

"Hey, man," Archer greets Reeves before his eyes fall on me. I wait for hatred to fill them, but it doesn't. He lifts his chin. "Hey. You want bacon?"

Sawdust clogs my throat, but I force it back. "Sure. Thanks."

He plates my breakfast and offers it to me. "Heard you had a rough night."

"Yeah," Reeves adds. "You should've seen him at SeaBird. The guy was fucking wasted."

"Thanks for the sympathy," I joke.

"Jaxon warned you, man. Gotta take it easy on the tequila before the season starts."

"The season doesn't start until the end of September. I think I'll be fine."

My eyes find Ophelia's. She's staring at me.

You thinking about last night, too, Goose?

Realizing she's been caught, she hops off the counter and sneaks a coffee cup from beside the stove, bringing it to her lips.

"You'll be fine once you get laid," Reeves argues. "And September, my ass. The girls need help with a fundraiser next week, remember? And Coach Sanderson already lined up a scrimmage against the Snappers too."

"It's next week?" I ask.

"Come on, man. Do you not hear anything Jaxon says?" he asks.

"Jax is the girls' coach, not ours," I remind him.

"Dude, he was at the bar last—" He shakes his head, not deeming my question worth the effort of a full explanation. He scrubs his hand over his face. "Remember the girls we met last night? A few of them are playing for the Lady Hawks this year."

The night's fuzzy as shit, so I don't even bother trying to recount the evening. Besides, I was too busy getting wasted in an attempt to erase the image of Lia smiling at me until realizing I wasn't Archer to pay attention to anything else.

Fuck, that hurt.

Instead of announcing it to the rest of the room, however, I prod, "So?"

"So, they want help building hype for their team since it's

their first year. We're in charge of an ice plunge, and the girls are doing a kissing booth at the Lockwood Heights carnival."

His words turn to a low buzz in my ears as I turn to Archer and demand, "You're going to let Lia kiss random guys?"

His eyes cut to Ophelia, proving we're on the same page, though I doubt he'd ever admit it out loud. He looks at me again, his eyes clouded with restraint as he lifts a shoulder and smooths his expression.

Rolling her eyes, Ophelia leans her hips against the edge of the granite countertop and announces, "Whether or not a kissing booth is dated and a little barbaric, the truth is, it sells tickets, and the girls' team needs tickets sold if I have any hope of breaking the stupid stigma and turning hockey into a respected women's sport. But the good news is, Jaxon said I can man the ticket booth, so you can take a chill pill, gentlemen. I'm not going to be kissing any random guys."

"And if someone calls in sick?" Reeves jokes.

"Then I'll have to take one for the team, which is fine because Archer and I trust each other." She gives him a pointed look. "Right?"

My brother snakes his hands around her waist and kisses her temple. "Right."

"Good. Now, if you'll excuse me, I'm going back to my place to shower." She takes a long swig of her coffee, sets the mug on the counter, and smiles at my best friend. "Reeves." Rising onto her tiptoes, she brushes her lips against Archer's cheek. "Archer." Her eyes find mine, and her heels hit the ground. "Maverick."

Her familiar scent hits my nostrils as she slips past me and walks outside, leaving me anxious and frustrated and so fucking confused I'm not sure if I'm still drunk or if I've actually processed what's going on.

"The Lady Hawks are seriously doing a kissing booth?" I demand.

"Dude, did you hit your head last night when I wasn't looking?" Reeves questions. "Yes. I already told you they're doing a kissing booth. Why do you care?"

Fuck.

"Because if it was Rory, I'd be shitting my pants," I argue, mentioning my little sister as I pin Archer with a look.

He nods his agreement and lets out a sigh. "Yeah, I get it. I'm not too excited about the booth either, but Lia worked her ass off to get here. I'm gonna support her however I can."

Support her?

That's bullshit.

It's also none of my business.

"You're a better boyfriend than I would be," I mutter, and I hate how he's proving it.

I wasn't always this jealous of an asshole. Before, it was different. I didn't care who she talked to or what she wore because I knew she was mine. I knew I was the only one touching her. The only one who knew what she tasted like. But it's not the case now, and it's driving me mad and turning me into a fucking asshole. One I can barely look at in the mirror most days.

"Yeah, well, at least I won't have to see it if she winds up participating," Archer says.

I tilt my head. "What do you mean?"

"I'm gonna be out of town again and won't get back until after the carnival, so..." He hesitates and clears his throat. "I'm gonna need you to keep an eye on her, Mav."

My head falls back, and I stare at the ceiling, convinced I've already died and gone to Hell for being put in these positions.

"Is it a problem?" Archer prods.

"If she heard you say that, she'd knee you in the balls," I point out.

"Then I guess it's a good thing she left. Look, I know you care about her. We all do. Think you can play nice for me?"

My short nails dig into my palms, and my jaw locks as I consider his request. I love my brother. More than anything. But it's times like this when I want to hate him too. For trusting me. For relying on me. For believing I'm better than I really am when we both know it's the furthest thing from the truth.

My molars grind, but I force a nod. "Sure thing, brother."

"Good."

"Still jealous you get to miss the ice plunge, Arch," Reeves chimes in from the fridge. "My balls are always freezing after that shit."

I grunt my agreement and grab the half-finished coffee belonging to Ophelia from the counter, throwing back the rest of its contents and heading back to my room.

Who knows, maybe a little ice will be good for my blue balls because they just might be the death of me at this point.

21

MAVERICK

"Maverick!" Coach calls. "Come here."

Sweat drips down my forehead and stings my eyes.

I can't. Fucking. Breathe.

Ripping my helmet off, I wipe the moisture from my face and head to the bench.

When I reach him, Coach asks, "You okay?"

"Fine," I pant. "Why?"

His eyes thin like he doesn't believe me. The guy's so old he even coached my Uncle Theo and Uncle Colt, but you'd never know it. Other than the shaved head and a few more wrinkles, he looks the same, or at least it's what my uncles tell me. The guy's as sharp as a tack too. And when his scrutiny is directed at you, well, it kind of makes you want to piss yourself.

"You look tired," he decides.

Tired? I feel like my heart might explode.

Reaching for my water bottle on the bench, I mutter, "Guess I partied too hard last night."

He glances down at his iPad littered with the team's stats.

"At the beginning of last season, you could sprint from one end of the ice to the other three seconds faster than what I just clocked you at. Three seconds, Maverick."

The team is still running drills, skating backward to the center red line, pivoting, and sprinting diagonally across the ice to the far corner. My muscles ache from simply watching it.

"Mav," Coach starts.

"I'll try harder."

"Look at me," he orders.

When I do, he hesitates, searching my expression. "You sure you're okay?"

I open my mouth to answer, but he tilts his head toward the bench. "Take a seat. Get some more water. From now on, no drinking the night before practice. Not if it's gonna fuck you up like this."

"Yes, Coach." Slipping past him, I collapse onto the long bench and rest my elbows on my knees, attempting to catch my breath and calm my unsteady, racing heart.

Today's a bad day. Like my body's been filled with sand-bags, and a semi-truck sits on my chest. But even my shitty body can't erase the impending ice plunge and kissing booth, my brother dating my ex, or why I feel like I'm crawling out of my skin.

Then again, it's just another day as Maverick Buchanan.

22
OPHELIA

The place is buzzing. Seriously. I had my first practice a few days ago with the girls, and they weren't kidding when they mentioned how much hype had been building around the yearly Lockwood Heights carnival. The fact they let us rent some booths with such short notice is a freaking miracle. Well, that, or Jaxon kissed up to the chairwoman and finally asked her on a date. Ms. Thompson might be a billion years older than him, but if it gives the girls' team an opportunity to earn some buzz, I won't judge. I was a little nervous, considering how fall semester hasn't started, but everyone is right. Lockwood Heights loves its hockey. If we're lucky, their love for the sport might also extend to the new female division.

I've been manning the ticket booth for about an hour, but my gaze won't stop falling on the oval blue bathtub set up on the grass beside the entrance. Sanderson keeps filling it with ice chunks, making sure the not-so-little cubes stay floating in the crystal-clear water.

The goal is to see if you can make it to twenty seconds. If you can, you win a free churro or cotton candy from the food stand, along with bragging rights. Or, you can use your ticket to send one of the players into the icy depths, making them earn the treat for you. The men's hockey team is all lined up, taking turns in the frigid pool as a timer counts down a few feet away. It's kind of brutal but hilarious, too, since I've only seen a handful of people who aren't on the team attempt the challenge. The guys are lucky it's blistering out here. At least they warm up relatively quickly, thanks to the hot sun hanging high above us. I lift the neck of my black tank top and fan myself. It's so hot the icy water is *almost* appealing as Everett grips the side of the bathtub.

"Three. Two. One," the petite blonde chants beside him. She must be the one who used her ticket to get him all wet and half-naked. As soon as she reaches zero, Everett makes like a bunny rabbit and hops out of the water. His mouth is the shape of a large "O," and his entire body shakes like a leaf while the rest of his teammates laugh at him.

Yeah, the ice plunge is a definite fan favorite, considering how many girls are circling it. Each of them takes a turn offering tickets to the players. Maverick's been in the water at least a dozen times and lost his shirt thirty minutes ago, letting the sun warm his tan skin as he hangs out next to the timer. Part of me still itches to take a closer look at his tattoos. I almost did when he was drunk off his ass. But it's strange. Seeing how different he is now. The tattoos are a reminder of exactly that. He isn't the same boy, and I can't help but miss him.

Maverick chats with Reeves when another girl offers him a ticket. "Do it for me, Mav," she begs. "Please?"

Gag.

I wish they'd scoot the ice plunge a little farther away so I wouldn't have to witness all the girls drooling over my childhood friends, but it seems I'm not so lucky. At least Archer isn't here, and I don't have to witness them drooling over my boyfriend too. I roll my eyes and turn back to the line of customers purchasing tickets.

A loud squeal distracts me as Maverick bends down and splashes the girl with a handful of water. I scoff, pulling his attention.

"There a problem?" he calls across the grassy ten-foot space separating us.

"No problem." I hand an old couple their change as Maverick passes the blonde off to Reeves and strides toward me.

When he reaches me, he asks, "You sure?"

I cross my arms, giving him my full attention. "Okay, but for real. Have *any* of the girls gotten in, or are they all playing the damsel in distress card?"

"Damsel in distress," he confirms, mirroring my stance and giving me front-row seats to the gun show.

Hello, muscles.

"Why do you ask?" he prods.

My attention slices from his biceps up to his face. "I don't know. No reason, I guess."

"You sure?"

"Mav," the girl whines from behind him. "Come win a churro for me!"

"I find it a little pathetic, is all," I rush out, attempting to drown out her nasally voice. "It's not like it's difficult to get any of you guys in your underwear or anything, so why pay for it with a ticket? Why not corner you guys at SeaBird?"

His mouth lifts. "You hate the ice bath."

"I don't hate it."

"Uh, yeah, you do. You loathe it and always lie to your coaches and physical therapists whenever they ask you—"

"Shush." I cover his mouth and look over my shoulder like any of my previous coaches might pop out at any second and yell at me for avoiding the ice bath like it's the Plague.

Maverick smiles against the palm of my hand as he grabs my wrist and slowly pries me away from him. "Do you wanna try it?"

"What? Cornering you?"

He steps closer. "I meant the plunge."

"Oh." I glance at the tub of water as Griffin and Everett each dump a fresh bag of ice into it. "I'm good."

He lifts a brow. "If you were good, you wouldn't have been rolling your eyes."

"Do you want me to do it?" I counter.

"I want you to do whatever you want, Opie."

"Fine, I'll do it," I snap. "If it'll get you off my back, then...fine."

The same stupid, amused smirk teases his lips until he hides it behind his hand. "Did you bring a swimsuit?"

I look down at my tank top and jean shorts and shake my head. "Nope."

"Here. You can use my shirt." He removes it from the waistband of his shorts and offers it to me.

Grudgingly, I take it. "What now?"

He lifts his finger in a *give me two seconds* motion and yells, "Yo, Reeves!"

Reeves jogs toward us. "Yeah?"

"Can you man the ticket booth for a minute? Opie wants to try the plunge."

"My name isn't Opie," I remind him.

He ignores me and points toward the bathroom. "Go change. When you get back, we'll see if you survive three seconds."

"And if I make it to ten?" I ask.

With another stupid smirk, Mav starts walking backward toward his teammates and offers, "I'll buy you two churros."

Before I can talk myself out of it, I march to the bathroom and slip out of my tank top and bra, sliding his shirt over my head. It smells like him. Like warmth and summer and cologne despite the dampness clinging to the soft material from one of his plunges. Resisting the urge to drag it to my nose and breathe in deep, I slip my shorts off and add them to my small pile of clothes, choosing to keep my underwear on for the plunge while deciding I'll go commando afterward because no one likes wet underwear.

No, thank you.

To be fair, going commando in jean shorts doesn't exactly sound like a walk in the park either, but letting Maverick think I'm a wuss isn't on my Bingo card today, so I'm going to pull on my big girl panties by...*not* wearing panties at all after the plunge.

Yeah, it makes perfect sense.

The sun heats my cheeks as I head outside again. Whistles ensue when the team sees me. I offer Maverick my clothes and pull my hair into a ponytail. When I do, the warm sun kisses my upper thighs, and Maverick's eyes heat, taking in my exposed skin. He steps in front of me, blocking his teammates' view of my body.

Once I finish, I mutter, "Thanks," and he faces me again.

"You ready?"

"For two churros *and* a cotton candy?"

"Someone's greedy," he notes.

"Confident," I clarify. "And, yup."

His mouth twitches as he bows at the waist and motions to the icy bath. "Ladies first."

Everett and Griffin reset the timer as I approach the tub. I dip my fingers into the frigid water, yanking them out just as fast.

"Cold?" Maverick questions with a quirked brow.

It's freezing. Like, freeze your tits off freezing with a side of frostbite, but I'm not about to tell him that. Thanks to playing hockey, I've been around my fair share of ice baths,

171

and maybe it's because Maverick's right, and I've found a way to avoid them *way* more than I probably should, but they never get easier.

Why, Ophelia? Why did you have to open your big, fat mouth?

"You can always back down, ya know," Mav suggests, moving closer to me. "Ask one of us to take the plunge for you if you wanna pull the damsel in distress card."

I glare back at him. "I think I can handle it."

"Oh?"

"Mm-hmm," I hum, but even *I* can hear the indecision in my voice.

"Wait, wait, I gotta film this," Griffin announces. He grabs his phone from the folding table with the giant timer and starts recording me.

With my head held high, I lift my leg over the edge, dip my toe into the water and yank it back, planting my foot on solid ground. It isn't even a choice at this point. My body's own self-preservation instincts are kicking in, making it impossible to sit in the water even if I wanted to. And I do want to. If only to prove a point. To prove I'm not a big fat baby like the girls Maverick has been flirting with all afternoon.

Man, you're pathetic, a tiny voice whispers, but I shove it aside, approaching the stupid tub again.

"C'mon, Lia. Get in," Griffin prods.

I glare back at him, and he laughs, keeping his phone lens pointed at me.

Sensing my frustration, Maverick steps between me and the stupid phone, dropping his voice so only I can hear him. "All right, Opie, I know you. And I know you wanna get out of this."

"I don't—"

"I also know you won't back down," he adds, "so I have a suggestion."

I pull my attention from the wet, matted grass beneath my feet to a pair of stormy blue eyes. "What type of suggestion?" I murmur.

"I get in with you. I'll go first, and you can sit between my legs."

"What does that prove?" I ask.

"It proves you're a badass with an overprotective boyfriend who said I need to get in the water with you."

My brows tug. "But Archer didn't—"

"Just take the offer, Opie."

Shaking my arms out as if preparing for battle, I answer, "Okay, fine."

"All right, guys, Archer didn't want me to make this a thing, but he insisted I keep an eye on Opie here, which includes helping her with the ice plunge. So if you wanna give anyone shit, give it to him." Maverick's steps are strong and sure as he climbs into the water without even flinching and motions for me to join him. If I wait too long, I'm pretty sure his toes will freeze off, so I force my legs to move and step into the tub with him. Ice shoots up my spine, pulling a gasp from me when Maverick sits down and tugs me with him.

My lungs freeze, refusing to work as his hands wrap around me, pressing my back to his front.

"Breathe," he orders against the shell of my ear.

I let out a tiny whimper, and he holds me tighter. "Breathe with me, Goose."

His chest expands on a breath, and I force mine to follow suit, breathing in oxygen as the timer counts down beside us.

"Give us another five," Mav orders.

Goosebumps race along my skin, and I close my eyes, focusing on the man behind me. His steady breathing. His strong arms. His thighs cradling me.

Breathe.

I force my muscles to relax further into his hold, stealing what little warmth I can from his chest and legs as the rest of the world slowly disappears, leaving me alone with Maverick Buchanan. Without the jabs. Without the baggage. Only me and him. And I hate how good it feels.

I don't know how much time passes. Honestly, it's a blur of molasses-coated quicksand, but soon, Griffin's sharp voice cuts through my focus as he announces, "That's it. You beat today's record!"

People whoop around us, and applause fires from all angles, but I don't hear any of it. All I hear is the slight rasp of Maverick's voice as he whispers in my ear. "It's over, Lia."

It's over.

I grasp the edge of the tub, a numbness washing over me. Both physically and emotionally. Every inch of my torso and legs feels like they're being pricked with tiny needles as I stand up. A low whistle sounds, and I look down, realizing Maverick's shirt has ridden up during the plunge and is plastered to my stomach, leaving my underwear and legs on full display. Warm hands grip the hem, tugging it away from my body and pulling it lower to keep my ass from hanging out. This time, I most definitely *am* wearing a thong. I look down to find the hands' culprit. Yup, my practically naked butt is inches from Maverick's face as he covers it with my—well, technically his—soaked shirt.

"Thanks," I whisper weakly.

Icy rivulets drip down my thighs, and I fold my arms, attempting to hold whatever warmth my body can produce close to me while keeping my freaking nipples from saluting every Tom, Dick, and Harry in the vicinity. I need to snap out of it. What it felt like to be in his arms again. To not have him acting like an ass or pushing me away. But it's hard. Being given a glimpse of the guy I fell for. The guy who would've never broken my heart over a stupid phone call... until he did.

Maverick climbs out from behind me, and I follow suit, exiting the tub. His discarded towel is on a chair, and he picks it up, wrapping it around me.

"You did good." He runs his hands up and down my arms in an attempt to warm me, but it's useless.

My teeth chatter as my head bobs up and down. "Thanks."

"Ophelia!" a voice yells.

My head snaps toward where it's coming from, and I find Jaxon jogging toward me. "Bad news. Archer might kill me, but I need you to man the kissing booth."

"But I thought—"

"I know," he interrupts. "It's Emily's turn, but she's fifteen minutes late for her shift, and I'm not sure how much more Morgan can handle. Can you cover for her?"

Maverick's grip tightens on my biceps, but I ignore him, holding Jaxon's gaze. "Sure thing. I'll be right there. I need to change really quick."

His gaze flicks over my half-naked body, and he nods. "Probably a good idea. Thanks." He turns to the main booth where Reeves is sitting. "You still good manning the ticket booth?"

Reeves gives him a thumbs up. "Sure thing, Jax."

"Thanks, man."

Slipping out of Maverick's grasp, I ignore his death glare branding my back, grab my folded clothes off the table and race back to the bathroom, changing as quickly as I can.

Apparently, I *will* be working the kissing booth.

Today keeps getting better and better.

23

OPHELIA

My teeth are still chattering when I reach the kissing booth to support the rest of my team. There's a short line. They bumped the age requirement up to eighteen, but otherwise, there weren't any stipulations other than the kiss has to be close-mouthed and all that jazz. Regardless, I don't miss my teammate's relieved expression when I approach her.

"Thank goodness." Morgan stands from her barstool and steps away. "The floor's all yours."

"Gee, thanks," I quip, taking the empty seat and gripping the edge of it with my hands. I've never volunteered for a kissing booth. Honestly, I didn't even know they were still a thing, but I shouldn't be surprised. Lockwood Heights is all about tradition, and apparently, a kissing booth makes the cut.

Shocker.

The first guy in line looks older than my grandpa as he hands Grace Temple a single red ticket. She's the designated collector for our booth and the Lady Hawks' left wing. After she takes it, the old guy faces me again and motions to his cheek. "Gotta support the Lady Hawks, am I right?"

"Of course." With a light laugh, I lean forward, giving him a quick peck on his weathered cheek. It's a little prickly and smells like aftershave. My smile widens.

Like seriously, how cute is he?

"Thank you, my dear." The man lifts my hand, kisses the back of it and leaves the stage, only to be replaced by another stranger who hands Grace a red ticket.

One by one, I start clearing out the line but eventually realize how much longer it is than when I first took over. And it isn't full of eighty-year-olds, either. Nope. These guys are starting to look like they might go to LAU with me this year. My nerves kick up a notch, and I twist my hands in my lap. A blonde with short-cropped hair offers his ticket to Grace and steps toward me. He's the freshman from Game Night. The one who cuffed me to Maverick. He grins at me, but a large, toned body cuts in front of him.

"What the fuck?" the blonde starts. Reeves faces him fully, and the guy cowers. "Oh, shit. Hey, Reeves." He steps back, giving Reeves his position at the front of the line. "Uh, yeah, you go first."

"Thanks, man." Reeves slaps his shoulder, turns, and gives me his full attention. "Hey, Lia."

"Aren't you supposed to be manning the ticket booth?" I question.

"Asked Cameron to cover for me."

"And he said yes?"

With a smirk, he admits, "I may have bribed him." Reeves hands his red ticket to Grace, and when their fingers brush, she practically swoons. I swear, Reeves wields *way* more charisma than any college guy should have at their disposal. So much so I'm pretty sure it'll bite him in the ass one day.

Once his payment is accepted, he swaggers closer to me, and I ask, "And why did you bribe Cameron?"

"I gotta shake things up a bit." He wedges himself between my knees. "Let's see if this gets under his skin."

"Archer's?" I ask.

His mouth lifts. "Sure."

Caught between confusion and amusement, I laugh lightly but let it go. My tongue darts out and moistens my bottom lip as I lean forward cautiously, preparing to kiss Reeves' cheek when I'm wrenched from the stool like I weigh nothing at all.

"Aaaand, you're done," a familiar voice growls.

Stumbling over my own feet, I brace myself for impact, but a pair of hands catches me, dragging me off the stage and around the edge of it until we're blanketed in privacy.

Glaring up at the culprit, I yank my arm free and seethe, "What the hell, Mav?"

"You said you weren't going to do the kissing booth."

"You heard Jaxon," I remind him. "Emily didn't show up for her shift and the team—"

"Fuck the team," he growls.

My back hits a steel post as I retreat a step. Crowding me against it, he glares down at me.

"Dude. What's your problem?"

"You have a boyfriend," he reminds me.

"Archer and I talked about this possibility before he left. This is for the Lady Hawks. He knows how much they mean to me and doesn't care—"

"I don't give a shit whether or not he cares." Maverick bends closer until we're nose to nose, our mouths a few mere inches apart. Shit, I can practically taste him. And the animosity in his eyes? It's razor-sharp, threatening to shred me to ribbons if I hold it for another second, but still, I do. "Seeing you out there?" He shakes his head. "I tried to stay away. I tried to let you handle your own shit. But I can't…I can't do it, Ophelia. Go home. Be done with this bullshit."

"Why do you care?" I ask as my attention slices from one molten iris to the other.

"Because it's wrong!" he spits. "If you were mine, there isn't a chance in hell I'd let you be up there kissing everyone on campus."

"Then I guess it's a good thing I'm dating your brother, isn't it?"

He scoffs. "Since, apparently, we're interchangeable to you, right?"

"I never said—"

"You didn't need to. I break up with you, and you wind up —" His mouth snaps closed, and he clenches his fists. "That's not the point."

"What *is* the point?" I demand.

"You really want a guy who doesn't mind you being passed around out there?" He points toward the stage, his muscles bunched and ready for battle.

"I'm not being passed—"

"You said so yourself." He backs away from me and starts pacing the small area like he's too amped up to stand still or hold a civilized conversation. "Kissing booths are barbaric and juvenile."

"I know what I said."

"Then why are you letting them touch you?" He stops pacing behind the stage and strides closer while my back stays glued to the metal post. The same fire he's been wielding burns along the top of my head like he's daring me to look up at him. To see his anger and disgust at what I'd been doing.

My lips fuse together, and I lift my chin, holding his stare, refusing to cower. But my words? My rebuttal? They're gone. I don't know what to say or how to feel. He's right. It's not like I enjoy kissing random strangers, let alone individuals I might share a class with in a few weeks. But even so, it isn't Maverick's job to drag me around like a Neanderthal. He has no right to tell me what I can or can't do. No, he lost that right the moment he broke up with me.

"You're being ridiculous," I finally say.

"You think I don't know that?" He grabs the side of his face and squeezes, proving how close he is to snapping. He fists his hands at his sides. "Look. You win, all right? Whatever game we're playing, you win."

"I'm not playing a game with you, Maverick." I hate how hurt he looks. How freaking unhinged, all because of a stupid kissing booth. And I hate how it makes me feel like he still cares about me. Like he still wants me. I lick my lips, trying to soften the blow. To soften the divot between his brows and the tension in his jaw. "If it helps at all, the kisses don't mean anything."

"So, if it was me?" He steps even closer, causing his chest to brush against mine. "If it doesn't mean anything, would you kiss me? Let me *pay* for it?"

I shake my head. "Don't make it sound dirty."

"It *is* dirty! It's—"

"Stop acting like an ass," I seethe, rising onto my tiptoes in hopes of it making me feel less small. Less inconsequential.

His lips gnash together, and he takes a deep breath. "I can't watch you out there."

"I don't know what you want me to say. Archer's—"

"Archer's cool with it." He grabs my chin and lifts it, demanding my full attention. "Good for him, all right? He's always been a better man than me, but I can't take it, so can you please just...*stop?*"

The pleading in his gaze almost does me in, but I stand my ground anyway.

"I don't owe you anything, Maverick," I whisper.

"You think I don't know that too? Fuck, Opie. Trust me, I know. But if I was your boyfriend—"

"Yeah?" My heels hit the ground, and defeat settles on my shoulders as I try to pull away from his touch, but he doesn't let me go. "Well, you're not."

"You're right." He drops my chin from his grasp like I've burned him. "My mistake."

Turning, he storms away.

24

OPHELIA

"Hey," I brush my lips against Archer's cheek as the music blares around us. He's finally home from his trip, and even though we texted the past few days since the carnival, I'm anxious to see him. To talk to him. To quiet the stupid voice in my head sounding a hell of a lot like Maverick ever since our conversation behind the kissing booth. I debated whether to text Archer about it but decided I wanted to see his reaction firsthand, but I'm seriously second-guessing myself.

Reeves thought it would be a great idea to throw another Game Night, and their place is packed with gyrating bodies, the alcohol flowing like a damn waterfall.

I almost didn't come. I probably shouldn't have since I've been testy all day, but the idea of seeing Archer, of having his presence quiet the growing doubt inside me, spurred me on. But it's too early to tell whether or not I'll regret it later.

"Hey." Archer's hands find my hips, and he pulls me against him. "Missed you."

The words leave a splinter in my sternum, but I shake off the strange response. "Missed you too."

"How was the carnival?"

"It was fine. I did the ice plunge," I offer.

"I saw." He smiles. "Griffin sent me the video."

"He did, did he?"

"Yeah." Archer kisses my nose. "I'm surprised you did it. You hate ice baths."

"I may have felt obligated to prove I'm not some damsel in distress."

"Ah, so you were pressured into it." He nods. "Next time, you'll have to do it without Maverick's help."

"Yeah, I will," I agree, swaying my hips to the ear-splitting beat surrounding us. "I did the kissing booth too."

"Oh?"

"Yeah. I was going to text you about it, but I figured I'd wait until you came home to tell you."

"No worries. Did you have fun?"

"Um, I guess?" Avoiding his gaze, I fiddle with the collar of his shirt while my nerves buzz like bumble bees beneath my skin. "Is it...a problem for you? Me doing the kissing booth?"

His expression pulls tight, and he drops his hands from my sides. "Should it be?"

"I mean, no," I say. "It's not like I made out with anyone, but I told you I most likely wouldn't actually man the kissing booth, so I thought you should know."

"Okay?" He chuckles, but it sounds forced. "Now I know."

"Cool. And you're...good with it?" I prod.

"I said I would be, right?" He stares over my shoulder, distracted by the ruckus around us.

"Well, yeah, but hypothetically versus reality are two different things." I stand on my tiptoes, putting myself in his line of sight while hoping to gain his full attention.

Catching on, he sighs and stares down at me. "Do you want me to be mad?"

I hesitate. "It's just…if I saw you kissing random girls, I don't think I'd like it very much."

"Yeah, but you weren't kissing random guys for no reason, and I knew it was a possibility beforehand. So, it's different. Right?"

"Yeah, it is, but…" My shoulders hunch. "I don't know… maybe I'm acting crazy."

The music continues blaring around us, and chairs scrape against the hardwood floor as everyone gets ready for musical chairs in the center of the family room. Meanwhile, Archer and I stand awkwardly in the hall, enduring our own staredown. He barely casts a glance as his friends greet him and move past us. He's too busy giving me a look and making me feel ashamed and stupid but kind of right too.

"Hey, man. Good to see you," Everett says as he lugs a handful of folding chairs from the basement.

"You too." Archer nods at Everett. Turning back to me, he keeps his voice low. "Why do I feel like I'm in the dog house for *not* being mad at you while I was gone, despite the fact we'd already discussed it all?"

He has every right to be confused. Honestly, it doesn't even make sense in my own brain, so how can I expect him to understand why I feel the way I feel when I'm as lost as he is? But I can't stop thinking about it. What Maverick said. The passion in his eyes. The barely restrained anger. The desire and desperation. It made me feel…wanted. Needed. Special. And Archer *not* caring makes me feel…replaceable almost.

"Lia," Archer prods.

"I dunno." I shrug. "I…I feel like you should at least somewhat care, ya know?"

"I do care."

"I know you do," I rush out. "I just…" I clench my hands at

my sides, attempting to stop the word vomit from spewing from my mouth. I shouldn't be talking about this. It's stupid. But Maverick got in my head at the fundraiser, and now I'm genuinely questioning things. I'm questioning everything when I have no right to. "Griffin sent you the video of me with Maverick, right? With his arms wrapped around me? Me in nothing but my thong and his T-shirt? Did you care about that?"

His eyes say it all. He saw it. The video. And he isn't pissed at me. He isn't pissed at Mav. No, his emotions are locked up tight right now. Like I'm talking to a statue instead of my own freaking boyfriend. And if he doesn't feel anger, what does he feel?

"It didn't bother you?" I push.

He takes a step toward me, but I back away.

"Lia, he's my brother."

"And I'm your girlfriend," I argue.

"What's going on with you?" Like a rubberband, his patience snaps and stings all at once. "Look, obviously, you're feeling heated, and I just got home from my trip. Let's take a break—"

"A break?" I scoff, basking in my frustration. And it isn't even directed at Archer. It's directed at me. Because I should feel sad or anxious to fix this. To talk to Archer. To apologize for acting like a crazy person, and I *am* acting like a crazy person. Instead, all I feel is confirmation. That I'm not even worth the energy of a heated conversation. He'd rather brush it aside than get his hands messy trying to figure out why I'm hurting and why I need to know if he cares about me. Even when it isn't logical. Even when it doesn't make sense. "Actually, I think it's a great idea. A break is exactly what I need." With a shake of my head, I put more distance between us. "I'm going to grab a drink."

"Ophelia," Archer calls, but I weave between a few people,

barely dodging one of the chairs set up in a large circle while blindly waving behind me as I find the kitchen.

An array of drinks is spread out on the granite island like the last Game Night. The drinks range from two-liter sodas to beer to hard liquor. Reaching for the gin, I pour a shot and swallow it back. My expression pinches from the burn, but I pour a second shot, then a third, and do the same thing. Warmth spreads through my chest as I splash some more clear liquor into a cup and add Sprite, giving it a swirl with my wrist. Satisfied, I drink it while moseying into the family room. A bunch of faceless people hang out in the main area with Archer's roommates.

Griff stands on the coffee table with the same stupid gold medallion wrapped around his neck Reeves wore during The Floor is Lava. Griff must've won last time. Now, he's explaining the rules for Musical Chairs, surrounded by already-wasted peers. Or at least, I think it's what he's doing. I'm not exactly paying attention. I'm too distracted by the lack of twins in the vicinity. Archer probably went to his room to cool down, but Maverick? I would expect him to be in the center of the room, helping coordinate tonight's game or, at the least, participating. But he's gone. I shouldn't care he isn't here—*and I don't*—but a small part of me? Well, it hates how I noticed. How I was reminded of exactly how different Archer and Maverick are. And how stupid I am for comparing them in the first place. It's what they hate most. Being compared to each other or feeling interchangeable with one another. And here I am, weighing their differences and how easy it would be to cherry-pick my favorite characteristics between the two of them.

But what's worse? It's the knowledge Maverick cared I was kissing some random guy at the kissing booth. He isn't even mine anymore and he *still* cared. And it isn't because he doesn't trust me or thinks I'd cheat on me. It's because the idea of anyone else's lips other than his being on mine is more than he can stomach. But if that's the case, why'd he throw me away?

And the way Maverick wrenched me away from the kissing booth? It should bother me. How he's bossy and forceful. It should repulse me. But I can't help feeling jealous. Because after being on the other side of the coin, I feel expendable. Meaningless. Inconsequential. Which is insane, I know, but I can't help it.

Why doesn't Archer care? Or if he does, why isn't he telling me?

Is it normal not to care?

Would I care if Archer was asked to kiss random girls under the guise of fundraising?

A ball of lead falls in my gut. Right now? I don't even know.

They must've started the game because the music keeps turning on and cutting off every minute or two. It's kind of jarring but entertaining too. Watching the chaos unfold. Sliding onto my ass at the edge of the room, I nurse the rest of my drink, letting the warmth from the alcohol spread over my limbs. There are so many people here. So. Many. People. A gorgeous woman with dark skin and black braids falls into Everett's lap as the music cuts off. They both laugh when Griffin calls her out, and she makes her way to the center of the room with the rest of the losers. She doesn't look too disappointed. No, she's now flirting with Cameron and having a ball. Reeves scoots in behind her as the music comes back with a vengeance. Meanwhile, Griffin continues walking in circles around the room, playing referee. I'm not sure how much time has passed, but he's checked on me a thousand times. Okay, maybe not a thousand. Honestly, I have no idea how long I've been sitting on my ass, but it looks like he's about to add another tally to the checklist when he rounds the corner and squats beside me.

"Hey, pretty girl," Griffin murmurs as the rest of the people either walk in a circle waiting for the music to cut off so they can snatch an open seat, or they're grinding against each other in the center of the room.

I give Griffin a dopey smile. "Hello again."

"You sure you don't want to play?"

"And potentially be yelled at for breaking the rules?" I chuckle into my almost empty cup, swallow the last drop, and set it on the ground by my hip. "I think I'm okay. Thanks, though. Now help me up." I lift my hand into the air, and he takes it, pulling me to my feet. Vertigo nearly knocks me on my ass again, and I grab hold of his arms, closing my eyes to stop the world from spinning.

"You feeling okay?" he asks.

Nope.

"Yup," I answer. "I'm gonna dance." I shake out of his grasp and head to the dance floor. Griff says something else —a warning, maybe?—but I don't pay attention. With my hands in the air, I sway my hips, letting the heavy rhythm wash over me. It's faster than the last one. More upbeat. I like it. Losing myself in the music, I block the rest of the world out and simply...feel. My eyelids are heavy. Then again, so are my arms. So is every inch of me. But I'm too tired to stop. Too tired to go home and sleep it off, knowing I'll be right back to square one in the morning. Or maybe I won't. Maybe I'll still be pissed. But is that any better? Any less depressing? The music continues cutting in and out every few minutes, and the makeshift dance floor in the center of the room is becoming more and more crowded. But I kind of like this too. The warm bodies pressed around me. The way it makes me feel invisible, but in a good way this time. Like I can do whatever I want. Be who I want to be. Without worrying about anything else in the world.

"Come on, Lia," a low voice mutters as warm hands find my waist and pull me into a heated body. Seriously, I could wrap myself up in it. The warmth.

Keeping my eyes closed, I twist in Archer's grasp but continue swaying my hips as I relish the song. It's slow and sexy.

"You jealous yet?" I slur.

"You have no fucking clue," he grumbles. "But you shouldn't be dancing like this."

"I'm mad at you."

"Me?"

"Mm-hmm," I hum, resting my head against his chest. "You're kind of an ass, Archer. You make me feel like you don't care."

His muscles tense beneath me as I nuzzle closer, desperate for his touch. His comfort. He smells different than usual. Maybe he showered? I don't know, but he kind of smells like—

Maverick pulls away from me, and the room spins, making my legs feel like a baby deer's. I almost fall on my butt, his hands finding my waist a second time.

"Come on," he grunts. "I'm taking you home."

Home.

It sounds pretty good right now.

My bed.

My pillow.

My blankets.

"Mmm," I hum, nuzzling against Maverick's chest again as he wraps his arms around me and guides me outside.

The air is cooler out here. Still warm but not blistering. I like it. It's almost…predictable. Unlike the man beside me. Why is Maverick being so nice after being a dick at the carnival? I can still hear his words after I told him he's not my boyfriend.

My mistake.

A deep ache flares against my ribs at the memory, but it's duller now. Probably because of the alcohol, but what do I know? And why did he call me Lia? He never calls me Lia. Not unless he feels guilty for something, or he's trying to get me to do something he wants.

I like it when he calls me Lia. I like it when he calls me Opie too. I shouldn't. I hate the name. But when it comes from him? Well, it hits differently. Like a shot of espresso or something. I like it almost as much as when he calls me Goose. Like I'm his other half, his ride or die when he's always been mine.

But that was before. Before he broke my heart. Before I broke his by dating his twin brother.

Why is he helping me? And why didn't he correct me inside when I called him Archer? They hate when people can't tell them apart.

A prickle hits the base of my skull, and I peek up at Maverick again, keeping myself tucked against him. They look so alike. I mean, most identical twins do, but Maverick and Archer? They're almost impossible to tell apart. Even people who have known them for years struggle sometimes. But me? I'd recognize the differences anywhere. And it isn't only their smells. It's the tightness in Maverick's jaw. The softness in Archer's eyes. The sharp lilt of Maverick's tongue. The understanding nods from Archer. They're opposites. But they still fit. Hell, they're best friends. Two peas in a pod. Two sides of the same coin. The yin to his yang. The Starsky to his Hutch.

And here he is, helping his brother's girlfriend to bed when he should be sleeping with a random girl like the rest of his friends, especially after he acted like an asshole at the carnival.

My eyes slide to his, the question shining up at him in my curious gaze as his hand finds my back, and he guides me to my front door.

Why are you here?

This is a dangerous game. One I shouldn't be playing, especially when I'm drunk. But if he didn't correct me when I called him Archer inside, would he correct me now?

"I'm sorry I yelled at you, Archer," I tell him.

His eyes flash with...something, but it's too quick for me to analyze. Disgust? Shame? Hurt? Regret?

He really thinks I don't know?

"It's fine," he mutters. "Goodnight, Lia."

"Help me into bed," I murmur. "I'm not sure I can make it to my room on my own."

The same tightness in his jaw greets me, but he nods and follows me inside. The front door closes with a quiet click behind us. It's louder than a fog horn in the otherwise silent house. Maverick's never been inside my place. Hell, Archer's barely been here thanks to his busy schedule, but still. I wait to see where Maverick guides me, curious if he'll give up the ruse and why he's playing it in the first place. Turning in his arms, I slide my hands along his chest and over his shoulders, memorizing the feel of him in my palms.

So similar. So different.

"I should go," he rasps.

"Will you kiss me, Archer?" I whisper.

The name feels wrong on so many levels. But I'm curious. Curious what he'll do. What he'll say. How far he'll take this, and if he really believes I can't tell the difference between him and his brother. If he thinks they really are so interchangeable.

The thought leaves a rancid taste in my mouth, but I force it back.

"Ophelia," he murmurs. His hands tighten around my waist, and his eyes look nothing less than tortured.

Using his massive frame for balance, I rise onto my tiptoes, keeping my movements slow and controlled—or at least as slow and controlled as I can, considering the alcohol swirling through my veins. I brush my lips against the underside of his chin. The slight scruff of his jaw tickles my lips, and I smile against him. I've missed this. Missed him.

This is a *very* dangerous game. But my thoughts are fuzzy, and so is my willpower. Especially when he's looking at me like this. Like he wants me. *Really* wants me. The same way I've always wanted him. The same way I thought he wanted me until something spooked him. Until something ripped him away from me. Archer never looks at me like this. Like he'd kill to have a taste. The passion? The torture? The agony of being away from me? It's never been there with Archer. And I'm not sure if he even knows it, but it's true. Maverick's the opposite, and he's proving it right now with a single look making me press my thighs together.

They say alcohol inhibits your ability to consider consequences. I don't know who *they* are, but they're not wrong. Because I want to see how this plays out. I need to see if he'll back down or continue pretending to be his brother. I have to know if he thinks so little of me to really believe I can't tell the difference between them.

"You taste different," I note, dragging my lips against his jaw and moving higher to nibble on the edge of his lip.

"You haven't tasted me yet," he rasps. His muscles are like stone beneath my fingertips. "Not recently."

Not a lie. But it's not a confession, either.

Are we still playing, Mav?

My fingers find the edge of his shirt as I whisper, "And why is that?"

I nibble the edge of his jaw one more time, pull away slightly, and peek up at him again, daring him to lie to me. To give in. To keep pretending.

Are. We. Still. Playing?

His eyes darken another shade. The lack of light in the entryway makes them almost black and reminds me of a wild animal, one I'm currently toying with. His fingers tighten on my hips, causing little indents in my flesh. A growled "Fuck it" echoes past his lips, and his palms are on my cheeks in an instant, his mouth devouring me whole. He's so much more forceful. More commanding than his brother. The way he dominates me with his kiss, shoving his tongue between my lips as he angles my head in the exact position he wants it. Heat pools between my legs, and I whimper as his teeth dig into my bottom lip.

I never thought I'd have this again. Never thought he'd give it to me. His kiss. His touch. His time. And it doesn't matter how desperate it makes me. To steal it. To possess it under these circumstances. I want this passion. I want it all.

Arching my back, I press myself against him and soak up the feel of his hard muscles against my curves, all too aware of how quickly it could be stolen from me. He picks me up and carries me to the nearest wall. My back hits the hard surface with a thump, and I gasp, tilting my head to one side as he trails kisses along my neck.

It's so good.

I've missed it.

This.

Him.

"Fuck, Mav—"

He freezes, turning into steel as soon as the words slip past my lips.

Mav.

Shit.

Slowly, I slide down his frozen frame while the alcohol in my veins evaporates instantly. The same darkness fills his eyes as he glares down at me while regret and shame flood every inch of my body, leaving me naked and exposed and guilty and...confused. So fucking confused it's not even funny. Once my feet are on the ground, a disgusted Maverick shakes his head, turns around, and leaves.

What. The. Fuck?

25

MAVERICK

"Hey," Archer greets me as he walks into the kitchen.

My head rests in my hands as I chew the tepid oatmeal at the kitchen table. I shouldn't have come home and gotten shit-faced, but I didn't know what else to do. The guilt was killing me. And now my head is killing me.

Karma?

Hardly, but I guess it's a start.

Slowly, I drop my hands to the table and look up at my brother. His hair is still wet from the shower, but the kitchen was clean when I woke up, so I have a feeling he's been awake for a while. I shouldn't be surprised. He cleans when he's stressed, like my dad does. The question is, is he stressed because Ophelia told him we kissed last night or is something else bothering him?

"Hey," I reply. I shove another bite of oats into my mouth and chew slowly as he pours himself a cup of coffee from the community pot under the microwave.

"Heard you took Lia home last night."

My heart throbs, and I choke on my oatmeal, coughing

into my fist. He knows I took Lia home? Who else saw us leave together? At the time, I didn't care. I wasn't hiding anything. I was only trying to help. Then she called me Archer and asked me to kiss her, and—

He slaps his hand against my back in an attempt to dislodge the oatmeal from my throat, his coffee cup resting on the counter behind him. "You okay, man?"

With a nod, I reach for my water and swallow the mush. "Yeah. Sorry."

"No worries." He grabs his coffee again and sits next to me. "I actually wanted to thank you."

I pick my spoon up and draw circles in the oatmeal paste, trying not to puke as I glance at him. "For what?"

"For keeping an eye on Ophelia last night. We got into a fight, and—"

"Don't worry about it." I spoon another bite of mush into my mouth and chew mechanically, careful not to choke this time. I've never lied to my brother. Not about anything.

Anything except *her*.

But, fuck. It's getting harder and harder to pretend around him. To appear unaffected. To act like I'm not in love with his girlfriend or pretend she wasn't mine first.

"I told her I wanted to take a break," Archer replies. "I meant from the conversation, not our relationship, but I think she took it the wrong way." He rests his elbows on the table and cups the mug with both hands, staring blankly at the dark liquid. "She was pissed I wasn't acting jealous about the kissing booth."

"What?"

His focus snaps to me. "Yeah."

So it *did* bother her. Our conversation behind the stage. Is it why she pretended I was Archer last night? Was it some kind of test to see if I still wanted her? No, she wouldn't do that. She might've been shit-faced, but she isn't a bitch.

So why did she kiss me?

And why the fuck did I play along?

"Should I act jealous?" Archer prods.

Dropping my spoon into the bowl, I wipe my sweaty palms against my dark sweats. "I'm not the guy you should talk to about this."

"You're my brother," he argues as if he has to remind me.

Trust me, I know.

"Fine." I lean back in the chair and sigh. "Why don't you get jealous?"

"Who says I don't get jealous?"

My brows pull. "I thought—"

"I said I wasn't *acting* jealous. I never said I wasn't jealous at all," he clarifies. "You know Ophelia. You know how much she means to me. The girl's fucking perfect."

My eyes fall to my half-eaten bowl of food, and he chuckles.

"Okay, perfect for *me*," he clarifies, completely misreading my discomfort. "She was my best friend before we started dating, and…I don't know. I guess I'm trying to give her space and shit, but sometimes it feels…*off*."

"Why?" I ask.

"It's complicated," he mutters. "Remember how I took her to prom a few months back?"

I nod, barely restraining my snarl as I scoop another heaping spoonful of oatmeal. Shoving it into my mouth, I mutter, "How could I forget?"

"Yeah, but here's the thing. She wasn't ditched by some random dick. Apparently, she'd been hooking up with the guy for a while, and he bailed on her for no reason."

I swallow the acid coating my throat but stay quiet.

"It messed with her," Archer continues. "Ever since, I feel like she's holding back. I don't blame her. It's gotta be hard to hand over your heart again after the first guy you ever dated tore it to shreds, ya know?"

I wipe my mouth and nod again.

"Exactly," he agrees. "So I've been trying to give her the space and time she needs to trust me and give me a real chance."

"Who says she isn't giving you a real chance?" I ask.

"Just…stuff," he deflects. "But I don't want to scare her away by being all possessive and shit."

"So you're hiding that you *are* possessive and shit?"

"I've cared about her for so long, of course, I feel possessive of her. But, do you really think I'm gonna waste my chance by scaring her away just because she might not be over the guy she was with before me?"

The pounding in my chest skips like a broken record, and I throttle my spoon to keep from rubbing at the ache. "Who says she isn't over him?"

"No one." His brows dip. "I guess I just feel it. Sometimes she's fine, and other times? She goes all quiet and…I dunno." He reaches for his cup again but hesitates before taking a sip. "Like she's lost in her own head or…like she's still thinking about him." He shakes his head and takes a long swallow of caffeine, licking his lips. "Like I said, her mystery man messed her up. Fuck, she can't even say his name. Won't even tell me who he is." He pauses. "But it doesn't really matter because I'm not gonna push her on it, and I'm okay with being patient. The problem is I don't know how to show her I care without making her feel like I'm smothering her. I dunno. Being in a relationship with Lia, it's…it's harder than I thought it would be."

I stay quiet, unsure what to say as I rub my tongue along my teeth.

The man looks lost. Like he's overthinking and overanalyzing in a way only my brother can. There isn't an easy answer. Not for Lia. Not for Archer. And there sure as fuck isn't one for me. But seeing him like this? Lost and shit? It sucks. This is why he's a better fit for Ophelia than I'll ever be. Because he's here. He'll always be here. He'll always look out for her in a way I can't.

The familiar defeat I've grown accustomed to makes me slump a little farther in my chair, but I force my vocal cords to work. "You're not gonna smother her, man."

A flash of hope ignites in his eyes. "You sure?"

I nod. "Yeah, I'm, uh, I'm sure. She just wants to know you care."

"You think?"

"Yeah."

"Thanks." He smiles. "Keep up what you're doing with Lia, all right? I need you on my side."

My muscles coil in my gut, making it hard to breathe as I force a nod, staring blankly into my bowl. "Sure thing, man."

"Speaking of," he adds. "Any chance you can pick her up from practice today?"

I don't even bother hiding my groan as I drop my head back and stare at the ceiling. "Arch."

"I don't want her walking back on her own, and I have a meeting I can't miss."

"What about Griffin or—"

"Mav."

"Fine." I stand and set my bowl in the sink. "What time?"

"Noon."

I grip the edge of the granite counter until my knuckles turn white. "Can't wait."

~

SHE'S LATE. I CHECK THE TIME ON MY PHONE AS I LEAN against my bike in the parking lot. The rest of the team filed out almost an hour ago.

What's taking her so long?

Annoyed, I head into the empty arena. Ophelia's on the ice, sprinting from one end of the rink to the other. Most of her pads sit on the half-wall separating the team bench from the ice, along with her helmet, gloves, and stick. Other than her, the place is empty.

I sit on one of the red spectator seats and wait for her to notice me, but she doesn't. Or maybe she does, and she's avoiding me. I wouldn't be surprised either way.

What am I doing here? And how do I handle this? By pretending? Sweeping shit under the rug? Fucking suffocating?

Yeah, the last sounds about right.

Maybe we're still playing the game of chicken, waiting for the other person to crack instead of actually talking shit out the way I know we should.

But my shit? It's not her baggage. She shouldn't have to carry it. Not now. Not ever. And last night? Last night made everything so much worse. Even now, I'm not sure how it happened.

I was buzzed. She was drunk. I was jealous of all the guys watching her dance in the middle of the family room, and I couldn't find my brother, so I decided she should go home and sleep off the alcohol. I didn't expect her to call me Archer, but I didn't correct her, either. It seemed easier than trying to explain why I wanted to help her at the party when I had no right to.

She isn't my problem.

Or at least, she wasn't...until she kissed me. Or fuck, I dunno. Did I kiss her? Yeah. I did. She called me Archer and begged me to kiss her, and because I'm a fucking prick with no restraint, I did it. I kissed her.

Fuck, I kissed her.

She was even sweeter than I remember. More pliant. But just as excited. Just as ready. Honestly, it's a miracle I pulled away. If she hadn't called me by my real name, I'm not sure I would've snapped out of it in the first place. And that would've been a fucking disaster.

But even then, I couldn't control myself. I went to my room and jacked off, imagining Ophelia riding my dick until I came in my hand like a little bitch.

Slush sprays the opposite goal as she skates to a halt, resting her hands on the top of her head while she catches her breath. Her strawberry blonde hair is twisted up in a messy ponytail, and her face is red from exertion. Even from here, I can tell she's never looked prettier.

"Are you going to keep staring at me like a creeper or what?" she calls without bothering to look at me.

"I'm not staring," I yell back at her.

"Just hiding in the stands while I run drills," she quips, finally gifting me with an amused smirk. It makes me want to fall to my knees and fucking worship her.

Not. My. Girl, I remind myself.

Standing, I reply, "I'm here to take you home because my brother asked me to."

Her scoff is loud and almost unhinged as she throws her head back and laughs. "You're joking, right?"

"Come on," I urge, but my feet take me down the steps instead of up them, leading me closer to the girl of my dreams as if they have a mind of their own. "Stop being an overachiever for once in your life. Let's go. The rest of the team left an hour ago."

She skates toward me, stopping at the edge of the ice. "Asshole Maverick's back, I see."

Gripping the half-wall separating us, I lean closer and give her a condescending grin. "Good to see you too. Come on. I wanna get out of here."

I start to push off from the half-wall, but she places her hand on mine. "Wait."

"Not in the mood, Opie."

"We should talk."

"Like I said," I flex my fingers beneath hers. "I'm not in the mood."

Slowly, she lifts her hands, plucking a few strands of sweaty hair away from her face and pushing them behind her ear. "Truth or dare?"

"What?" My eyebrows raise.

"Truth. Or. Dare?" she repeats.

"I'm not playing this game." I turn around, ready to get the hell out of Dodge.

"Fine," she calls. "I'll tell your brother what happened last night."

"And fuck up your own relationship?" I laugh and face her again. "I doubt it."

"Dammit, Maverick!" she yells at me. "Why are you so stubborn?"

"Why not?" My shoulders lift, and I head back up a few more steps, but my curiosity gets the best of me.

This girl.

This fucking girl.

Facing her again, I tuck my hands into my pockets and grunt, "Fine. Dare."

"I dare you to grow a pair and come back here so we can talk about this."

My nostrils flare, but I take the final steps separating us and lean forward, stealing her space as she keeps her heated gaze on me. "Pretty sure you already know I have a pair, and you were reminded of them last night when I was nestled between your pretty little thighs."

"Technically, it was your dick I felt, which is fitting by the way, since you've basically created your entire persona around being one."

My lips lift with amusement, and I growl, "My turn. Truth or dare?"

"Truth."

"Are you in love with my brother?"

She pulls back slightly. "Of course, I love your brother."

"*In* love," I clarify.

Confusion twists her pretty little face, and she tilts her head. "What?"

"You can love hockey. You cannot be *in* love with hockey."

"Fine," she concedes. "I don't know if I'm in love with him or not. Is that what you want to hear?"

I don't know anymore. What I want. What the repercussions will be. Because it isn't only me. It isn't only her. It's him too. It'll always be him.

When I stay silent for too long, she asks, "Truth or dare?"

"Dare," I repeat, keeping my expression—my feelings—on lockdown.

Her eyes flash with frustration. She wants me to say truth. She wants me to open the door and let her ask me things I've been refusing to answer.

"Fine," she seethes. "I dare you to tell me why you pretended to be your brother last night."

These aren't the rules. I know it, and so does Ophelia, but I answer her anyway. "You assumed—"

"And you didn't correct me," she interrupts. "I want to know why."

"Because you were drunk, and I didn't feel like confusing you."

Her upper lip curls. "You're lying."

"I'm not," I lie. *Again.* "Truth or dare?"

"Dare," she snaps.

"I dare you to tell me how long it took you to figure out it was me walking you home instead of Archer."

A dry, sarcastic laugh slips out of her. "You really think I don't know you?"

"Was it before or after the kiss?" I push.

"You think you're so interchangeable, Maverick? You think I wouldn't know you by your eyes? Or your smell? Or the way your jaw tightens? Or the way my name rolls off your tongue compared to your brother's? I didn't need to kiss you to know it was you."

"Then why did you?" I rasp.

Her tongue darts out between her pretty, full lips. "It isn't your turn."

"Answer the question."

"It isn't. Your. Turn," she seethes. "Truth or dare?"

"Truth."

She hesitates, a gleam of fear and uncertainty swirling in her pretty caramel eyes.

When she's quiet for too long, I push, "Don't stop now, Goose. You have me right where you want me."

A spark consumes the fear, and she holds my gaze, her voice never wavering. "Why did you stop kissing me when I called you Mav?"

My eyes fall to her lips as I damn near drown in want and guilt and fucking need. "Because my name had never sounded sweeter. I'll meet you out front."

I turn to leave, but she calls out, "I don't need a ride."

"I don't care," I reply. "I'm gonna give you one anyway."

Then I get the hell out of there.

2 6

OPHELIA

You know what really sucks? Being in a fight with your best friend all because you started dating him and picked a fight, ending said romantic relationship over something as stupid and juvenile as a kissing booth.

We still haven't spoken. Instead, I've been lying in bed while my phone blows up with messages from my hockey teammates.

The same teammates who were at SeaBird the night Maverick got shit-faced.

Yeah. Group texts? Sometimes, they suck too.

GRACE

So...I need everyone's advice. Ever since we went to SeaBird, I can't stop thinking about Maverick Buchanan. I saw him on his motorcycle earlier today, and *fans self* I'm dying over here. What I wouldn't give to climb into his bed and screw his brains out right now...

EMILY

I told you to hook up with him that night!

GRACE

I didn't want to come on too strong.

MORGAN

Yeah, Mav seems like a guy who enjoys the chase.

EMILY

Hey, it's the twenty-first century. We're allowed to chase the people we're interested in every once in a while. ;)

GRACE

Maverick definitely seems like a guy worth chasing.

MORGAN

Totally. You could always hire Reeves to take you out. It might make Maverick jealous.

EMILY

What do you mean "hire Reeves"?

Good question. I was wondering the same thing.

MORGAN

You don't know?! Apparently, Reeves is like a male escort or something. It's super hush-hush, so I don't know all the details.

GRACE

If it's hush-hush, how do I ask Reeves to take me to make Maverick jealous?

EMILY

I never said I was the criminal mastermind behind the operation. It's just a suggestion.

GRACE

You mean like how you suggested I slip
Maverick my number the other night?!

EMILY

Yes! That was amazing lol Has he called yet?

GRACE

No

MORGAN

He will, don't worry. You're gorgeous, and
Maverick would be lucky to have you.

My nose scrunches as another text comes through.

GRACE

Maybe. Ophelia, you're dating Archer, so you
probably know Maverick better than any of
us. Does he really seem like the jealous type?
And if not, how do I get on his radar?

I stay quiet, stewing in my own misery as I read over the
messages without bothering to respond. Then again, there's
no need because Emily is especially chatty tonight.

EMILY

You could always hook up with him. There's
no way he'd turn you down if you offered up
a no-strings-attached arrangement.

Bile floods my throat, and I toss my phone onto my bed,
roll out of it, and head to the kitchen.

I'm annoyed. I shouldn't be, but I am.

After our impromptu truth or dare session at the rink
today, I can't stop thinking about Maverick. About our kiss
yesterday or how he admitted his name had never sounded
sweeter after I whispered it during said kiss.

It's confusing and so freaking infuriating I don't know

what to do with myself. But what's worse? It's the fact that Archer and I are currently drowning in the biggest fight of our relationship, and even now, I'm too caught up on all things Maverick to care.

What is wrong *with me?*

Grabbing the book I've been reading from the kitchen table, I tuck it under my arm, snatch a sleeve of Oreos from the pantry, and open the sliding glass door leading to the back patio, anxious for a distraction from my screwed-up thoughts.

Thankfully, the guys aren't having a game night tonight, so it's quiet. And boy, do I need it. I have no idea what time it is, but it must be late because the men's side of the house is quiet too, and their kitchen light is off. As the stars twinkle above me, I tiptoe across the patio when I notice a shadow on the steps. My lungs seize, and I stop short.

The shadow turns around and faces me, an unopened six-pack resting beside him.

"Opie," Mav grunts.

"Of course, you're out here," I mutter to myself, turning back to the door.

Seriously, I cannot catch a break.

"Wait," he calls.

I freeze, and my head falls forward. "I'm not in the mood, Mav."

"Mood for what?"

"For whatever hot and cold bullshit you want to throw at me."

"Someone's feeling sassy this evening," he notes. "What are you doing out here? It's almost three in the morning." The stairs creak softly as he pushes himself up and strides toward me. "What's wrong?"

My nostrils flare, but I force myself to turn around and

face him. His aftershave teases me, so I breathe through my mouth to keep from salivating at the familiar scent.

"Seriously, what's wrong?" Mav prods. "You look pissed."

"Grace Temple is interested in you," I announce.

His brows wrinkle. "Who?"

"Grace Temple."

"Am I supposed to know who she is?"

"She's my teammate, and she's interested in you."

"Oh." He hesitates. "Okay?"

"Apparently, she gave you her number at SeaBird the other night."

Confused, his forehead wrinkles and he lifts one of his shoulders. "So?"

"So." I juggle my book and Oreos in my grasp, folding my arms. "I'm doing my due diligence as her teammate, and I'm curious if you're interested in her."

His chuckle is sardonic at best as he pinches the bridge of his nose. "Is that what you're doing? Your due diligence as a *friend?*"

I hate how he can see right through me. But what I hate even more? It's how I care enough about his answer to keep pushing when I know I shouldn't.

With my head held high, I argue, "Yes. I'm doing my due diligence. Are you interested in her, Maverick?" As the words tumble out of me, the Oreos slip from beneath my arm and crash to the ground like a puck hitting the ice. I flinch but don't bother picking them up. I'm too amped up from our conversation. Too invested in his potential answer and what it'll do to me.

His eyes fall to the cookies, but he finds my gaze again. "You really want to know?"

"Yeah, I really want to know."

His shoes brush against my bare toes as he steps closer,

careful not to step on them. "No, Opie. You can tell your teammate I'm flattered but not interested."

He's not interested.

I shouldn't be relieved, but I am.

Ignoring the feeling, I push, "Why not?"

"Because I'm not."

"Is there someone else?"

He cocks his head. "Are you asking if I'm seeing someone?"

I open my mouth to respond, but he cuts me off. "No, Ophelia. I'm not seeing anyone."

"*Were* you seeing someone?" I whisper. "Is that why you broke things off?"

His expression falls. "Opie—"

"Just answer the question, Maverick."

It comes out as a plea, and I hate myself for it. The way I need to know if there's someone else. If there's ever been someone else.

His movements are slow as he raises his hand and brushes his fingers along my jaw. "Where is this coming from, Opie?"

"Just answer the question," I repeat.

He lowers his hand again, like he's just remembered I'm not his to touch or to comfort. It only hurts me more.

"Of course I wasn't seeing someone else," he murmurs.

"There wasn't some…girl here?" I run my thumb along the edge of my book and look down at the battered pages, unable to hold his penetrating stare for another second. "Some girl who caught your attention or something?" The thought leaves a trail of bitterness on my tongue, and my nose wrinkles. How had I never considered this possibility? That he was seeing someone else? That I didn't matter.

"Opie, look at me," Maverick orders.

My teeth dig into the inside of my cheek as I steal the courage to look up at him. To actually communicate with the asshole in front of me instead of dancing around the subject like we always do.

His eyes soften in the moonlight. "The only girl who's ever held my attention is you."

The last of my resolve crumbles, and I close my eyes, soaking up his admission no matter how much it hurts. I believe him. Maybe I'm stupid, but I do. And the truth is...the feeling is mutual. I tried being all-in with Archer. I've done everything in my power to move on and to be happy with someone who, by all accounts, is perfect. It's done nothing but made me more miserable, more defeated, and more sure of my feelings for the man in front of me, even when it doesn't make any sense. Even when I'm better off running in the opposite direction.

But the idea of fighting those feelings for another second is more than I can bear.

"Listen," I whisper. "After the kissing booth, you said you were done playing this game. And...well, so am I." I take a deep breath, forcing my lungs to work.

"Lia—"

"I still care about you, Mav."

Panic flashes in his eyes, but it's replaced with resignation almost as quickly. With a soft shake of his head, he breathes out, "Don't say that."

"Yeah, well, me *not* saying it hasn't exactly changed my feelings over the last few months either, so..."

"Ophelia—"

"Can we please talk for once? Like, actually talk?"

When he stays quiet, I push, "Last night, before we..." I lick my lips. "Before we kissed, Archer and I fought, and we kind of took a break." Taking a deep breath, I add, "And the crazy part is...I haven't felt torn up about it. How messed up is that, Maverick? Your brother and I break up, and I'm okay with it?"

"Ophelia—"

"I'm gonna make the breakup final." The words feel cleansing almost. Cathartic, maybe. Like they've been on the tip of my tongue ever since I witnessed Maverick's eyes flaring with heat when I was lying out in the hot sun. Hell, even before. I'll always love Archer. I know I will. But he deserves more than a girl still hung up on her ex—even when he knows about said reservations—and this isn't fair to him. I need to see where things go with Maverick. For real this time. It's like we've been dancing around each other for years. *Years.* And he's always been too much of a coward to see it through. Even when we finally dipped our toes in the possibility of something real between us, he bailed, and I don't know why. But I don't even care about the reason anymore. Not when it's clear he hasn't let me go, either. The push and pull over the past few weeks? It means something. I know it does. And I'm done hiding. Done running. Done waiting. Done playing this stupid game.

"Did you hear me, Mav?" I ask. "Archer and I are finished dating."

His expression shuts down almost instantly. Like he's finally chosen to pick a side when all he's ever done is walk the line, teasing me, toying with me, playing with the idea of what we could have if we simply...tried.

"Don't," he orders, giving me his back and taking the short set of stairs to his six-pack waiting for him. When he pulls a beer out and pops the lid off, I almost laugh.

"Seriously? You're drinking right now? Classy, Mav."

"Never claimed to be the classy twin, Opie," he mutters against the rim of his bottle as he brings it to his lips.

It isn't the first time he's said it, but he's right. He's never been anything but himself. Even when it makes him an ass.

Squaring my shoulders, I announce, "Archer deserves to

know I'm still interested in you. I'm tired of stringing him along. It isn't fair to him."

"Then stop being interested in me."

I grab his arm, attempting to make him actually look at me, but when he does, I wish I hadn't. Because the indifference in his eyes? It fucking burns. Making me feel like a crazy person. An obsessed person. A freaking stalker who's fabricated every single interaction between us, turning it into something it isn't. Like attraction. Connection. Something real. Something worth fighting for.

As if I've been scalded, I let him go, allowing my hand to fall. "Are you serious right now?"

"Breaking up with Archer is a mistake."

"How can you say that?"

"Just because I haven't been seeing anyone else doesn't mean you should break up with Archer. You and me? It's... it's not in the cards, Ophelia." His jaw sets. "You don't belong with me."

The sharpness of his words leaves me sick, but I shove the feeling aside, refusing to give in or back down. Not again.

"Bullshit," I spit. "I belong with who I *want* to belong with."

"Trust me. I wish it was that simple, but I—*you* can't..." His Adam's apple bobs. "You can't control everything, Lia."

"You mean I can't control *you*," I conclude.

He shakes his head as if he's talking to a toddler. "You don't get it. You and Archer are...you're perfect together."

"Are you serious right now?" I repeat, shaking my head, convinced I'm actually going crazy. "Mav, you kissed me."

"I also said it was a mistake," he mumbles, bringing the beer back to his lips.

"Look, I love Archer. I do. He's amazing and sweet and kind and patient and every other great quality you could want in a guy. But—"

"No." He lowers the beer bottle to his side, his muscles bunched beneath his T-shirt as he faces me fully. "No buts. That's it. He has every quality you could want in a guy and can give you the future you want. There. The end."

"But he isn't *you*," I finish.

Maverick lifts the bottle again, taking a long pull and wiping his mouth with the back of his hand. Turning to me, he gives me his full attention. "Trust me, Ophelia. You don't want me."

"Maybe it's time you stop listening to whatever baseless insecurities you have and trust what I want for once."

"I know what you want."

Shifting my book in my hands, I fold my arms. "And what do I want?"

"You want a hockey career. And a successful husband who worships you. You want kids and a dog and a house close to your parents and your little sister, no matter how much you two like to fight." His mouth lifts, but it isn't happy. It's sad. So freaking sad, I can feel it in the pit of my stomach as he licks the moisture from his bottom lip. "You want things I can't give you, Lia. So, why drag this out when it'll only end with you in shambles?"

"You're being unfair," I argue.

"Just saying it like it is."

"Do you have any idea how much this is killing me? How much *you're* killing me?" I yank the bottle from his hand and keep it out of his reach, demanding his full attention. "By being hot and cold and messing with my head until I'm convinced I'm going fucking crazy? Or am I the only one who remembers your tequila dick rearing to go not so long ago? Huh? So what? I'm good for a solid fuck, but an actual relationship is out of the question for you?"

"Never said I wasn't a fuck-up."

"Touche," I snap. "You're also selfish."

"Check."

"And stubborn."

"Check."

"And with a heart so fucking rotten you can't even let yourself be happy."

Resting his hip against the railing, his eyes close for the briefest of seconds. He nods. "Check again, Opie."

"You don't get to play it both ways," I seethe. "You don't get to be hot and cold. You don't get to break my heart an hour before you were supposed to take me to prom, then be pissed at me when your brother took me instead. You don't get to tell me I should stay with your brother when I see the hurt in your eyes whenever you see us together. It isn't fair."

"Don't talk to me about what is or isn't fair, Ophelia. He might be the better choice, but you can't hold it against me for hating it when I see you with him."

"You ended things with *me*." I jab at my own chest while fighting back tears of frustration. Because it hurts. It hurts so much. To see everything we could be, everything I want, if we could only…take it. "You don't get to be jealous," I add. "You don't get to play the victim or pretend I'm the one who broke your black heart."

"You're right." He nods, digging the dagger a little deeper as he cuts the distance between us until his chest brushes against mine. "Now run along back to my brother's bed where you belong."

"His bed," I seethe. "Because it's where I belong?"

"It's not like you haven't already been there. Tell me, how long did you wait after we broke up until you fucked him?"

"I thought we never dated," I argue.

He lets out a low, humorless laugh and pinches the bridge of his nose but doesn't answer me.

"And I haven't fucked him," I add.

He scoffs. "Don't lie to me."

"I haven't," I repeat.

"You sleep in his bed," he reminds me as if he has all the answers, and it only feeds my need to knock the arrogant asshole down a peg or two.

Lifting my head, my upper lip curling, I jab at his chest, driving my point home. "You think you know everything, don't you? Yes, I sleep in his bed. I like being held, and he likes holding me. But actually fucking him?" A bitter laugh scrapes up my throat. "Call me a prude or a lovesick puppy, but I've been holding back."

He leans down, his nose an inch from mine and his eyes gleaming with arrogance as if he doesn't believe me, even now.

"You're lying," he grits out.

Tears burn in my eyes as I shake my head. "You know, at this moment, I really wish I was."

"Fine, I'll bite," he growls. "Why haven't you slept with him?"

"Excellent question, Mav." My voice cracks, and I dig my nails into my palms. "Maybe it's because the guy I gave my virginity to turned out to be an asshole who tossed me aside without an actual explanation." I blink away the ache behind my eyes. "Maybe it's because I was afraid it might hurt you. Maybe it's because I know if I cross that line, there's no going back."

He steps closer, crowding my space. "My brother—"

"Is patient, and kind, and a fucking saint. I told him I was a little hesitant to go all the way, but he's had no issue waiting until I'm ready, and trust me, I've been far from ready. I've been a fucking wreck all because of you. So maybe it's time you stop assuming shit. Did you ever think of that?"

As if I've slapped him, his expression tightens with pain, and he pulls away, giving me some room to actually breathe when all I want to do is drown in his embrace.

"You're lying," he repeats. This time, it's less resolute. Less sure. It only breaks my heart more.

"You know I'm not," I whisper. "But you know what, Mav? You're right. I don't know what's been holding me back when you've made it clear I mean nothing to you. I'm going to give your brother all of my love because he isn't going to toss it aside or make me feel like I'm not enough. And when I do, you're going to look back on this moment and realize exactly how much you screwed yourself over. So buckle up, asshole. You might wanna invest in some noise-canceling headphones." I hesitate, and a dark, twisted laugh bubbles out of me. "Actually, scratch that. I'm not going to give you a performance because even though you deserve to have your nose rubbed in the fact you're letting me go right now, I'm not doing it to get back at you for stringing me along. I'm doing it because your brother deserves me. *All* of me. And I'm tired of holding back, hoping and praying you'll pick up the pieces you broke and put me back together again."

His eyes dim, the blackness swallowing the blue I've come to love until only indifference shines back at me. It shreds the last of my hope as he turns his head toward the grassy space in front of him. "Have a good night, Opie."

Fuck. Him.

27
OPHELIA

I walk into Archer's bedroom and slam the door behind me, not giving a shit it rattles the walls and potentially wakes the rest of the guys.

I don't. Fucking. Care.

The lump on the mattress jerks to life as a muffled curse sounds from beneath the sheets. Archer scrambles for the lamp on the nightstand, but before he can flick it on, I push at his shoulder and climb onto his lap, kissing him with every single piece of me left.

It's rough and messy and angry. My eyes ache. My heart pounds. My hands tremble. But I force myself to keep going. To erase Maverick and everything he's put me through, even if it kills me. I shove my tongue between Archer's lips as his hands find my waist. I can feel his hesitation with every brush of his lips. Like he's holding back. Like he's knocked off kilter.

Angry, I tangle my fingers in the hair at the nape of his neck and grind myself against him, my heart fucking breaking all over again.

It feels wrong.

Why does it feel wrong? Why can't it be easy? Why can't I love him the way I love his brother?

He kisses my lips and slowly pulls away from me, a deep wrinkle between his brows. "Whoa, whoa. Lia, slow down."

Angry tears well in my eyes as I shake my head and kiss him again. Harder. Needier. Angrier. The moisture slides down my cheeks, but I don't wipe it away. I hold onto Archer's shoulders for dear life, kissing him with all my broken pieces. With everything I have left. Salt clings to my lips, and he must taste it because he squeezes my waist and leans back, ending our kiss again. "Lia, are you crying?"

I wipe my mouth with the back of my shaking hand. "I think we should break up."

He flinches back. "What?"

"Indefinitely," I clarify. Sucking my lips between my teeth, I bite hard. A metallic taste spreads across my tongue, but I don't relieve the pressure. I hold onto the pain. The hurt. The fucking agony. Because this is too much. It's too hard. Everything is.

I messed up.

I messed up so badly. So many times. And I don't know how to fix it. How to slow down. How to go back in time and erase my mistakes.

Archer's knuckle brushes against my chin, and he tilts my head toward him, commanding my attention. When he has it, he runs his thumb along the seam of my lips, pulling them free from my teeth. "Shit, you're bleeding."

"I want us to stay broken up," I repeat.

His eyes lift from my wound to my eyes. "Lia…"

"I'm still a mess," I whisper. "I'm still a mess, and it isn't fair to you."

"Where is this coming from?" He shakes his head. "Look, I know I should've told you I didn't want you kissing other guys, and I'm sorry, but—"

"Archer." My bottom lip wobbles, and I lean into the hand cradling my face. "I'm being unfair to you, and I'm not okay with it anymore."

His expression falls, the pleading in his gaze acting like a noose around my heart. "I told you I can be patient."

"I know." I pull away from his gentle touch and give him a sad, pathetic smile. "That's the problem. I don't deserve your patience, and I can't keep stringing you along and putting our friendship on the line until I know I can be all-in for real instead of just..."—I climb off his lap— "pretending."

"*Pretending*," he repeats. His voice is laced with disbelief as he slouches on the bed and stares out the window. "This is about your mystery man, isn't it?"

My heart plummets. "Archer..."

"Did you see him around campus or something?" He looks at me again. "Is that where this is coming from?"

"It doesn't matter."

"I think it does."

"No, it doesn't because I'm *still* a mess," I argue. "It hasn't changed since prom night. And trust me when I say I really have been trying to let him go and move on, but you deserve more than tying yourself to a mess like me."

His chin dips in a subtle nod as if he's processing our conversation. Finally, Archer asks, "Who is he?" He isn't angry. Isn't disappointed. Only curious. And it makes me love him more.

If only I could tell him the truth.

My tongue grows thick as I even consider mentioning Maverick, but the name never comes. It would hurt too much. Not only me, but Archer. It would ruin more than my friendship with him. It would destroy everything. His relationship with his brother. Our families' relationships. *Everything.* And for what? I have no future with Maverick. He's made it clear, so why rock the boat? Why air out our dirty laundry when there's no reason to?

"Still not gonna tell me?" Archer prods.

"It doesn't matter," I repeat. "My...*whatever* with Mystery Man is one hundred percent over. I know it. He *clearly* knows it. But my heart hasn't gotten the memo, and it's still holding on for dear life. And even though you've been way more patient than I ever deserved, I can't keep doing this to you. I can't keep making you wait for me to figure my shit out." I thread my arm through his limp one and squeeze it tightly, resting my head on his shoulder. "You've always been amazing at putting our friendship first, even above our relationship, and I think it's time I do the same."

He nods slowly, but it's mechanical. Robotic. "So you're breaking up with me."

Lifting my head, I look up at him. "I'm your best friend protecting you from a shitty girlfriend who's been taking you for granted."

His smile doesn't reach his eyes as he tucks my hair behind my ear. "You're not a shitty girlfriend, Lia. Only a confused one. But if you want to take a step back, I get it. Whenever you're ready, I'll be here."

"Arch—"

"It doesn't mean you're obligated to give me another chance. It means I'm a guy who knows what he wants, and I want you, Ophelia Taylor. Broken pieces and all."

"Arch," I repeat, my heart squeezing.

"You should get some rest."

With a nod, I glance at the bedroom door, and my bottom lip trembles. I don't want to run into Maverick. I don't want to face him and be rejected all over again. But staying here isn't exactly an option either.

Shit.

I wish I'd thought this through.

"Stay the night," Archer offers, proving yet again he's the most amazing man I've ever met.

I wipe at my tear-stained cheeks. "Arch—"

"You can sleep in my bed. I'll sleep on the floor."

He grabs his pillow from the top of the bed, tosses it to the ground, and heads to his closet, where a few folded blankets are stored.

"You don't have to," I whisper. "I can sleep on the couch in the family room or—"

"Lay down on the bed," he orders. "As your best friend, I insist."

He lies on the floor and spreads the olive green blanket over his long legs, pulling it up to his chin. But he doesn't close his eyes. He simply stares at me with a look telling me, *if you don't listen, I will spank your ass.*

It works.

With a smile, I murmur, "You really are the best. You know that, right?"

He chuckles. "Yeah, I know. Goodnight, Ophelia."

"'Night, Archer."

28

MAVERICK

My brother must be shit in bed because I didn't hear a sound last night other than a few whimpers early on. Regardless, it didn't quiet my imagination. What she's doing with him. What he's doing to her. If she likes it. If she's comparing him with me. The possibilities have been on a constant carousel in my skull, driving me crazy until I can't take anymore.

It's different this time. Knowing they're having sex. Knowing she was holding back because of me. Because I was her first and only.

Until last night.

When she let me go for real, and I did nothing to stop it. Hell, I pushed her into his waiting arms.

It fucking wrecks me.

Rubbing my hand over my tired face, I head toward the bathroom when the door opens. Steam billows around a freshly showered Ophelia. Her long, strawberry blonde hair hangs in ropes around her shoulders, down her back, and her makeup-free face, showcasing the freckles along the bridge of her nose I could draw from memory. The little knot of cloth between her breasts is the only thing keeping her perfect body from me. My hands fist at my sides. It would be so easy to reach up and tug at it. To let it fall at her feet. To drink her in. Every inch. Every curve. Every freckle.

She probably just finished showering off her fuckfest with my brother. The realization makes my stomach curdle.

"Mav," she whispers.

I blink slowly. "You done?"

"Done?"

"With the bathroom."

"Oh." She swallows and nods, stepping aside so I have plenty of space to slip past her.

"Thanks," I grunt, closing the bathroom door behind me.

It feels like the four walls surrounding me are closing in, leaving me dizzy and nauseated. I rest my head against the door and take a slow, controlled breath as memories I'd give anything to keep hidden rise to the surface.

∼

"We should play Truth or Dare," Finley announces. "Come on, guys!"

We're all hanging out in the back of Griffin's house. His parents, Ash and Colt, insisted we come home for Thanksgiving. Grudgingly, we agreed, giving up our freedom for a few days so we could catch up with everyone while Everett's family's in town.

"Truth or Dare?" Griffin asks. "What are we, twelve?"

I laugh at his response, well aware of the game nights we've thrown at LAU and how many times we've played Truth or Dare with our friends.

"Ah, come on," Finley begs. "It'll be fun. Please?" She presses her hands together in a begging motion, and Dylan does the same. With a laugh, Ophelia and her little sister, Tatum, join in, giving us their best doe eyes.

"Fiiiine," Everett grunts.

Archer shoves at my shoulder and tilts his head toward the side of the pool where the girls are all gathered. "Come on, brother. For old time's sake."

Old time's sake.

Yeah.

We've been playing Truth or Dare for as long as I can remember. Aunt Blakely taught us the rules one summer when we wouldn't leave the parents alone during a get-together. Looking back, I don't blame them for providing a distraction. Then again, after all the reckless dares we've thought of, I bet they regret showing us the ropes.

Too late now.

"Come on, Griff," Finley prods. She pats the patch of pavement beside her. "You can sit by me."

"Yeah, no," Everett protests. He takes the spot and stretches his legs in front of him.

"Everett!" She slaps her brother's shoulder.

Everett grunts, "Just be grateful we're playing," and makes himself comfortable.

Despite the fact all of us guys are over eighteen, we give in and sit our asses on the cool pavement beside the pool, forming a circle with the girls.

"All right, who starts?" Dylan asks.

Everett shrugs and turns to Griffin. "Truth or dare?"

"Dare," Griff answers.

"I dare you to jump into the pool with your clothes on."

With a smirk, Griffin stands up, wipes his hands on his jeans, and races toward the edge of the pool in the backyard, cannon-balling into the deep end. The girls squeal as water sprays over them, and the guys laugh as he pushes himself out of the pool, soaked from head to toe. It's been a warm autumn so far, and the water's heated, but it doesn't mean his balls won't freeze off within the next hour or so. Then again, the consequences of Truth or Dare make the game entertaining. I find myself smiling as Griffin shakes the water from his shaggy brown hair and takes his seat again.

"All right, Archer's turn," he announces.

"Oo, I'll do it!" his little sister, Dylan, pipes in. "Archer, truth or dare?"

"Truth," my brother answers.

"What's the craziest thing you've done at LAU?"

"You do know you're asking the more stable Buchanan twin, right?" Opie interjects.

"You think I can't be crazy?" Archer quips, his smile spread wide.

Not missing a beat, Opie grins back at him. "Mm-hmm. I'm sure you're a real loose cannon, Mr. Buchanan."

Dylan's eyes light up. "Oo, what if we compared—"

"They hate being compared," Opie reminds everyone.

"Uh, we're right here," Archer adds.

"Actually, I kind of like this idea." Finley waves her hands around the circle, completely ignoring my brother's response. "As self-appointed Truth or Dare commissioner for the evening, I decree that for tonight, the Buchanan twins shall be a package deal, and both are required to answer or perform any obstacle for the rest of the game. All in favor, say, 'I.'"

"I," everyone yells.

I scoff and shake my head, taking a sip of the rum and Coke I'd stolen from inside.

Clearing her throat, Dylan sits up a little straighter and repeats her question. "So, Buchanan boys, what is the craziest thing you've done during your time at LAU?"

"I know Mav's," Everett offers. "He had a threesome."

"Ew!" A wave of groans echoes from the girls.

Dylan gives Archer a pointed look. "And you?"

"I may have hooked up with one of my teacher's assistants."

"Day-um," Finley says. "No wonder you have straight A's. Okay, Mav. It's your turn. Truth or dare?"

"I just went," I point out.

"Come on, just answer the question."

"Fine," I mutter. "Truth."

Sitting up a little straighter, Finley asks, "Do you now, or have you ever, had a crush on anyone here? And remember, this is for both you and Archer."

"Two for one," I grunt. "Yeah, you've made the rules clear. Arch, you go first."

His eyes find Ophelia sitting cross-legged on the cool autumn pavement, then he turns back to Dylan. "Maybe."

Finley argues, "You have to say yes or no."

"Fine," Archer grumbles. "Yes."

"Oo, who is it?" Dylan asks.

"Can't ask two questions for one truth," Finley reminds everyone, eating up her position as Truth or Dare commissioner like a crack addict. When she turns to me, she asks, "Mav? What's your answer?"

"Now or ever?" I clarify.

"Ever," Finley replies.

Squeezing the back of my neck, I avoid the opposite side of the circle and shift on the pavement. "Then yeah," I answer. "I think we all have, right?"

Finley rolls her eyes but doesn't deny it.

Everett calls, "Ophelia, it's your turn. Truth or dare?"

Ophelia looks up from the pavement. She's been drawing pictures on the concrete with her finger, using the puddle of pool water as her paint. Honestly, she's been so focused on it I'm surprised she's still paying attention. Wiping her finger on her jeans, she answers, "Dare."

Finley slaps her brother's chest again and says, "I dare you to kiss one of the twins."

"We have names," I remind Finley.

Finley waves me off. "She knows what I mean."

"Yeah, I know what she means." Ophelia licks her lips, her attention shifting from Archer to me and back again with those damn caramel eyes. Her strawberry blonde curls have fallen around her face despite the majority of it being pulled up in a ponytail. She's changed over the past few months since I've been away.

Grown up, though she'd smack me for thinking it.

I'm not the only one who's noticed.

Archer's had a thing for Ophelia for a while now. We both have, but I'm more subtle about it. It doesn't help how our families like to joke about them ending up together, acting like they're a match made in heaven or some shit without even giving me a chance to shoot my shot.. To be fair, they've always been pretty close. He's the soft one. The patient one. The nice one.

Me? Yeah, I'm kind of an ass. Have been since we were little. But I think it's why I've been so interested in her. Because no matter what I throw at Ophelia, she still puts up with my shit and isn't afraid to push back. To tell me like it is. To step up and keep me in check.

"Either of them?" Opie's attention bounces between me and my brother by my side as she chews her bottom lip.

With a grin, Finley leans back on her hands and confirms, "Yup. You pick."

Ophelia pushes herself onto her knees and crawls through the middle of the circle toward me and Archer. The sight makes my cock stir, surprising the shit out of me, and my heart thumps faster and faster. Who's she gonna pick? And why am I delusional enough to think I'm even on her radar?

I've been an ass to her since we were little. In the beginning, it was because I was a dick, but as we got older, it almost became a game. I wanted to see how many buttons I could push until she snapped. She'd keep her composure in check until she couldn't take it anymore and would explode. Then I backed off, and we started *all over again. After all these years, she's slowly become less of a hothead and takes each and every jab without a second thought. It's only made me want to push her more.*

To crawl under her skin the same way she's crawling toward me right now.

Pretty. Innocent. Ophelia.

She's looking like a fucking snack when I have no right to see her like this. Like anything other than my brother's best friend and my parents' friends' daughter.

When she reaches my brother and me, Opie hesitates, her eyes holding mine for an extra second. Her lips part, and she turns to Archer, giving him her full attention. I feel Archer's muscles tense when he realizes she's picked him.

Fuck, mine do too.

I shouldn't be surprised—and I'm not—but...

With a smile, she murmurs, "Hello, friend."

"Hey, Lia," Archer replies.

He stretches his legs out, making room for the girl in front of him. She scoots closer, sandwiching herself between us. She faces Archer fully until all I see is the back of her head and my brother's grin over her shoulder. The scent of her shampoo hits my nostrils, and I breathe her in, shifting a few inches back so she has room to fulfill her dare. Her fingers grab my brother's chin as she leans closer. Slowly. Cautiously. My stomach twists with jealousy. Every disappearing inch between their mouths only fans my confusion at the foreign feeling. At the last second, she forces his head to the side and kisses his cheek.

Laughter, groans of disappointment, and smartass ribbing echo throughout the backyard as Ophelia lets Archer's chin go.

She slides back onto her haunches and looks around the group. "I believe the commissioner only stated a kiss. She never specified where." She sits on her ass, making herself comfortable between me and my brother, and when her thigh brushes against my knee, I stare at the contact, surprised she doesn't pull away. Neither do I.

Instead, I relax my leg even more, giving the innocent touch more pressure. More presence.

Staying where she is, Ophelia leans back on her hands and turns to Dylan. "Truth or dare?"

The rest of the night goes by in a blur. By midnight, Griffin and Dylan disappear into the house, retrieving blankets and pillows for everyone. Another hour or two later, the laughter turns to hushed whispers, and before we know it, everyone is fast asleep in the backyard.

Everyone but me.

I rest my hands behind my head on the rooftop, looking up at the expanse of stars in the sky. It's dark but bright too. There are so many stars. So many planets and solar systems. Worlds among worlds. A soft rustle grabs my attention, and I turn toward it. Opie's tiptoeing on the roof, careful not to wake anyone below us on the lawn, as she makes her way toward me wrapped in a flannel blanket. When she catches me staring, she freezes.

"What are you doing?" I ask.

"Sh!" She places her finger against her lips.

I bite the inside of my cheek to keep from grinning but stay quiet. Satisfied with my silence, she starts moving again. Once she reaches me, she spreads the blanket on the cool gray shingles, plops down beside me, leans back on her elbows, and looks at the sky. I don't follow her line of sight. I'm too busy staring at the girl beside me.

Amusement toys at the edge of her lips. "So, a threesome, huh?"

I chuckle under my breath, sitting up and resting my elbows on my knees. "Guess so."

"Why am I not surprised?"

"Is that why you kissed Archer instead of me?" I ask.

Her caramel eyes shift from the sky to meet my gaze. "Technically, I think I still owe you."

My brow arches.

"You know, since the Buchanan twins are a package deal and

all," she explains. "Then again, I know how much you hate being compared to your brother, so..." Her attention falls to my lips, her tongue darting out to moisten hers.

This is a bad idea.

During the game is one thing. It can be written off as peer pressure and shit. But finding me afterward? Looking at me like this? Like little Ophelia Taylor wants to kiss me? It's a bad idea. A stupid idea. But I've never been known as the smart brother.

"What do you say, Mav?" She tears her attention from my lips and pins me with her stare. "Are you a package deal for the evening?"

"Commissioner's rules," I confirm. "I guess I can make an exception for tonight."

"Oh, you do, do you?" Her pouty lips tilt up as she watches me scoot closer to her. "How diplomatic of you."

"I'm very diplomatic."

"You never answered the who question, by the way," she adds.

I frown. "Who?"

"Who you had a crush on in the group...or is it have?" She taps her finger against her chin as if deep in thought.

"Not sure it matters," I point out.

"Why not?"

"Because dating anyone in the group is a bad idea, don't you think?"

"I mean, seriously dating, sure," she concedes. "I can see how it could make things messy if things didn't work out, but hooking up for fun in secret?" Her shoulders lift. "I can see the appeal."

"If I was gonna cross the line with someone in the group, I'm pretty sure my parents would want it to be serious. And so would her parents."

"Mm-hmm. You make a good point. Her parents are probably pretty protective. But what about her older brothers?" she asks.

I know what she's doing. She's baiting me. Curious to see if I'll throw her a bone and confirm whether or not she's the girl I'm interested in since she's the only one of her friends without over-protective brothers watching her every move.

"Funny," I mutter. "I don't think Archer had to answer these questions."

"Archer is...Archer." She shrugs. "He doesn't play games."

"And I do?"

"You love games," she murmurs. Her tone is laced with amusement as she peeks at me again. "You love the chase, Maverick. The competition. The rush. The question is...what happens when you win? Do you move on to the next thing without appreciating the spoils, or do you bask in the glory?"

"Since you know me so well, you tell me," I reply.

She nods, inching even closer. "I think it doesn't matter. Not if you and the girl are on the same page."

"And what page is that?"

"Let's find out." The scent of flowers invades my space and clings to her messy waves, but I don't pull away. The organ in my chest pounds faster and faster as she shifts her upper body until she's fully facing me. She wets her bottom lip, and her eyes fall to my mouth. Without hesitation, she kisses me. Fuck, she feels like silk. All soft and supple. Unsure almost. It only turns me on more. Grasping the side of her face, I tug her into me further, dragging my tongue against the seam of her lips, and she opens for me, letting me taste her.

A soft groan rumbles through my chest as I lay her down on the blanket and press my weight against her when a tiny voice of reason echoes in the back of my mind.

Eighteen.

Family friend.

Archer's best friend.

Fuck.

My fingers flex against her jaw, but I let her go and roll off her. Subtly, I shift my throbbing cock in my jeans, well aware of the blue balls I'll be sporting by morning.

Pressing her fingers against her lips, she watches me carefully, a fog of wariness clouding her amber eyes.

"Why'd you stop?" *she asks.*

"I'm not gonna fuck you here." *I shake my head.* "Not gonna fuck you anywhere."

"Why not?"

"Because you're Uncle Theo's kid. You're my brother's best friend. You're..." *I close my eyes, praying for clarity.*

"I'm what?" *she whispers.*

"Fucking perfect." *Grabbing her face, I kiss her again. Hard. Rough. Needy. I shouldn't. Fuck me, I shouldn't. But I can't help it. The way I crave her. The way I need her. To touch her, to talk to her, to be inside her.*

"This is a bad idea," *I remind her. The last of my logic and restraint slowly dissipates as my blood rushes south.* "You sure you want this?"

"Pretty sure we've been dancing around this for a while now."

She grabs the hem of my shirt and tugs me to her mouth, but I stay strong, staring down at her. She looks like a fucking buffet. One I want to devour. Her hair is sprawled around her, and her shirt's ridden up, giving me a glimpse of her pale, toned stomach. I smother a groan of frustration and cage her in, using my forearms to hold my weight so I don't smother her. "Doesn't mean it's a good idea."

"That's future Lia's problem," *she announces.* "But present Lia? Past Lia? Well." *She spreads her thighs and cradles me against her core.* "She's been waiting for you for a lifetime."

"You want me, Opie?"

"Yes."

"Even if it's only for tonight?"

She nods again. "Even if it's only for five minutes. I want you. And I'm not gonna regret you."

"Promise?"

"I know you, Maverick. And I know you aren't one to think five *years from now, let alone five minutes. As long as our families don't find out and turn this into a bigger deal than it really is, I'm okay with it."*

She grabs the edge of my shirt and drags it up, trailing her hands down my spine, but I grasp her wrist and cock my head. "I think I can do better than five minutes."

With a smirk, she brings me a breath from her lips and dares me. "Prove it."

~

TO THINK IT STARTED THAT LONG AGO. ALMOST NINE MONTHS. At first, we pretended like nothing had changed. Hell, she barely looked at me afterward. Didn't make a fuss. Didn't have any expectations. Didn't text me or tell me she missed me. I went back to campus thinking I'd hit the lottery. A girl who understood I wasn't ready to settle down, and she was okay with it. She knew me. The ins and outs. And instead of trying to change me, she embraced it. What I could offer.

It made it impossible to stay away from her when I came home for Christmas, and we wound up in each other's beds again. And when I left for school a few weeks later, I sent her a text. I'm still not sure why. I'd never missed a girl before. But Ophelia? She was different. On and on it went, our relationship shifting from enemies, to friends, to friends-with-benefits, to casual dating, to secret love, to heartbreak, to...*this.*

Fucking strangers barely holding it together under the guise of family ties.

It's a bitch.

29

OPHELIA

When Archer and I decided to give a romantic relationship a shot, I was terrified. Terrified I could lose my best friend if things didn't work out. I should've given Archer more credit. This morning, he made me pancakes and dropped me off at practice. He even managed to make me smile—twice—after I ran into Maverick outside the bathroom, proving he can move mountains and achieve the impossible.

He really is perfect.

And I really am a fool.

Everything is so messed up. I don't know how to fix it. How to forget what it felt like to be in Maverick's arms so I can fully let him go and appreciate how amazing it could feel to be in Archer's.

I wasn't lying when I told Maverick I love his brother.

I do. Archer's my best friend. My rock. My constant. And if Maverick wasn't in the picture, I have no doubt I'd marry Archer in the long run. And I'd be happy. I would. He's *that* perfect.

So why the hell won't Maverick just…disappear? From

my thoughts. My day-to-day life. I dunno…maybe the LAU campus altogether? There's no escaping him. Maverick will *always* be there. Haunting me. I'm sick of it. The pull I feel with him. The way he crawls under my skin and burrows deep. The way I catch him looking at me even when he shouldn't. The way tingles spread through my entire body whenever his thigh touches mine when we're sitting on the couch or how he acts jealous whenever someone even *looks* at me, yet he's too stubborn to claim me for himself.

It's screwing with my mind, and I'm not sure what to do about it.

At least hockey practice is a welcome distraction. The physical strain from Jaxon's utilitarian coaching has left me sore and satiated. The aches and pains dull my thoughts, along with the banter from the rest of my team. They're nice. My teammates. Well, when they aren't talking about hooking up with Maverick, anyway. And they're not afraid to put in the work to prove we're ready to make a splash this season, which is all that matters. It gives me hope for something in my future since my personal life feels like it's up in smoke.

Hiking my gym bag over my shoulder, I make my way toward our duplex across campus. Airpods in place, I follow the winding path, stopping short when a familiar silhouette comes into view on the black asphalt in front of me, though he's still fifty yards away. My heels dig into the ground, and I squint my eyes.

Nope. Not Archer. I'm not surprised. He's been so insanely busy with his internship he's lucky to hit practice, let alone make time for a random run on a Tuesday afternoon.

No, the Buchanan twin in front of me is definitely Maverick. He hasn't noticed me yet, but it's him. He seems… off. His chest heaves, and he looks two seconds from passing out, which is weird, considering the bastard's health and how close we are to our duplex. Sweat collects along his hairline and seeps into his running shirt, the sun reflecting off of him, reminding me of the *Twilight* movies, if Edward was sickly and on his deathbed. He looks pale. Really pale. Like a ghost or a walking corpse.

Something's wrong.

Something's very *wrong.*

I start jogging toward him. "Hey," I call. "You okay?"

It's like he doesn't see me.

"Mav?"

Gasping, his pace slows, and his eyes roll back, showcasing the whites while torching my panic and turning it into an inferno.

"Mav!" I yell.

With a skull-cracking thud, he hits the pavement, and I drop my gym bag to the ground, racing toward him.

Once I reach his side, I call out breathlessly, "Mav!" The pavement bites into my bare knees as I lift his head into my lap, tapping his cheek repeatedly. I was right. His forehead is sticky with sweat, and I wipe it away with the hem of my shirt, repeating his name over and over while choking on my own helplessness.

"Mav. Mav, wake up." Careful not to jostle him too much, I search my pockets but realize my phone is in the gym bag fifteen feet away. Patting Maverick's gym shorts, I find his phone and pull it out, preparing to call an ambulance when his heavy lids raise. The whites of his eyes are still on full display, as the phone slips from my fingers, falling onto Maverick's sweat-soaked shirt and clattering to the asphalt. I gasp at the view as he blinks again, his eyes gaining focus.

"Lia?" he croaks.

"Mav? Mav. Hey. Are you okay?"

His brows pinch in discomfort as he closes his eyes again. "Fuck."

"Are you okay?" I repeat.

"What happened?"

"Y-you fell."

"Fuck," he repeats, forcing his lids open another time and sitting up. My hands tremble and ache to pull him into me again, but I fist them instead, placing them in my lap as I watch him helplessly.

Resting his elbows on his bent knees, he takes a few deep breaths, looking utterly exhausted.

"What's your phone's code?" I find his cell on the pavement and pick it up again. "I'm calling an ambulance."

"Don't," he breathes out.

"Mav, you just passed out."

"I'm fine, Opie."

"Clearly, you're not fine. Healthy people don't simply collapse."

"I pushed myself too hard. That's all."

"Too hard?" I balk. "We're what? A mile from home?" I scoot closer to him and touch his shoulder. "There's no way—"

"Can you drop it, please?" he seethes, but he doesn't pull away from my touch. If anything, he leans closer, his strained muscles soft beneath my fingertips.

"I'm not going to drop it," I tell him. "I'm going to call—"

"Fucking hell, Opie," he grits out, but the words are still woven with exhaustion as he lifts his head from his palms and glares at me. "I said I'm fine."

My attention bounces around his face, taking in the sheen of sweat still clinging to his forehead and the pale color of his cheeks.

"You're lying," I decide.

"I'm not."

"You are. What's going on?"

His head hangs off his shoulders, and he lets out another

slow, controlled breath. "Will you help me up, please?"

"Only if you promise to tell me what's going on."

"There's nothing to tell."

"Mav—"

"After our conversation last night, I got wasted and pushed it too hard on my run. I'm dehydrated and exhausted, and I passed out. That's it."

I hesitate, a fresh wave of guilt hitting as I consider whether or not he's telling the truth. He looked like shit this morning when I ran into him in the hallway after my shower. Hurt too. And it isn't the first time he's drowned his sorrows in alcohol. I know what it's like to exercise while dehydrated and hungover.

Maybe he's telling the truth?

Sucking my lips between my teeth, I push to my feet and sigh. "You promise?"

He gulps and nods. "Yeah, Opie. Promise."

"Fine." I offer him my hand. "But you're done with your run."

"No shit." He rubs at the back of his head, winces, and checks his palm for blood. "At least I didn't split my skull open."

"This time," I argue. His weight feels like a thousand pounds as he takes my hand and I help him up. "You can't do that. You can't treat your body like shit, then be surprised when it gives out like this."

"I'll be sure to keep it in mind." He brushes his thumb along the back of my hand, lets me go, and clears his throat. "Now, if you'll excuse me, I gotta go invest in some noise-canceling headphones like you suggested." He gives me a little salute. "See ya around, Opie."

He turns and leaves.

And instead of calling him out and correcting his assumption, I let him.

"**H**ey, man," Archer greets me as he pushes my bedroom door open.

I'm lying on my mattress, staring up at the ceiling. After sending Coach a shitty excuse as to why I was missing practice, I took a long nap in hopes of resetting my body. My limbs still feel heavy, and my thoughts are foggy, proving the extra sleep didn't do shit, which is the last thing I need. I still can't believe I passed out in front of Opie. If she knew what was going on, she'd kill me herself. Lying to her didn't exactly make me feel better, either. The lies, in general, are becoming so copious I'm not sure how much more I can take.

"Why weren't you at practice?" my brother asks.

"Migraine," I lie. Really, I feel like shit all over, and my run kicked my ass, but explaining everything to Archer is more effort than it's worth.

He nods. "That sucks. Are you feeling better?"

"Sure," I mutter.

I can tell he wants to call me out on my lie, but he stops

himself. With his arms crossed, he leans against the door-jamb, his brows pulled low like he's deep in thought.

"You need something?" I prod.

"Did you see Lia talking to anyone yesterday?"

Sitting up, I swing my legs over the edge of the bed and rub at my tired eyes. "I don't know, why?"

"I think she ran into her ex."

My stomach tightens. "What makes you think so?"

"We broke up last night," he mutters.

The room spins, but I shove my dizziness aside, convinced I'm hallucinating. "What?"

"We broke up," he repeats.

"Shit." I wait for the relief, but it doesn't come.

"Yeah." A low, humorless chuckle reverberates in Archer's chest as if he doesn't believe it. "It fuckin' sucks. Don't get me wrong. We're fine," he adds. I'm not sure who he's trying to convince. "But she needs a break. Some space, I guess. Don't say anything to anyone. We agreed not making an announcement or some shit would, I dunno, make things easier."

"You're not telling anyone?" I confirm.

He shakes his head. "Nah. Maybe later, but neither of us wants to hear I told you so from the family, so we're taking a breather until shit settles a bit. Have you talked to her?"

I shake my head. "Not really. I bumped into her on my run before my migraine hit, but she didn't mention the breakup."

His head bobs. "If you see her talking to anyone, will you let me know? I want to make sure she's all right and her asshole Mystery Man doesn't fuck with her head any more than he already has."

My teeth grind, but I force my jaw to relax and pick my phone up, pretending like I give a shit about the outside world when this conversation holds more weight than my brother could ever know.

"She's a big girl," I remind him.

"I know," he mutters. "But I'm not gonna give up on her. This isn't it for us. It can't be."

I know this side of Archer. When he's determined. Stubborn. It's what got him his internship. What pushed him to get a 4.0.

I want to tell him to back off. That she's made her choice. But it isn't what I want, is it? Fuck, after passing out and the reminder of how messed up my life is right now, I don't even know anymore. Should I be selfish? Should I put her first? Should I give in and fight for her? Should I leave her with Archer? With a guy whose world isn't spinning out of control?

I don't. Fucking. Know.

"Thanks for letting me vent," Archer adds.

"No problem." Sitting my phone back in my lap, I look up at my brother. "I'm sorry."

I don't know what else to say.

He nods. "Yeah, me too. Do you need anything? Any aspirin or Advil?"

If only aspirin could fix this.

"I'm good, thanks," I reply.

"All right." He taps his knuckles against the doorjamb and disappears down the hall.

MAVERICK

The guys went to a movie. Archer went to the office. And me? I paced my room for thirty minutes, digesting Archer's revelation.

I head to the kitchen in search of a drink. As I fill a glass with water, I spot Ophelia in the backyard. Earbuds in place, she pushes the lawn mower up and down the grass. She shouldn't be. All the guys agreed to take the outside chores so none of the girls would have to lift a finger this next semester, but Lia's stubborn. When she wants something, she isn't afraid to grab onto it with both hands. Setting the half-full glass of water onto the counter, I walk outside. The sun beats down on us, and sweat collects on my brow within minutes as I stand on the patio watching Ophelia's lips mouth the lyrics to whatever song she's listening to.

She hasn't noticed me yet.

I like it this way. Seeing her in her element. Relaxed. Focused. Distracted. Since our breakup, she's been on edge with me. I don't blame her. I've been a dick, pushing her away, fighting the pull between us, making her hate me so it'll soften the sting of my absence in the long run. Or at least, that was the plan. Now? Now I don't fucking know what I'm doing anymore. Not since prom.

When she catches my presence in her periphery, her muscles tighten. She does a double take, shakes her head, and stares at the grass in front of her like I don't exist.

She's still upset with me.

For pushing her away. For my dick comment about the noise-canceling headphones. For telling her to stay with my brother when we both know I want every piece of her.

It's complicated. More complicated than she realizes, and I don't have the heart to tell her everything. To make her understand why I'm putting us through hell when I'd prefer to do the opposite. If only I could control the world around me and the future fate fucked over.

The question is, why didn't she tell me she broke up with Archer?

And why do I care when it doesn't change anything?

With a huff, she pulls her AirPods out and cuts the lawn mower off. "Is there a problem?"

"Where's your boyfriend?"

Her eyes thin. "Not sure why you think I'm your brother's keeper, but—"

"So he's still your boyfriend?" I challenge. My steps are slow but steady as I walk down the small set of stairs leading to the grass and head straight for her.

When I get close enough, she tilts her head up at me and folds her arms, standing her ground. "Is there a problem?"

"Just curious when you were going to tell me you broke up with him."

"It's none of your business."

"I told you breaking up with him was a mistake." Her chest heaves beneath her oversized T-shirt, but even the ugly-ass stained fabric does shit at covering her perfect tits. I tear my attention from what I know is hidden beneath and hold her gaze. "I told you your future is with him."

With a quiet scoff, she glances at the house behind me and gives me her full attention. "One, fuck my future."

"Lia," I growl.

"I'm serious. I'm sick of mapping everything in my life out when none of it goes according to plan anyway. If it did, we would've wound up together, and you wouldn't have broken my heart. And two, do you know what's funny? I hear it from everyone. How Archer and I are perfect together. How we belong together. And maybe we do," she adds. "But for someone so adamant about hating the future your family has pushed you into, you seem to be having a hell of a time playing the part and encouraging me to do the same."

Fuck.

I'm so stunned my tongue ties and my brows pinch.

She's right. I've hated it. From the beginning. The way everyone pushed Lia and Archer together. Like they were a match made in heaven. I never realized she felt the same pressure or how heavy a burden it must be for her until now.

"You're right," I mutter. "I'm sorry."

She glares at me, but the corners of her eyes soften a fraction. A moment later, she doubles down and lifts her chin in defiance. "You should be."

"I am," I repeat.

"Good."

Shit, she's cute when she's fired up.

My mouth quirks, defying my willpower as I mirror her stance and fold my arms. "Good."

"Stop smiling at me," she demands.

My grin widens. "What's wrong with my smile?"

"Other than it being annoyingly perfect?" she quips. "*Everything.*" She throws her arms in the air and marches toward a tree at the edge of the property in hopes of hiding in the shade from the ruthless sun beating down on us.

"What's that supposed to mean?" I call.

"It means it's another morsel."

"A morsel?"

"Yeah. A stupid morsel."

I chuckle in spite of myself and follow her toward the edge of the property. "You're gonna have to spell it out for me, Opie."

"Morsels are little things like…your smile."

"My smile?"

"Yes," she huffs. "It messes with my head and confirms my decision to break up with your brother because his smile doesn't do what your smile does. Which doesn't even make sense, by the way. You guys are identical twins. Most people can't even tell you apart, but my stupid heart? Yup. It's well aware of the difference, and it isn't fair."

I sober slightly, her distressed rambling hitting me square in the chest. I've put her through so much. Dragged her through the dirt. Held things against her when I had no right to.

I'm an ass.

Scrubbing my hand over the top of my head, I admit, "You're right. It isn't fair."

"He's a good guy, Mav. He really is. He's thoughtful and patient and understanding. Too understanding sometimes. He gave me everything I could ever want." Her eyes slice to mine. "But you? You give me butterflies. You give me what I need—er, *gave* me what I needed until you started acting like an asshole," she clarifies. "And even *I* can't understand the difference. The logic behind why I feel the way I do when, let's be honest, there isn't any logic to it in the first place."

"Ophelia…"

"But I think that's the most confusing part," she continues. "Because, even when I recognize the ludicrousness of the situation, it doesn't erase the fact I still need you, Maverick. Even when you refuse to give me all of you, the little morsels —the fucking crumbs—are still enough to make me come back for more each and every time and..." She licks her lips, her eyes turning hazy. "What does that say about me?"

"It says you're too good for me."

A breath of laughter slips out of her, but it's tainted with sadness. Still, the little crumb of amusement brings her back to me instead of keeping her lost in her thoughts as she points out, "And not good enough for your brother."

She's too good for my brother, too, but I don't tell her. Instead, I press her against the giant maple we're hiding beneath, memorizing the feel of her curves as they mold to my front. When she doesn't push me away, I grasp her waist, the last of my restraint snapping like a rubber band. My hands dip beneath the hem of her top. Her bare skin is soft and supple and warm. So fucking warm, I want to wrap her around me. Crawl under her skin the same way she's crawled under mine.

"Maverick," she whispers.

"I don't wanna talk about my brother anymore."

"Good, because neither do I." Her eyes meet mine. "I want to know how you do it."

"Do what?"

"Put your future aside and just...be."

My brows pull down, and my hand stalls on her hip. "What do you mean?"

"I mean the way you don't think about your future. How you can focus on the here and now without even considering the long-term repercussions or how they might affect you."

I close my eyes. "Trust me, Goose. I think about them more than you know."

"Then how do you fake it?" she pushes.

"I'm not faking anything. Not with you."

"Do you ever wish you could go back? To before prom? I mean, yeah. We were hiding our relationship, but it was so easy. I enjoyed the morsels you sent my way, and I didn't have to think about our family or drama or what people would think. We could just...*be*. Do you ever miss it?"

She has no clue.

My fingers make tiny indents on her hips as I squeeze her curves roughly, the proverbial carrot she dangled acting like gasoline on an open flame. "You want it again? You. Me. And nothing else? No pressure, no future, just—"

"Stolen moments and little morsels," she finishes for me. Her smile is sad as she nods. "Yeah, Mav. Even if the fallout was a bitch, I miss it. Those moments. I wouldn't give any of them back, even if it could take away the pain from the last few months. I wouldn't give them up for anything."

I dip closer, resting my forehead on her shoulder as her soft, sweet scent washes over me. "I'm sorry."

"You've already apologized," she reminds me.

"I don't know what else I can do," I whisper against her skin, nuzzling deeper into the crook of her neck while knowing exactly how much I don't deserve it. To be here. To hold her. To want her when she deserves so much more. "I'm not gonna lie and tell you I can give you everything you want, Goose. No matter how much I want to."

Her cheek brushes against the side of my head as she nods. "I know."

I drag my nose along the column of her throat, breathing her in. My movements are slow. Controlled. Giving her plenty of time to reject me. And fuck knows, I deserve it. But she doesn't. She lifts her chin and waits, her pulse thrumming against my lips.

Thump-thump. Thump-thump.

"Tell me they're enough." I lift my head and hold her gaze. "The little morsels."

"They are." Her tongue peeks out along the seam of her mouth, and she licks her bottom lip. "Enough for now."

For now.

The words hang in the air, but I push them away. Because *for now* is all I have to give. I lean closer, holding her gaze as I brush my lips against hers. Her breath hitches, and she returns the kiss. Softly. Carefully. Like she's afraid I'll leave her again.

Fuck me, Goose. I don't want to.

I close my eyes and tilt her head up, kissing her deeper as I fight for control. Of my words. My body. My future. *Our* future. Her hands find my chest. She slides them along my pecs, wraps them around my neck, and presses herself against me. I kiss her harder, claiming her mouth with mine as she melts into me, the last of her restraint evaporating. She tastes like heaven. Soft. Sweet. I groan against her lips, pushing her against the rough bark of the tree.

"Tell me no one's home," she begs.

"Everyone's gone."

"Good." She tugs at my shirt, yanking it up and finding my hot skin beneath. Her hands are on me. My chest. My stomach. They slide lower and fumble with the button of my jeans.

"Lia—"

"I want to," she murmurs as the metallic zip of my pants being undone cuts through the air. "I want to see you still need me, even if it's only for a minute."

She slides to her knees, but I shake my head and pick her up despite her protests. When her back hits the tree with a soft thump, she gasps, and I wedge myself between her thighs.

"Maverick…"

"Sh…" Lifting her chin with my knuckle, I press my forehead to hers. "Let me make something very clear to you, Ophelia. I need you more than you will ever understand, and even though I love fucking your mouth, let me give you something more."

"Mav…"

"A girl who's so quick to get on her knees for me, but you won't let me get on mine?" I challenge. My fingers find the top button of her jean shorts, and I undo it slowly. Her eyes hold mine, but she shifts her hips slightly as if the thought alone is enough to drive her crazy. I take full advantage, tugging her shorts and underwear off her ass and down her thighs until she's left bare. Kneeling in front of her, I grab her hips and kiss the outside of her thigh.

"What are you doing?" she whispers.

"I've been craving you for months. Do me a favor. Open up, and let me have a taste."

Slowly, her muscles relax, and I lift one of her legs onto my shoulder. Once she's spread wide, I dip my head between her thighs. Her skin is dappled with light as the sun cuts through the tree's branches above us, spotlighting her perfect pussy. My mouth waters. I drag my thumb along her slit, part her folds, and let my tongue follow suit.

Fuck, I missed her taste. The way she whimpers. The way she lifts her hips and shies away like she can't decide if she wants to pull me closer or push me away. I continue licking, dipping my tongue into her center and trailing it up to her clit. So hot. So wet. So needy. I glance up at her as I spread her folds with my fingers. Her eyes shine with need, watching while I eat her out like she's my last meal.

Fuck, I'd make this my last moment if I got to choose.

My cock is so hard it hurts, but her breathless moans spur me on, and I push my forefinger inside her. Her core squeezes me as I pump it back and forth, circling her clit with my tongue, her thighs quivering around me. Knowing her only leg on the ground might give out at any second, I grip her ass with my opposite hand and lift her up. She hooks her other leg over my shoulder and grabs one of the lower branches for leverage. I lap at her, kissing her entrance and clit with my lips, my tongue, my everything.

"Mav," she breathes out. "Fuck, I'm gonna—" Her words end on a gasp as she comes, squeezing my finger as I drag it in and out of her while rolling the tip of my tongue against her clit. Without giving her a chance to ride it out, I unhook her legs from my shoulders, determined to feel what it's like to be inside of her again. Once her feet are on the ground, I finger her slowly, pulling another moan from her as I stand and unbutton my pants the rest of the way with the hand not inside her. My cock aches. I pull it out and rub it from base to tip while she catches her breath.

"You have no idea how many times I've dreamed of this," I murmur.

She grabs my wrist and rolls her hips against my hand. "Ditto. You gonna fuck me now?"

I chuckle against her mouth, pulling my fingers from her center. "You still on birth control?"

"Yes."

"Turn around, Goose."

She smiles against my lips. Complying, she faces the tree with her back arched and her pussy dripping and ready for me.

Fuck, she's perfect.

I grab the base of my dick and run it along her slit, pulling another whimper from her as she peeks over her shoulder and pants, "Any day now, Mav."

"Someone's impatient."

"Just craving another little morsel."

"A *little* morsel?" I challenge.

She grins back at me. "I mean, my memory's a bit hazy, but if you feel like reminding me—" Her words die on parted lips as I shove myself inside her. Her body jerks forward from the force, but she stretches around me, squeezing me so tight it's almost hard to breathe.

"Fuck, baby," I groan.

"Love it when you call me baby."

I thrust inside her again.

"And Goose," she whispers.

I pull out, then force myself inside once more.

She gasps, adjusting to my size, adding, "And Opie."

"Gonna have to think of a new nickname," I grunt as I pick up my pace while the sound of our skin slapping echoes throughout the otherwise silent backyard.

This is stupid. And reckless. Anyone could catch us like this. With my pants around my ankles and Ophelia's tossed aside. But I don't give a shit. I want her. Today. Tomorrow. The next and the next. I want every moment she can give me until my dying breath.

Ophelia pushes into me, her back arching as she takes my cock like a good girl. Whimpering and moaning and cursing under her breath. Together, we chase our orgasms, and when I come, she squeezes me tight, pulling another groan from me as we fall over the edge together. Bending closer, I rest my forehead along her spine, my cock pulsing inside her. With my hands wrapped around her torso, we catch our breath slowly. When I slip out of her, my cum follows suit, landing on the dirt as Lia straightens and covers her face, a light laugh on the tip of her tongue.

"I can't believe we just did that."

Neither can I.

"Oh, so *that's* the little morsel you mentioned," I joke, kicking some dirt over my cum with the toe of my shoe.

She laughs even harder and turns around, wrapping her

arms around my neck. "And you say you're not the classy brother." Rising onto her tiptoes, she kisses me softly and adds, "But I feel like I should mention just because I finally like your nicknames, it doesn't mean you need to think of a new one."

"Maybe I like getting under your skin." I dip down and pick her underwear up off the ground.

As she slips her feet into the leg holes, she asks, "Why?"

"It makes it even." Pulling the flimsy material up her legs, I redress her and kiss her nose.

She smiles. "So I'm under your skin, too, huh?"

A chuckle hits the back of my throat. "You have no fucking clue. Now, go inside and shower."

"What about the grass?" she asks.

"I'll take care of it."

"I think I know how to mow a lawn."

"Which you've already proven." I motion to the half-trimmed yard. "Let me do this for you."

"You sure?"

"Yeah, I'm sure."

"Okay." She smiles, pushing her hair away from her face. "And, uh, don't tell Archer about...*this*. Especially when we've both agreed it's only morsels...or whatever. It'll only hurt him."

My chest aches, but I shove the feeling aside and dip my chin. "Secret's safe with me."

"Good. I guess I'll, uh, I'll see you around?" Her question hangs in the air, highlighting her insecurities as she waits for me to take the lead. To tell her what the plan is and how we should navigate it.

"Yeah, of course." I pull her into me and kiss her again, shoving aside the voice in my head reminding me how much this might hurt her in the long run. Because I'm selfish and greedy, and I want her. Ophelia Grace Taylor. I want her more than anything. "As long as we both agree to keep this simple and…"

"As little complicated as possible?" she offers against my lips.

With a nod, I let her go. "Yeah. I guess we're in agreement."

"Good. I'll see you around," she repeats. Her hips sway as she heads back to the house, my chest squeezing with every step.

"See you around, Opie," I murmur.

32
OPHELIA

If my Midol doesn't kick in soon, I might actually cry. I feel like I've been stabbed in the uterus. Seriously. Like someone stuck a knife above my pubic bone and twisted it with the force of a…I dunno. What's strong? A giant? Sure. I feel like a giant is sawing at my insides with a rusty machete.

After hockey practice, I caught a ride home from Morgan, one of my teammates, popped a handful of painkillers, and am now neck-deep in lukewarm water. To be fair, it started out scalding. But I forgot to bring a towel in here, and I don't have the energy to drag myself out of the bathtub, making a watery mess across the floor and into the hallway in search of one. Especially not when I feel like I'm dying.

Why do periods suck so bad?

My phone buzzes on the edge of the tub, and I stick my bottom lip out in self-pity as I shake off the water clinging to my hands and reach for it to see who's trying to get in touch with me.

ARCHER

Hey, where are you?

I reread the message, confused.

ME

I'm sorry, am I supposed to be somewhere?

ARCHER

Shit. Sorry. I guess I figured one of the guys invited you, or at the very least, you heard the commotion and would come over. There's a game night tonight, and I'm actually here for it for once. Do you want to come hang out?

Yeah, I can definitely hear the commotion. The pictures on my bathroom wall have rattled more than once, and the constant thump of the bass would drive any sane person mad. It's a good thing I'm on the other side of the duplex instead of a grumpy old ninny, or I have a feeling the cops would've been called within ten minutes of tonight's shenanigans starting. If I felt better, I'd even join in.

With a sigh, I type my response.

ME

I can't tonight. I'm sorry.

ARCHER

You sure?

ME

Yeah, I'm sure. Thanks for the invitation. It means a lot, Arch.

ARCHER

I feel like I haven't seen you in forever.

ME

It's been one week. :)

ARCHER

I know, but with everything that went down, I want to make sure you're not avoiding me.

ME

I'm most definitely not avoiding you, but I'm on my period and would rather hang out alone tonight. We'll catch up soon. I promise.

ARCHER

Fine, but I'm only giving in because I know how stubborn you can be.

ME

You know me too well. :)

ARCHER

I'm going out of town for a little while. Leaving tomorrow morning. What if I come over next week? Maybe the night before the Snappers game? I'll bring takeout, and we can watch a movie or something.

The Snappers' game. Man, I almost forgot about the scrimmage Sanderson set up in hopes of helping create more buzz for the Lady Hawks this upcoming season.

ME

Sounds fun. Let's do it. :)

ARCHER

It's a date.

My eyes widen, but another text follows almost immediately.

ARCHER

I meant in a platonic sense. My bad.

With a soft laugh, I let out a long breath of relief and reply.

ME

lol, I figured. Have fun tonight. Tell the guys hi for me.

ARCHER

Will do.

My phone buzzes again with another text, but instead of seeing Archer's name flash across the screen, I find a familiar one I haven't seen in a long time. It's a text from Mystery Man. The nickname makes me smile.

MYSTERY MAN

You're not coming?

Slipping a little further into the lukewarm water, I type my response.

ME

Why, if it isn't the infamous Mystery Man.

MYSTERY MAN

Mystery Man?

ME

I haven't changed your name in my phone since last fall.

MYSTERY MAN

Why not?

ME

I didn't think I needed to. It's not like I planned for you to message me anytime soon.

MYSTERY MAN

Not the forgiving type, huh?

ME

I mean, I did let you come inside me the last time we hooked up. If that isn't forgiving, I don't know what is.

As I press send, I laugh, imagining what his face must look like. Turned on? Embarrassed? Shocked? Entertained? The possibilities are endless, but I don't regret any of them, especially if he's at the party, surrounded by his friends who have no idea who he's texting or what the person said to garner that kind of response.

MYSTERY MAN

Fuck, Opie. Way to say it like it is.

ME

You're surprised?

MYSTERY MAN

You're right. I forgot who I was texting. Where are you?

ME

Home, why?

MYSTERY MAN

Archer said you weren't coming.

ME

I told him I wanted a night in.

MYSTERY MAN

So, you're really not coming?

I look around my bathroom, the view hitting a little differently from my position in the bath as I consider his request. He wants me to go to Game Night? Yeah, not

259

happening. I haven't even washed my hair since practice. The idea of blow-drying it, doing my makeup, and putting on anything other than sweats sounds miserable and *way* more effort than it's worth.

ME

Nope. Although, I appreciate how you sent your brother to do your dirty work and gain intel on me.

MYSTERY MAN

You should come.

ME

I can't make it.

MYSTERY MAN

Why not?

ME

1- hanging out with my ex-boyfriend/best friend AND his brother/my...whatever this is when we both agreed to keep this under wraps sounds like a bad idea all around. And 2- because I'm not feeling so hot.

MYSTERY MAN

What's wrong?

ME

Nothing's wrong.

MYSTERY MAN

Tell me.

ME

Pretty sure you're a dude, and the last time I checked, dudes don't wanna know about why I'm not feeling so hot, so...

MYSTERY MAN

Let me guess. You're on the rag. The Crimson Tide came for a visit. You're checking into the Red Roof Inn. It's shark week. Mother Nature dropped off a gift. You have a visit from Aunt Flo. A little Carrie Flarie comin' at ya, and you're taking a little ride on the Cotton Pony. Am I right?

ME

What the hell's a cotton pony?

MYSTERY MAN

No idea.

ME

Did you just Google different terms for a girl's time of the month?

MYSTERY MAN

I did, and I do not recommend it.

PS- Don't click on the images.

With a laugh, I type my response.

ME

Look on the bright side. At least I'm not pregnant after the little morsel you gave me.

MYSTERY MAN

Don't toy with me.

ME

Why? Because pregnancy freaks you out so much?

MYSTERY MAN

Nah, because you love my little morsels. ;) Can you imagine everyone's faces if I knocked you up?

> ME
>
> I hope you're joking.

> MYSTERY MAN
>
> Come on. You'd be a cute mom. Your belly all round and shit.

Keeping my phone above water, I dip my head beneath the surface and scream. Because this guy? Well, it's been a while since I've seen him—er, heard from him. But I know this Maverick all too well. And it's a little scary being privy to this side of Maverick Buchanan when it's clear he doesn't want anything more with me. The one who teases. Who's thoughtful. Who talks about the future as if he wants one. As if he thinks about it the same way I do despite our agreement to keep things…simple. It gives me hope. And if I've learned anything since prom, it's hope is a dangerous thing.

My phone buzzes in my hand, and I sit up, my head breaking the water's surface as I gasp for air and read his new message.

> MYSTERY MAN
>
> What? No response?

> ME
>
> Who are you, and what have you done with Maverick Buchanan?

> MYSTERY MAN
>
> Smartass.

> ME
>
> There's the Maverick I know.

> MYSTERY MAN
>
> Just because I'm not being a dick anymore doesn't mean I'm a different guy. I'm still me, Opie.

That's what I'm afraid of.

A loud knock echoes from the front door, and my phone buzzes in my hand with another text.

MYSTERY MAN

Answer the door.

ME

I can't. I'm in the bathtub.

I wait for another loud knock or maybe another message to make my phone buzz, but nothing happens. Only silence. Shifting in the bath, I set my cell on the edge of the tub when the bathroom door opens, revealing a sexy-as-sin Maverick in a dark, fitted T-shirt and jeans.

"What are you doing here?" I cover my boobs with my hands and tuck my feet under my ass to hide my lady bits as much as possible.

Maverick chuckles. "Pretty sure I've already seen everything you have to show me, although it's cute when you're shy."

Heat floods my cheeks, but I ignore it and rest my chin on the ledge of the tub, peeking up at him through my lashes. "Let me repeat myself. What are you doing here?"

"I'm here to take care of you."

"Take care of me?"

"Yeah."

"You don't take care of people."

He clutches at his chest. "One. Ouch. And two. You're not *people*. You're Ophelia."

Swoon.

Praying he doesn't notice I'm most definitely blushing, I tuck my chin to my chest and suck my lips between my teeth. Getting a grip on myself, I clear my throat. "How did you get into my house?"

"There's a spare key in case of emergencies."

"And this constitutes an emergency?"

Lifting his hands in defense, he says, "Hey, I don't make the rules. Here. I brought you something." He offers me the grocery bag hanging from his arm, but I don't take it.

"How did you go to the grocery store so fast?" I ask.

"I didn't. I stole Reeves' stash from under his bed."

"Reeves' *stash*?"

"The guy has a sweet tooth like nobody's business." He sets the bag on the counter and wipes his hands on his jeans, looking helpless. "What else can I do?"

"I don't...uh," I look around the bathroom, feeding off his anxiety. "I don't know? You don't have to be here, you know. You can go back to the party."

"Not gonna happen."

"Mav, I'm serious. We hooked up. It doesn't mean you need to miss out on a party and take care of me."

"I'd want to take care of you whether or not we hooked up, Opie."

"You sure about that?" I ask. "No offense, but you haven't exactly been welcoming since I moved in. You'll have to forgive me for having whiplash."

With a sigh, he squeezes the back of his neck. "I know I've been a dick. I've had some personal shit going on, and I was taking it out on you. It wasn't fair, and I'm sorry."

Nibbling my bottom lip, I nod slowly. "Dating your brother probably didn't help."

He chuckles dryly. "Yeah, not so much, but it's still no excuse."

"I guess not."

"Let me turn over a new leaf." He sits on the edge of the tub. "Be the guy I was before?"

Before.

Before prom. Before he broke my heart. Before he made

me question my sanity, along with every single interaction we'd ever had. Part of me wants to ask why. Why he ended things. Why he broke my heart. The other part? Call me a coward, but I'm not sure I want to know. Not when it doesn't do me any good. We can't go back. And with us agreeing we're okay without labels or complications, why stir the pot? Besides, it's easier not knowing. Like a barrier. One I know I need to get through if we have any hope of this turning into something more. Having it here? The barrier? It's a good reminder of the past. Of the things I can't change about Maverick Buchanan, even if I wanted to. Dealing with the truth is a problem for future Ophelia, and I'm tired of worrying about it.

"Can I get you some medicine or something?" he prods.

I hesitate, unsure whether I should be flattered or annoyed. Maverick's always been a *rub-some-dirt-in-it* kind of guy and has always left his nurturing instincts on the back burner. The fact he's here and offering to take care of me is... new. Even when we were secretly dating, he was away at college and couldn't come by at the drop of a hat. So this? Caring Maverick? I'm not sure how to handle him without going into full-blown swoon mode.

"Why are you looking at me like I have my pants down?" he asks.

"Nothing," I laugh. "It's just...this is a new look for you."

"What is?"

"You being concerned."

"You can blame Rory," he replies, mentioning his little sister. "As soon as she hit puberty, she wouldn't stop complaining about how bad periods are, so I guess I have a soft spot for girls during shark week."

"Oh, so it's nothing personal?" I quip.

His mouth lifts in the corner as he reaches for the glass of water I brought in when I took my painkillers. After emptying it in the sink, he scoops up some bath water from the tub and orders, "Lean your head back."

I tilt my chin up and wait. He pours the water on my head, careful not to get any in my eyes while wetting my roots. I should be embarrassed. My hair is gross from hockey practice, but I'm too curious about the man in front of me to care. Once he's satisfied it's wet enough, Mav squeezes some shampoo into his hands, scrubs his palms together, and digs his fingers into my hair. His touch feels incredible as he massages my scalp, turning the shampoo into a rich lather. I close my eyes and almost moan. The tingles along my skull are so good I could lie here for hours.

"Does this feel okay?" he asks.

I open one eye and quirk my brow. "What do you think?"

His lips curve up. "I think you like today's morsel."

I laugh as he dips his hands in the water and begins rinsing the suds from my hair.

"And I think you've upgraded your morsel game since this spring," I tell him.

Maverick's smile fades, and he picks up the conditioner, squeezing a dollop of lavender-scented goodness into his palm and focusing on my ends. "It's all about the little things, right?"

"Mm-hmm," I hum. "I like the little things."

His eyes fall to mine. "Me too."

I want to wrap myself up in the softness of his voice. The slight rasp. The careful brush of his fingers. The warmth in his gaze. It's comforting to see him open up to me again, even if it's only a little bit. I like the way he dotes on me. His attention to detail. His non-sexual touches and how they manage to still leave me tingling.

Once he's finished washing my hair, he finds a towel in the hallway and drapes it around my shoulders. "Here."

"Thank you," I murmur as he rubs his hands up and down my arms, drying me off.

"You're welcome. Why don't you get dressed, and I'll get a movie started."

"A movie?"

"Unless you want to do something different," he adds.

I shake my head. "A movie's fine, but…"

"What?"

"You don't have to stay or take care of me or…" My shoulder lifts. "Whatever. You already more than fulfilled your morsel quota for the day."

"I think we both know I'm an overachiever." He winks at me as he heads into the hallway. "I'll pick a few options and order some food. Are you craving anything?"

Other than you, nothing comes to mind.

"What about the party?" I ask. "They'll know you're gone."

His head pops back through the door. "Reeves is covering for me, so don't worry. We'll be fine."

"Reeves knows about us?"

Mav shakes his head. "No, but he knows how to have my back when I need him to. Now, answer the question. What do you want to eat?"

"I'm good with whatever."

"Good." He pulls his phone from his pocket and heads back down the hallway, calling out, "Supreme pizza, it is."

So he *did* remember.

Interesting.

I hide my smile beneath the edge of the towel, the stupid butterflies wreaking havoc on my insides. I head to the toilet, grabbing a tampon from the counter.

Yup. It's official. Maverick Buchanan might be the death of me.

Then again, I think I already knew he would be.

But what a way to go.

33
OPHELIA

"**P**ractice ended an hour ago," Maverick calls.

"And yours doesn't start for another two," I reply, gripping the back of the net and lowering myself into a dip then extending my arms. My triceps burn, but it's my second to last set, and I want to make them count, which would be a heck of a lot easier if Maverick wasn't watching me from the bench.

Closing my eyes, I finish my reps, counting in my head.

Eighteen. Nineteen. Twenty.

With a deep breath, I stand and shake out my arms.

"Damn, Opie. You never quit."

"I'm almost done. One more set of dips, a set of lateral hops, and I'll probably call it a day."

"Probably?" he questions.

"Depends."

"On what?"

"On whether or not you're still bugging me." I give him a cheeky grin and rest my gloved hands on my hips. I ditched the mask an hour ago, along with the majority of my pads. Now I'm in a slim black jacket, my gloves, some leggings, and my skates, yet I still feel warm. "Why are you here, anyway?"

"Wanted to take you home."

"Only to turn back around so you can practice with your team?"

He tucks his hands in the pockets of his athletic joggers and shrugs. "I was thinking of skipping so we could hang out."

My eyes widen. "You want to skip practice? Mister eat, sleep, and breathe hockey?"

He chuckles dryly and squeezes the back of his neck, looking boyish and way too tempting for my own good if I have any hope of finishing my workout.

"Maybe I found a better way to spend my time," he murmurs.

"And what's that?"

With a smirk, he steps further onto the ice. "By appreciating how hot you look right now."

"Smooth, Mav. Real smooth," I note, starting another set of dips on the bar. My triceps are screaming before I even reach my tenth rep while Maverick watches from the center line with folded arms. Once I'm panting, he questions, "Are you pushing yourself too hard?"

"Always," I reply. "Now stop distracting me. I wanna keep my heart rate up and finish strong."

"I can think of a few ways to keep your heart rate up." He glides toward me, his skates half-laced. The same devilish smirk is still firmly in place and cranks up the heat with every slice of his blades through the slush.

When he reaches me, I grab onto the edge of his fleece jacket, toying with the material while fighting the ever-present pull between us. But it's weird. How much his presence affects me. Makes me want to wrap myself up in him. Delve under his skin and stay there forever.

"So that's why you're here," I note. "Hoping to get lucky on the ice, Maverick?"

He lifts one of his shoulders. "I could use a bit of luck."

"Oh, you could?" I cock my brow. "Where were you this morning, anyway?"

"You came looking for me?"

"Maybe."

"Well, here I am, Opie. How can I be of service?"

"Not gonna tell me, huh?"

His eyes dip to the ice. "I had an appointment, but I like the idea of you looking for me."

"I'm sure you do."

"Now, how can I be of service?" he repeats.

"For starters, you can head back to the bench so I can finish my workout."

"Or…" He holds onto my hips and starts spinning us around on the ice. It's slow and leisurely. Comfortable. And it makes me want to lean into him.

"Or what?" I push.

"Or you can let me give you another little morsel to tide me over until after practice."

"To tide you over?" I laugh. "What about me?"

"Been missing your taste for months."

"You tasted me last weekend," I remind him. "And six more times since. And let's not forget last night when you snuck into my room. Pretty sure when my parents gave you guys a spare key, they didn't think you would use it to hook up with their oldest child."

"I won't tell if you won't." He guides me toward the penalty box, skating backward while keeping his hands planted on my waist. "And if we're gonna be technical, I tasted your *mouth* last night." He nips at my bottom lip. "Now I wanna taste this." His hands slowly lower, cupping my sex and making my lips part.

"You're joking, right?" I glance at the tunnel, but we're still blissfully alone as he opens the penalty box and guides me inside.

"I never joke about oral, Goose." He boops my nose with his finger and closes the glass behind us.

"Practice just ended," I remind him. "I'm all gross."

"Trust me, Ophelia. You're perfect."

"And you're horny." I push against his chest to keep a few inches of distance between us, but he simply swats my hand away and continues his pursuit.

"Let me taste you," he begs.

My mind is dizzy with exhaustion and curiosity and lust. The combination makes it almost impossible to think straight, especially when his hands and mouth are on me, tasting the column of my throat.

"And what happens if I say yes?" I whisper.

"I go down on you right here."

"And then?"

"Then, we pick up takeout, go back to your place, and watch a movie."

"So, no practice?" I question.

He nips at my bottom lip. "Why are we still talking?"

"Because you're deflecting."

"You'd seriously rather I go to practice than ditch and hang out at your place?"

"I'd rather you not get in trouble with Sanderson all because you want to get laid."

"Hockey isn't everything."

With a laugh, I ask, "Since when?"

He tugs me toward him. "Since you gave me another chance."

"Well, I'm pretty sure I'm not making you choose between me and hockey, so why don't you pick up some food after practice, and I'll be waiting at my place—naked—when you finish. And if you're still feeling needy, we can watch a movie and snuggle afterward."

Looking thoughtful, he notes, "I *am* a sucker for snuggling."

"I may have pieced that together over the past couple of weeks," I reply, remembering how many times he's snuck out of his place only to slip into my bed to hold me.

His mouth lifts. "Fine. But only if you let me make you come right here, right now." His fingers toy with the edge of my pants and dip inside. He slides even lower, playing with my entrance.

"That's"—I gasp as he finds my entrance—"kind of you."

What am I doing?

Oh, right. I'm appreciating the morsels Maverick's been delivering in spades ever since the backyard incident by letting him eat me out in LAU's arena.

He drags his lips along my neck, pausing beneath my ear. Then he presses his forehead to mine and groans. "You're fucking soaked."

"Should I apologize?" I ask.

"No," he grunts. Sliding to his knees, he shoves my pants down to my ankles. The majority of the board blocks most of my lower half from the tunnel, but even so, this is dangerous. Really dangerous.

"What about the cameras?" I ask.

"Already turned them off."

"How—"

"Will you shut up and let me eat you out?" His tone is laced with humor, pulling an exasperated laugh from me as I shake my head back and forth.

Why does he have to look so good right now? On his knees? His eyes gleaming with want. It makes me want to give in. To ride his mouth right here. Right now. Damn the consequences. And yeah, there are quite a few of them. Someone could walk in. Someone could see us.

"Mav—"

"Hold on."

"To what?"

He spreads my legs wide and dips his head even lower. I scramble for the edge of the penalty box, using the ledge of the barrier to keep from falling on my ass and preparing myself for the best fucking morsel imaginable. Because it's what Mav does. He teases me. Toys with me. Plays with me. Turns me into nothing but a puddle of want and need until he fulfills every single desire and blows all of my expectations out of the water. And even though it's stupid—really freaking stupid—I can't help but play along. Waiting. Anticipating. Craving. Whatever crumb he's offering at any given moment. Even when it's a terrible idea.

His hot breath kisses my pussy as his hand continues to draw circles around my entrance, spreading my wetness to my clit and making me want to crumble.

"Do you know how good you smell?" he asks, looking up at me while keeping his mouth an inch from my core. "How much my mouth is watering? How much I've missed this? Missed you?"

I tangle my fingers along the back of his head and tug him closer, my desperation making me reckless. "I think it's time you put your money where your mouth is, don't you?"

With a grin, he latches onto my core, the heat from his mouth causing my jaw to drop as he uses the flat of his tongue against my slit. Lapping at me, he spreads my folds with one hand and slips his fingers into me, pumping them in and out while his tongue finds my clit. He uses the tip to flick it softly, and my back arches. Sweat clings to my heated skin beneath my clothes, and I look at the tunnel again, confirming we're alone as he eats me out like I'm a feast curated only for him.

"Oh," I moan.

He groans, spreading me even wider. My thighs tremble beneath his touch as he kisses my center, dipping his tongue into me and sucking on my lips, then turning his attention back to my aching clit. He runs his teeth along the sensitive bud while his fingers play with me again like I'm his own personal toy. This time, he adds a second finger, stretching me.

This is so wrong. So dirty. Anyone could walk in. Anyone. And they'd see me with my pants around my ankles and my ex-boyfriend's brother's head between my thighs.

My hips shift against Maverick's mouth as I shake my head back and forth with my back pressed against the glass.

I'm close.

So fucking close.

My breathing turns shallow, and his kissing grows deeper as he tongues my slit and latches onto my clit one more time. Stars appear behind my eyelids, and I gasp, coming on his mouth and holding him against me until I'm pretty sure I'm smothering him, but I don't care. Not right now. Not when I'm coming apart like this.

Warmth spreads from my core and out to my limbs, leaving me limp and satiated. Little ripples of pleasure continue pulsing as he keeps licking at my juices, tasting me, eating me. I push him away when the sensations are too much against my sensitive clit. With one final kiss against my pubic bone, Maverick stands and situates my clothes until I'm covered.

He kisses me greedily. "Do you taste it?" he asks. "How fucking sweet you are?"

I open my eyes, taking in the flecks of navy surrounding his dark pupils.

"Best fucking morsel I'll ever have." He pecks at my lips again. "That's a promise. Now. Let's get going."

He moves toward the exit, but I grab the hem of his sleeve and tug him back to me. "Only if you promise not to change your mind about skipping practice once we get home."

"Home, huh?"

I roll my eyes. "You know what I mean."

"Fine. I'll drop you off and come back for practice. Happy now?"

"Mm-hmm," I hum. "And when you're finished, I'll be waiting for you in my bed. Naked."

"And dinner?" he questions.

"I thought you just ate?"

He chuckles as his hand finds the back of my neck, and he pulls me into him, kissing me roughly. "I'll pick up tacos."

Smiling against his lips, I whisper, "Deal."

34
OPHELIA

Dragging my fingertips along Maverick's bare chest, I trace the dark ink and snuggle closer to him on the couch in the family room. My friends will kill me when they find out I've been using the community sofa for sex, but we had a blanket down, and it's not like we were planning to screw each other's brains out. We'd been watching a murder documentary. That has to count for something, right?

Yeah, they're definitely gonna kill me, but that's a future Ophelia problem.

The entire left side of his torso looks like a black and tan page stolen from those iSpy books my mom used to read with me. There's so much to look at I could spend days studying the damn thing and *still* find something new hidden in the swirling ink. Gotta give the guy credit. They look awesome.

"So when did you get these?" I ask.

His abs flex as he lifts his head from the armrest, watching me trace his tattoos. "After prom."

"Duh." There's a tiny hawk the size of a quarter by his

sternum, and I trace it softly. "I think I'd remember if you had them before you blasted my heart to smithereens."

"Never gonna let me live it down, huh?" he grumbles.

"Not a chance."

A breath of laughter hits the top of my head, and he squeezes his arm around me. "I was going through some shit and decided scratching ink into my skin was a good distraction."

"A good distraction from what?" I ask.

"Life." He lifts his head from the armrest again, kisses my hairline, and settles back into the cushions as I stay sprawled beside him. Honestly, I'm surprised we fit, but I've never been more comfortable.

We've been doing this a lot lately. Screwing each other's brains out and snuggling in my house, talking about everything and nothing at all. There's only so much a secret couple can do, but I'm not going to lie. I love it. If I didn't know any better, I'd say Maverick and I have fallen right back into our old habits, playing boyfriend and girlfriend in every way without the title or the spotlight.

It should feel weird or like we're taking a step back in our relationship, but instead, it feels like visiting a favorite destination. I'm not dumb enough to think I can stay here forever, not when he hasn't made me any promises. But who doesn't want a chance to revisit their favorite place? To soak up every moment while you can until reality calls you back home and you only have the memories to keep you warm at night.

Oof. That just took a turn.

I clear my throat and examine a delicate skull I hadn't noticed until now. "So, what do they mean?"

"Some mean nothing. I just thought they looked good."

"And the others?" My fingers pause on an itty-bitty

silhouette of a bird hidden between a hockey stick, a rose, and Maverick's jersey number.

He stays quiet while I study the hidden pieces making up Maverick Buchanan in all his messy glory.

"Seriously, the detail is insane," I add. Sitting up, I throw my leg over his lap and straddle him, letting my curls fall around us in a curtain of strawberry blonde. He threads his fingers through the locks and pushes them over one shoulder, tugging softly on the ends as he stares up at me.

"I was right." I tap my finger against the bird silhouette. "This is a goose."

He doesn't even bother looking at which tattoo I'm referring to. "Is it?"

"Uh, yup. It most definitely is." My cheeks pinch as I grin down at him, squinting at the dark smudge over his heart. Yeah, it's definitely a goose.

No. Freaking. Way.

"That's weird," he replies.

Tearing my attention from the tattoo to his eyes, I quirk my brow. "Weird? Or adorable?"

"I think *you're* adorable."

"And I think you got a tattoo to remind you of me."

"Maybe it's a coincidence."

"Mm-hmm," I hum, unconvinced. "Or maybe you like me."

"You know I like you." His thumb skates across my jaw, and I swear it has a direct line to my libido.

I tilt my head and bite on the pad of his thumb, pulling a smirk from him.

"Okay, maybe you like me more than you like to let on," I clarify.

His mirth is contagious as his hands find my waist, and he squeezes me. "I guess we'll never know."

"Mm-hmm," I repeat, my eyes narrowing. "I have a hunch

we'll find out this weekend when you can't sneak into my house and realize how much you miss me."

"What's this weekend?"

With a look telling him he's crazy, I answer, "Uh, the scrimmage against the Snappers. Ring a bell?"

His head falls back on the armrest. "Shit, I forgot about it."

My eyes bug out. "You *forgot* about it?"

"I've been a little preoccupied." He lets my waist go and squeezes my thigh instead.

"Too preoccupied to remember the first practice game of the season?"

"Apparently," he mutters under his breath as his fingertips dance along the outside of my bare thighs.

"Did you also forget you aren't allowed to sneak into my place afterward because my little sister's staying with me?"

"*That,* I remembered," he grunts and doesn't look very happy about it.

With a laugh, I reply, "Glad to see you have your priorities straight."

"I'm not so sure," he mumbles. "You still good with us not telling anyone about this?"

"I don't know how we can. Not without pouring gasoline on—"

A loud knock sounds from the front door a few feet away, and my brows pull.

Mav tugs my very naked body onto his chest and dips lower into the cushions, hiding us from the front door's side windows and whoever's outside.

"Who's at the door?" Mav asks.

"No idea."

"You don't know?"

My phone dings on the coffee table, and I reach over,

picking it up while making sure I'm still hidden from the front window.

ARCHER

Hey, I brought takeout. Come answer your door.

"Shit," I whisper.

"What is it?" Maverick's head dips to one side, trying to see who messaged me, but I slide off his lap and fall to the ground.

My ass lands on the floral rug with a thud, and I rub at the tender spot while keeping my voice quiet. "I made plans with Archer a week ago and totally forgot." I look at the front door as another loud knock reverberates through the house, and I shove my hair away from my face. "He's here."

Maverick blanches. "Shit."

"Exactly."

"Lia?" A voice calls through the door. "Lia, are you in there?"

I grab Maverick's discarded shirt and boxers from the ground and throw them at him, searching for my own clothing, but they're missing.

"Where are my clothes?" I seethe.

He shrugs, looking down the hallway while sliding his boxers on. "I don't know? We started in the kitchen."

"Shit." Yup. If memory serves me right, my shirt is on the counter next to the microwave, and my bottoms are on the floor in front of the fridge.

"Take my shirt." He slips it over my head, causing my mess of curls to pop out on the other side. Once I'm halfway decent, I crouch low and point toward my bedroom. "Hide in there."

"He'll see," Maverick grits out.

I look at the front door and the thin window panes, giving a perfect view of the hallway leading to my bedroom.

Dammit!

"What do we do?" I ask helplessly.

He looks toward the ceiling like he's silently cursing what decisions got him here, crawls into the coat closet, and shuts the door behind him, locking himself inside.

"Lia, it's me!" Archer calls. "I can hear you in there. You okay?"

"Just a second!" I run my fingers through my messy hair, confirm I can't see Maverick through the skinny slats in the closet door, square my shoulders, and unlock the front lock.

Archer stands on my porch dressed in his usual work clothes. The top button on his white shirt is left undone, and his sleeves are rolled up to his elbows as he cradles a brown bag in his arms, looking every bit the sexy businessman he's grown to be.

With the scent of curry and warm spices wafting through the air, he gives me a concerned look. "Hey. Everything all right?"

My fingers throttle the edge of the door as I force myself not to look at the closet door to my left. "Uh, hi. And, yes, I'm good. Sorry, I was napping on the couch, and it took me a second to realize I wasn't in a dream."

"No worries. You look…" His eyes slide up and down my body, hesitating on my bare thighs for the briefest of seconds, and find my face again.

"Like I was ready for a night in?" I offer, tugging at the hem of Maverick's shirt in hopes of adding three inches to the dark fabric. It's from his great uncle's band, Broken Vows. All of us have plenty of apparel with the band logo, but even then, it's like ten sizes too big, so I blurt out, "It's my dad's shirt."

"Figured." Archer chuckles. "You look good in it."

"Why, thank you." I give a little curtsy in hopes of disguising my nerves, though I doubt it works. "How was your presentation?"

"Good. Really good. I think they'll want to hire me full-time after graduation."

"That's great, Arch!" I wrap my arms around his neck and hug him, feeling his free hand splayed against my lower back.

Does he always touch me this low, or am I being sensitive because a certain brother may or may not be watching?

I shake off the thought and let Archer go, shifting back a few extra inches hoping to create more space. If Archer notices, he doesn't comment.

"Thanks." He gives me a boyish grin and lifts the brown bag, waving it back and forth. "You didn't answer your text when I asked what you wanted me to pick up, so I grabbed Indian food. I hope it's okay?"

"Oh." I nod, peeking at my closet door and the tiny slats hiding Maverick from view. I have no doubt he's looking directly at me.

"Did you forget I was coming over tonight?" Archer asks, sensing my hesitation.

I turn back to him and fold my arms, rushing out, "No, no, no." I pause when he tilts his head in a silent challenge. "Okay, yes, I forgot," I concede. "But I'm not mad you're here. My brain's taking a second to catch up with everything since I just woke up."

His frown deepens. "You sure?"

"Yeah. Totally." I dig my teeth into the inside of my cheek and tuck my hair behind my ear, unsure if I should ask if he wants to come inside or if I should pretend I'm sick so I can get out of this as soon as possible. When the thought crosses my mind, the muscles in my stomach knot. This is Archer. My Archer. He's my best friend, and I haven't seen him in so long. Between his internship, hockey practice, and me sneaking around with Maverick, we've been busy.

"I've missed you," I admit, and honestly? It's the first truth I've said since he showed up on my porch.

"I've missed you too, Lia." Archer's voice is like a caress and warms my insides, settling my anxiety with a simple lift of his lips. "I guess I'm trying to figure out how to wade through all of this since the...break."

"Yeah, me too," I murmur.

Resting his shoulder against the doorjamb, he prods, "How've you been?"

"Good. Really good," I clarify. "Uh, busy, obviously. But... I've missed you," I repeat.

His smile widens. "Do you mind if I come inside?"

"Uh," I look down at Maverick's shirt swallowing my body and grimace. "What if I get dressed and meet you at your place?"

He rocks back on his heels. "Yeah, sure. Whatever you want."

"Okay. I'll, uh, I'll see you in a few," I promise.

"See you." He steps forward and kisses my cheek, pulling away with a sweet smile while backing up. His long legs eat up the eight feet of distance between our doors, and he steps inside, leaving the porch empty, but it doesn't do anything to calm my racing heart.

Once he's gone, I close my door and lean my back against it, letting out a long, slow breath.

The closet door opens with a quiet squeak, where I find Maverick watching me. "So, this is it for us tonight," he mutters.

"I'm sorry. I forgot."

"Don't worry about it." He moves closer, crowding me against the front door, bending down and brushing his lips against the opposite cheek his brother had. And it's fascinating. How similar their movements can feel sometimes, and how wildly different my body reacts. His breath is warm as it hits my cheek, and I lean into the innocent kiss, forcing him to hold it longer than he planned. When he pulls away, he doesn't look amused. He looks...torn.

Looping my fingers in the edge of his jeans, I keep him close and whisper, "What'd I do wrong?"

His eyes fall to my lips. "Nothing."

"Then why do I feel like I did?"

He stays quiet, his gaze bouncing around my face as if committing it to memory. "Sometimes I forget I'm not the only guy who sees how perfect you are." He kisses my forehead. "But it isn't a bad thing. Promise."

My fingers fall from his jeans as he steps back and runs his hand along the top of his head. "I'm gonna sneak out the back. I'll see you later."

I nod. "Okay."

As he turns around, heading through my house, I call out, "Wait. You forgot your shirt."

I reach for the hem as he faces me again and shakes his head.

"It's not mine. It's your dad's, remember?" He smiles, but it doesn't reach his eyes as he turns and walks away.

35

MAVERICK

The doctor clicks a few buttons on his computer as he checks the data from my last appointment and compares it to the results from today. His white, bushy eyebrows are bunched behind his glasses as he leans closer to the screen.

I should be used to this. Being poked and prodded. Having my blood drawn and feeling like a lab rat while my doctor looks over the latest test results.

He was out of town last week. It felt like a vacation for both of us, though I'm not sure it's a good thing. The lapse between visits was almost long enough to make me forget my reality. Allowing me to believe I was normal. The past few months were nothing but a nightmare, and my days with Ophelia are my sweet, sweet future.

"Any new symptoms?" he asks without bothering to look at me.

I shake my head. "Nothing more than the usual. Dizzy spells. Shortness of breath. My memories are foggy sometimes."

He nods. "Those are to be expected. Have you told your family yet?"

I wipe my palms against my thighs and shift slightly on the crinkly paper beneath my ass. "Not yet."

His eyes shift from the screen to me. "Mav—"

"I know."

"Your dad still believes this is physical therapy?" he prods.

I nod. After passing out on the ice last season, I came in for some tests, but since I'm over eighteen, my parents can't access my medical records. However, they do receive the monthly bill from Dr. Scott's office. I knew this would be the case, so I lied before my father even had a chance to question it, telling him I was coming to physical therapy for my knee. And because I've never lied to him, he bought it.

Dr. Scott turns the computer screen off, giving me his full attention and steepling his fingers in front of him. "And you're still playing hockey, I assume?"

I nod. "Yeah."

"I heard about the game this evening."

"Uh, yeah," I repeat. "It should be a good one."

Slipping his glasses off, he sets them on the small desk tucked in the corner of the office and faces me again. "Maverick, there's a fine line between using exercise to stay healthy and pushing yourself too hard."

"I'm aware."

"Hmmph," he grunts under his breath as if he isn't convinced.

"Just say it, Doc."

He sighs. "It's time, Maverick. I know you've been holding off on this for as long as possible, but the pressure playing hockey puts your body through is... Well, it isn't sustainable."

"I'll keep that in mind," I mutter.

"It isn't enough—"

"This isn't your decision," I remind him. "You aren't affiliated with LAU, and thanks to HIPAA laws, this is between you and me, and *only* you and me unless I decide otherwise."

He bites his tongue, his frustration palpable. We've had this conversation a hundred times since my diagnosis, but he still manages to bring it up each time I come in for an appointment. I get it. He's a doctor for a reason. He wants to help people, and I'm making his job especially difficult. I feel for the guy, but this is my life. *Mine.* He doesn't have to understand my decisions. However, he does need to accept them.

"What happens when the team physician decides to perform another physical, Maverick?" Dr. Scott pushes. "Your condition didn't show up on the results from your prior years because they didn't know what to look for, but after today's test…" He shakes his head. "They will find this, Maverick. Honestly, it's a miracle they haven't already."

Staring blankly in front of me, I run my tongue along the top of my teeth. "Like I said, I'll keep it in mind."

He nods. "Fine." Turning back to his desk, he grabs his glasses and stands, offering me his hand. "I'll have the nurse call in your new prescription."

"Thanks, Doc." I shake his hand.

"Be careful." He tugs me closer, leveling me with his stare. "I'm serious."

I let his hand go and give him a mock salute. "Will do."

3 6

OPHELIA

I stayed at Archer's until almost two in the morning. It was fun. Catching up and making plans. He also made me promise to let him drive me home after today's game, but I'm not complaining. It's not like I can catch a ride with Maverick or anything, not when all our families will be here.

Today is going to be interesting. Finley's coming into town, along with everyone else. Well, everyone except Dylan because she has an eye appointment. *Lame.* To be fair, she was bummed too. She wanted to be here to support the boys' first game, even if it isn't an official one. The girl loves hockey as much as I do, but thanks to a puck to the head when she was little, she doesn't play anymore, and if she puts her appointment off, she'll wind up with a few nasty migraines. No one wants that.

She'll be here soon, though, and I'm excited to see Finley. I've missed her more than she knows. The guys left for the game an hour ago, but I decided to stay at my place so Finley and I could drive over together. As I flip through the upcoming class schedule I already memorized, a loud knock echoes from the front door.

Practically skipping to it, I yank the door open and gush, "You're here!"

"You really think I'd miss my brother's first game?" Finley pulls me into a quick hug. "*And* I get a chance to hit on Griffin and make him uncomfortable, so win-win."

When she lets me go, I challenge, "And what does your boyfriend think about you hitting on someone who isn't him?"

She waves me off. "Dude. Drew has nothing to worry about. And Griffin is...Griffin. He's fun to tease, but only because it pisses Everett off. Can you imagine anything actually happening between us?" She snorts. "Yeah, not likely." Her brows dip as her gray-blue eyes trail down my body. "Wait. Is this what you're wearing?"

I look down at my black and red LAU T-shirt with a hawk along the front and shrug. "Something wrong with it?"

"Where's Archer's number?" She grabs my arm, spinning me around. "Yup. Just what I thought. Nowhere."

"So?"

"So, he might not be your boyfriend anymore—which everyone is still in the dark about, by the way, so you're welcome—but he's still your best friend. Who else are you going to support out there?"

I open my mouth to answer and close it just as quickly. It's not like I can say Maverick. But guys can get weird about jerseys, especially when Maverick made me promise I'd only wear his number before he broke up with me on prom night. He might not even remember asking me to make the promise, but still. The idea of wearing Archer's feels like a betrayal.

But is it?

Honestly, I have no idea.

"Exactly," Finley smirks as if my silence proves her point.

"It's a good thing I came prepared. Come on." Grabbing my arm, she tugs me inside my place and heads straight for the bathroom with her massive purse dangling from her shoulder. She gets right to work.

～

THE ARENA IS PACKED. I SHOULDN'T BE SURPRISED. LAU's hockey team is practically royalty at this point. It's been this way since forever, even before my father and his friends were on the roster.

Everyone's here to show their support. My parents. My younger sister, Tatum. The twins' parents, Henry and Mia. Not to mention Uncle Colt and Aunt Ashlyn. They're here to cheer for Griffin and check on Jaxon. Oh, and let's not forget Uncle Mack and Aunt Kate who are here to support Everett. Yup. The place is packed. It would've been a full house no matter what, but as soon as a few reporters announced the possible appearance of my dad and his friends to support their kids at today's game, the tickets sold out almost immediately. My familial alumni even received a standing ovation after the national anthem was performed.

And their wives wonder why they have such big heads.

With a deep breath, I attempt to stop my knee from bouncing and smooth out the wrinkles in my jersey. Well, *technically*, it's mine, but the number scrawled across the front and back in red and black ink belongs to Archer. His name is plastered along my shoulder blades, and his number adorns my cheek, thanks to Finley's face-painting skills. When my mom saw her handiwork, she full-on applauded. Not because she doesn't support my relationship with Archer, but because she's a sucker for an excellent face-paint job and, apparently, Finley's handiwork earned her stamp of approval. It feels all kinds of weird, though. They don't know

I broke up with Archer. I almost forgot I hadn't told my mom. I haven't told anyone. Archer wanted to wait a little while, hoping if we could prove nothing really changed, we'd save ourselves from hearing I told you so from everyone.

But that was before I started hooking up with Maverick again.

Now it just feels...wrong.

I need to have a chat with Archer about it. And soon.

However, if I wanted to prove I don't belong to Maverick Buchanan, I'm pretty sure the face paint and jersey are doing a bang-up job.

Wearing Archer's number when both Buchanan twins are on the ice makes me feel like I'm betraying Maverick some-how, even when he knows I'm still close with his brother. So it's fine.

Right?

"Come on," Mom prods from beside me. "Stand up so you can see the ice. You, too, Tatum."

My little sister's nose is buried in a book. It's the unabridged version of *The Count of Monte Cristo* and is girthy as shit. The pages are weathered and frayed along the edges, proving she's read it at least a dozen times. I'm not surprised. She's always been a sucker for reading, and I doubt she'll tear her eyes from that monster until she's finished, especially since our parents are forcing her to spend the night with me. They're hoping I can convince her to apply to LAU next year instead of putting all her eggs in one basket that starts with an H and ends with an arvard, which is funny when you consider how stubborn my sister is. No one can convince her to do something she doesn't want to. No. One. So I'm not sure why my parents think I'll be able to.

It doesn't really matter.

She'll hang out with me and the boys, go to bed, read in her room all day, maybe eat a granola bar or two, and unknowingly cock block me for forty-eight hours until our Uncle Colt takes her home once he's moved all of Dylan's things in this weekend. But, hey. Whatever floats her boat.

Besides, I have more important things to focus on. Like how I'm supposed to enjoy today's hockey game when I feel like I might puke if Maverick sees me wearing Archer's number.

My mom's right. I can't see anything in this position. Everyone in front of me is on their feet, blocking my view as the Hawks take the ice. But it means Maverick's view of me is blocked, too, and I'm not against keeping it this way. I feel guilty about last night. About hiding him in my closet like he's my dirty little secret. Like I wasn't proud to claim him, which is ridiculous. He's the one unwilling to claim me. If only things weren't so convoluted, maybe—

"Lia," Mom snaps.

My legs shake as I force myself to my feet. Yup. There they are. Ten feet away. Of course, my family has seats two rows up from behind the glass, making the team nearly impossible to miss.

Finley bumps her shoulder with mine and murmurs, "Dude, your boy looks fine in his gear."

"Yeah," I breathe out, my gaze following Maverick as he takes the ice.

"Oo, he's looking at you," she adds.

I tear my attention from Maverick to Archer, who's grinning from ear to ear. He motions to his jersey, gives my own a pointed look, and bounces his eyebrows up and down. With a laugh, I mouth, "Good luck!"

"Thanks!" he mouths back at me.

My attention slides to Maverick beside him. Again. Because I can't help myself even when I'm trying to appear unaffected by the bastard. He's watching me, his expression unreadable as he makes his way to the bench and sits down.

That's a lie.

I know exactly what he's thinking. What he's feeling.

Disgusted.

Annoyed.

Betrayed.

Archer follows my stare, smiling at his brother beside him on the bench and nudging him with his elbow. Maverick barely budges. A moment later, he shoots to his feet and stands next to his coach, giving me his back. Within minutes, the game starts, and he charges onto the ice. It doesn't take long until he's shoving the Snappers' center into the boards. A ref guides him to the penalty box. But he doesn't look over at me. Not once. He shouldn't. I know it. But I want him to. If only so I can have a glimpse as to what he's thinking and why he looks like he wants to rip the world apart all because of a stupid number painted on my cheek. Or maybe I'm being ridiculous. Maybe something else pissed him off. Something having nothing to do with me.

It's possible. Honestly, it's more than likely.

Feeling confident with my conclusion, I cup my hands over my mouth and cheer for the Hawks as Griffin passes the puck between a Snappers' defender's legs. Everett catches it near the goalie and slips it into the bottom left corner, scoring the game's first goal.

Finley and her parents go wild, and so do the rest of us.

Another few minutes pass, and both Maverick and Archer are on the ice, cornering the Snappers' center again. The center dodges Maverick, but Archer slams into him in an instant, knocking the guy on his ass as the Snapper's left wing steals the puck from between Maverick's skates.

Shit. That's not good.

Maverick darts toward him, but he's slow. Winded almost, despite it being the first period of the game. When the left wing chips it off the board, Archer checks the right wing into the glass. The crowd loses their mind from the brutal hit, screaming at the top of their lungs as Archer steals the puck and passes it to Griffin, who scores seconds later. Archer finds me through the glass and points at me.

"That was for you!" he mouths with a grin.

I laugh and roll my eyes when another body slams into his from behind. Archer's neck snaps forward, but all I see is a flash of red and black scuffling next to the glass. Which makes no sense because the Snappers' colors are green and blue.

"What the hell?" Mom mutters under her breath.

My grimace deepens as I notice the attacker's jersey number.

It's Maverick.

His gloves are on the ice, and his fists fly into Archer's stomach and skate across his jaw. Catching on to what the hell's happening, Archer blocks the next punch, throwing a few of his own while the referees attempt to break the chaos apart. Maverick rips his jersey out of Archer's grasp and throws another punch at his own flesh and blood.

In an instant, Henry charges down the arena stairs and is on LAU's bench in the blink of an eye. With his hands cupping his mouth, he yells at the boys, but I can't hear what's said. I can only see the frustration and embarrassment etched into Henry's features. It's too loud in here. Too chaotic.

His boys look just like him. Tall. Broad chests. Brown, wavy hair. Sharp jaws. Ruthless expressions. The referee blows his whistle one more time, finally ripping the brothers apart. They're escorted to the locker room as the rest of their team watches in shock. And the silence that follows? It chills me to my core. Because I have a feeling it's all my fault.

37

MAVERICK

"**W**hat the fuck was that?" my dad spits as soon as we enter the locker room.

I take my helmet off and chuck it against the lockers, but it doesn't erase the fire in my veins. After last night, then this morning, I'm...I'm fucked. I shouldn't have gone to my appointment before the game. The results messed with my head, confirming my fears for the thousandth time and stealing what little hope I managed to collect since the previous appointment. I was already wound up. Already drowning. Then I saw her. Ophelia. Saw the way she smiled at Archer. The way she looked in his jersey. The way my brother fucking lit up when he realized it was his number painted on her cheeks. His last name on her back. And what did he say to me when he saw her?

"Damn, she looks good with my name on her, doesn't she? Calling it now, brother. I'm gonna marry that girl."

It killed me. But what's worse is how I responded by doing the exact opposite of what I should have.

It's fucked-up. I know it is. I shouldn't have hit him. I

shouldn't have hidden in my room while Ophelia hung out with my brother all night. I shouldn't care that she's wearing his jersey, wishing it was mine instead.

I shouldn't have done a lot of things.

But the real problem is I wouldn't have if it wasn't to protect her in the long run. I care about her more than I should and more than I want to. And if a relationship isn't in the cards for us, why do I fucking care if she smiles at Archer? Why do I care if she's wearing his jersey? Why do I care if he's experienced her optimism and her lips? Why do I care if he loves her and she loves him, even if it's only platonic?

I hit the locker again, this time with my fist, and my knuckles scream in protest as my chest heaves.

Why do I fucking care?

"Calm the hell down, Maverick," my dad orders.

Archer's quiet. He's sitting on the bench with his head in his hands, preparing for the inevitable lecture we both know is coming.

"Are you twelve? Ten? Five?" my dad continues. "What is wrong with you two?"

Archer drops his hands to his lap and pins me with a glare as I pace the locker room. "Ask Maverick. He's the one who attacked me."

Folding his arms, my dad turns to me and waits.

A million reasons rise to the surface, but I press my lips together, knowing none of them are enough.

"I fucked up," I mutter.

"No shit," Archer starts, but our dad lifts his hand, silencing him.

"Why'd you hit your brother?" he demands.

I scrub my hand over my face, my teeth gnashing. I don't know what he expects me to say. Not about this.

"Nothing to say?" he prods. "Nothing?"

"I don't have a reason," I grit out. "Not a good one."

"On that, we agree," my dad mutters. He adjusts the white sleeves beneath his dark suit. "Look, if you want a future in the NHL, you need to keep your anger in check." The vein in his forehead is throbbing as he looks at me, his eyes brimming with disappointment. "Especially when it's against your own fucking teammate, let alone your brother. It's you and him, Mav." He points to my brother on the bench. "You and Archer. You know that."

"I know," I mutter. He's right. I know he is. And I know it isn't fair for me to be pissed at either of them. Archer doesn't know about my past with Lia. He doesn't know how the future was ripped away from us or how we've been sneaking around behind everyone's backs again, only for her to openly wear his number and let everyone—our friends, our families—think she still belongs to him.

Doesn't she, though?

I bang my head against the locker, then drop my chin to my chest. "Sorry, Arch."

"Me too," he replies.

"You're lucky you're signed with the Lions," my dad continues, "after a stunt like that. What about your future?"

Tension explodes at the base of my skull, and my upper lip curls. "Fuck my future."

"Don't say—"

"Fuck. My. Future." I push myself away from the locker and pace the space like a caged bull. It isn't fair. I know it isn't. To take it out on them. They love me. They want me to be happy. But I can't help it. It isn't fair. That I don't get to keep her. That she's going to belong to Archer when she belonged to me first.

"What's going on, Maverick?" my dad orders.

Adrenaline and rage sizzle beneath my skin, making me

want to scrape at it with my fingers, but I keep my hands fisted because if I start, I'm not sure I'll be able to stop.

"Maverick," Dad prods. It's sharp. Direct. So is his stare.

I look down at the ground, my muscles trembling. "Nothing's wrong."

"Don't lie to me." His tone softens. "This isn't like you. You've been on a slippery slope for a while now. Ever since the end of last season. It's like you don't even want this anymore."

"Maybe I don't," I say numbly.

"Don't say that," Archer spits from the metal bench between the lockers.

Fine. I won't say anything at all.

I stop pacing and face my father again. "Do you need to say anything else?"

"You aren't going to talk about this with me? With us?"

"Do you need anything else?" I repeat through clenched teeth.

Another wave of disappointment flares in his eyes, but he shakes his head. "No, son. I don't."

"Good." *Say it, Maverick. Just spit it out.* "I'm done with hockey."

A divot forms between his brows, and my dad cocks his head as he stares at me. I wait for his disappointment, his disgust. But only confusion shines back at me in his blue eyes that match Archer's and mine.

"What do you mean?" he finally asks.

"I mean, I'm done," I repeat. My doctor's comments from earlier urging me to finish. To fucking say it. "I'm done with hockey. With LAU. The NHL. All of it."

My father pales as if he doesn't even know me anymore. As if I'm a stranger instead of his own son. "Maverick…"

"I quit, Dad. And there isn't anything you can say or do to change my mind." I don't give him a chance to yell at me or demand we talk about this some more. I head to the showers and turn the water on, wishing the icy spray would ease the guilt on my shoulders and wash away the regret clinging to my heated skin. But it doesn't do shit.

Nothing does.

Fuck.

38
OPHELIA

I'm freaking out.

Freak. Ing. Out.

Maverick isn't answering my texts, and I haven't seen him since he disappeared into the locker room with Archer. Now, here I am, in the passenger seat of Archer's car, going out of my mind with worry and confusion.

Archer's quiet. He hasn't said much, and I have a feeling it has something to do with whatever happened in the locker room with his brother and his dad.

The question is, what happened?

"You played well," I offer, twisting my hands in my lap while fighting off the helplessness growing in the pit of my stomach as Archer drives us home from the arena. He's been acting off ever since he returned from the locker room without his twin.

I have no idea where Maverick is.

It's only stressing me out more. I feel like I'm sitting on pins and needles. Like an overinflated balloon is lodged in my chest and could pop at any second. Like something's wrong. Something's seriously wrong. And I don't know what it is.

"I'm sorry Maverick hit you," I add.

Archer's chin dips slightly as he flips the blinker on and turns onto the main road. LAU lost 1-2. My parents offered to take the team out to dinner, but the guys wanted to come home and lick their wounds. My sister's in the backseat. Her nose is less than six inches from the pages of her book. She's staying with me for the next couple of days until she can steal a ride home from Dylan's parents after they officially move Dylan's things into our place. Finley went home, too, promising she'd be back by the end of the weekend with her boxes. Personally, I think it's because she wanted to sneak in one more night with her boyfriend before they head to opposite ends of the country for their freshman year. But what do I know?

Besides, I have bigger things to deal with.

Like finding out why Maverick hit Archer and why I feel like it's all my fault. I shouldn't have given in to Finley's suggestion. I shouldn't have worn Archer's jersey. It doesn't matter how we both agreed to keep our relationship hidden from our family. Maverick's pissed, and he has every right to be. Things are still messy between us, but I hate how Archer is the one caught in the crosshairs.

Archer's hands tighten around the steering wheel as if he can read my thoughts, and he mutters, "Maverick quit."

Confused, I crane my neck toward the driver's side of the car. "He what?"

"He quit. He said he's done playing hockey."

I shake my head. "Why would he…?"

"I don't know." Archer sighs. "I have no idea what his problem is, but he won't talk to me."

He won't talk to you because he's pissed at you, and you have

301

no idea why, I want to say, but I don't. It would only make things worse.

Touching my fingers against my lips, I play out a thousand scenarios, but none of them fix this. None of them mend the fraying relationship between the two brothers, all because I wound up falling for both of them.

"I'm sorry, Archer," I whisper. "I know how much you love your brother."

"I do," he agrees. His iron grip loosens on the steering wheel, and he glances at me. "How are you doing?"

"Just bummed you guys lost," I reply as he turns into the driveway and cuts the engine. Tatum climbs out of the backseat, closing the door behind her with a soft thud as if afraid of interrupting us.

Maybe she's not as oblivious as I assumed.

I reach for my handle, but Archer stops me with a gentle touch on my knee. "You're worried about Mav, aren't you?"

With a sigh, I let the door handle go and settle back in my seat. "Mav and I bonded over our love of hockey. The idea of him quitting doesn't make any sense."

"Something's going on with him, but I don't know what, and the more I dig, the more he retreats."

It isn't surprising. Maverick's good at pushing people away. I should know. I'm his favorite victim. But he's never pushed Archer away, not really. And his parents? They've always been close.

Archer squeezes my thigh, and I stare at his touch. "I hate it," I whisper.

"Me too. I'll figure it out, though."

"You sound so confident."

"I'm his brother," Archer reminds me. "Now, enough sad shit." He picks my hand up and kisses the back of it. "Let's go get shit-faced. After the fight with my brother and tonight's loss, I could use my best friend to help me drown my worries in alcohol."

I smile back at him, surprised by how much lighter I feel. "That, I can do."

39

OPHELIA

"**N**ot gonna play the game tonight, huh?" I murmur from the open study room window. The soft breeze ruffles my hair around my shoulders as I grab the edge of the window sill and lean over the threshold. I debated coming out here. Confronting Maverick. Attempting to comfort him. But hanging out on the main floor with all our friends and no Maverick? It was more than I could stomach. So here I am. Hoping and praying he doesn't push me away.

He's on the roof like I knew he would be. With his jean-covered ass planted on the slightly-sloped pitch and two empty beer bottles by his hip, he grasps a third by the neck, staring out at the skyline.

When he hears my voice, Mav glances over his shoulder at me as he brings the bottle of beer to his lips and looks back at the view. I don't blame him. It's quite the sight. Lockwood Heights isn't exactly a big town, and since we're pretty close to campus, there are rolling hills. Further away are the twinkling lights from most of the city. Not to mention the stars above us. They're beautiful tonight without a cloud in the sky. And, in a weird way, it reminds me of the first time we hooked up. When he took my virginity after a stupid game of Truth or Dare.

It's funny.

I thought that would be it between us. A single night and nothing else. That's all it was initially. Until the next time he came home, and it happened again. He surprised me by texting me the next day. And the next. And the next. We grew closer over inside jokes, late-night conversations, and the occasional secret rendezvous whenever he was home from campus. Until almost a year went by, and I thought I'd found myself in an actual relationship. Or at least the closest thing to it I'd ever experienced. And yeah, they were stolen moments. But they were *our* stolen moments. Moments I treasured. Conversations I cared about. About our future. About life and goals and hopes and dreams, and now, he's given up on his biggest one.

Hockey.

It doesn't make sense.

Everyone's downstairs getting drunk and playing UNO. It's been fun or at least it would be, if I wasn't too distracted by Maverick's absence to really focus on anything else. Maverick loves hockey. He's loved it all his life. So, why? Why would he quit? Why would he throw in the towel after hitting his brother during the first scrimmage game before his senior year even has a chance to start? I should've known something was off when he offered to skip practice and hang out with me instead. But I simply thought he was being a regular guy and thinking with his dick, not that he was done with hockey in general.

"Care if I join you?" I prod.

"You should go inside," he says without bothering to look at me. "I'm not in the right headspace, Lia."

Careful not to bump my head, I ignore his suggestion and

climb out the open window without waiting for his invitation, well aware I won't get one.

"Where's Archer?" he adds.

"Downstairs with Tatum and the guys."

He nods, taking another sip of his drink. "How'd you find me?"

"You've always been a sucker for rooftops."

His smile is sardonic at best as he brings the bottle to his lips again. "True."

Thankfully, the roof isn't too sloped, but I watch my step and make my way toward him. "So, why'd you quit?"

"Arch has quite the mouth," he notes. "But I bet you liked that about him."

"Mav," I warn, sitting next to him.

"Why'd you have to show up in his jersey, Ophelia?" he growls. But it isn't angry. It's...sad.

"Telling Finley I can't wear my best friend's jersey because it might make his brother jealous is kind of a red flag, don't you think?"

"He isn't me," Maverick breathes out.

The words hit like a wrecking ball, and I jerk back slightly.

It hurts.

Fuck, it hurts.

The defeat. The slight undertone of jealousy and resentment. The surrender.

"Pretty sure we already proved you two aren't interchangeable," I remind him. "You know I'm well aware of how different you are."

Whatever relief I hoped to find from my reassurance is absent as he stares at the bottle in his hands. "You should go inside, Opie."

"No."

"Why?"

"Because I'm not finished."

His nostrils flare, and he faces me fully. "Fine. *Finish*."

"Don't quit," I tell him.

"Pretty sure it's not your decision."

"You love hockey."

"So?"

"So, if you love it, why let it go?"

His chest expands on a deep breath, and he rumbles his hostile amusement. "I've let go of a lot of things I love, Opie."

"Why?"

"Because I have no future in hockey."

"Says who?" I push. "You have your entire career ahead of you. You can't just…quit."

"Pretty sure it's exactly what I did," he returns dryly, bringing the stupid beer bottle to his lips and finishing the rest of the amber liquid off.

"Look at the big picture, Mav," I beg. "Look at a year from now. Two years from now. Five years from now."

"There is no five years from now."

My frown deepens. "What do you mean?"

He gulps and scratches his chin. "I mean, shit changes. Shit out of our control. We're not guaranteed tomorrow, let alone five years from now. Life doesn't work that way, no matter how much you like to plan for it."

"So it's easier to quit?" I demand. "To throw in the towel?" *Man, I want to shake him!* "Look, I know you have a short attention span and all, but your future—"

His jaw sets, and he shakes his head. "My attention span has nothing to do with this."

"Then what is it?"

"Maybe I wanna have one fucking ounce of control over my life." He turns to me, his eyes dark and clouded. "Ever think of that?"

"What are you even talking about?" I whisper. "You're not making any sense."

"Go inside, Lia."

"No." I shake my head. "What's going on with you? Yesterday you were fine, then—"

"Then Archer showed up."

I pull back, surprised. "Is that what this is about?"

"Fuck." His head hangs, and he pinches the bridge of his nose. "No. That isn't what this is about. I'm being a dick, okay? You should go inside."

"What's going on?" I beg. "I feel like we took a hundred steps back after making so much progress over the last little while. What happened? What changed? It's like a switch flipped or something. I feel like you aren't…" I hesitate.

"I'm not what? The guy you fell for?" he finishes for me. The darkness in his eyes practically swallows me whole.

I pull my hand away from him and place it in my lap, hating the iciness in his gaze and how it makes me feel. "I guess not."

"Guess it's good you found Archer, then, isn't it?"

"Did you hit your head or something, Maverick? Because I'm not sure if you remember or not, but for the past little while, I've been in your bed, not his."

"No, I've been in *your* bed and *your* closet."

"So that *is* what this is about," I assume. "How you had to hide in my closet since we agreed not to tell anyone about us?"

"No, it's…" He grinds his molars, his muscles fucking vibrating beside me. "He knows you. He knows what you taste like. What you feel like. Do you have any idea what it does to me?"

My eyes thin. "You can't keep throwing my relationship with your brother in my face."

"I'm not—"

"You are," I push. "And it isn't fair because you're the one who broke my heart, Mav. Not the other way around."

His head falls, and for the first time since I climbed onto this roof, I can see a crack in his armor. A glimpse of the guy I fell in love with not so long ago, only to have my heart broken by the same man.

"Then, why do I feel so damn broken?" he asks.

The words hang in the air, practically choking me. Because they're filled with desperation. With want. With resignation.

"Tell me what's wrong," I whisper.

"I can't."

"Then tell me why you were jealous at the game. It's a stupid jersey, Mav."

"You were mine first," he admits, as if I've forgotten.

"I'm still yours," I remind him.

Defeat shines in his eyes, and he meets my gaze. "For how long?"

"Don't you get it?" A pathetic laugh slips past my lips. "For as long as you'll have me, Maverick."

"It doesn't work like that."

"And how does it work?" I push. "Because for someone who likes his control, you're sure as shit giving it up easily. You want me? You have me. I'm right—"

He grabs the back of my neck and pulls me to him, kissing me with a fervor and impatience I haven't experienced in months. It's desperate and deliberate and filled with a raw determination I feel all the way to my toes. This kiss tastes just like him. Just like Maverick, the first boy I ever loved despite myself.

I open for him, letting him take what he needs while understanding whatever this is—whatever he's going through—is only the tip of the iceberg, and it seems I'm not the only one who's ruined. He feels the ache from our lost time as much as I do, and the reminder of our lost time was more than he could bear earlier today. It's why he snapped. Why he hit Archer. Why he's pushing me away yet holding on to me for dear life at the same time.

It ruins me.

In a way, I think I've been ruined for a while now. My thoughts. My relationships. Everything.

Carefully, I shift on the roof, lifting my leg and straddling Maverick's waist while keeping our mouths fused together. I'm scared Maverick will push me away again. Terrified he'll end this.

Not again.

Please, not again.

His hands slip under my shirt. He drags them up my spine and follows the same path to my hips. I've missed his hands. The rough callouses. How delicate they make me feel. He squeezes my waist, and I grind against him, hating my clothes now more than ever. I want him. All of him. His skin. His muscles. His erection. His soul. I want it all. Inside of me. Around me. I want it to seep into my skin, tattooing me. Branding me. Marking me as Maverick's and *only* Maverick's. *Always* Maverick's.

Sensing my desperation, he lifts his hips, letting me rock against the bulge in his jeans as his hands find my breasts beneath my shirt. He pinches my nipples through the thin cotton of my bra, and I moan against his mouth.

"That's it, baby," he rasps against my lips. "Bet you could come just like this, couldn't you?"

I rock myself against him more, the seam of my jeans rubbing through my panties and against my clit in the most delicious way possible. Fuck, he's right. I could come like this. Because it's Mav.

After shoving my bra up, he leans down and sucks my

nipple into his mouth, swirling his tongue around the bud while guiding my hips with his hands, urging me on.

"You have no idea how good this feels," I whimper.

He releases my nipple with a soft pop and shifts beneath me, letting me feel his cock and exactly how hard he is. How ready he is. "Bet you're so wet, aren't you, baby?"

"So fucking wet," I whisper, squeezing my eyes shut.

He scrapes his teeth against the side of my neck, and I arch my back as his palms find my breasts. I soak up the heat from them and the roughness of his touch.

"I might not be able to give you forever, Goose, but I can give you this. I can give you these little morsels. And it's enough. Right, Lia? Tell me it's enough."

"Yes," I whisper because if I don't, he'll stop. He'll push me away. I know he will. And I can't let him. Not when I just got him back. The truth is, I'm not sure if these little morsels *are* enough anymore. I want more. I've always wanted more. I've wanted every single piece of Maverick Buchanan since we were teens, and I'm not sure I'll ever stop. But if I tell him, he definitely will.

And I can't lose him. Not again.

"I need you naked, Goose. I need to taste you and lick you and put my tongue inside you."

"God, yes."

"You gonna ride my face, baby?"

I nod, rolling my hips in long, slow motions as he lets go of my left breast and slides his hand into my hair, knotting it with his fingers.

"Fuck, Lia. You have no idea how pretty you look. With your hair in my hand. Do you have any idea how many times I've pictured this? You and me again? I wanna see you suck my cock long and deep. I wanna see you ride it, throwing your head back and rolling your hips. I want—"

"Fuck," I choke out as my orgasm hits me harder than I anticipated. My thighs quiver, and my lips part on a gasp.

He slams his mouth against mine again, swallowing my moans while I slowly come back down to earth. When the flick of the study room's light paints the roof, our heads snap in its direction.

"What the hell are you guys doing?" Tatum spits.

My heart lodges in my throat, and Maverick rushes to pull my shirt down, covering me. But I don't move. I can't. I'm fucking frozen. "Tatum, we weren't—"

"Don't you *dare* try to lie your way out of this." Her look of disgust will forever be etched into my mind as she crosses her arms and shakes her head. "Archer is the best thing that has and *will* ever happen to—"

"We broke up," I announce. My pulse pounds in my ears, fucking galloping so fast I can barely see straight. "It was a little while ago, but—"

Her dark, venomous laugh cuts me off. "You think it makes this any better? Maverick is Archer's brother. His *twin* brother." Her nose wrinkles in disgust. "It doesn't matter how much time passes, you fucking Maverick will *never* be okay, Ophelia."

"You don't get it," I rush out. "You remember Mystery Man? It was Mav—"

"You mean the dick who broke your heart an hour before prom?" she mocks. "You're really stupid enough to give him another chance after how he treated you?"

"You're being unfair."

"Did he even tell you why?" she demands.

I pale.

"He didn't, did he?" She waits for my response, but when I don't give her one, she lets out a sour laugh. "So let me get this straight. He didn't commit then, and you honestly expect him to commit to you now?"

"We're…" I lick my lips, unsure what to say.

With a nod, she rolls her eyes. "Let me guess, you're not putting a label on things, right? Just hooking up for shits and giggles without bothering to think about how it might hurt those around you?"

"Tate, you don't know what you're talking about," Maverick interrupts, but my sister doesn't even bother acknowledging him.

She simply stares at me. *Glares* at me. "Don't get me wrong, Lia. I know we've always been pretty different, but this?" She flicks her hand in my direction. "You really think Maverick's gonna settle down and give you what you want? You broke Archer's heart so you could be his brother's fuck toy for a little while, and you fell for it. Pretty sure I've never felt more ashamed to call you my sister in my entire life."

"Tate—"

"Archer deserves so much more than you've ever given him it's not even funny, and this is how you thank him for it?"

"Tatum," I beg.

She shakes her head, her eyes narrowing into slits. "If you don't tell him about this, I will." She turns on her heel and disappears from view.

And just like that, the euphoria from minutes ago explodes into an eruption of shame and remorse and *fear* until I'm left gasping for air.

What if she tells him?

And why does the idea of him finding out make me feel like I might *literally* puke?

I cover my mouth and slump into Maverick, my muscles heavy and useless and stiff and fucking *mush* as the realization of what transpired hits me square in the face. I just dry-humped my ex, who happens to be my *other* ex-boyfriend's brother, on the rooftop while he's one floor away, and instead of having the decency to tell him beforehand, I've been hiding it. From Archer. From everyone.

I rest my forehead against Maverick's and squeeze my eyes shut.

What did I just do?

It doesn't matter that Archer and I aren't technically together anymore. I've been keeping this from him. And this isn't a little secret. This is me and Maverick. He'll think I planned this. That I broke up with him for his twin brother. It doesn't matter how he'd be wrong. The way it looks? It's bad. Really bad. What if he hates me forever? What if he hates Maverick forever? What if he never forgives his own brother because of me? Because of what we've been doing behind his back? And for what? For a few solid orgasms without any actual future?

"Sh...," Mav murmurs. "It's gonna be all right. I'll talk to—"

"Don't."

My thighs quiver as I climb off Maverick's lap and shove my hair away from my face, bringing my fingers to my lips. I think I'm going to be sick. I think I'm going to hyperventilate and pass out. I think I'm going—

"Whoa, whoa, whoa, Opie. Breathe." Maverick rubs his hand up and down my back.

My chest heaves, and I shake my head. "What have we been doing?"

"We—"

"We really thought we could hide this?" My voice cracks. "Thought we could pretend everything's okay, and it wouldn't hurt Archer to see us—"

"Stop," he orders.

"She's right. Tatum's right. What did I just do, Mav?" I ask. My eyes plead with his, begging him to tell me it didn't happen. To tell me I didn't break his brother's heart or ruin his trust or make him feel like he's anything less than perfect.

Maverick's touch is gentle as he grabs the side of my face and forces me to look at him. "Breathe, Goose."

My bottom lip trembles, and I blink the moisture making my sight hazy away as I pull out of his grasp. "I need to go."

"Let me help you—"

I slap his hand away as he tries to steady me. "Stop. I can't. I can't do this right now. How could we do this to him? How could we... How could we not actually consider the consequences of who this would hurt, especially for a casual fling that doesn't feel so casual anymore? Not to me," I whisper. My shoulders sag a little more. "Tatum's right. I might've ended things before all of this, but it doesn't matter. He's your fucking brother, Maverick. Who does that?"

His lips are nothing but a slash of white on his face as he stares at me helplessly.

We did.

"Opie—"

"I—I need to go."

"Lia," he pleads.

I hesitate. Unable to look him in the eyes, I stare at his messy brown hair instead. The same hair I'd been running my fingers through. I wipe my palms against my jeans and fold my arms. "I need to deal with one fucked-up relationship at a time, Mav. Looks like you'll have to wait your turn."

I head back to my place, and by some miracle, I don't run into Archer on my way out. But it doesn't mean I won't have to face him at some point. And when I do? I'll have to tell him the truth.

Clutching the edge of the toilet, I puke what little I'd eaten into the bowl, my eyes watering and my vomit choking me.

I fucked up.

Tatum's right.

I screwed up.

After catching us, she sent my dad a text saying she had the flu, and a little while later, he picked her up without hesitation while I hid in my room, pretending to have the same stomach bug.

It was for the best.

I can barely look myself in the eye right now, let alone my sister. How did I let this happen?

I'm better than this.

I know I am.

So is Maverick.

He wouldn't hurt a fly, not really. Let alone his twin brother.

But he touched me anyway.

And I'm not the one caught in the crosshairs.

Archer is.

There isn't anything I can say or do to take him out of it.

We pretended like we could go back to before. Like we could hook up in secret without it hurting anyone. But we forgot one key piece of the puzzle. His brother. My best friend.

I knew it would hurt him. Maverick knew it would hurt him. But we did it anyway. We were selfish. Cowards. He deserves to know.

As the hours passed, I tossed and turned, unable to quiet the voice inside my head screaming at me to tell him. To tell Archer what I've done.

He deserves to know.

This is going to suck.

I SHOWER SLOWLY, PROCRASTINATING LIKE A CHAMP. SLAPPING on my hand-me-down baseball hat, I hope it'll help me sieve off a bit of my father's courage. Without bothering to see what a mess I look like, I head to Archer's. I had the foresight to text him last night, telling him I wasn't feeling well, and I went home so he wouldn't worry. He bought the lie easily since Tatum used the same one.

I woke up to soda crackers on my porch and a note telling me to feel better soon. It only made me feel worse.

He's perfect. And way more thoughtful than I'll ever deserve.

My hands shake, but I fist them into tight little balls, keeping my head held high as I knock on the boys' front door. My stomach twists when Maverick opens it a minute later. His shirt is missing. His tan chest and inked skin on full display, acting like salt on an already oozing sore.

When he sees me, he glances behind him, preparing to meet me outside. "Hey."

"Is Archer here?"

He hesitates, his brows tugging down in the center. "Uh, yeah. Sure."

"Thanks." I slip between him and the doorframe, but he grabs my wrist, and I lurch to a halt.

"Listen, about what Tatum said—"

"Not now," I whisper, staring at his hand. The way it encompasses my entire wrist. The way his dark, even-toned skin contrasts with my pale, freckled complexion. The way his callouses tickle my sensitive flesh and the way his simple touch sends goosebumps racing along every single inch of me. I feel like I'm fraying. Every touch. Every look. I can't take it.

"Ophelia," he rasps.

My gaze snaps to his from beneath the brim of my hat. "Like I said last night, Mav. One fucked-up relationship at a time, okay?"

I start to shrug out of his hold, but his grasp tightens even more. It isn't painful. It's insistent.

"Don't," he breathes out.

"I'm not going to lie to him."

"Let me tell him."

"It isn't your responsibility to clean up my mess."

"It's *our* mess, Ophelia."

I shake my head. "There is no *our*. No us. Tatum's right. You've made it very clear, remember?"

"It's complicated."

"Is it?" I challenge. "I thought I was okay with the little morsels. Thought I could pretend I didn't care about my future. But after realizing the fallout from even casually hooking up with you is going to cause, I've decided I'm not okay with it anymore. It isn't fair to Archer. It isn't fair to me or our families. You either love me, or you don't. You either commit to me, or you don't. That's it. And until you can figure it out, I'm... I'm done." I pull away from him, and by some miracle, Maverick's grasp loosens this time, and he lets me go. But I can still feel his eyes on me as I walk down the hall toward Archer's room.

The heat. The regret. The desire.

When I reach Archer's closed door, I let out a slow, controlled breath and lift my hand, tapping my knuckles against it.

The floor creaks on the opposite side before Archer appears. His mouth pulls into a smile, and it kills me.

"Hey, how are you feeling?" he asks. "I was worried about you."

Concern creases his eyes and only fans my guilt, so I look at the ground instead. "I'm fine," I murmur. It couldn't be further from the truth. "Thank you for the crackers."

"Always."

I wipe my sweaty palms on my jean-clad thighs and tuck my hands into the crooks of my elbows.

I don't want to do this.

"You sure you're okay?" he prods.

Shame eats at me, but I force my gaze to his. "Any chance we can talk for a minute?"

He nods and opens his bedroom door the rest of the way. "Yeah, sure. Come on in."

Arms folded, I step over the threshold and wait for Archer to close the door behind me. My hands are still shaking as I pray for the strength to get through this when all I want to do is run and hide and pretend last night never happened. Or maybe I want the last few months, in general, to disappear. So I can go back to my prom night and tell Archer no. He can't take me to prom. He can't treat me right. He can't waste his time on me when his brother still owns my heart.

I should've stayed home. I should've climbed into bed and watched a corny rom-com or a gory horror movie. I should've done so many things. But instead, every single decision I made led me here. To Archer's room. Feeling like I'm the most terrible person in the world.

"What's going on?" he asks, watching me from the edge of the room as I stare out his bedroom window. I'm not sure how much time has passed, how long I've been lost in my own head, but his words are tense. Tight. Like he can feel the same shift in the air I can, and fuck, it hurts.

Tearing my attention from the large tree in the front yard, I face Archer again.

"Lia," he breathes out, his expression twisting with...*fear*? He reaches for me, but I shake my head.

"I've been doing something I need to tell you about," I whisper.

His brows pull. "What did you do?"

"I..." I lick my lips.

Just say it, Lia.

"I've been hooking up with Maverick," I finish, forcing myself to look at him. "It was after we broke up, but I'm not sure if the timeline really matters. I messed up, and..." My teeth dig into my bottom lip as I fight back tears. "I can only imagine how it must make you feel. I'm so sorry, Archer."

A mask slides over his features almost instantly, hiding Archer's emotions as he stares at me. The silence is stifling. The indifference hiding the hurt I know is hidden beneath it.

"Archer," I start.

"You had sex with my brother?"

The words hurt, making it hard to breathe, but I don't cower. I take the hit and wipe the moisture from my eyes. "Yes, I've been having sex with Maverick." I move toward Archer, but he leans back, keeping the distance between us. My heels dig into the ground, and I nod my understanding. Of course, he doesn't want me comforting him. I suck my cheeks between my teeth and bite hard. But the pain doesn't ground me. It doesn't ease the sharp ache in my chest or the white-hot guilt I'm drowning in. I did it. I ruined the one constant in my life. The one relationship I never wanted to tarnish. My friendship with the man in front of me.

"Archer, I'm... I'm so sorry."

"You wanna know what I felt when I saw the video of you and Mav?" he interrupts numbly.

I shake my head, confusion flooding my already withered brain. "W-what are you talking about?"

"The video of you and Mav doing the ice plunge," he clarifies. But he isn't looking at me. He's looking at his feet. His strong arms are folded over his chest as if closing himself off from the rest of the world. From *me*. "You were pissed at me for not acting jealous, remember?"

Acid floods my mouth, but I swallow it back. "I remember."

"Do you wanna know what I really felt?"

"What?" I whisper.

"Fear." His eyes slice to mine. "I felt fear, Ophelia. Fear that you'd be taken from me, or if I overreacted, I'd scare you away. I feared you were never mine to begin with. That you still belonged to your fucking Mystery Man, so why should I worry about my own flesh and blood when we had bigger obstacles to overcome than an innocent crush you'd been hiding for as long as I can remember?"

He knew about my crush on his brother? The realization acts like a hot poker, leaving me raw and burning.

"Archer..."

"Thank you for telling me." The same numb indifference engulfs his words. Like I've announced two plus two is four, or the weather's nice today. Like I didn't just break his heart when I know I did.

I pull back, rubbing my hands up and down my bare arms. "That's it?"

"What else do you want me to say?" He scrubs his hand

over his tight jaw. "You did your due diligence. You broke up with me beforehand, so thanks for that, I guess."

"You're not going to yell at me? To—"

"I need you to go, Lia." He looks down at his bare feet again and rocks back on his heels.

I step closer to him and touch his cheek. "Don't be a gentleman about this. Don't take the high road. Don't let me off the hook because you're my best friend. I deserve every vile thought and name you want to fling at me. And trust me, none of it can be worse than what I've been thinking since the moment I—"

"I don't want to know." His eyes close, and he leans into my touch. "And I don't want to fling anything at you," he rasps, circling my wrist and lowering my hand from his face.

"I'm sorry, Archer. I know how much I screwed up. How much this must hurt you. I still love you so much. You're my best friend. My superhero. My—"

"You should go," he repeats.

I nod, hating the shameful tears in my eyes. He looks so hurt right now. So broken. And I'm the one who caused it. His pain. I ruined everything.

I'm so sorry.

I brush the moisture away with my fingers and nod again, forcing my feet to move. To give Archer the space he wants. The space he needs. In a rush, I leave his room and slide past a silent Maverick in the hallway. Or at least, I think it was Maverick. I didn't exactly look him in the eye. I'm not sure I can. But I'd recognize those black biker boots anywhere. I don't know how much he heard. And honestly, I don't care. Not right now. Because this isn't about him. This is about me and Archer and everything I ruined. Everything I gave up. Everything I lost. My legs feel weak as I walk back to my house. Then, I collapse on my bed and cry.

41
MAVERICK

Her cheeks are red and shiny. She tries to hide them beneath the bill of her hat, but they're like a beacon, highlighting every mistake I've made in the past few months despite my best attempts to keep them at bay for both our sakes. Tiny trails of tears stain her perfect complexion as she slips past me in the hallway, leaving me alone without a backward glance.

Resting my back against the wall, I fold my arms and wait, unsure what to do or say. I fucked up. More times than I can count, but this takes the cake. This ruins my brother. This hurts Ophelia. This burns down the two most important relationships in my life, and there isn't anything I can do about it but wait, hoping I can at least clean up the ashes.

Hope.

It's a funny word.

Four letters.

Like a curse.

And I've been cursed for years.

Last night was reckless, but I don't regret it. I don't regret any moment I've been lucky enough to hold her. And after everything she said, I've decided to give in to the beast inside me. The one who loves Ophelia with every fucking fiber of his being. Giving in is calming almost. Soothing. Even now, with the aftermath ahead of me, ahead of *us*, I can't bring myself to regret a single moment I've shared with her.

I've been drowning for months. Floundering in a sea of chaos and depression. And the past few weeks felt like I was finally given a breath of fresh air. The idea of being pushed under again is more than I can stomach.

I just need to get through this.

Ophelia closed Archer's door behind her when she left, but even now, I can hear my brother pacing in his room on the opposite side of the wood separating us. He's the calm one. The collected one. The logical one. Ophelia poured gasoline all over his emotions. His future. *Their* future. And now, he's trying to figure out how to fix it. How to clean it up. How to mend it regardless of the dagger in his back. The one I helped place there.

I hate it.

Even now, after everything that's happened, after knowing everything that's going to happen, I don't want him to fix it. His relationship with Ophelia. At least not the romantic side. I want it to stay burned. Torched. Ashen. I want every speck of their relationship to be obliterated so I can continue piecing her back together. So I can have another chance to claim all of her despite the reason why I broke things off in the first place. It's glaring at me, reminding me how fruitless of an effort it would be. For us to work things out. How it would only wind up hurting her in the end, just like the first time. I never claimed to be the selfless brother, though. Not once. I tried it, and it clearly didn't stick.

Still, this is low, even for me.

But she's right. I either love her or I don't. It's that simple.

And fuck me, I love her with every fiber of my being. I know it's selfish, and I shouldn't because, in the end, it'll destroy her.

But I tried. To step back. To let her go. Obviously, it didn't work for either of us, and I can't bring myself to do it again.

With my head resting against the wall, I look at the ceiling. My own self-loathing reaches a feverish pitch when the hinges on Archer's bedroom door squeak. He yanks it open but stops short as his gaze lands on me.

The air grows thick, nearly choking me as I stare back at him. Waiting. For him to yell at me. To throw a punch. To tell me I'm a waste of space. He isn't wrong. And he wouldn't be wrong if he beat the shit out of me. But only if he promised to stay away from her afterward.

"You gonna hit me?" I ask.

He scoffs and drops his chin to his chest as his hands clench at his sides, fisting and unfisting.

"You should," I push. "I deserve it."

"Yeah." A dry laugh escapes him, but he doesn't look at me. "You do."

"Hit me." I push myself away from the wall and stride closer to him. "Hit me, Arch."

His eyes snap to mine, but I continue my pursuit, crowding his space until we're chest-to-chest and nose-to-nose.

"Hit. Me," I growl, pressing my forehead to his as I silently beg and plead for him to let me carry the weight, the burden, the pain I inflicted by kissing Ophelia last night and so many others before it. By grabbing her hips and spurring her on. By letting her rub herself against my cock until she came on top of me, moaning my name—not his—as she did.

"Why?" Archer spits. "So I can make you feel better for touching her? For touching what's mine?"

Mine.

The word curdles in my stomach, ripping a snarl from my throat and causing my guilt to transform into full-blown rage. "Careful, Archer."

"About what? About telling you the truth and calling out your bullshit?"

"She isn't yours."

"Bullshit," he spits. "She's always been—"

I shove at his chest, and he stumbles back, hitting the door trim. Regaining his balance, he charges at me. His shoulder slams into my gut, and the air whooshes from my lungs, knocking the wind out of me in an instant. But I like the burn. I crave it. Digging my fingers into his shirt, I try wrenching him away from me, but he doesn't let me go. Instead, we tumble to the ground. He straddles my waist and hits me in the jaw. My head swings to the side, and I swear I taste blood as he lands another punch. And another. And another. But I savor these too. The pain. The reminder I'm alive. The reminder I have something worth fighting for. Ignoring the black dots marring my vision, I let him land one more punch, then block his fists with my forearms as I shift beneath him, shoving him off me and cocking my arm back. My expression twists with fury as my knuckles skate across his cheek and crunch against his nose. Blood pours down his face.

Shit, the fucker's broken. I know it.

The crimson liquid snaps some sense into me, and I let him go, climbing off him and resting my back against the wall as my chest heaves.

He wipes beneath his nose with the back of his hand, assessing the damage with a hostile laugh. "You fucking broke my nose."

"You deserve it."

His brows lift. "*I* deserve it?"

"Yeah."

"You hooked up with my girlfriend," he reminds me.

"*Ex*-girlfriend."

"So it was only the one time, huh?" he challenges.

"You don't know what you're talking about."

"So there were other times," he assumes.

"I'm not gonna talk bullshit timelines with you," I growl. "And I'm sorry about what happened. I really am. But she isn't yours."

"Fuck that."

"She isn't," I repeat through clenched teeth.

"Is that how you justify it, brother? Because we broke up, she was, what? Fair game?" He shakes his head, letting the blood drip off his chin and onto his shirt without giving a shit about the inevitable stains like he normally would.

"Tell me this," I add. "Are you pissed she moved on with *me*, or are you pissed she moved on at all?"

"You think I didn't see how she looks at you?" he questions. "You think I didn't notice the way she stared? I figured, hey. Look at the bright side. My girlfriend must be attracted to me physically since she can't stop staring at my twin. That's gotta count for something, right? But she wouldn't *do* anything. It's Ophelia. The girl doesn't have a thoughtless bone in her body, and I'm her best friend. She wouldn't do that to me. And my brother? My fucking *twin*? There's no way he'd stab me in the back by touching her." Another scoff slips out of him as he pushes to his feet. "Guess the joke's on me."

He closes his bedroom door, leaving me alone in the hallway with nothing but my guilt as company.

Fuck.

42

OPHELIA

I've been lying in bed for hours, unable to move without bawling my eyes out. Then again, even when I'm not moving, I'm still a sobbing mess.

This sucks. Everything sucks. After sending a quick text to Jaxon, telling him I had the flu so he wouldn't wonder why I wasn't coming to the team's four-mile run today, I curled up into a ball and tunneled under my covers, only slipping out of bed to grab food from the kitchen or to use the restroom.

Right now, I want nothing more than to disappear. I want to not exist for a little while. I want to go back to the way things were before prom. Before Tatum caught us on the roof. Before I let boys and bad decisions take over my life and turn me into a shell of the person I know I am. I feel like I'm a stranger. A stranger who betrayed one of my best friends. A stranger who led two brothers on and pushed the future she wants more than anything aside so she could justify hooking up with one of them when she knew he wasn't ready for anything serious. I feel like I'm a stranger who's even avoiding hockey, which is so unlike me it's not even funny.

It's almost noon. I should be out of bed. I should've already attended practice. I should be showered. I should be getting ready for my friends to arrive since Dylan and Finley are moving in today. But instead of doing any of these things, I'm a pathetic lump on my mattress, and I don't know how to find the will to make it better.

As I lie awake in bed, I stare at the ceiling while recounting the last few weeks when my phone buzzes on the nightstand. It's a text from Mystery Man.

The name brings another fresh wave of tears to my eyes, and I change the name in my contact directory and read the message.

MAVERICK

We're not done, Opie.

And I think about the future all the time. About you and me. About everything I want. What I'd give up to have what I want.

My phone buzzes again.

MAVERICK

You have no idea how much not tracking you down is killing me.

I want to, just to clarify. But I already punched my brother twice this weekend, and I'm not sure either of us is ready for round three.

My chest squeezes as memories of their fight on the ice assault me. It's all my fault. I wipe the moisture from the corner of my eye, too weak and curious to keep myself from responding.

ME

Why'd you punch Archer the second time?

MAVERICK

Because he said you were his.

A tear skims down my cheek, and I squeeze my eyes shut when my phone buzzes again.

MAVERICK

You were right. I'm so sorry I've put you in the middle, Ophelia. I know I've messed up more times than I can count, and I want to tell you everything. But doing it over the phone doesn't feel right, and tracking you down when I know my brother's hurting in the room next to mine doesn't feel fair, either.

ME

None of this feels very fair.

MAVERICK

You're right. It doesn't. But sitting here makes me feel fucking helpless, Goose. I don't know what to do.

I grab another tissue from the box on my nightstand and blow my nose, wadding it up and tossing it onto the decent-sized pile covering my bedspread.

ME

Ditto.

MAVERICK

Reeves is throwing another party next weekend. Can you make it?

A party? He has to be joking.

ME

I'm not exactly in the party mood, Maverick. Besides, Dylan and Finley are moving in today, so I'm not sure what our plans will be or if Archer will want to see me.

MAVERICK

Bring them along. I'm sure Reeves would love to meet them.

A soft laugh slips out of me.

ME

But the real question is, would Everett and Griffin love their little sisters to meet Reeves?

MAVERICK

Hey, if it'll move the spotlight from us for once, I'm not complaining.

True.

It doesn't make me feel any better.

MAVERICK

You should come.

Please? I need to see you so I can explain everything. And seeking you out before Archer has a chance to cool down makes me feel like a bigger dick than I already am. If I at least have something to look forward to, I might be able to get through this week without tracking you down.

ME

Yeah, but a party? Are you sure it won't make us look like we're bigger dickheads?

MAVERICK

Hey, don't lump yourself in with me, Ophelia. Dickhead-singular. Not plural.

ME

After everything that's happened, I think it's debatable.

MAVERICK

Don't talk like that. Archer wouldn't want you talking like that, either.

ME

Also debatable.

MAVERICK

I know it seems like a party's a bad idea, but avoiding each other won't fix anything. Not for me. Or you. Or Arch. I'll even keep my distance so it doesn't piss him off. But we need something to break the tension. And like I said, it isn't until next week. Plenty of time for him to cool down.

A lot can happen in a week. But the possibility of Archer cooling down within that timeframe is slim to none. He must hate me.

ME

You sure Archer would want me to come over?

MAVERICK

He's gonna see you at brunch next Sunday anyway.

ME

Not sure I'm going to make it to family brunch, Mav.

MAVERICK

Running from your problems doesn't make them go away. Trust me. I would know.

ME

Doesn't make it any easier to face them.

MAVERICK

> You're right. But none of us can run from facing each other for the rest of our lives, so we might as well get it over with. And I prefer to do it away from our families' eyes.
> Don't you?

I roll onto my side, weighing the pros and cons without being able to deny his logic, no matter how crazy it sounds.

ME

> Good point.

MAVERICK

> So, you'll come?

ME

> I'll think about it.

MAVERICK

> Good. And afterward, we're gonna talk.

ME

> Not sure I'm ready, Mav.

MAVERICK

> We'll get through it, Opie. Promise. Miss you.

My heart seizes in my chest, and I rub at the ache, hating how much it hurts to be away from him, even after the shitstorm from the last couple of days. Honestly, it doesn't even make sense. Loving him the way I do. But I can't stop. I've tried.

Before I can talk myself out of it, I type my response and groan as the bubble shows "delivered."

ME

> Miss you too.

My phone buzzes seconds later, and this time, it's a call.

I slide my thumb along my screen and bring the phone to my ear. "Hey, Dylan."

"Hey," she greets me. "I wanted to call and give you and Tatum an ETA for today since my dad's still planning to bring her home after he's finished delivering me and all my boxes to the house. I'm thinking three o'clock or close to it. Does that work for you?"

"Yeah, three o'clock is fine, but Tatum's not here," I tell her, "so your dad doesn't have to worry about taking her home."

"She's not there?"

"She, uh, she got the flu, so my dad picked her up early," I explain, but even I can hear the dullness in my words.

"Oh." She hesitates. "Did you get it too? No offense, but you sound...*off*. Are you okay?"

I clear my throat. "Yeah. Uh, I'm not feeling so hot, either."

"Aw, man. That sucks."

"Yeah, it's a real bitch," I mutter.

"It's too bad I didn't move in yesterday, so I could already be there and make you some soup," she mentions. "Actually, that's a lie. We both know I don't cook. But I'm a hell of a DoorDasher. I could order you some mean soup."

I smile despite the tears gathering in my eyes. "That actually sounds pretty awesome. I've missed you."

"Ditto," she replies. "Although I'm still a little peeved we're next-door neighbors with my brothers and all."

Rolling onto my side, I point out, "Jaxon found a place of his own, so he won't be a problem, and Griff isn't *that* bad. If you want to feel sorry for anyone, you should feel sorry for Finley. She came to the game yesterday, and Everett spent the whole time barking at his teammates for even looking at her."

Dylan chuckles. "Everett's always had a stick up his ass, so I'm not sure why anyone's surprised when he acts like that."

"Good point."

"Speaking of the guys, why don't you have one of them bring you soup, or do I need to pull Archer's *Best Friend of the Year* award? Actually, I take it back. We both know I'm the one with the title. But seriously, you should make him take care of you until I get there."

I look down at my comforter, rubbing the thin cotton sheets between my fingers as the reality of my situation washes over me. "I'm not exactly on Archer's good list right now, so I don't think it's possible." The words hit me hard, and my voice breaks. The ache. For our friendship. Everything.

"What happened?" she prods. "Fill me in."

"I will when you get here."

"Come on, don't make me wait. At least give me a little something to tide me over."

"Let's just say Mystery Man popped back up on my radar, and things got messy."

"Wait, like *the* Mystery Man?"

I grimace. "Yeah."

"Yikes. I mean, I knew he was at LAU, but... Okay, I'm totally making my dad drop me off early so I can hear all the details."

"Don't tell them, please? Your parents," I clarify.

"About what?" she asks.

"All the drama," I mutter, clearing my throat. "I'm...not ready to face the consequences yet."

"Sure thing, Lia. Your secret's safe with me."

"Thanks. I'll see you soon."

~

DYLAN SHOWED UP EARLY, BANGING ON MY DOOR AT ONE IN the afternoon with her parents and a small trailer in tow. After Uncle Colt carried everything inside and Aunt Ashlyn stocked our freezer with Ben & Jerry's ice cream, they made us promise we'd be at brunch next weekend and kissed us goodbye.

A few minutes later, I experience deja vu with Finley and her parents until boxes litter the family room, and I'm pretty positive I'll never have another moment of peace for the rest of my college career.

"I can't believe we're all finally here!" Finley squeals. She pulls me into a hug, reaches for Dylan's arm, and forces her to join in.

Dylan laughs but throws her arms around us in the middle of our family room. When I nearly trip over one of the boxes, we all laugh a little harder. I like it. A lot, actually. Because I don't feel so alone anymore. The house doesn't feel quiet. It feels lived in. Like together, we can make it an actual home.

Letting me go, Finley rubs her hands together. "Okay, so once we're all finished unpacking, I was thinking we should go to one of the infamous Game Nights I've heard so much about. What do you guys say? I've been dying to attend one of these as soon as Griffin let it slip."

"When did Griffin let it slip about Game Nights?" Dylan asks.

Finley picks at the split ends of her dark, shiny hair and avoids Dylan's gaze. "I may or may not text your brother on occasion." With a flick of her wrist, she tosses her hair over her shoulder and adds, "But it's not like it's a big deal or anything."

"Does your older brother know you text his best friend behind his back?" I quip.

Finley's perfectly filled-in brows dip, but she waves me off. "What Everett doesn't know won't hurt him."

"Yeah, because that's a super smart idea," I note. "Keeping secrets from everyone."

"Like you're one to talk," she replies. "A little bird told me you're hiding a doozie."

Dylan preens beside me, and I shove her in the shoulder. "Dylan!"

"Hey! I didn't say *much*. Besides, we both know when we say a secret is safe with us, we mean everyone but each other, right? And all I said was I'm clearly your favorite cousin since I was the first one you told."

"Uh, who says it makes you her favorite?" Finley argues.

Lifting her hands, Dylan smirks and steps back. "Hey, the proof is in the pudding."

"Baloney. What proof?" Finley asks Dylan.

Dylan gives me the side-eye, waiting for me to spill the beans. I scrunch up my face, blurting out, "Fine! I'll tell you everything, but only if you promise to keep it between us."

Finley zips her lips, tosses the imaginary key away, and waits.

"For real, this time," I say, giving Dylan a pointed look.

"Yeah, yeah. I know," Dylan replies.

Satisfied, I take a deep breath and announce, "You already know Archer and I were taking a break, and we were kind of keeping it between us because we didn't want to stress our families out."

"Yeah, we know. Now, get to the juicy stuff," Finley prods.

"Mystery Man popped back up on her radar," Dylan tells her.

Sitting up a little further, an intrigued Finley asks, "Wait, the guy from senior year?"

"Yup," Dylan answers for me.

Finley's jaw drops. "The Mystery Man Cherry-Popper showed up again this summer?"

"Please don't call him the cherry-popper," I groan, covering my face with my hands.

"Did he, or did he not take your virginity?" Finley prods.

Flashes of the night I found Maverick on the roof after a game of Truth or Dare assault me. I collapse beside Finley on the couch and let my hands fall to my lap. "No comment."

"That's a yes." Dylan slaps Finley's feet off the coffee table and sits her ass in front of us. "But I think the real question is...are you finally ready to announce Mystery Man's true identity? Because we're bound to find out when we catch him sneaking out of your bedroom with us all living together."

"Let's not get ahead of ourselves," I mutter. "After the shit-storm I created, I'm not sure what's going on with Mystery Man, but I'm done hiding things from you guys. I'll tell you who he is on one condition."

"Yes?" they answer in unison.

"You guys *have* to promise to keep this between us. And I mean a cross-your-heart-and-hope-to-die kind of promise."

Finley and Dylan exchange glances, and both zip their lips like Finley did moments ago.

With a sigh, I admit, "Okay. So...Mystery Man is... Damn, I can't even say it." I suck my lips between my teeth and take a deep breath in through my nose. "Mystery Man is"—I cringe—"*Maverick*."

Gasps ensue, and they cover their mouths, their eyes practically jumping out of their skulls as they stare at me, speechless.

I curl a few more inches into the cushions while praying they swallow me whole and grumble, "Stop looking at me like that."

"Like what? Like you've been keeping a beyond massive secret from us?" Finley offers.

"Yeah, I know. And I wanted to tell you," I add, propping my feet onto one of the cardboard boxes labeled "girly stuff" in pink, glittery Sharpie marker I assume belongs to Fin. "It's just...at first, it was casual. And when things started feeling a little more serious, I was the one who wanted to keep it a secret, and Mav was the one twisting my arm, begging me to tell everyone we were seeing each other. Then prom happened, and we broke up, and I didn't think his identity mattered anymore." I take a deep breath, forcing myself to lay out the entire scenario in all its fucked-up glory. "Until I broke up with Archer, started hooking up with his twin brother—again—and told Archer about it because, let's be honest, it was way past due."

There. Now it's all out in the open.

"Wait," Dylan interjects. "Archer knew about Mystery Man, right?"

I nod. "Yeah, why?"

"Does he know Mystery Man is *Maverick*?" Finley prods.

I shake my head.

"So he thinks you're hung up on *two* guys?" Dylan demands.

Yeah, that makes it feel even worse.

"Maybe?" I hesitate. "Probably. Honestly, I'm not one hundred percent sure what's going through Archer's head. We aren't exactly on speaking terms right now."

"Duh," Finley replies. "Why didn't you tell him Maverick's your Mystery Man?"

"I don't know?" My head falls in my hands as another wave of shame rolls through me. "I felt like I was going to puke, and honestly, I was just trying to get everything over with as quickly as possible. I also didn't want to hurt him any more than I already had, and—"

"Pretty sure that ship has already sailed," Finley interrupts.

"Yeah, no shit," I mutter, puffing my cheeks out and dropping my hands to my lap. "I know it's messy, and I know I screwed up. Maverick suggested we come to a game night next weekend to kind of air everything out, and even though it sounds terrifying, I think it's a good idea to see Archer before family brunch. What do you guys think?"

"I think it's probably a smart idea, but does this mean you and Maverick are still together?" Dylan asks.

I chew on the inside of my cheek, offering a shrug. "Honestly, I don't know. After I broke up with Archer, Mav and I agreed to hook up without any labels and not to make it anything serious. But after seeing the repercussions and how much it's potentially hurting those around us, I've realized if he isn't interested in an actual relationship, I'm out."

"Damn," Dylan mutters.

Finley adds, "Good for you."

"Yeah." I offer a sad smile. "I also told him to be patient until I could figure out what's going on with Archer. He agreed it's probably a smart idea and promised to keep his distance this week until the party. He wants to talk afterward."

"Well, that's good, isn't it?" Dylan prods.

"I dunno." I shrug. " I'm kind of terrified to hear what he has to say."

Finley eyes me warily. "Why are you so scared to talk to him?"

Giving up, I stare at the ceiling. "Because if I do, I'll have to ask why he broke up with me."

Dylan frowns. "Don't you want to know?"

"Of course, I want to know."

"So, why haven't you asked him?"

It's a good question. I was wondering the same thing long before Tatum brought it up.

Nibbling on the little patch of skin between my thumb and thumbnail, I admit, "I'm scared of what his answer will be. If it's for a stupid reason, I have to face the fact that even if I'm in love with Maverick Buchanan, he'll never feel the same way, and I'm wasting my time with a guy who doesn't want the same things I do."

"And what if it's a good reason?" Dylan prods carefully.

"Then it's even worse," I admit. "Because…if we couldn't be together when things were easy, when his brother wasn't my ex-boyfriend and all we had to worry about was our families accepting our relationship, who's to say we can be together now?" I thread my fingers through my hair and push it away from my face. "Things are so much messier, you guys. I'm honestly not sure how we can come back from it all. And that's…terrifying."

"We get it," Dylan murmurs. "You have every right to be scared."

"Thanks," I sigh and attempt to shake off my morose thoughts. "But one relationship fix at a time, right? Once I smooth things over with Archer, I'll be able to figure out what to do with Mav. Or at least, that's the plan. Do you guys want to come with me to a game night next weekend?"

"Uh, duh." Finley bumps her shoulder against mine. "I already told you I'm dying to attend one of those things. The question is, should I bring popcorn when I get front-row seats to your first interactions with the bone brothers?"

"Do *not* call them the bone brothers," I warn.

"Come on, it's kind of fitting," she returns with a smirk.

"Doesn't make it any funnier," I argue. "And technically, Archer and I didn't bone."

Finley's eyes pop, and she shares a look with Dylan. "Seriously? You guys were together for like...a couple months, right?"

"I told him I wasn't ready," I admit when my phone buzzes in my lap.

"Who is it?" Dylan asks.

A message from Reeves shines back at me from the screen.

"It's Reeves."

"Who's Reeves?" Dylan asks.

"He's one of the roommates," I tell her.

"Oo, is he cute? He has to be cute," Finley answers for herself. "All cute guys hang out together. It's like a rule or something."

Ignoring her, I open Reeves' text.

REEVES

Hi.

ME

Hi.

REEVES

I heard I'm throwing another Game Night next weekend.

And, yes, I'll do it for you.

ME

Who said it's for me?

REEVES

Silly, Ophelia. You think I don't see the drama you've created?

I grimace.

ME

Is it obvious?

REEVES

You have no fucking idea. ;) I have one condition.

ME

What's your condition?

REEVES

You bring your new roommates.

ME

Since when do I have roommates?

REEVES

Since I saw them unloading their shit earlier.

ME

Caught that, did you?

REEVES

I like to stay up to date on my neighbors' comings and goings.

I snort and type my response.

ME

Of course you do. Fine. I'll bring them.

REEVES

You gonna introduce me to them?

ME

Do I have to?

REEVES

Obviously.

ME

You're a horn dog.

REEVES

Would you expect anything less?

As I catch myself biting back my amusement, my phone vibrates with another message.

REEVES

And that wasn't an answer, by the way.

ME

Yes, I'll introduce you.

REEVES

I knew you were my favorite. Do you have any preference for what game we play?

I look up at the girls and ask, "Any preferences for what game you want to play during Game Night?"

"Oo, we can pick?" Finley asks.

I look down at my phone and reread Reeves' message. "Apparently."

"What about Sardines?" Dylan offers.

Finley's eyes light up. "Oo, how 'bout Spin the Bottle?"

"Yeah, 'cause your brother will totally approve," I quip.

"Or your boyfriend," Dylan jokes.

Finley counters, "Har, har. I suggested it so you could finally get someone to kiss those virgin lips."

Dylan huffs, "Hey, I've been kissed before."

"Yeah. Twice," Finley reminds her. "And you're eighteen. It's both adorable and supremely pathetic. Come on, Dylan. The more you do it, the less scary it is."

"For you, maybe." Dylan shivers. "The last guy I kissed passed me his bubble gum."

My face sours. "Gross."

"You have no idea," Dylan deadpans.

"Yeah. And let's not forget her first kiss, shall we?" Finley chimes in, not even bothering to hide her amusement. "I still can't believe you got so drunk, when he stuck his tongue into your mouth, it triggered your gag reflex, and you almost puked all over him."

Dylan glares back at her. "I'm so glad I told you the story."

Finley grins wider. "So am I."

"Anyway," Dylan turns back to me. "What about Truth or Dare?"

"We always play Truth or Dare."

"Duh, because it's a classic," Finley says. "But if you're not in the mood, we could always do Never Have I Ever."

"Oo, I like that one!" Dylan chirps. "I always win."

"Or lose since you always end the night sober," I say without bothering to smother my amusement.

She pouts. "Good point. I haven't done anything fun."

"You've done lots of fun things. But not many of them are called out when we play Never Have I Ever," I tell her. "That being said, I think it's a good starting game. Do you guys agree?"

"Yup," they reply.

"Okay." I look back at my phone and type my response.

ME

The girls voted for Never Have I Ever. Thoughts?

REEVES

Classic. It's good for big groups. I'll get the ball rolling.

ME

Thanks.

REEVES

Anytime, Lia.

43

OPHELIA

It was a long week of radio silence. Maverick texted me a couple of times, but I told him I felt guilty texting when his brother refused to respond to any of my messages, so Mav told me he'd back off, but only if I promised to give him a chance to talk tonight.

And because I have an addiction to all things Maverick Buchanan, I agreed.

The place is packed, making previous parties look like small get-togethers compared to the bodies jammed into the boys' house. I had a feeling it was crazier than usual when I was getting ready, and my bathroom wall was shaking with the music, but this is something else. Their front door is propped open, and the front porch is practically spilling over with people.

If only I liked crowds more.

I tear my attention from a couple making out on the grass outside and nudge a discarded cup from my end of the porch to the boys' side.

"I guess summer break's over," I mutter under my breath

as I slip between two bodies blocking the entrance, the girls moving in behind me.

People are everywhere. The nooks. The crannies. The couches. The hallway. Almost every inch feels like it's filled with hot, gyrating bodies while music plays over the speakers.

Finley grins and grabs my arm, squeezing it softly. It's like her excitement is literally more than her petite frame can handle. Dylan, however, hesitates. "Yeah, I think I'm gonna—"

"Nope!" Finley loops her arm through Dylan's. "You're not going anywhere. Come on."

Jutting her bottom lip out, Dylan lets out a groan. "Seriously, are you and Aunt Kate even related? My mom says she hated parties when they were in college, and you're her daughter."

"Dude, my parents ask the same thing all the time," Finley says with a laugh. "I think you can blame my half-sisters. The age differences made for some *fun* experiences growing up." She tugs Dylan inside. "Now, come on. Let's go find some fun."

Reeves is busy making out with a girl in the corner. Trevor Cameron, the blonde asshole on the men's team, is chatting with a few of the other players while Griffin is talking to a brunette with long silky hair that reaches her back. As for Archer, Maverick, and Everett? They've yet to make an appearance, but I'm sure they'll be around soon.

Not that I want them to be. I'm not sure who's aware of my breakup with Archer since I've basically been hiding in my house whenever I'm not at practice, and I don't know if he's told anyone about my little hookup with Maverick, either. The combination makes me dread and second-guess every single look cast my way. I can't hide away in my house anymore, though, which means I need to pull up my big girl panties and face the fallout of…everything, even when it's terrifying. I just wish I knew what Archer was thinking.

Sliding my phone from my back pocket, I send him another text.

ME

Hey. Just got here. I hope it's okay.

I stare at the screen, but he doesn't reply.

Of course not.

"Okay, so where's the alcohol?" Dylan asks. "I need a drink to get through this night."

"Whatever, this is going to be fun," Finley promises. "I bet they have some drinks in the kitchen."

Acting as if she owns the place, Finley leads us into the kitchen and pours herself some Diet Coke. Finley doesn't drink alcohol since it can trigger her epilepsy, but with enough sass while sober, she's never needed the liquid courage. Unlike Dylan, who looks like she might puke if anyone tries to talk to her. My hands feel sweaty, so I wipe them against my jean shorts and grab a seltzer from a red cooler beside the table leg. It fizzles against my tastebuds as I take a sip. I let out a slow breath, waiting for its warmth to spread and hopefully calm my anxiety.

Resting the cool can against my lips, I scan the space. When a familiar profile grabs my attention from the hall, my brows pull, and I examine it closer.

It's Mav.

He looks good. His dark T-shirt stretches across his pecs and hugs his biceps. He pushes his wavy hair away from his face as he scans the family room and gives the kitchen his full attention.

When he catches me staring, he dips his head in greeting and strides toward me.

Shit.

I'm not ready. Not when Archer could be anywhere. Could see us together. Could hold it against me.

My spine turns into a steel rod as I freeze in place while he approaches. When he gets close enough, he pulls Dylan and Finley into quick side hugs. I wait for him to give me one as well, but he doesn't touch me. He only offers me a smile. "Opie."

"Mav," I murmur.

The same swell of butterflies bat their wings inside my stomach, and I fold my arms, hoping to calm the stupid things.

It doesn't work.

His smile widens, but he doesn't comment. "I'll see you outside, yeah?"

I nod. "Okay."

He slips past me, letting his fingers brush against mine as he heads to the back door and onto the patio. I ache to grab hold of his hand and link it with mine. Instead, I watch him leave, wishing I could pull him aside and ask what he wants to talk to me about. What he wants to say. If he really misses me the same way I've missed him, despite the short span of time it's been since we've been together.

An arm is tossed around my shoulder, and Reeves yanks me into his side, pulling me from my thoughts.

"I see you're making yourselves at home," he notes.

Snapping myself from staring at Maverick's backside, I turn to Reeves and give him my full attention. "Hello to you, too, Reeves."

With a boyish smirk, he asks, "Care to introduce me to your friends?"

Friends. Right.

Clearing my throat, I shrug out of his grasp and motion to my cousins. "Reeves, this is Finley, Everett's little sister, and Dylan, Griffin's little sister. Fin, Dylan, this is Reeves."

349

Shamelessly, his eyes roll over each of them. "The family's all here, I see."

"Would you expect anything less?" Finley grins, taking a sip of her drink.

"Of course not." Reeves' chuckle is low and throaty as he looks at me. "How are you doing?"

Act. Normal.

I force a smile. "Never better. You?"

"Could be a little better. Your boy has his panties in a twist." He lifts his chin toward the back patio.

"Oh?" Finley interjects. "Which one?"

I glare at her, and she grins. "I'm teasing."

"No, she isn't," Reeves jokes. "And now that you mention it, I guess I meant both of them. Wanna tell me what it's all about, Ophelia?"

I clear my throat and take another sip of my drink. "No comment."

His eyes shine with amusement as he watches me. "Of course not." When he realizes I'm not willing to spill the beans anytime soon, he scratches the scruff of his jaw and turns to my friends. "So, are you guys ready for your first Game Night?"

"Probably not," Dylan mutters into her cup.

Finley elbows her in the ribs, adding, "She's lying. We're definitely ready. Bring it on."

"You don't like games, Dylan?" he asks.

She chokes on her drink, and Finley slaps her back as she coughs violently.

Surprised by her response, Reeves steps forward to help her. "You okay?"

"She's fine," Finley answers. "She isn't used to guys talking to her."

"Finley!" Dylan snaps.

"What? It's true!"

"So help me, Finley, I will hide a frog in your bed if you keep talking," Dylan threatens under her breath.

With a gasp, Finley clutches at her chest. "You wouldn't dare."

Dylan pastes a fake smile on and directs it to an eavesdropping Reeves while reaching for the back of Finley's elbow and pinching. "Make it *two* frogs."

Eyes wide, Finley gasps. "So help me——"

"You know I would," Dylan seethes.

"Okay, okay." Finley turns to Reeves and smiles. "I was lying. Dylan is totally used to talking to guys and isn't acting weird right now. At. All."

His mouth lifts with amusement as Reeves leans closer to the chaos, holding Dylan's attention hostage. "Don't worry, Dylan. I like making my girls squirm."

She gulps but doesn't comment.

With another deep chuckle, he adds, "Yeah, you're gonna be fun. I can tell." He steps back, giving her room to breathe, and rubs his hands together, tacking on one more devilish smirk for good measure.

Cupping his hands around his mouth, he yells, "Game Night is about to start! If you're interested in playing, join us out back with a full cup of your favorite beverage of choice." He heads toward the exit, and a crowd follows him.

"Dude," Finley gushes. She fans herself with her hand while balancing her drink with her opposite one. "Am I the only one hot and bothered from that interaction or what?"

"Yeah, it was a *lot* of fun," Dylan mutters.

"Aw, come on. I think he likes you," Finley argues.

Dylan scoffs. "And *I* think he has player written all over him."

"There's nothing wrong with hanging out with a player." Finley nudges Dylan with her shoulder. "As long as you keep your heart in check—"

"No offense, Fin, but I'm not you," Dylan interrupts. "I can hardly talk to normal guys. You really think I want to attempt to keep up with someone like *him?*" She snorts. "I might be naive, but I'm not delusional." Throwing the rest of her drink back, Dylan adds another heavy splash of rum into her cup, grumbling, "Come on. Let's get this party over with."

"That's the spirit," Finley says dryly when Everett approaches us with a sour look.

"What are you doin' here, Fin?" he demands.

"Uh, hi, big brother." She grins and gives him a quick squeeze. "I was—"

His eyes fall to her drink. "Are you drinking alcohol?"

Tilting her head, Finley replies, "What do you think?"

"I think you're underage."

"And I think we both know I'm not stupid enough to drink, but even if I *was,* this is the best place for me to mess with alcohol, don't you think? Where I'm safe, and you can keep an eye on me?" She bats her lashes at him innocently and pats his chest.

Clearly, he doesn't buy her bullshit, but he shoves her softly toward the back patio anyway. "Come on, smart-ass."

With another light squeal of excitement, Finley sticks her tongue out at him over her shoulder and heads outside while the rest of us follow them.

"I see you're in the mood to play nice," I quip.

"Hardly," Everett mutters as his hand finds my waist and he guides me outside. "I'm too buzzed to deal with her right now. Besides, Never Have I Ever is pretty harmless compared to the other games we play, so I'm gonna let it slide."

"Until they start asking sexual questions, and you see what your little sister's done while you've been away," Dylan points out. "It'll be a real hoot, am I right?"

"At least I won't have to worry about you on that front. Right, Dylan?" he returns.

She glares back at him but doesn't deny it as she steps over the threshold into the backyard, the warm summer breeze ruffling her long blonde hair. Chairs are set up in a large circle, and another table is by the back door, littered with liquor. Most of the seats are already taken, but there's a small cluster still available. Dylan and Finley take the first seats, leaving an open spot sandwiched between Dylan and an unsuspecting Maverick, who's already talking to Everett on his opposite side.

Seriously?

Pressing my lips together, I square my shoulders, walk to the empty spot, sit down, and clutch my can of seltzer in my lap. When Maverick's conversation continues, and he doesn't slip his arm around my shoulders, I slowly relax. Pinning my drink between my thighs, I pull my phone out and check my texts.

Archer still hasn't replied, so I send him another message.

ME

> Where are you? I don't want you to feel like you can't be at your own party just because I'm here. Do you want me to leave?

I hit send, waiting for the three little dots notifying me he's responding. I don't receive anything but silence.

Tension hits the side of my face a moment later. My cheeks burn, and I peek up at Maverick, finding him staring at me. His expression is almost unreadable.

Except I know him.

And I know exactly what he's thinking.

He's worried about his brother too.

"He's in his room," Mav mutters. "Maybe he'll come out once the game starts."

"Maybe," I whisper, not exactly convinced.

His eyes darken as they drop to my lips. "Do you have any idea how much it's killing me not to kiss you right now?"

"Mav…"

"Yeah, I know. One fucked-up relationship at a time." He shakes his head and stands. "All right. Rules are simple. Never Have I Ever. We go in a circle. If you've done the thing someone expresses, you take a drink. If you haven't done it, you don't drink. Last one standing wins. Any questions?" He barely waits a beat, adding, "Good. Everett will go first."

Everett says, "Never have I ever had a period."

A round of amusement hits. Every girl lifts their drink and takes a sip.

Reeves lifts his untouched glass into the air and adds, "Never have I ever kissed a guy."

The girl next to him smacks his arm. "You trying to get me drunk, Reeves?"

Reeves grins shamelessly back at her. "Drink up, Britney."

"Whatever," she replies but takes a long gulp from her red Solo cup.

I do the same.

"Never have I ever ice skated," she says.

I take another drink, finishing the last of my beverage. Seemingly out of nowhere, a freshman offers me a plastic cup with amber liquid.

The guys are good at hosting and seem to think of everything, including refills. I'll give them that much.

"Thanks," I murmur as I take the beverage, and he nods, heading to the opposite side of the circle where a few girls look close to finishing their drinks.

"Never have I ever sucked a cock," Cameron says beside Britney.

Most of the girls take another drink, but a few keep their cups in their hands, including Dylan, who gives me an awkward smile, resting her barely-touched drink in her lap. As I do my shot, I catch Reeves staring at her, his gaze openly curious. To be fair, I'm pretty sure he doesn't have a subtle bone in his body. Everett's staring at her, too, but his expression is unreadable until he catches Finley taking a sip, and his jaw tightens.

Sorry, dude. Your sister likes guys. Deal with it.

The game continues, and if the boys keep this up, I'll be shit-faced before it's even my turn. Then again, maybe it's for the best. Archer still hasn't shown up, and the idea of tracking him down so we can hopefully rip the Band-Aid off and talk to each other makes me feel like I need the liquid courage.

This is going to be a long night.

44

OPHELIA

Tapping my finger against my already half-empty mystery drink, tasting a lot like whiskey with a splash of Diet Coke, I bounce my knee up and down while attempting to focus on the game instead of the guy sitting beside me.

Seriously. How can one man smell so good?

We continue around the circle, taking turns drinking or waiting for the next question. When it's almost Finley's turn, a shadow grabs my attention from the patio, and my breath stalls.

Archer.

His hair is a mess, like he's been running his hands through it, and his eyes are nothing but slits as he searches the grassy area. I clench the cup harder in my grasp, itching to run toward him and apologize. For his nose. For hurting him. For loving his brother even though I shouldn't. Instead, I keep my butt in place and wait. Maybe this was a bad idea. Maybe I should go home.

And maybe you should grow a freaking backbone, Ophelia.

When his eyes land on me, Archer steps off the stairs but hesitates when Maverick shifts beside me in his seat.

Tension thickens the air around us as my attention shifts from one Buchanan brother to the next. Maverick's messages mentioned he hasn't spoken to his brother, but they live together, and it's been a week. Is it really so easy to avoid someone?

Archer looks sloshed. Like he's already had at least five shots as he continues toward the circle and plops into an open seat beside Griffin. Black swallows the blue in his eyes, making him look even more like his twin. His friendly demeanor has morphed into a cold, detached villain. It only feeds my anxiety, making it almost impossible to sit here and do nothing. Say nothing. Explain nothing.

Griffin takes his turn, but I don't hear it. Cups are lifted. Shots taken. Laughter echoes around the circle. I don't register any of it. I'm too busy being ripped apart by my best friend across from me.

"My turn," Archer announces, leaning back in his seat and stretching his legs out in front of him. Everyone looks at him and waits. "Never have I ever kissed brothers."

My eyes thin as he stares at me, making his intentions clear. He isn't here to talk. He's here to embarrass me. To make me feel an ounce of the pain I've inflicted on him. And since he's clearly already drunk, his thoughts are a jumbled mess. Any hopes of speaking with the calm, level-headed friend I love go up in smoke. But if this is what he wants, what he needs to help him forgive me, so be it. Britney drinks from her cup, and my hand shakes as I lift mine to my lips, taking a small sip of my beverage. Even if someone sees me, it's not like they know my history. I could be thinking about any brothers. Hell, I'm pretty sure I've kissed Jaxon and Griffin during Truth or Dare and Spin the Bottle at some point or another. They were on the cheek, but still. This sip doesn't have to relate to the Buchanan twins.

Right?

Beside him, Everett looks around the group, confirming we're all ready to move on. "Never have I ever worn a thong."

The girls all take drinks. Then it's Finley's turn. "Never have I ever gone skinny dipping."

A few of the guys and several girls chuckle, each lifting cups to their lips and drinking.

Once everyone finishes, Dylan goes next. "Never have I ever...gotten an F."

With the exception of Finley, Dylan, and Archer, everyone lifts their cups.

Now, it's my turn. My hands still tremble as I throttle my nearly empty cup. I don't want to play this game anymore. I want to talk to Archer. I want him to listen to me. I want us to have an actual conversation instead of being the recipient of his glare from across the yard. But I also don't want to simply walk away. So, where does it leave me?

"Your turn," Dylan murmurs, snapping me out of my staring contest with the pissed-off Buchanan brother on the opposite side of the circle.

My turn.

Right.

"Never have I ever...broken a girl's heart," I offer in an attempt to pick something relatively safe.

Archer's sharp voice cuts through the circle. "Broken plenty of guys', though. Right, Lia?"

My gaze snaps to him again. He doesn't take a drink from the glass bottle dangling from his fingers between his thighs.

Ass.

However, all the other guys chuckle lightly into their cups, each confirming their player status. From the corner of my eye, I catch Maverick lifting his drink to his mouth. He brushes the back of his hand against my knee. It's subtle. Practically innocent. But laced with an apology I didn't know I needed until now. At least someone cares about this messed-up situation. I close my eyes for a brief second, savoring the feel of his warm skin on mine until it disappears. He leans forward, resting his forearms on his thighs.

Confirming he has everyone's attention, Maverick announces, "Never have I ever embarrassed a girl on purpose or made her feel guilty for something she has no reason to feel guilty about."

Shit.

I glance at Maverick again, but he isn't looking at me. He's glaring at Archer across the circle.

"Mav," I whisper.

The tension radiates off him and seeps into my skin, triggering my fingers into motion. I reach for him to sit back in his chair. To relax. To *not* make a scene.

Archer's gaze darkens as it falls on my hand resting on Maverick's stiff shoulder, and he says, "I wanna go again."

"It's not your turn," Maverick grits out.

"And I don't give a shit, *Mystery Man*."

A gasp slips past my parted lips as his words wash over me.

Mystery Man.

He knows.

I don't know how he knows, but he does.

Shit.

This is why he's so pissed. Why he's acting the way he is.

Archer shoves to his feet, not even bothering to hide his irritation anymore. His chair topples over onto the grass, and his chest heaves. I've never seen him like this. So angry. So unhinged. So volatile.

"Archer," I call out, desperate for privacy. For a chance to explain myself. But he raises his hand, silencing me.

With his tortured focus glued to his twin, Archer spits, "Never have I ever kissed my brother's girlfriend."

Shit.

Shit, shit, shit, shit.

Maverick lifts the cup to his mouth and drinks it as the crowd stays silent, watching the exchange. It doesn't matter how I broke up with Archer before Maverick kissed me. Again, accuracy isn't the point. Archer's goal is to shine a light on what happened. It's to paint a big, fat A on our chests like in *The Scarlet Letter*. And Maverick's giving his brother exactly what he wants.

Once he's finished, Maverick says, "Never have I ever taken a girl for granted."

Archer grins but doesn't drink any of his beverage. He lifts a brow as if waiting for Maverick to eat his words and take a shot. When Maverick doesn't, Archer shifts his attention to me, and all I see is contempt. "Never have I ever cheated on my boyfriend with his twin brother."

Silence.

Fucking silence.

It's so loud my ears ring as every single person around the circle stares at me. My chest tightens, and my lungs give out, but I don't move. I don't even blink. I can only stare at my best friend. Shocked. Hurt. Sickened. I'm blindsided and feel like I'm not even in my body anymore. It's as if I'm watching the entire scenario unfold from a distance, and all I can think is, *Poor girl. I can't believe he would do that to her.*

As I stay frozen in my seat, Archer's eyes hold mine hostage, daring me to *not* take a sip. To not out myself in front of everyone. It's embarrassing. And rude. And uncalled for since I didn't cheat on him. We weren't together anymore. But it doesn't excuse my behavior or the pain I've put him through. Nothing does.

"You gonna take a sip, Lia?" Archer challenges. His tone is downright lethal.

So this is how it is.

It doesn't matter what I have to say or how I've been trying to talk to him in private. Right now, he wants a show. He wants to embarrass me the same way I embarrassed him by falling for his brother.

Fine.

Without bothering to explain myself, I lick my lips and throw the rest of my drink back. The bitter alcohol goes down like water, but even its warmth does shit to defrost the frigid gaze holding me in place from across the lawn. When my cup's completely empty, I stand and head inside without a backward glance.

Footsteps follow me as I make my way past the kitchen.

"Ophelia," a low voice calls, but I don't answer.

"Ophelia," he yells again.

It's Maverick. The deep growl. The hint of impatience.

I can't face him right now.

I don't want to.

Not when everything is such a mess. Not when I feel so ashamed. I chose to go to prom with Archer. I chose to date him despite knowing I was still hung up on his brother.

This is on me. But it's on Maverick too. For breaking my heart in the first place. For playing with me—toying with me —when he damn well knew I still wanted him even though I shouldn't. And I'm not ready to face him. Not when I don't know what I can have or what I've already lost, thanks to everything that's happened.

Ignoring him, I rush out the front door and take a sharp turn into my own house, locking the door behind me. The girls have their keys, but I'm not in the mood for anyone else. Not tonight.

A loud knock pounds on the solid wood as I rest my back

against it, sliding to the ground while my mind replays what just transpired.

My dirty laundry was aired out in front of everyone. Everett. Griffin. Reeves. Let alone a few of my new team-mates and a cacophony of strangers I'd hoped to turn into friends one day. Now they know the truth. I love two broth-ers. One in nothing more than a platonic way, and the other I'm so in love with, it hurts. But it doesn't take away the gravity of my feelings for either of them.

And even though I'm pissed at Archer for putting me on the spot, I deserved it, and I'm still the catalyst. The one who screwed up in the first place. He didn't deserve this, and neither did Maverick. To be caught in the crosshairs. To be pitted against each other. To be turning their frustration on each other when I deserve it. I deserve it all.

Closing my eyes, I listen for Maverick's retreating foot-steps, but I don't hear any.

I can't even blame Archer for being a dick. I knew all his bottled-up frustration was going to come out at some point. In a way, I was at the party so it *would* come out. Like drawing poison from a snake bite. I knew it was necessary. Inevitable. But I didn't think it would happen in front of everyone. At least it wasn't in front of our parents. That has to count for something, doesn't it?

"I know you're in there, Goose," Maverick murmurs.

Softly, I knock the back of my head against the door, wishing it would bring clarity.

"Talk to me, Ophelia," he begs.

Speaking of drawing out poison.

Pushing to my feet, I turn around, unlock the door, and open it before I lose my nerve. "Why did you break up with me?"

"What?"

"I want to know why you broke my heart before prom."

The front lawn is surprisingly empty. Everyone is still at the back of the house playing Never Have I Ever. It only amplifies Maverick's silence to my question. The gutted look on his face etches itself into my memory as I wait for him to say something. Anything.

When he doesn't, my blood boils. "You said you wanted to talk."

"I do, but—"

"Just answer the question, Mav."

"Ophelia..." He sighs, squeezing the back of his neck. "I will, but it's a long, complicated story, and after everything that happened tonight..."

"Fine." I nod. "Goodnight, Maverick."

I start to shut the door, but his palm slaps against it, preventing me from closing it as he stares at me with so much conviction, so much hurt, it nearly brings me to my knees.

"I didn't wanna do it this way," he murmurs.

"Do what?" I demand. "Tell me the answer to something I deserved to know months ago?"

His head jerks back a few inches, but he reaches for my arm. I shy away from his touch. He doesn't get to do this. To try to make things better by touching me when we both know our physical response to each other has never been the issue. It's this. Communicating. Actually talking instead of shoving our problems under the rug.

Helpless, Maverick runs his hands through his wavy hair and looks down at his dark biker boots. "You're right. You deserve to know the truth."

"Yeah. I do." I fold my arms and wait, refusing to invite him inside no matter how much I want to. "Tell me why you broke up with me."

His eyes snap to mine. "Tell me where you see your life in five years."

My mouth dips at the corners, and I hesitate as a heady sense of whiplash washes over me. "What?"

"You're the one always talking about the future," he pushes, moving closer to me, and this time, I let him. "Tell me where you see yourself in five years."

"Can we stay on topic, please? You and I—"

"Humor me, Lia," he begs. "Tell me where you see yourself in five years."

"Fine. Uh, graduated, obviously. Probably in a serious relationship. Hopefully still playing hockey. Why?"

He steps even closer and cages me in, leaning his elbow along the doorjamb behind me. "Ask me where I see myself in five years," he demands.

"Mav—"

"Just ask me."

I don't know what stupid game he's playing, but it's getting on my nerves. With a huff, I ask, "Where do you see yourself in five years?"

"I don't."

My brows knit. "What?"

"I don't see myself in five years."

"Why? Because you suck at thinking about your future?" I assume.

His expression falls. "Because I don't have a future, Lia."

I pull back, surprised. "What?"

His Adam's apple bobs, but he doesn't pull away. "I don't have a future."

"Mav—"

He gives me another helpless, almost resigned look as his chest caves. "I'm dying, Opie."

45
OPHELIA

The words crash into me like a wrecking ball. They nearly knock me on my ass as I stand in front of him, replaying the words over and over again in my head.

I'm dying, Opie.

I'm dying.

Dying.

Clutching the edge of the door behind me for balance, I whisper, "What?"

His eyes shut, and he shakes his head. "Don't make me say it again."

"No. It's not possible," I argue. "There's no way—"

"You really think I'd make this shit up, Lia?"

He's right. He wouldn't. No one would. You don't joke about death. You don't joke about dying. But the alternative makes me queasy and lightheaded. It's not true. It can't be. Acid burns my throat, but I swallow it back, sucking my quivering bottom lip into my mouth.

Attempting to maintain a semblance of composure, I slip

my hand between us and tuck my hair behind my ear, ignoring the way my body trembles. "H-how do you know?"

"I'd been feeling really tired and shit, even passed out during practice at the end of last season, remember?"

My lips part, and I nod. "I remember."

"I'd been getting winded and dizzy at practice, so I went to the doctor, and—"

"Before prom," I finish. The memory is both hazy, yet so sharp and vibrant, it feels like it happened yesterday.

He dips his chin. "Yeah. The, uh, the doctor discovered I have HCM."

The letters are meaningless to me, so I ask, "What's HCM?"

"Hypertrophic cardiomyopathy."

"I don't"—I peek up at him—"I don't know what that means, either."

His chuckle is almost warm but defeated, too, as it ruffles the hair along the top of my head. "My heart's hyper-trophying."

The words jumble together like Scrabble pieces, leaving me just as confused. I shake my head, wiping at the corner of my eye and the moisture collecting there. "You're gonna have to spell it out for me, Mav."

He grabs my hand, dragging his thumb along my finger-tips in hopes of erasing the evidence of my tears. Bringing them to his lips, he kisses me. "The tissue in my heart is getting thicker," he clarifies, "making it harder for my heart to pump and work properly. For most people, it's not life-threatening. They can go on to live normal lives as long as they keep their blood pressure in check and their doctors keep an eye on them."

"Most people?" I swallow back the stubborn bile, but it still coats my throat. "I assume that doesn't include you?"

"Doctor said I got the shit end of the deal."

Squeezing my eyes closed, I let a tear slip free as his words wash over me. "W-what do you mean?"

"It isn't only a portion of my heart." He sighs. "It's the entire thing, Lia. My entire fucking heart is hypertrophying, and it's only a matter of time until it stops beating entirely."

Angrily, I tear my hand from his and wipe the stream of tears from my cheeks, but they're only replaced with more, making my attempts useless. I hate the acceptance in his voice. The resignation. The way he's giving in and refusing to fight. "S-so we find you a new doctor. We get you some medicine—"

"Medicine doesn't fix this."

"Then we get you a new heart."

"Not exactly an easy ask, Ophelia."

Frustration floods my system, and I fist my hands at my sides. "I didn't say it would be easy, but—"

"I'm doing everything I can."

"Do your parents know? Does Archer? What about your little sister? Or Reeves, or—"

He shakes his head. "You're the only one."

I shouldn't be surprised, but I am. Maverick's always been a bit of a lone wolf, but he hasn't told *anyone*? Hasn't let anyone else help him carry this burden? Not a single soul?

My back hits the edge of the door, and I start to collapse when his hands find my waist. He guides me inside, closing the door behind us. It's dark, but neither of us bother to turn on any lights as my ass finds the ground in the middle of the small entryway. I cover my mouth, the weight of the situation finally hitting its mark and making it almost impossible to think straight, let alone breathe. I feel like I've been punched in the gut. Like this a dream. A nightmare. And I'd give anything to wake up from it.

"You need to tell your family," I decide.

Towering over me, he shakes his head. "I can't."

I lift my head and look up at him. "Why not?"

Maverick sits beside me and rubs his hands along his thighs, staring blankly in front of him. "You think I want to look in my parents' eyes and see them mourn me before I'm even gone?"

"So you'd prefer to blindside them?"

He jerks back as if I've sucker punched him, but I don't stop. I can't. Not now. Not anymore.

"How dare you, Maverick? I know you probably think I'm being selfish or whatever, but if I have to protect you from you, I will. How dare you hide this from everyone you know and love? How dare you carry this all on your own when it's the last thing any of your family would want, and it's the last thing you deserve? You have your friends, your parents, your little sister. Archer. Me. You're not alone, and whether or not you want to hurt us by sharing this burden, you deserve to have your family and friends rallying behind you every step of the way."

"Opie."

He reaches for me, but I shy away from him again, my tears falling freely now. "No!"

"Opie." He reaches for me again, pulls me into his lap, and cradles me like I'm a child. Wrapping my arms around his neck, I cry, letting my heart break for the man in front of me as every hope and dream dissipates. It isn't fair. None of this is. It's Mav. My Mav. My everything. He can't leave me. He can't die. He can't. My hands fist the soft cotton of his T-shirt as sobs wrack my body. His arms tighten around me, his entire body enveloping mine in a cocoon of warmth and Maverick. His cologne clings to his shirt, and I breathe it in, committing it to memory.

"Sh…," he coos against the top of my head. "Sh… It's okay."

It's not okay. It isn't. He knows it as well as I do. But

sometimes life isn't fair. Sometimes it isn't a fairytale. Sometimes, it's a tragedy. And my love story with Maverick Buchanan? It's exactly that. A tragedy. One I'll never recover from.

"I hate seeing you hurt, baby," he whispers.

My head bobs up and down in the crook of his neck.

"I'd give anything to take this away." His chest rumbles against mine. "Anything."

"Promise me you'll tell them," I beg.

The familiar rhythm of his hands running along my spine ceases. "Ophelia…"

I pull away from him and look up. "Promise me, Mav. They deserve to know."

"Do you have any idea how much it guts me to see you like this?" he demands. "To see the way your lashes are clinging together from crying and how red your face is?" He rubs his thumb along my left cheek, erasing the tracks of moisture. "You really think I wanna see my mom like this? My dad? My brother? My fucking baby sister?"

"They deserve—"

"I know what they deserve," he grits out. "They deserve a healthy son. A healthy brother. They deserve grandchildren and nieces and nephews. Just like how you deserve a husband who can give you kids and stability and a fucking future."

"No one can guarantee the future, Mav."

"Says the girl obsessed with hers," he counters with a sad smile, pushing my hair away from my forehead. I grab his wrist and lean into his touch on my cheek.

"Wanna know something crazy?" he whispers.

I nod.

"Most people never find out about their diagnosis with HCM."

My breath hitches. "What?"

"Most people never even know."

I pull away from him again but stay seated in his lap in the middle of the dark room while the world continues spinning around us.

"They just what?" I ask. "Drop dead one day when their heart stops working?"

I take in his strong jaw and how his molars grind as he stares over my shoulder at nothing at all. His hair is messy, but otherwise, he looks fine. Healthy as ever. Gorgeous. Untouchable. Like a Greek god. A workhorse. An athlete who has his entire career ahead of him. Or *would've*, if he hadn't quit.

Slowly, Maverick's head bobs in a single nod. "Sometimes I wonder if it'd be easier that way. To not know."

"How can you say that?" I breathe out.

His eyes slice to mine, and the sadness swirling in the navy blue depths kills me. "Because if I didn't find out, we'd still be together, Goose. I would've taken you to prom. I would've told you I love you. I would've claimed you in front of both our families." His chest heaves, and he sniffs quietly. "I would've had a future with you."

A future.

Our future.

"This is why you broke up with me," I realize as everything clicks into place. "Because you found out about y-your condition."

All this time, all this heartache, all this questioning. None of it would've happened if he'd never received his diagnosis. If he'd never pushed me away all because he was trying to protect me. My house blurs around me as I press my fingers to my temple and attempt to calm my unsteady pulse, no matter how useless it is.

"It's not a condition, Opie." Maverick's forehead falls to mine. "It's a death sentence."

"You broke up with me because you were scared."

"I broke up with you because you deserve more than tying your future to mine."

"So instead, you let me tie it to your brother's."

His jaw tightens until he forces the muscles to ease and murmurs, "I tried to."

"Why would you do that if you still cared about me?"

"Because I felt guilty," he growls. "I *still* feel guilty for wanting to build a life with you while knowing I won't be there to help see it to fruition. You always talk about your future, Ophelia. With me, you don't have one. Only an expiration date hanging over our heads without knowing when it'll hit."

"Don't say that," I beg.

"But it's true." He squeezes my hips and tugs me closer. "And it makes me feel helpless, Lia. I've been trying to talk to you since you let me touch you behind the house. Trying to figure out a way to tell you I'm a selfish sonofabitch who wants you anyway. Despite the expiration date. Despite the complications. Despite my own fucking brother being in love with you. I want you. All of you. For a day. A week. A year. I love you, and I want you. I know I can't be your forever, but I'm begging you to be mine." He brings his hands to my cheeks and frames my face, his eyes desperate. "Please?"

He wants me. He wants me for as long as he can have me. For as long as he's still on this earth. He wants me to be his forever.

Stupid man. I've always been his forever, and we would've had so much more of it if he'd have simply opened up to me instead of pushing me away.

With a sad smile, I blink away the burn behind my eyes and rest my head in his hands. "Did you really think you had to ask?" I whisper. "It's always been Goose and Maverick, right?"

"Lia…"

"Something as silly as having HCM isn't going to get rid of me so easily, Maverick." A sad chuckle slips out of him, and I shake my head. "Not a chance. But I'm going to tell you something, and I don't know how much you'll like it."

"What is it?" he asks.

"I'm not going to lie to your family, Mav. I'm not going to keep this from them. Not when they deserve to know."

His palms fall from my face, but I grab them just as quickly, lacing our fingers together while refusing to let him go.

Looking down at our entwined hands, he murmurs, "Give me some time. Please?"

"Fine. But if they ask? If something happens? If they even give me a questioning look, I will scream it from the rooftops. We clear?"

His head falls in defeat. "Yeah, Opie. I hear you."

"Good." With another sniff, I let his hands go and wipe the rest of my tears from my cheeks, drying them and smoothing out the wet cotton against his strong chest and shoulder from my earlier meltdown. "I think I ruined your shirt."

He looks down at the mess as his mouth lifts at the edges. "Yeah, you kind of did."

"You should probably change."

"I don't care about my clothes, Ophelia. I only wanna hold you."

He is holding me, but I don't point it out. Honestly, I kind of want to crawl beneath his skin and stay there for the rest of my life. The rest of *his* life.

I know I should act normal. I know I should pretend everything's okay, or it'll only make him second guess telling his parents even more.

But I can't help it.

I'm drained. Physically spent. Emotionally spent. I've been put through the wringer. But Mav's had it so much worse, so what do I have to complain about? My bottom lip quivers as I nod and choke back tears, pulling a sad smile from the man in front of me.

"Come here, baby."

He pulls me closer and tilts my chin up, brushing his lips against mine.

It's a goodbye kiss. A welcome home kiss. An I-missed-you kiss. An I'm-going-to-miss-you kiss. It's toe-curling and heart-melting. It's soft and slow. It's everything a girl could want in a kiss and everything a girl could hate too. Because it's a promise. A warning. An apology.

It's Maverick.

The good.

The bad.

And the ugly.

And I've never craved anything more.

46

MAVERICK

Neither of us heard from Archer. I didn't expect us to. He was an ass last night. His actions were so unlike him, he's probably at home licking his wounds and drowning in self-loathing. He should be. I'm pissed at what he said to Ophelia. The way he made her feel.

If he wants to blame someone, he should blame me.

We'll get through it, though.

I spend the next day in bed with Ophelia at her place, and when the late afternoon hits, I invite her on a motorcycle ride. She says yes without hesitation. We take the long way, Ophelia's arms wrapped around my waist, and a familiar hum from the warm breeze surrounds us. It makes conversation nearly impossible. But it's nice. Cleansing almost. We make our way up the mountain on the winding road with Ophelia's front pressed to my back. Trees line both sides, but the view waiting for us spurs me on. I rev the engine, craving the adrenaline rush. I slowly brake as we approach the end of the road and the break in the treeline I know is coming.

I've been here dozens of times—hell, maybe a hundred—since my diagnosis. I craved the isolation. The peace. The beauty. It was like my soul needed the reminder not everything is shitty, and maybe, just maybe, someone out there has a plan. Someone who knows what they're doing. Then again, maybe there isn't.

But with a view like the one I know is coming, I can't help but wonder.

And for a guy who's dying, it's enough. The possibility. The potential. The *maybe.*

Different shades of orange, pink, and purple began painting the sky a few minutes ago, making the drive almost dreamlike. Or maybe it's the surreality of last night and today. I can't believe I told her everything. I can't believe she knows the truth. I can't believe she's here with me. With her arms wrapped around my waist and her desire to be my forever, even when she knows I can't be hers.

When we break free from the treeline, the colors grow even more vibrant, and I pull off to the side of the road, taking in the sun hidden beneath a blanket of clouds as it slowly sets. Once the tires meet dirt, I cut the engine, and it stops rumbling beneath us. Ophelia slips her helmet off, and her strawberry blonde hair cascades around her shoulders. It's even more red as the sunlight glints off it, framing her face and making her freckles pop off her porcelain skin.

When she catches me staring at her over my shoulder, she shies away with a soft smile playing at the edge of her lips. "What are you looking at?"

"You really are gorgeous, you know."

"Wanna talk gorgeous?" She tears her attention from me and looks out at the skyline. "This sunset is..." She whistles. "Am I right?"

"Yeah," I agree. "It's nice."

"Nice? My good sir, it's picture perfect." Pulling her phone from her back pocket, she scoots closer to my back and raises her cell into the air, framing us on the screen. The background is a canvas of colors, and she kisses my cheek while snapping a picture.

"Look at the camera," she orders.

I do.

"Smile," she adds.

A grin tugs at my mouth, but I'm no longer looking at my reflection. I'm too busy staring at the girl behind me on my bike. The girl doing her best to act normal despite everything I told her in the last twenty-four hours. It makes me love her even more.

She snaps a few more pictures and rests her head against my back, letting out a soft little sigh of content-ment. It's as if it soaks into my skin, releasing the constant ache in my chest ever since I found out about my death sentence, and I look out at the watercolor landscape in front of us.

With another click of the camera, she announces, "There. Perfect. Now, on to the next order of business."

"What business?"

"Well, the whole rumble of the engine and snuggling against a good-looking guy's back for the last forty-five minutes has me all hot and bothered." She swings her leg over the back of the bike and takes a few steps toward the ledge while still facing me with her arms open wide. "You gonna help a girl out or what?"

The last rays from the sun make her practically glow and highlight her curves as she cocks her head, waiting.

"Is this your way of coming on to me?" I ask.

"I'm sorry, was I being too subtle?" She hooks her thumbs in her jeans and shimmies them down her legs until I'm gifted with a view of her long, lean legs and smooth, silky skin. "Maverick, I want you to ravage me on this mountain and make me come at least two times," she challenges. "Was that direct enough for you?"

She's lucky this road is always empty, or I'd throw her over my shoulder and spank her ass for being so brazen.

"Yeah, I think it'll do." I climb off my bike and dig into the leather saddle bag, pulling out a small checkered blanket and spreading it on the grass.

"Do you always carry a blanket?" she asks.

"I do now."

With a laugh, she strides toward me and kneels in front of me. Her thighs are spread a few inches, showcasing the thin scrap of baby blue cloth covering her lower half as she smooths out the checkered fabric. "Now, do I keep undressing myself, or will you help me out a little?" She peeks up at me through her thick upper lashes. "Then again, I kind of like this position. Maybe it's you who's wearing too much clothing." Slowly, she slides her hands up her thighs and reaches for the top button on my jeans. My dick strains against the zipper, but I keep my hands fisted at my sides as she slowly slides it down.

A smile teases her lips as her tongue darts out and moistens the edge of her bottom lip. "Not gonna lie. I missed this." Her eyes lift to mine. "Missed you."

"Missed you too, Opie."

"My name isn't Opie." She slides her hand along the ridge of my cock through my boxers and pulls my hard length free from the black material. Slowly, she runs her hand up and down my shaft, but her eyes don't leave mine. My dick jerks in her palm as she leans closer, pressing a soft kiss against the tip. Leaning back a few inches, she blows against the head.

Fucking hell. She has no idea how often I dream of this. I drop my head back, staring at the swirling sky as I thread my fingers through her hair. Wet heat wraps around the head of my cock, and I close my eyes, lost in the feel of her mouth on me. I missed this. Ophelia. Her mouth. Her sass. Her silky hair. The little mewls she makes. The way she smiles. We were only apart for a little while, but it felt like a lifetime. Fuck, even before. Ever since my diagnosis, I've been holding back. Pretending I'm not obsessed with the girl in front of me in hopes of protecting her. But with everything out in the open, I feel like I can finally breathe.

My heart pounds in my chest harder and harder as I let her take the lead, sucking me off like a good girl. She takes me deeper, moaning softly. The vibration is almost more than I can bear. When I touch the back of her throat, her hands squeeze the base of my dick, and my balls tighten.

"You trying to kill me, Goose?" I rasp.

She looks up at me but doesn't stop swallowing my cock. Her head bobs up and down while her hand slides from the base of my dick to my balls. Driving me to the brink of insanity, she massages them, tugging gently and rolling them in her palm.

I tilt my head, studying her. "You *are* trying to kill me."

She slips back and smiles against the head, swirling her tongue around the tip, her eyes never leaving mine.

"It's working," I note. Her hair is like silk as I tangle my fingers in it, tugging tenderly.

Hollowing her cheeks, she sucks me harder, releases me with a soft pop, and gets right back to work on my erection.

"But what a way to go," I grunt. I brush my thumb against her wet lips while she continues rubbing her hand up and down my length, resting the head of my cock against her cheek as if she knows the image of her on her knees with those swollen lips will be branded into my memory for the rest of my measly existence.

But I don't want to come down her throat. Not yet. Not today. I want to savor this. Savor her. Commit it all to memory. Every touch. Every whimper. Every fucking kiss.

And even though it kills me, I slowly slide onto my knees

beside her, and she stretches out, laying back and resting her weight on her elbows as she looks up at me.

"Ah, so the man doesn't want my mouth anymore," she quips.

"Oh, I want your mouth." I crawl over her body, caging her in on both sides and capturing her lips with mine. I kiss her deeply, swallowing her soft moan and rubbing my bare cock against her center while my jeans hang around my ankles. Her damp underwear separates us, but the heat from her core seeps into me, and I drop my forehead to hers.

She has no idea how many times I've imagined this. Being with her again. Without any secrets. Without the questioning look in her eyes I put there the moment I broke up with her.

It's as if the last of our barriers have finally been broken down, leaving nothing but Ophelia Grace Taylor and Maverick Bud Buchanan. Only us in this moment. And if impending death has taught me anything, it's to grab hold of it with both hands.

I kiss Ophelia again, flicking my tongue along hers as my cock jerks against her core. Precum drips from the head, and I have no doubt it'll probably leave a wet spot on her underwear, but the idea only makes me harder. I want to mark her. Make her mine so no one ever questions who she belongs to, even if it's only for a little while.

"You're fucking perfect," I rasp. "You know that, right?"

She smiles against my lips. "Ditto."

I grind into her again, the heat from her pussy making my cock ache against her. "Do you have any idea how wet you are, baby?"

She squirms beneath me. "I think I have an idea."

My bare length rubs against her center as I shift my hips into her, causing her eyes to roll back and my own to become heavy with pleasure.

"Fuck, you have no idea how good you feel, and I'm not

even inside you." Chuckling, I torture us both with one more roll of my hips, kissing the edge of her mouth and scooting lower. Her shirt has already ridden up, giving me a glimpse of her toned stomach, but I push it the rest of the way off and palm her breasts in my hands.

"Fucking perfect," I growl.

"You said that already." She laughs and lets her thighs fall open. The damp spot at her core teases me, confirming my suspicion while her eyes shine with mirth as she bites her bottom lip.

"Doesn't make it less true," I mutter.

Dragging her fingertips along my spine, she murmurs, "I think it's time for another game of Truth or Dare."

My attention snaps from the scrap of cloth covering her to her eyes. "Right now?"

"Mm-hmm."

"No offense, baby, but I think we're a little busy."

"And I think I'll make it worth your while," she replies. "Besides. You want to make this last, right?"

"Fine," I grunt. "Truth or dare?"

"Truth," she replies.

"On a scale of one to ten, how does it feel when I do this?" I hold her gaze, slowly moving down her lithe body until her center is an inch from my lips. Leaning closer, I cover the damp fabric with my mouth and blow all the hot air in my lungs against her slit.

"Ten," she moans, tangling her fingers in my hair and tugging me closer.

I tease her clit through the scrap of cloth. Backing away, I mumble, "I believe it's my turn."

Her glare pulls a chuckle from me as I remind her, "Hey, this was your idea, not mine."

She grumbles, "Truth or dare."

"Dare," I say with agrin.

"I dare you to take my panties off without touching me."

"Sounds like it's torturing you more than me, but..." I slip her underwear off, my teeth digging into the inside of my cheek. She's pink and wet and—

"I take it back," I rasp. "Baby, let me touch you."

My fingers dig into the inside of her thighs, but she slaps them away. "I choose dare."

My eyes slice to hers. "I dare you to keep your hands at your sides."

She fists the blanket in her hands but lifts her head, watching as I move closer to her center. Slowly, I spread her folds with my fingers and play with her entrance, barely dipping a finger through her heat and carefully circling her clit with the tip of it.

"Oh," she moans.

"You like that, Lia?" I glance at her hands on either side of her hips. Her knuckles are white, and the blanket is bunched, barely covering the ground around us except where we're lying.

"Tell me it's your turn," she begs.

"I choose dare," I answer against her pussy.

"I dare you to make me come with your mouth."

"And I dare you to keep quiet while I do."

"Fuck," she breathes out as I keep playing her with my fingers, her juices trickling down to her ass as her hips lift to meet me. "Okay, deal."

"That's my girl."

Instead of bending down, I reach for the back of her thighs and lift her up, scooting closer until her back is off the ground and only her shoulder blades and head are on the blanket. Then, my mouth is on her. I keep her pussy pressed against me, thrusting my tongue into her dripping entrance and flicking it softly against her clit. She's so sensitive. A whimper escapes her, and I pull away with a silent warning.

With wide eyes, she stares up at me and breathes out, "Fuck, you're serious."

"Dead serious. You stay quiet, and I'll keep going. You make a sound, I stop."

"But this is torture," she whines.

"You're the one who suggested we play," I remind her dryly. "Now, be a good girl, and let me eat you out."

With a glare, she shifts in my hold, throwing her legs over my shoulders, leaning her head back again, and covering her mouth with her hands. Part of me wants to call her out for moving her hands, but I keep it to myself, unable to hide my amusement.

I pull her closer, tonguing her entrance as she stares up at the sky, her back arching with every movement. It's darker now. A lot darker. Stars have started making their appearance, but I don't bother looking at them. I'm too entranced by the girl spread out beneath me. The flush of her skin. The tremors of her muscles whenever I circle her clit with the tip of my tongue. She's beautiful. She's always beautiful. She'll always *be* beautiful.

Fuck, I'm gonna miss her when I go.

Lapping at her folds, I watch as her breathing grows ragged, and she squeezes her eyes shut, biting into her palm to muffle her scream.

She's close.

Any second now.

I move one of my hands between us and scissor her entrance with my fingers as I flick my tongue against her clit, knowing it'll push her over the edge. Coming, she clenches around me, the last of her restraint dissipating, and she chants my name over and over.

When she's finished, I set her back on the ground. She scrambles to her knees, shoves me onto my back, and she's on top of me, lining up my dick with her entrance and lowering herself onto it. A low moan fills the air as she drops her head forward, savoring the feel of me stretching her as she watches our bodies connect.

"Mav," she whimpers.

"Move for me, baby."

Her head bobs, and she lifts herself up a few inches, her hands pressed to my chest for balance. Slowly, she slides back down, and my dick jerks inside her.

"You still trying to kill me, baby?" I ask.

"Pretty sure that joke isn't funny anymore."

"It was funny a minute ago," I point out.

"Only because my mouth was full of your cock."

I laugh and hold onto her waist, keeping us connected as I roll her onto her back. Hooking her leg a little higher on my waist, I piston in and out of her, the sound of our bodies mingling with the crickets in the grass and our heavy breathing.

"Fuck, you feel good," I rasp.

"Ditto," she pants. "Pretty sure I'm gonna come again."

"That's my girl. Squeeze me tight, baby."

I swallow her moan as she starts to come around me, milking my cock like a fucking vice. It pushes me over the edge, and I spill inside of her. I collapse on top of her tiny body. So small. So delicate. But even if she wasn't, I'd still love her. Still care about her. Still hold her and worship her.

It's her soul I'm in love with. Her soul I wish I could keep forever.

"Pretty sure I could break you," I say against the column of her throat.

"Pretty sure you will break me," she returns. "But I gotta give you credit. You fulfilled your end of the bargain. Those were some pretty freaking amazing orgasms. Just sayin'."

I chuckle. "Glad I could be of service." Rolling off her, I

pull her against my chest, letting the moon act as our lantern high above us.

She drags her hand against my bare chest as her muscles melt into me. "I want this, Mav. Whether it's a day, or a year, or ten. I want this."

"I want this, too, Opie."

"Then we're gonna do this for real," she murmurs. "And it might be ugly telling our family or getting Archer's support. But I'm not going to waste time by overthinking things anymore or putting off the future I want. Not this. Not you and me."

"I'll talk to him," I promise.

"I want to talk to him first."

My brows dip. "You sure?"

She nods against my chest. "Yeah. I'm sure."

"Whatever you need."

"Thank you," she whispers. "Although, if you want to call your mom and convince her to not hate me, that'd be great."

I chuckle and pull her closer. "I'll see what I can do."

"Thanks." I can almost hear her rolling her eyes. Suddenly, her breath stalls, and she murmurs, "Do you think Archer told your parents about us?"

"I don't know," I answer honestly. "I haven't really talked to any of them lately."

"Why not?"

"Guess I've been a little preoccupied." I pause, dragging my fingers along her bare arm. "Truth be told, I haven't really talked to them since my diagnosis."

Her brows pinch as she lifts her head from my chest. "You haven't?"

"No. I guess it's easier pushing them away than lying to their faces."

She sinks against me even more. "You need to tell them."

"I know," I sigh, the familiar pressure in my chest making it hard to breathe. "I will. One shitstorm at a time."

"I guess so," she concedes, not looking too happy about it.

"We could always skip brunch altogether," I suggest.

Her lips purse. "No more running from our problems, Mav. Isn't it what you told me?"

I sober. "Guess so."

"But"—she leans down and kisses the tip of my nose—"I agree with waiting to tell the families about us until we have a better idea of how Archer's going to play everything. I don't think we should walk in together and act like a couple when we don't know where Archer's head is."

"Agreed."

"Good. So we get through brunch, I chat with Archer, and you chat with your parents. We keep a wide berth while everything settles, and we all live happily ever after."

"Sure. It'll be a walk in the park."

She grins back at me. "Exactly. Also, don't tell my dad I've ever been on the back of your bike, or he'll never let me go anywhere with you again."

My smile widens. "I'll keep it in mind."

"Good." She kisses my nose again. I roll her onto her back and deepen the kiss.

It's like she said. I'm not gonna waste another minute with her. And I want her again. Here. Now. Under the stars. In my bed. Wherever I can have her.

I want her.

I want her forever.

47

OPHELIA

I didn't know what to expect when I arrived at brunch with Finley and Dylan, but everyone pretending everything was hunky dory was the last thing I anticipated. I'm pretty sure I'm going to break out in hives if I have to stay in this house for another second, but it's not like I can ditch out on brunch when I just got here. Oh, how I wish I could, especially since my parents decided to switch the location from my house to Archer's and Maverick's childhood home late last night.

Everyone's here. My parents. Their siblings. Everyone's kids. There are at least fifty people packed into this place. All I can say is it's a good thing the Buchanans are loaded and can afford a massive mansion like this one, or there's no way we'd all fit in one house.

Thankfully, the huge home also has a large patio overlooking their backyard, and I've managed to find an ounce of privacy, but I'm not naive enough to think it'll last. It is pretty, with rolling hills, tall trees, green grass, and a perfect view of the city.

But even the gorgeous view isn't enough to distract me

from the fact no one has mentioned Archer's outburst during Never Have I Ever, and no one has mentioned my relationship with Maverick, either. Why haven't my parents said anything? It's not like Tatum would've kept it to herself. And what about Archer's parents? They have to know, right? But if they do, why haven't they approached me and yelled at me for screwing everything up?

A wet nose hits my thigh, and I nearly jump out of my skin. Squatting down, I say hello to the Buchanan's family dog.

"Hey, Kovu," I murmur, scratching the fluffy German Shepherd behind his ear. "You scared the crap out of me." After Uncle Henry bought Aunt Mia one when they were dating, the breed stuck, and the Buchanans have owned a German Shepherd ever since. He licks my palm, and his tongue lolls out on one side while his long tail swishes back and forth as he greets me.

At least someone is genuinely happy to see me.

"Ophelia!" a warm, feminine voice calls from the sliding glass door.

I look up, barely holding back my gasp of surprise as I stare at Archer and Maverick's mom. I've been avoiding her —well, everyone, actually—since I first arrived, but it seems my luck has run out. Why am I not surprised?

Wiping my sweaty hands against my shorts, I stand and lean my hip into the wrought-iron railing lining the gray Trex patio.

"Hey," I greet her, but my voice comes out squeaky like a mouse.

"What are you doing hiding out here?"

Gripping the railing behind me, I answer, "Just, uh, getting some fresh air."

With a nod, Aunt Mia glances back into the house, steps outside, and closes the sliding glass door behind her. As she sways toward me, her flowy, white dress leaves her tattoo sleeve on full display, blowing in the summer breeze. She has other tattoos sprinkled over the rest of her body, but the sleeve is a thing of beauty. When I was little, I often crawled onto her lap and traced the ink with my fingers while she told me the stories behind why she chose each and every design. I always loved those moments.

Aunt Mia is pretty much the opposite of who you'd expect a suave billionaire like Henry to marry, but they couldn't be more of a perfect fit for each other. If I wasn't raised with her, I'd say she's one of the most intimidating people I've ever met, simply by the way she holds herself. Her head is always held high, and she doesn't take anyone's bullshit.

She's also one of the people I look up to most, and the idea of disappointing her by admitting I broke one of her sons' hearts is terrifying, especially when I don't know what Archer told her or what kind of villain he painted me to be.

"I could use some air too," Aunt Mia replies. "There are a *lot* of people in my house. So, how are you? What's new? Are you having fun with the Lady Hawks?"

"Uh, yeah." I lift a shoulder. "Jaxon is keeping the girls' team busy, and I'm trying to mentally prep for classes starting next week while juggling hockey and, uh…yeah," I repeat, well aware of how stupid I sound, but I can't help it. I stare at my feet and suck my lips between my teeth.

"You're going to do great," she gushes. "How's Archer handling his internship?"

My brows tug, but I recover quickly. "I think he's okay? Actually, from what I've seen, he's killing it," I clarify as another shot of remorse hits me. A better friend would be up to speed on the internship. But me? I was too distracted with his twin brother to ask him any detailed questions.

"Aw, that's good," Mia returns. "And how's Mav?"

My pulse spikes. "Uh, I don't—why do you ask?"

"You know how those boys are. They love their mama but also have a habit of being shitty at giving details." She smiles and mirrors my stance, resting her lower back against the railing. "So, here I am, recruiting my son's girlfriend to keep me in the loop. Tell me all the things."

Girlfriend. As in...*current*.

Archer still hasn't told her. I mean, I haven't told my parents yet, either, but I figured he would've thrown me under the bus by now. He did with our friends. Why stop there?

But she doesn't know.

Why doesn't it make me feel any better?

Twisting my fingers together, I lie, "I'm not sure there's much to tell."

"Well, have they been nice to you? Looking out for you and everything?"

I nod. "Yeah, they've been great."

"Good." She pauses and adds, "You seem distant lately."

I look at my feet again, unsure what to say. I have been distant lately. With everything going on, most days, I feel like I'm a chicken running around with my head cut off, but it doesn't make it okay.

"I'm sorry," I murmur. "I guess I've been overwhelmed trying to prepare for fall semester and figure out where I belong with hockey and friends and...everything else."

"I totally get it. Trust me, I was the queen of pushing people away when I was overwhelmed during college. Actually, pushing people away, in general, was kind of my forte," she clarifies dryly. "But I'm here for you if you need anything. Even if I *didn't* think of you as my daughter, I'd still be here." Her mouth lifts. "And so are my boys."

"Thanks," I reply. "And yeah, Archer and Mav are really

great guys. Pretty sure I don't deserve either of them with how often I test their patience."

"Don't worry, my boys get their patience from their dad," she quips. "And Henry has the patience of a saint for putting up with me all these years."

With a breath of laughter, I argue, "Give yourself a little more credit, Aunt Mia. You're kind of awesome."

"Fine, but only if you give yourself a little more credit too." She nudges her shoulder with mine. "You're going to do excellent at school, both on and off the ice."

"I'm trying," I admit.

"I can tell." Her touch is gentle as she pats my hand clinging to the railing as if she can feel my nerves buzzing beneath my skin and wants to soothe them. "But don't be afraid to ask for help if you need it. Your family's here for you. I'm here for you. And my boys are *definitely* here for you."

"Thanks," I whisper. "Some days, I feel like I don't deserve them."

"You do," she asserts, "but I get it. They're good eggs."

"Yeah, they really are."

Her eyes bulge. "Shit, the eggs. I gotta go. We'll catch up some more later." She rushes inside, and I start to laugh, but the sound catches in my throat when a familiar face replaces Aunt Mia's retreating form in the doorway.

Archer.

My breath stalls, and I stay frozen in place, unsure of what to do or how to act. I haven't texted him since the party, and he hasn't bothered to reach out to me. But now, I'm here, and it's obvious he's *still* keeping his parents in the dark regarding our relationship, along with everything else, leaving me with more questions than answers.

But after everything I've put Archer through, do I even deserve an explanation?

I feel like there's a stick of dynamite strapped to my chest, and Archer's finger is on the trigger as he slides the glass door closed behind him and strides toward me on long, muscular legs.

His expression is tight. Guarded. But the malice from the party is missing, and a small ember of hope flares inside me. Maybe we'll get through this. Maybe he'll be able to forgive me.

"I take it you didn't tell her?" he asks.

I swallow and shake my head. "You mean about my relationship with Mav or my relationship with you?"

Mirroring my movements, he shakes his head and mutters, "Both."

Kovu perks up when he recognizes his family member approaching us, and his tail swishes back and forth, hitting my calf. Archer gives him a half-assed scratch behind his ear, stands, and throttles the railing. His knuckles are white from the pressure as he leans against it and faces the rolling hills.

His silence kills me. We've never struggled with communication. With telling each other how we feel. With anything, really. We've always clicked. And now we're not. It sucks.

"We agreed to keep things under wraps from our families to prove we were still friends, remember?" I smile tenderly. "I guess I'm still holding out for it." Peeking at him, I start, "Archer, I'm—"

"Don't say it. Not after the shit I pulled at the party."

I nod, sucking my lips between my teeth while staring at his tight, set jaw. But the silence is too much. Too thick. Too heavy.

"We've both made a lot of mistakes, but I'm pretty sure messing with Maverick takes the cake," I point out.

"I shouldn't have outed you the way I did. It was between you and me, and I messed up." He runs his tongue along his teeth but keeps his focus glued in front of him as he adds,

"I'm sorry. I don't know what came over me. You know I don't usually drink, so when I found out Mav was your mystery man, and I saw you sitting next to him, I—"

"How did you figure out he's Mystery Man?" I interrupt.

His teeth grind, but he forces out, "Tatum told me."

Tatum.

My own little sister.

I should be mad at her, but I can't drum up the energy.

Besides, Archer deserved the truth, even if I was too much of a coward to give it to him. I should've told him Maverick was Mystery Man from the beginning. I should've told everyone. If I had, we wouldn't be in this mess. None of us would.

Reading my silence as anger, Archer argues, "Ophelia, I deserved to know."

"I know you did," I rush out. "I was so ashamed of falling for him in the first place and how he broke my heart, I figured if I ignored what he meant to me, I could let him go. But…" I shake my head. "It doesn't matter. What matters is I hurt you," I continue. "I wasn't trying to cause drama, but I'm so sorry. Mav and I, we—"

"I don't want to hear it, Lia. I know it makes me sound like a dick, but…" His voice trails off, and his chin drops to his chest.

"I get it," I tell him.

"I'll tell my parents about the breakup after everyone leaves, then you and Mav can…do whatever the fuck you want." The pain in his voice kills me.

"Archer," I start.

"I'm not gonna say anything about you and Mav. I talked to the guys too. They won't say anything, either."

My eyes widen, and I turn to face the same direction he is, gripping the stupid iron railing with all my might. "Why?"

"I'm trying to protect you," he grits out, and his shoulders hunch. "And him."

Him.

As in Maverick.

His brother.

Twin brother.

The elephant in the room and the catalyst in all of this mess.

Why would Archer want to protect us?

"Can I ask you something?" he mutters.

"Of course."

Turning back to the view in front of us, he lets out a long, deep breath. "Was I always the lesser brother?"

His words pierce my chest, making it hard to breathe, let alone stand here and let him think he's anything less than amazing.

"You know you're not," I argue. "And after everything we've been through, I'd like to think you know me better than that."

"Honestly, Lia, I'm not so sure right now."

Ouch.

I hurt him.

I know I hurt him.

And I know only time will heal something like this, but it doesn't make it easier. Seeing the pain I've caused him while knowing there isn't anything I can do or say to fix it. To put him back together again.

"Look, I know I messed up, but you're still my best friend." I touch his hand, praying it'll soften the death grip he currently has on the stupid railing. He softens—barely—and I continue. "I know it doesn't make any sense, and I know it's no excuse, but no matter how much I've fought it, there's always been a pull between me and Maverick. Always. I guess we both forgot to fight it when I came to LAU, and…and it ruined everything. But trust me when I say you're pretty freaking close to perfect, Archer, and any girl would be lucky to have you. But Mav is…Mav."

He nods, digesting my words with the same weight of calculation he does everything else in his life.

Steeling my shoulders, I add, "I wasn't going to do this here, but I think it's time we have a long overdue conversation."

His mocking laugh cuts me off. "I think it might be a little late."

"Sorry, but I can't accept that."

"Not everything is up to you, Ophelia."

"You're right," I concede. "But you're my best friend, Archer, and even though I screwed up by taking *boyfriend Archer* for granted, I refuse to lose *best friend Archer* too."

The weight in my words does its job, and his head falls forward. "Ophelia…"

I turn around, sit on the top stair leading to the vast back-yard, and pat the space beside me. "Please?" I beg. "Five minutes. I promise."

Grudgingly, he lets go of the railing and sits next to me.

I give him a smile and bump my shoulder against his. "Do you remember when we were kids and I would always say, *'Secrets, secrets are no fun, secrets are for everyone?'*"

He nods.

"Well, as your best friend, I was wrong to keep so many secrets from you, and you deserve to hear them from the source, aka me, if we have any hope of our friendship making it through the clusterfuck I created. So." I take a deep breath. "I'm going to tell you a story, and you're going to listen to the whole thing. Deal?"

"Do I have a choice?"

"Obviously, the answer's no, you do not have a choice," I joke, hoping it'll lighten the mood, but the same downturn of his lips is all I get in return. Sitting up a little straighter, I clear my throat, forcing myself to continue. "Once upon a time, there was a princess named Ophelia."

"You hate princesses."

"Will you let me finish?" I quirk my brow, and he presses his lips together. Satisfied, I continue, "Ophelia grew up with two amazing princes who were twins. Okay, one of them was amazing, the other one was an ass for a little while, but I'll get there," I clarify. "These two brothers were opposites in every way. At first, both of them loved pulling Ophelia's pigtails and telling her she sucked at hockey, but it didn't take long until Prince Archer started looking out for her. He was kind and gentle and patient and every other swoon-worthy description regularly used to describe a knight in shining armor." His mouth lifts, but he doesn't comment. "The other brother, however, was sarcastic and competitive and loved driving Ophelia crazy."

"Sounds about right," he mutters.

I smile softly, attempting to squash the blossoming hope in my chest because if we don't make it through this, it'll break me. "Anyway, Ophelia befriended the first brother almost instantly. She loved his tenderness. His protective-ness. The way he was always there for her whenever she needed him most. They became almost inseparable, and she could tell him anything, knowing her secrets were safe with him. However, there was one secret she was afraid to tell, and it wasn't because she didn't trust him, it's because…" I hesitate, licking my lips. "I think in a way, she knew it would hurt him. He was her safe space. Her protector. And she was…she wanted to be young and irresponsible and reckless. And the knight didn't need any of those things. He was too busy building his future, and man, was he good at it." His lips lift again, but he stays quiet and stares at his lap. "So…she fell in love with his sarcastic—and sometimes annoying—

brother, the jester. And she fell hard," I add with a laugh of disbelief. "Last year, the princess and the jester started seeing each other in secret. She didn't tell a soul. Not even her knight." Sobering, I grab Archer's knee and squeeze. "Looking back, Ophelia wishes she would've told her knight because she thinks it would've saved him a lot of heartache in the end. Instead, she kept it a secret because she was terrified of the fallout, scared she was being stupid for opening her heart to a silly jester who was known for being spontaneous and...not one for settling down. One day, the jester broke her heart the night of a very big, very fancy ball, like a small part of the princess knew he might. The princess was broken, obviously, and the jester stole a few pieces of her heart, taking the shards with him as he escaped to a far-off land."

"Lia," Archer starts, but I shake my head.

"Sh. Let me finish." Resting my head against Archer's shoulder, I say, "When her knight found out she'd be missing the ball, he came to the rescue in an instant. He was sweet and kind and every other swoon-worthy description regularly used to describe a knight in shining armor, just like before." I lift my head and smile at him. "And this time, the princess embraced it, wanting to feel happy. She wanted his warmth and his kindness, and he gave it to her willingly. She loved this knight, Archer. I promise you, she did. But the jester still owned a piece of the princess's stupid heart. Even if he didn't know it. Even if she refused to admit it to herself. He still had a hold on her."

"Lia," Archer repeats. It's pained and tortured.

"I'm almost done," I promise, threading my arm through his and squeezing his bicep tightly. "A little while later, the knight took the princess back to his kingdom at LAU. She loved spending time with him when he wasn't away, but the jester? He was there too. And it didn't matter how hard he tried to keep his distance from the princess. It didn't matter how hard she tried to keep her distance from him. They were drawn to each other, and I'm afraid there wasn't anything they could do about it. Nothing could keep them apart, and trust me, they tried."

"Enough with the story, Lia."

"I—" I lick my dry lips again and sit up. "You're right. I just…I need you to know I love you, Archer, and I'm so sorry. I'm so sorry you were caught in the crosshairs of a very messy situation. But you're my best friend, and we knew even if it didn't work out between us, we still wanted to keep our friendship, remember? I know I'm the one in the wrong. You really are perfect," I repeat. "And I know it's selfish, but I need you. I'll always need you. I didn't mean to hurt you. I don't want to hurt you. But this thing with Maverick and me… I'm afraid it isn't going anywhere, and despite knowing I don't deserve it, I don't want to lose you. I don't want to come between you and your brother, and I don't want to have to choose." My voice cracks, and I close my eyes, begging, "Please don't make me choose."

"You want me to support your relationship with my brother?"

I nod, forcing myself to hold his sad gaze as the sun hangs high in the sky. "Yeah. And I know I don't deserve it. I know Maverick doesn't deserve it. But I'd give anything to have your support, Arch. I still love you. I do. I will love you forever, and there isn't a single thing on this earth that will change that."

"Ophelia—"

"Now, I know there are different kinds of love," I clarify. I'm rambling, I know I am, but part of me is terrified this'll be the last time he talks to me. The last time I have a chance to state my case and fight for his brother *and* my best friend in the same breath. The last time I'll have the opportunity to fix this. To fix us. "And I know sometimes those different kinds of love are hard to tell apart or whatever, but I love you, and instead of dissecting it until I'm blue in the face, I only want to say, when I picture my life, you're in it, and so is your brother. It's that simple. Okay?" I kiss his cheek. "I love you, and I'm really hoping you'll forgive me." I sniff. *"Please* forgive me."

He stays quiet, probably overanalyzing my word vomit like he usually does. Then, he closes his eyes and rests his cheek against the crown of my head as we face the back lawn. I have so many memories here. When we'd pull out the slip 'n' slide and squirt dish soap all over it. When we'd play Hide and Seek and Truth or Dare. When he'd comfort me after a bad game, or I'd give him girl advice after a crappy date.

So many memories.

I don't know how long we sit like this, but the silence is nice. Soothing almost. And he isn't pushing me away. That counts for something. Honestly, it counts for more than he knows.

Maybe we can fix this.

Maybe we can get through this.

"I really do love you," I repeat.

A brush of lips hits the top of my head, and his deep voice rumbles, "Love you too, Lia. Just give me some time, all right?"

"Yeah," I whisper. "We have all the time in the world."

If only it was true.

"I'm, uh, I'm gonna head inside." Brushing off my jean shorts, I stand and give Archer the space I know he needs, even if he's too unselfish to take it for himself. I slip back through the glass patio door and down the hall toward the bathroom, anxious to lock the world out and how shitty it can be sometimes, even if it's only for a minute.

48

MAVERICK

Ophelia disappears down the hallway, and my feet move of their own accord, following her down the long hallway and away from the party. I know we agreed we wouldn't act like we're together, but the distance is killing me, and if I can steal a moment with her, I will. It's like I'm already a ghost, and I can't take it anymore. When she reaches the guest bathroom at the opposite end of the house and closes the door behind her, I twist the handle before she has a chance to click the lock into place, shoving the door open.

When Ophelia realizes it's me, her grip tightens around the edge of the door, and she blocks me from opening it fully. "What are you doing?"

"Let me in."

"Mav…"

"Let me in, Ophelia."

She peeks over my shoulder, scanning the hallway and stepping aside so I can join her in the small space.

I close the door behind us, grab her waist, and press her

back against it, holding her in place. "What did Archer say to you?"

"I'm the one who did most of the talking," she mutters. Her expression twists. "I hate how I hurt him, Mav."

"We both did."

Her smile is sad as her eyes find mine. "I'm sorry."

"For what?"

"For...everything?" she offers, giving me a pathetic, half-assed shrug as she stares blankly at my chest. "I feel like this is all my fault."

"Come here." I pull her into me and rub my hands along her spine.

She melts against my chest, releasing a quiet sigh. "I love it when you hold me."

"I love holding you," I whisper as her curves mold against me.

The girl is fucking perfect.

Her breath of laughter seeps through my shirt as her hand finds my hard-on pressed against her stomach. "I can tell."

"Careful," I warn.

She lifts her head and tilts it to the side, watching me. "Is this why you followed me in here? Thinking you could sneak in a quickie until you realized your girlfriend's an emotional wreck?"

I smirk and lift her chin a little higher with my knuckle. "It wasn't the plan, but if it gets you to smile and stop carrying all the guilt for something we *both* did, I'm not afraid to take one for the team."

"How generous of you."

"I think we both know how generous I can be."

Her teeth dig into her bottom lip, but it doesn't stop her mouth from stretching toward the ceiling. "You're joking, right?"

"I was, but then your smile reached your eyes. Come here,

baby." I cup the side of her face and kiss her. It's soft and playful and tugs at my chest. It turns more heated as her hand on my dick squeezes.

"Is this another game of Truth or Dare?" I rasp against her pouty lips. "Because if it is, we both know I'm gonna win."

"Pretty sure we'd both be winning."

I press her further into the door and grind against her hand as she closes her eyes.

"This is such a stupid idea," she whispers.

"Never claimed to be the smart one." I lift her up, set her on the bathroom counter, and spread her legs wide. "Lean back."

Resting her elbows against the granite, she lifts her hips, and I shimmy her underwear and jean shorts off her long, lean legs.

"Think you can be quiet?" I ask as I unzip my pants and shove them off my ass, lining the head of my cock up with her entrance.

"Is that a dare?" she challenges.

I chuckle dryly, yank her to the edge of the counter again, and lift her torso until we're chest-to-chest. Burying my head in the crook of her neck, I bite down hard.

With a gasp, she arches her back, and I smile against her skin. She's fucking dripping against the head of my dick, her wet heat tempting me like never before. Resting my forehead against her shoulder, I push into her slowly, watching as her pussy swallows every fucking inch of me. It's the hottest thing I've ever seen.

"Mav," she whimpers. Her fingers claw against the nape of my neck, and she squeezes her eyes shut, lost in the feel of me stretching her. Of me filling her. Of me claiming her the only way I know how. The only way I can.

"Do you have any idea how good you feel?" I ask.

"If it's anything like how good you feel, yes." She looks up at me and smiles. "I think I have an idea. You should probably get moving so we don't get caught."

Grabbing her hips, I slowly pull out of her and thrust back into place. Her heat makes it hard to concentrate on anything else, but I do my best, pushing into her over and over while sliding one of my hands between our connected bodies and playing with her clit.

She moans against my lips as I rub her gently, making sure to time the pressure with my thrusts as my heart pounds in my chest, leaving me winded, but I don't stop. She likes it. Her lips part with a soft whimper while her pussy tightens around me. I'm lightheaded, but I blink the black dots away, keeping my breathing in check.

Not now.

"You have no idea how good you feel," she whimpers, tugging my head into the crook of her neck. I smile against her skin again, realizing I've never felt closer to heaven than at this moment. With her in my arms. Her moans grow louder and louder as I continue fucking her, and the sound is like music to my ears. I should tell her to be quiet. If I had any self-preservation, I would. But part of me wants them to know she's mine. That I make her feel this way. Even when I have no right to. My hand covers her mouth as sweat drips down my back. But I'm close. I come inside her, shoving the tunnel vision aside, and she follows right after, squeezing me like a vice while moaning into my palm.

As we catch our breaths, she laughs. "I got you all worked up, didn't I?"

I force a smile, feeling like I've just finished an Iron Man, and I take in the messy curls framing her face. "You have no idea how gorgeous you look right now," I murmur.

She peeks into the mirror and smacks my shoulder. "I look insane!"

"You look like you've been thoroughly fucked." I nip at

her bottom lip between pants. Kissing her harder, she smiles against my mouth.

"So you like this look, I take it?"

"Mm-hmm." The sound rumbles through my chest, pulling another grin from her as I wait for my pulse to steady.

"Too bad," she notes. "Because there's no way in hell I can walk out of this bathroom looking like this."

"If you think this is bad, just wait."

Her brows crease, and her amusement falls. "For what?"

Slowly, I pull out of her, and my cum follows, dripping out of her slit. Her eyes widen. "We didn't use a condom."

"We've never used a condom," I remind her.

"Well, yeah, but *here*? I don't have anything to change into."

"Doesn't matter where we are, Goose. I'm gonna keep coming inside you until my dying breath. And you're not gonna clean yourself up or change. You're gonna walk around with my cum dripping out of you for the rest of the day."

Her eyes widen. "Oh, I am?"

"Yeah." I chuckle. "Do you wanna know why?"

"Why?"

I cup her cheek and run my thumb along her silky skin. "Let's get through brunch first."

With a smile, she leans into my touch and asks, "And then?"

"Then..." I lean against the counter and let out a slow breath.

"Hey, you okay?" Her forehead tugs.

I nod. "Yeah, I'm good. Just winded." I give her a wink, continuing, "And *then*, after brunch, we're gonna tell our families everything, and I'm gonna shout from the rooftops how it's you and me. It'll *always* be you and me. Right, Goose?"

I grab her hips and slide her off the counter. Once her feet touch the tile, I pick the shorts and black underwear up from the ground, dragging the fabric up her silky skin until she's covered. I slip her bra on and pull her shirt over her head. Satisfied, I tug her toward me, kissing her one more time as my hip finds the edge of the counter, and I lean against it.

"You should get back out there," I suggest.

"Fiiiine." She rises onto her tiptoes, kisses me one more time, and slips out the bathroom door. She doesn't have a chance to close it as she screeches to a halt, her muscles turning to steel. "Oh. Hi, Aunt Mia."

She slams the door behind her.

49

OPHELIA

I slam the door closed behind me to shield Maverick from his mother's view, preparing myself for the inevitable while my fingers bite into the round handle and my knees threaten to give out.

Shit.

Shit, shit, shit.

"What in the—" Aunt Mia gasps as she takes in my disheveled appearance, her expression hardening on the solid wood behind me. "Who's in there, Ophelia?"

"I—"

She steps closer. "Move aside, Lia."

I squeeze my eyes shut and shift to the left, giving her access to the bathroom door. She pounds her fist against it.

Maverick opens it immediately, his skin paler than usual. "Mom—"

"What. The actual. Fuck?" she spits, though she has the decency to keep her voice quiet as she glares at her son, demanding an explanation.

I suck my trembling lip into my mouth and look at

Maverick, but he's as quiet as I am. Just as speechless. Just as blindsided.

"How could you do this to your brother?" she demands. "He's loved Ophelia since you were both kids. And you." Her disappointment taints the air and tears well in her eyes as her attention slices to me. "How could you do this to him, Ophelia? Archer loves you. He would never do something like this to you."

"I know," I rush out. "I know he wouldn't."

"How can you…" She bites her tongue and shakes her head. "I'm sorry. I don't even know what to say right now. I'm so shocked and—"

"Mia," Uncle Henry calls. He appears at the end of the hallway, his brows knitting when he catches us staring back at him. God, he looks so much like his boys. It only shreds me more.

"Everything all right?" he asks.

"Dad," Maverick starts.

Uncle Henry's frown deepens as he takes in Mia's glassy eyes. Striding toward us, he demands, "What's going on?"

"I. We. Uh." My mouth snaps closed. My tongue feels as worthless as my apologies lately and makes my defense useless as Uncle Henry's heavy footsteps echo off the walls.

"Mia?" Uncle Henry prods. "What's going on?"

Mia shakes her head and waves her hand at Mav. "Anything you want to say?"

Scrubbing his hand over his face, Maverick's shoulder hits the hallway wall, and he rasps, "I know how this looks."

"It looks like you're sleeping with your brother's girlfriend."

"We're not…" My voice trails off, and Maverick shakes his head.

"Mom, I know I fucked up."

Mia touches her pursed lips, the repercussions of our

actions almost more than she can bear. She shakes her head back and forth, allowing a tear to slip down her cheek. Disappointment. Shame. Pain. They all fight for the spotlight. I don't blame her. Archer and Maverick are her boys. It doesn't matter that they've moved out and they're adults. She wants to protect them. I don't think the feeling ever really goes away.

Dropping her hand to her side, Aunt Mia whispers, "There's no excuse, Maverick."

Maverick blinks slowly but doesn't deny it.

I notice the shade of his lips. They're a purple-ish blue.

Something's wrong.

"Mav," I whisper.

He lifts his hand like he wants me to stay in place. Like he wants me to keep my distance. Like he wants to hide the fact he's struggling to remain standing. It freaks me out even more.

Shit.

I take a step toward him, but I'm not fast enough. His legs give out, and he crashes to the floor, a loud thwack vibrating off the walls and into my bones. Falling onto my knees, I roll Maverick onto his back and check his pulse. It's gone.

Where the hell is it?

His eyes are rolled back in his head as I begin chest compressions right away, grateful my Uncle Mack made all of us take CPR classes when we were younger, no matter how much we complained at the time.

Don't give up on me, Mav. Don't you dare *give up on me.*

Blood pours from his chin, dribbling down his jaw and pooling on the floor while cries echo around me.

I don't look up to see who they belong to as I continue performing CPR, feeling more helpless than I've ever felt in my entire life.

A warm body hits my side, and Archer shakes his brother's shoulder. "Wake up, brother. Wake up!"

"Call an ambulance!" I yell. Tremors of fear race down my spine, but Archer catches on almost instantly and pushes me aside, taking over chest compressions as I watch Maverick's lifeless body lay unmoving.

Another voice yells at someone in the kitchen, but I don't register what's said as my father's strong arms encircle me.

"Sh…, baby," he coos. "Sh… It's gonna be okay."

Seconds later, Uncle Mack kneels beside Archer and Maverick. A crumpled napkin falls from his hand as he reaches for Maverick's neck, checking his pulse, his brows knitting in concern.

Macklin's a paramedic—one of the best—and he's seen a lot of shit. He's also a rock and thrives under pressure more than anyone I've ever seen. But even this knowledge doesn't ease the panic racing through me.

"Let me take over," Macklin orders.

Archer falls onto his ass beside me, looking as wrecked as I feel. I reach for his hand as I sob against my dad's chest, every single heart-wrenching scenario flashing through my mind, one after the other, leaving me a shell of a human being. I'm a mess. I can't breathe. I can't think. I can't do anything but cry.

"What happened?" Archer begs. "Ophelia, what happened? I didn't—"

I shake my head, unable to form words. Unable to form a coherent thought in general. I need him to be okay. I need him to wake up and say everything is all right. I need—

Paramedics storm through the front door with a stretcher, and everything fades away as I watch them load him into the back of the ambulance, taking my heart with him.

50

OPHELIA

The steady *beep-beep* from the machine Maverick's hooked up to is the most confusing sound in the world. It's reassuring, sure, but every millisecond of silence between beeps causes my own heart rate to spike, and I catch myself holding my breath more than once.

The paramedics rushed Maverick to the hospital. His heart had stopped, but they were able to bring him back. He's weak. So weak. His lips are still a soft shade of purple, but there's more pink than blue now.

That has to count for something, doesn't it?

Progress, maybe? I'm not sure who I'm trying to convince as I watch his heavy lids open.

I rode with Archer and their little sister to the hospital. His parents were in the ambulance with Mav. Now, here we are, surrounding his hospital bed. Well, everyone except Uncle Henry. He's busy yelling at the nursing staff, demanding someone tell him what's going on. They told him they were still waiting for the test results and for the specialist to arrive.

It only pissed him off more.

Maverick's awake. It should make me feel better, but it doesn't. When his eyes meet mine, they're full of apology as he licks his parched lips and rolls his head to his mom beside him.

I know why he's avoiding me. It's because he's scared. Scared I'll blow his cover. Scared I'll tell his family about his diagnosis. Scared I'll break and blurt out the truth to every single person in this hospital room without giving a shit about what he wants. He's right. I don't. Not anymore. Not after a scare like today's. Instead, he'd prefer to sweep it under the rug, making everyone in the room question their own sanity after witnessing a healthy college athlete have a heart attack during brunch.

I want to be mad at him. I want to be understanding. But what I want most? Is for him to be okay, and I have no idea if it's even possible anymore.

Maverick's hair is matted with blood and sweat. He needed fourteen stitches in his chin. The angry slash only added to my fear. There was so much blood. I look down at my hands, expecting them to still be stained with red despite Archer helping me scrub them before we drove to the hospital.

I blink back a fresh wave of tears and scan the crowded hospital room when my phone buzzes with a text.

UNCLE MACK

> You wanna tell me why you started doing chest compressions as soon as Mav went down?

I wipe my sweaty palms against my jean shorts and tuck my phone back into my pocket, ignoring him.

He knows something's up.

I think the rest of the family does, too, even if they're afraid to admit it. To face the truth.

Aunt Mia has refused to leave Maverick's side. She's sitting on the edge of the hospital bed, pushing his hair away from his face and running her palm along his cheek, careful not to touch the stitches on his chin.

"Mom, I'm fine," Maverick grumbles.

"You're not fine."

"Mom—"

"It doesn't matter how old you are, Maverick. I'm your mother. I'm allowed to worry about you, and after this…"

"Mom," Maverick repeats. "Can you please just…"

She stops fussing with his wavy hair and twists her hands in her lap. "I'm glad Ophelia started compressions right away," Aunt Mia adds, tearing her focus from her baby boy to me. "How did you know to do that?"

My lips smash together, and I hold my breath, knowing if I open my mouth, I'll tell her the truth. I'll tell all of them the truth. I haven't been able to stop crying since the drive. My face is blotchy and red, and I can't keep the hiccups at bay for the life of me. And it isn't because he's hurt or because he passed out. Okay, that's a lie. It's definitely because he had a heart attack. But it's also because they don't know. How can they not know? I need him to say something. I need him to tell them this isn't a fluke. To tell them something is seriously wrong, and he needs their support. Because I can't do this. I can't keep this secret. Not from them. Not when it's clear they care about him the way they do. They need to know.

Tell them.

Tell them.

Sensing how close I am to breaking, Maverick tilts his head. "Lia, I'm fine."

"Maverick." His name is a plea as our eyes stay locked in silent battle.

"Lia," he returns, the same lilt in his voice as mine. He sits up further in his hospital bed.

411

"What's going on?" Archer demands.

"Nothing," Maverick says while I repeat his name at the same time. "Maverick."

"Say something," Archer demands. "Someone—"

"He has HCM," I blurt out.

Maverick's expression falls, and his head hits the pillow behind him.

Guilt blooms inside me, but I force it away and reach for Maverick's limp hand on the edge of the bed. When he lets me touch him, some of my anxiety eases, and I sit next to his hip, ignoring his family surrounding us and looking *very* confused.

"I told you I wouldn't lie for you," I remind him. "And I'm not going to. Not after today. They deserve to know."

"Know what?" Aunt Mia asks.

Maverick's jaw tics, and he winces, the stitches in his chin tugging. "I have a rare heart disease. It's called HCM. Long story short, my heart is shit, and it's gonna give out sooner rather than later. I'm seeing the best doctor, but there's no cure. I'm sorry I didn't tell you. I didn't want you to look at me differently, and that's about it."

Aunt Mia covers her mouth with a gasp. She collapses against him and pulls him into a hug. I blink back tears and push to my feet, making my way to the hallway so he can have some privacy with his family, who I have no doubt are reeling from the news. I don't blame them. I'm still reeling.

I shouldn't have done it. I shouldn't have blurted it out. But if I hadn't, he wouldn't have told them. They would've continued thinking he passed out from dehydration or some other bullshit excuse he could come up with.

"Hello," a doctor greets me. Or at least, I assume he's a doctor. He's wearing a white lab coat and blue scrubs.

Feeling awkward, I curl in on myself and wipe beneath my eyes. "Um, hi?"

"Hi," he repeats. "Do you think they'd mind if I...?" His voice trails off, and he tilts his head toward the open doorway leading to Maverick's room and his crying family.

I peek into the room, lifting one shoulder. "Oh, I–I dunno. They just found out some pretty"—I sniff—"some pretty crappy news, so..."

"He finally told them, I take it?" the doctor offers.

"I, uh, I'm sorry, who are you?" I ask.

"Are you Maverick's family?"

I nod. "Uh, yes. No. I–I'm Maverick's..."

"Ah, I see." His eyes gleam with understanding. "Well, come in. I'm sure he'd like you to be included in the update as well." With a soft touch against my upper back, the doctor corrals me into the hospital room, announcing, "Knock, knock."

Everyone's heads snap in our direction as the doctor steals some sanitizer from the dispenser beside the light switch.

"I found a stray in the hallway. I hope you don't mind if she joins us," he adds.

"Not at all, Doc," Maverick mutters.

The doctor's mouth lifts. "Good to see you, too, Maverick." He turns to Aunt Mia and Uncle Henry. "Hello, I'm Dr. Scott. Nice to meet you."

They take turns shaking his hand. Once the pleasantries conclude, his bushy brows lift at Maverick. "Do I need to clear the room so we can discuss everything going on, or...?"

"They know," Maverick grunts. He doesn't look too happy about it.

"About damn time." Dr. Scott nods. "I'm sure you have plenty of questions. What has Maverick told you?"

Maverick's parents take full advantage of their opportunity, peppering Dr. Scott with questions as I sit on the edge of the bed beside Maverick's hand. He lifts it, making more room for me, and places his palm on my thigh. I stare at his innocent touch, surprised by how much I need it. Then, I peek at Maverick on the bed. I assume he's listening to whatever Dr. Scott says, but instead, he's staring at me. Curious. Hesitant. Unsure. And looking so damn tired, I want to snuggle against his chest and shut the rest of the world out for at least twenty-four hours.

"I'm sorry," I whisper.

"Don't be." He squeezes my leg. "You were right. It's not like I can run from this forever."

"The good news," Dr. Scott announces, "is your name has officially moved up the list. Thanks to today's event, you're our top candidate for a transplant."

"Doc," Maverick warns, but Aunt Mia cuts him off.

"He's already on the list?" There's hope in her voice as she turns to Mav. "You're already on the list?"

"Mom—"

"I had to twist his arm," Dr. Scott admits, "but, yes. He's on the list and has been for a while now. As I said, he was initially quite low on it, but considering how quickly your son is declining, the board has decided to honor my recommendation. Now, it's simply a waiting game until a match becomes available."

"How long?" Uncle Henry questions. He steps closer to his wife and wraps his arm around her waist, tugging her into him.

The doctor hesitates, lifting a shoulder. "Unfortunately, there's no way to know how long it will take or how quickly Maverick's heart will continue fighting, but I'm hopeful."

Not a promise. Not a firm answer.

It isn't exactly comforting, and I fight the burn behind my eyes.

"So what's next?" Aunt Mia prods. "What do you need from us?'

"Your insurance is excellent, and he's already been preapproved for the transplant," Dr. Scott continues. "For now, you breathe, you keep your hope in check, and you convince your son to take it easy until we get the call there's a match. Depending on how stable Maverick is, I can release him from the hospital, and he can go home, take it *easy*,"—he gives Mav a pointed look—"and keep his phone close by. We continue treatment the best we can, we continue monitoring him, and we prepare for surgery. Any further questions?"

Maverick shakes his head, looking as overwhelmed as the rest of us feel.

Dr. Scott's chin dips, and he steps backward toward the door. "Well, you have my number in case you think of anything. Nice meeting you, Dr. and Mrs. Buchanan. Your son's a good kid."

With a watery smile, Mia sniffles. "Thanks. We kind of love him."

He chuckles. "I can see why. I'll be back soon to check on you." He gives Maverick another pointed look from behind his glasses. "I'm serious, Maverick. Take it easy." Then he leaves.

5 1
MAVERICK

The beeping from the hospital machine sounds like nails on a chalkboard as I lie in bed. Ophelia's asleep on the chair in the corner of the room. Her feet are tucked under her ass, and a scratchy maroon blanket covers her body. She stole her dad's hat when her parents came in to check on me before heading out with everyone else. They wanted to stay—everyone did—but my dad had enough foresight to see how much I hated the attention and looks of pity. He sent them packing, promising them my mom would reach out with any updates. It took some arm twisting, but Archer convinced Mom and Dad to head home too. Our parents deserve to sleep in their own bed, and since my little sister has school in the morning, they eventually caved. Besides, a hospital is the last place a thirteen-year-old should hang out.

Now, it's me, Archer, and Ophelia. I tried to push them into leaving, too, but they refused, and even though it pissed me off, I'm kind of grateful they were too stubborn to give in.

I don't want to be alone.

Other than the constant beeping, it's quiet. Too quiet.

Archer's ignoring me.

He hasn't said more than two words to me since Dr. Scott stopped by.

I don't blame him.

It's fucked-up.

Everything is.

But the silence? It's even worse.

Beep. Beep.

I glance at my brother again. His feet are propped on the edge of Lia's chair, and he's leaning back on his own, staring at the ceiling. The angry bruises from our fight over Ophelia have faded to yellow, but they're still present, making him look even more exhausted.

Beep. Beep.

It'd be better if he was playing with his phone. If he was sleeping. If I couldn't feel the tension clinging to his clothes. His expression. His tight fists.

Beep. Beep.

"I'm sorry I didn't tell you," I rasp, keeping my voice low.

"Tell me what? That you were seeing Ophelia last spring or you're dying?"

He's pissed. He has every right to be. But it doesn't make this easier.

Scrubbing my hand over my face, I mutter, "Both."

He nods but doesn't say anything else.

Beep. Beep.

"I know it isn't enough," I add. "I know I fucked up. But I'm sorry."

"All right." His eyes are vacant and dull as he looks at me. "Anything else?"

I stay quiet, and he nods again, turning his vacant stare back to the ceiling.

"I know you feel like I betrayed you," I continue.

Beep. Beep.

"And you're right. I did. We're brothers. I should've told you—"

"Yeah, you should've." He pulls his feet from the edge of Ophelia's chair and sets them on the ground, shifting in his seat as his forearms find his knees. "If you had told me…" His molars grind. "I wouldn't have touched her. I wouldn't have done that to you. I would've had your back."

"I know."

"If you had told me, I would've been here, brother. I would've taken you to every fucking appointment. I would've—" His mouth snaps closed, and he sniffs. The betrayal in his eyes is enough to put me in my grave right here, right now. And so are his unshed tears.

Beep. Beep.

Fucking hell.

"I know," I repeat. "You've done nothing wrong."

"Yet, I'm still the one who's gonna carry all the regret." He pushes to his feet and wipes his palms against his jeans, looking like a little kid. Like when we used to play roller hockey in the driveway, and he'd get worked up, ready to bash heads in, only this time it's mine.

"Don't feel guilty," I murmur. "About any of it. You didn't know."

"But I should've. I should've seen the signs. You were always in better shape than I was. How did I not notice the way you were slipping? The way you were always more tired than you used to be? If I hadn't been so preoccupied—"

"Don't do this. Don't play this game."

Head hanging, he starts pacing the small room, drowning in his guilt. "If I hadn't been so preoccupied, I would've noticed the way she wanted to keep her distance from you. I would've noticed the way you were with her. I would've—"

"Stop," I beg as my eyes fall to Ophelia.

Beep. Beep.

She's still asleep. Still blissfully unaware of our conversation. Good. I don't want her overhearing any of this.

Archer follows my gaze, confirming she's still out. He scrubs his hand over the top of his head, tugging at the roots as his face twists with regret. "She was always yours."

"She wasn't," I argue. "She still isn't. She belongs to you, too, man. Always has. Always will. I think we both know it." My stomach twists. "I kept my distance because I didn't want to hurt her. The funny thing is, I wound up hurting her anyway."

Again, he looks at Ophelia, and his mouth lifts for the briefest of seconds. But it's sad. Torn. "She's stubborn."

"Yeah," I breathe out. "She really is. So stubborn she's refusing to let me go."

"Good." His gaze finds mine again. "She should refuse to let you go because you're going to be fine."

"Stop," I order.

"No."

"I'm serious, Arch," I snap. "Do you know how many things have to line up for a fucking heart transplant? To find a perfect match? To get the heart in time? To go under anesthesia and have a successful transplant, let alone my body not rejecting the organ even if the surgery *is* successful? It's…it's like winning the fucking lottery, Archer. We both know I'm not that lucky."

"Have a little faith," he pushes. "The doctor sounds optimistic."

"He's supposed to sound optimistic," I counter. "But you can't blame me for wanting to plan for every outcome in case it doesn't work out the way we want it to."

"It will."

"But if it doesn't," I argue, "I need you to promise me something."

He sighs, taking his seat again, the exhaustion getting the best of him. "What is it?"

"Gonna need you to promise me that when I..." I swallow. "When I'm gone—"

"*If*," he interrupts.

My nostrils flare. "Fine. *If* I go, I need you to promise me you'll take care of our girl."

His expression falls, and he shakes his head. "Don't say shit like that."

"I need to know you'll look after her."

"Mav—"

"I get her for now. You get her in the future."

"Fuck you, Mav," he rasps, but there isn't any malice in it. Only...defeat.

I swallow the lump in my throat, forcing myself to continue. "Even if you fall in love with someone else. Even if you move on and get married and shit. Promise me you'll look after her. You'll invite her over. Make sure she's happy. Watch over her. Make sure she's okay."

"Mav—"

My hands vibrate as I grab his shirt and yank him closer until his ass nearly falls out of his seat. "Promise me, Arch. It's the only way I'm gonna be okay. The only way I'm gonna be able to come to terms with...with everything. Promise me."

He closes his eyes and slumps in my grasp, his fight dissipating entirely, leaving a shell of my brother. When he opens his eyes, a single tear falls. "I promise."

My hold eases, and I collapse on the bed. "Thank you."

A beat of silence follows, and his low whisper hits my ears. "Anything, brother."

52

MAVERICK

I t's been a weird week.

I was discharged from the hospital a few days ago with a gadget to monitor my heart to track any inconsistencies, and I've been to Dr. Scott's office twice. My parents attended the first appointment with me and Ophelia. Now, Archer's driving me home from my most recent one. Ophelia had practice, so despite the fact she insisted on tagging along, I told her we'd catch up afterward. Grudgingly, she agreed.

Dr. Scott tested Archer for HCM. He doesn't have it. His heart's as healthy as a horse's, or at least it's what the doc said. I didn't realize how much the news would bring me relief, but it has.

We're identical twins. The odds of us sharing the good *and* the bad genes aren't exactly a stretch, and the idea of my brother having the same fucked-up heart as I do was more than I could stomach.

"Thanks for driving me," I murmur.

Archer glances at me from the driver's seat. "No problem. How are you feeling?"

I hate this question. I've been asked it a hundred times since everyone found out about my diagnosis. Even the Lady Hawks insisted on decorating my bike when word got out.

But the answer is hard to explain. It's like I'm living a nightmare I can't wake up from. And in a way, I don't want to wake up from it because if I do, does it mean I'm dead?

"I think that's the most fucked-up part, man." I scrub at my tired eyes. "Other than feeling tired, I feel...normal. Like none of this is real."

He nods, but stays quiet as he stops at a red light.

"Can I tell you how done I am with being poked and prodded, though?" I grunt.

He glances at me in the passenger seat again, then turns back to the intersection. "I can imagine."

"I'd kill for some normalcy."

He nods, lost in thought. "What if we do a game night or something? I have another conference and fly out tomorrow morning, but we could do it tonight if everyone's free."

The idea sounds better than he knows. I've been so bogged down with my appointments and shit, being able to simply hang out with our friends sounds perfect.

Shifting in my seat, I pull my phone from my back pocket. "I always knew you were the smart twin," I joke. "I'll text Reeves and the rest of the guys right now."

"Don't forget Fin and Dylan," he adds.

I tilt my head. "You really think Finley would let me—or anyone for that matter—forget her?"

He laughs dryly. "Good point."

"And Lia," he continues.

We haven't talked about Opie since the hospital, and I've tried to keep a respectful distance between me and her whenever Archer's in the same room with us. It's been hard, considering my impending expiration date, but the idea of creating more friction between everyone is more than I can handle.

Still, Archer mentioning her feels like an olive branch, and I'm grateful for it.

"Sure thing," I reply.

As I finish sending out invites, Arch pulls into the driveway and turns the car off, but he doesn't reach for the door handle. He simply stares at the steering wheel.

Setting my phone in my lap, I unbuckle my seatbelt and wait.

People talk about how twins can read each other unlike anyone else. It's hard to explain, but it's true. We've always been in sync. And right now, my brother has something he needs to get off his chest.

"Listen," he starts. "I think we can both agree it's been a fucked-up few days."

I chuckle dryly. "Yeah, you could put it that way."

"But now, with things beginning to settle and shit, I, uh, I want to talk about Lia."

My shoulders fall, and I stare at my lap.

How did I fucking know?

"Look, Arch." I sigh. "You know how sorry I am—"

"That's the thing," he interrupts. "Yeah, not telling me you were her mystery man was a dick thing to do, but…" He scratches the scruff along his jaw. "I don't know, man. Even without you in the picture, we were still…off. I wanted her to be *the one*, but I was too busy forcing it to see the truth. And after our conversation in the hospital, I need to get this off my chest." He pauses, taking a deep breath. "You made me promise to take care of her. And I will," he rushes out. "But I don't want you feeling guilty for how shit went down."

"I'm always gonna feel guilty for how shit went down," I admit.

"Yeah, well, stop," he orders. "Time's too short for that."

He's right. It is. The heart monitor strapped to my chest is the perfect reminder of how I'm a ticking time bomb, and we'd be fools to squander the time we have left.

"I'll see what I can do," I mutter.

His mouth lifts. "Thanks. And I want you to stop walking on eggshells around me when it comes to you and Ophelia too."

"We haven't been walking on eggshells—"

"Bullshit," he laughs. "I'm not blind, man. You've been walking on eggshells from the beginning. I know it's because you were looking out for me—you're *still* looking out for me —and I appreciate it, but if I've recognized anything from all of this, it's Lia and me? We weren't meant to be. Not"—he gives me the side-eye—"romantically, anyway."

The tension in his expression makes me laugh, and the tightness in my muscles softens. "You have no idea how good it feels to hear you say that."

"Aw, come on." He shoves at my shoulder. "Don't be a dick."

"I'm just saying," I offer. "Hearing you weren't physically connecting with Lia is like music to my fucking ears, brother."

"Yeah, yeah, I know. She's your girl, not mine, but if you hurt her,"—he lifts his brows—"I'll beat the shit out of you."

Another laugh rumbles up my throat, and I reach for the door handle. "I wouldn't have it any other way."

And fuck me, I mean it.

53

OPHELIA

I t's a quiet game night. Okay, maybe not quiet, but relatively...small? And the usual accompanying chaos is absent since we kept the guest list to our closest friends. Everett, Griffin, Jaxon, Archer, Maverick, and Reeves sit cross-legged on the carpet along with Finley, Dylan, and me across from them. The coffee table is covered in black and white Cards Against Humanity cards, along with a few Sharpies, and we've laughed our asses off for the past hour.

The rules of the game are simple. Everyone has ten white cards with silly answers on the front. There are also black question cards. One person reads a question card aloud, and the other players anonymously pass a white answer card to the person. The person then reads all of the answers aloud and chooses which one is the best answer for their question.

However, a few years back, we started tweaking and personalizing the answer cards, depending on who's playing. Some include familiar names. Others have certain words replaced with something else. It's hilarious and *highly* inappropriate, especially for a girl like Dylan. But watching her blush as she reads the cards is probably my favorite thing ever.

"Okay." She picks the black question card up and reads it aloud. *"What would Dylan find disturbing and oddly charming?"*

Reeves snorts and grabs a silver Sharpie from the center of the table, scrawling something on his answer card. Satisfied, he places the cap back in place and tosses the altered card face down toward her. The rest of us do the same until she has a not-so-neat pile of answers in front of her. Her nose scrunches as she scans the first one, slipping it back into the original jumble without a word.

"Not gonna read it out loud, Dylan?" Reeves questions across from her. He's sporting a shit-eating grin making *me* want to squirm. I can only imagine how much Dylan's dying inside from his attention.

Her eyes thin at him. "Why do you want me to?"

"It's part of the game," he reminds her.

She picks the silver Sharpie up from in front of him and tosses it into his lap. "Pretty sure writing on the cards is against the rules, so…"

"Pretty sure we make our own rules here." He tugs the silver Sharpie's lid off with his teeth and starts drawing a tattoo on the inside of his forearm next to a giant octopus, the tentacles wrapping around his wrist.

"Fine," she huffs.

"Read the question one more time," Finley suggests.

Dylan clears her throat. "The question is: *What would Dylan find disturbing and oddly charming?"*

"And the options?" Reeves pushes, mumbling his words around the marker cap still pinched between his teeth.

She flips through the cards and shows one to the table. "Men." I snort, and she picks another card up. "Everett's personality." Everett chuckles and lifts his chin in acknowledgment as she adds another option to the pile. "Finley after watching a crime documentary."

"'Sup." Finley flashes a peace sign with her fingers.

"That *is* accurate, by the way," Dylan acknowledges, adding another few cards to the pile. When she reaches the one she initially pursed her lips at, she looks at Reeves and sets the card in the center of the table. "*What would Dylan find disturbing and oddly charming?* Reeves' dick."

He wiggles his brows at her as Everett interjects, "Disturbing sounds about right."

"And charming," Reeves reiterates.

"And disturbing," Dylan tosses back at him.

"To be fair, I'm pretty sure all dicks would be disturbing to our dear Dylan," Finley teases.

"Hey!" Dylan shoves her shoulder, but it only makes Finley cackle harder.

"And why are all dicks disturbing?" Reeves questions, clearly intrigued.

"Because Dylan's never seen one," Everett answers. His eyes slide to hers. "Right, Dylan?"

Her cheeks turn a soft shade of pink as she tucks her blonde hair behind her ear and mutters, "No comment."

"No shit?" Reeves pops the cap back onto the marker and tosses it on the table. "You've never seen a dick? Not even on TV?"

"I'm sorry, what shows do you watch that include dicks?" she challenges.

"I dunno? Porn?"

Dylan shies away from him. "Ew."

"Okay, *Game of Thrones?*" he adds. When Dylan's face stays blank, he leans forward. "Fuck me. You've never seen *Game of Thrones?*"

"I mean, I've heard of it," Dylan offers. "Isn't it like…kind of old?"

"No fucking way." Reeves shakes his head again like he can't believe it. "*Old*? It's a classic, Dylan. There's a difference."

"Mm-hmm," she hums.

"Aw, come on," Reeves continues. "Put a white wig on you, and you're practically Daenerys Targaryen."

Maverick tilts his head, studies a squirming Dylan, and nods. "You know, I think you're onto something."

"Right?" Reeves points his index finger at Griffin and Jaxon, who've been shockingly quiet considering the topic of conversation. "I want you two to know you failed as older brothers." He turns back to Dylan. "We're watching it. You and me."

"No thanks."

"Why not?" he asks.

"Because she doesn't want to," Everett announces. "Now, pick a card, Dylan. Finish the turn."

"Okay." She picks my card and lifts it in the air. "*What does Dylan find disturbing and oddly charming?* And the answer is... Finley after watching a crime documentary."

"Yes!" I do a short victory dance and grab the card pinned between Dylan's two fingers, adding it to my pile so we can tally up whose cards were chosen the most once the game is finished.

By the end of the night, my stomach hurts from laughing so hard, and Maverick's deep chuckle is like a balm to my soul. They were right. This is exactly what we needed.

The fourth episode of *Game of Thrones* plays on the screen, and I snuggle against Maverick's chest. He's asleep. Actually, I'm pretty sure everyone's asleep, and I'm seconds from joining them. The day has finally caught up to me, and I'm exhausted. Covering my mouth, I let out a yawn when I catch Archer standing from one of the armchairs in the corner of the family room.

Careful not to wake him, I slip out from underneath Maverick's arm and follow Archer to the kitchen.

"Hey, where are you going?" I whisper.

Hooking his thumb over his shoulder toward his bedroom, he answers, "I gotta pack."

"Pack?"

"Yeah, I have a flight this morning."

"Ah, man. I thought it was tomorrow."

"It *is* tomorrow," he clarifies. The light from his phone screen practically blinds me as he shows me the time with the same boyish grin I love so much.

"Damn," I concede. "So, where are you going?"

"I have a presentation in California with my Uncle Jake."

"Do you need a ride to the airport?" I offer.

"Nah, I got it." Slipping his phone back into his pocket, he adds, "I'll hire an Uber or something."

"You sure?"

He nods. "Yeah, no big deal."

"Okay." I rock back on my heels. "Well, give me a hug goodbye." I wrap my arms around his waist. "I'm going to miss you."

"Same." He kisses the top of my head. "This is the last business trip until I'm officially hired next year, so I'll get a little break."

"Good." I squeeze him tightly. "You need one."

He chuckles. "Yeah. I guess so."

If there have been any positives to Maverick's diagnosis, it's the tension between Archer and me dissipating. It's like we've finally bridged the gap I created. Like we finally found our rhythm again after it initially blew up. And it's been nice. Really nice. Honestly, it's more than I deserve, but I'm not going to question it.

I need him.

And I think he needs me too.

Letting go, Archer gazes down at me, and I tilt my head, waiting for him to spit out whatever he's thinking.

When he stays quiet, I ask, "You okay?"

"Yeah." He nods. The moonlight filtering in through the kitchen window highlights his sincerity as he keeps watching me with a look I can't quite put my finger on. He resembles his brother so much right now it's not even funny.

"You sure?" I press.

"Yeah," he chuckles. "I'm sure." His blue eyes soften.

"Seriously, out with it," I order. "You're making me feel all shy and stuff."

"It's nothing," he says with another quiet laugh. "It's... Well, I didn't think I'd be able to accept you and Mav, you know? But it makes so much sense. Honestly, I don't know how I didn't see it. I'm happy for you, Lia. I really am."

I pull back, surprised by his sincerity. I didn't know I needed to hear those words, but with them spoken, I kind of want to hug him all over again. Because I know I put him through the wringer. I know I don't deserve his forgiveness. Not really. But hearing his acceptance of...everything? It's more than I've ever deserved. My eyes burn, and I blink quickly, trying to get rid of the stupid feeling as Archer watches me carefully.

"Aw, don't cry, Ophelia." He pulls me into another hug.

I burrow into his chest, stealing his warmth. His comfort. And his acceptance.

"You really are perfect, Archer," I whisper.

"Gotta give my brother something to aspire to, right?" He lets me go, giving me a wink, reminding me way too much of his twin, who's still asleep on the couch.

"Well, you're nailing it," I tell him, waving my hand around to showcase him fully. "All this? Perfection."

"Mm-hmm," he grunts dryly. "Thanks for taking care of him for me."

With a tiny curtsy, I say, "Glad I can be of service."

"I'm serious." He steps closer, dropping his voice an octave. "He might act like he's the strong one, Lia, but he needs you."

I sober and fold my arms as my gaze falls to the lump on the couch who's oblivious we're talking about him. Turning back to Archer, I murmur, "I know."

He pulls me into one more hug. "Get some sleep. I'll text you when I land." Then, he lets me go.

"Love you, Arch."

"Love you, Lia." He gives me one last smile and heads down the hall toward his bedroom.

After watching him disappear, I go back to the family room, grab a knitted blanket from the back of the couch, and snuggle against Maverick's chest as the rest of our friends snore quietly around us.

BUZZING FROM A SILENCED PHONE WAKES ME A LITTLE WHILE later. Rubbing at my tired eyes, I search the couch cushions for my phone but find Maverick's instead. Aunt Mia's calling.

Patting Maverick's pec, I whisper, "Hey." He's still out cold, so I nudge him harder. "Mav, wake up. Your mom's calling."

With a yawn, he takes the phone and answers it, tossing his opposite arm over his eyes to block out the cell phone's light in the dark family room.

"Hello?" he croaks.

His forehead scrunches, then his eyes widen, and he sits up fully, causing the knitted blanket to fall onto his lap. "*What?*"

Pause.

"Wait, say that again."

Pause.

"Mom, slow down. What's going on?" He stands up and starts pacing in what little space isn't littered with our friends' prone bodies.

They're all sprawled out on the ground, having fallen asleep while watching *Game of Thrones* like Maverick and I did. They start to stir as Maverick's voice raises, causing panic to claw at my insides.

"That's not possible," he argues. "He's here. I was with him last night."

"Mav, what's going on?" I whisper. Pushing to my feet, I step in front of him and block his path with two hands pressed against his chest.

Ignoring me, he squeezes his eyes shut. "No. It's not—" He clears his throat. "It's not possible."

Pause.

"No, Mom, I can't—"

Pause.

"Hey, Dad."

Pause.

"Uh, yeah." He sniffs and wipes at his face, his navy eyes turning glassy as he clears his throat again. "Yeah, we'll be right there."

His limp hand falls to his side. The call is still connected, and I can hear sobbing on the other end of the line. The sound embeds itself in my memory, and my body goes rigid as it washes over me.

Something's wrong.

Something's very wrong.

"Mav?" I question.

His phone clatters to the floor, and he shakes his head.

"Mav," I repeat, but he won't look at me. He won't look at anyone. Our friends are wide awake, each motionless on the ground. Watching. Waiting. Holding their breaths and preparing for…what? I'm not sure. And I need to find out because not knowing? Well, my imagination has to be worse than any actual scenario. Doesn't it? Yeah. It'll be fine. Everything is fine.

"Mav," I say quietly. My touch is gentle as I cup his cheek, hoping he'll open his eyes and look at me. "Mav, what is it? What happened?"

"Archer was in an accident. He's…" Maverick pinches the bridge of his nose, but I don't miss the glassiness in his bloodshot eyes before he has a chance to wipe them away. "Fuck!" He twists out of my grasp and punches the drywall, leaving a hole in the shape of his fist.

I flinch in surprise, covering my mouth as the fight seeps out of Maverick's body, and he hangs his head.

There's something about watching a strong person crumble. Something about seeing the humanity and vulnerability cripple them. The way it makes you feel helpless. Hopeless. Useless. Like your hands are tied, and you're drowning. You can kick. You can squirm. But nothing. Absolutely nothing keeps you from slipping beneath the surface. From preventing your lungs from filling with water. From watching your world as it's ripped from you. From everyone you care about. Leaving you with nothing.

Nothing.

"Mav, you're scaring me," I whisper.

Staring at the ground, Mav chokes out, "He's dead, Goose."

My hands shake as we enter the hospital. I'm not one hundred percent sure why we're here instead of the morgue, but I'm not about to question Maverick or his dad's instructions. The low buzz in my ears drowns out every sound in the cold, white, sterile building as Maverick guides me down a well-lit hallway. A doctor steps in front of the door separating us from where Aunt Mia and Uncle Henry told Maverick to meet them. It's strange. Only registering bits and pieces of the conversation. I think my brain is shutting down in a way to protect itself, and all I hear are little snippets from the doctor's warning. Brain-dead. Car accident. Broken. No hope. Goodbye.

On the drive here, Maverick filled me in on his conversation with his parents. They already told us he's brain-dead, his body is bruised and broken, and any hope we could possibly possess should be left at the door because there isn't any coming back from this. The only reason we're here is to say goodbye. To make peace with his passing.

It's bullshit.

No one makes peace with something like this.

I assume the doctor's repeating the same speech.

It doesn't fix anything or have any hope of easing the blow I know is on the other side of this wall.

This can't be real.

I'm not ready to say goodbye.

Please don't make me say goodbye, Archer.

Maverick says something to the doctor, though I don't register a single word. I simply stare straight in front of me, reminding myself to breathe.

In.

Out.

In.

Out.

A few seconds later, the doctor gives a soft nod and motions to the doorway leading to my best friend, along with his little sister and grieving parents. Maverick's grip is like a vice as he grabs my hand. But he doesn't move. He doesn't follow them. He simply stands there, listening to his mother's sobs echoing from inside. My heart squeezes even tighter, and salty tears glide down my cheeks, dripping off my chin onto my LAU T-shirt.

This can't be happening.

Please don't let this be happening.

I just saw him. Hours ago. We talked. We laughed. We hugged. This isn't possible. It can't be. He was fine. He was smiling and happy and talking about his job. It just... He can't be gone.

I keep my feet planted where they are, unable to move. Unable to step inside the room. To see the reality of the situation and how impossible it feels to accept it.

I can't lose both of them. I can't.

We received Maverick's diagnosis such a short time ago, and now this? I don't know how much more I can take.

"Come on," Maverick murmurs, though I'm not sure who he's talking to.

He takes a deep breath and squeezes my hand even tighter. Like I'm the only reason he's holding it together when I know for a fact he's mine. My legs feel useless. Heavy. But I force myself to follow Maverick as he finally finds the courage to face the scene we know is waiting for us. But even the knowledge, the phone call, and the doctor's warning aren't enough to prepare me for what's inside the room.

Maverick's pursuit ceases instantly as he enters the room, and I almost run into him. Peeking around his body, I take in the scene in front of me, all the while wishing I hadn't. The main lights are off, and the lights from the machines keeping Archer's body alive cast shadows along the white walls and the two silhouettes surrounding the hospital bed. Aunt Mia's on her knees, clutching Archer's hand as she cries. Uncle Henry's beside her. He's sitting on the edge of the bed, his chin touching his chest and his shoulders heaving. A soft squeak sounds from the opposite corner of the room. Rory's on the ground, hugging her knees to her chest and burying her head against them. She looks so broken. So sad. My heart cracks even more. I'd offer to comfort her, but I know Rory better than that. She has one comfort blanket. One. It's been this way since she was a baby. The only person capable of consoling her is Jaxon Thorne.

He's already parked outside. Whether she sent him a text or he knew she'd need him and came without an invitation, I'm not sure. Honestly, it wouldn't surprise me if Aunt Mia or Uncle Henry called and asked him to come so he could comfort their daughter, but at least she's one person I don't have to worry about. The rest of us? Well...I'm pretty sure we're fucked.

I avoid the lifeless body connected to the machines with

every fiber of my being, focusing on Maverick's parents, no matter how much the scene unfolding kills me. They're two of the strongest people I know, and their world is being ravaged. My throat closes as I try to keep my grief, my pain, my heartbreak in check, but it's impossible.

I don't want to look at the bed. I don't want to look at Archer. I don't want to look at anything, really. I want to go home. I want to erase today altogether and start from scratch. If I close my eyes, I can still see him smiling. The way his eyes crinkle in the corners. The way his mouth lifts like he has a secret. The way his husky laugh is warm and inviting. I can still see him walking into his bedroom to pack. I just saw him. He was fine.

How?

How is this even possible?

Wiping the wetness from my cheeks with my free hand, I take a deep breath, hold onto Maverick's grasp, and force myself to search for what's left of my best friend. Cuts and bruises marr his arms and the side of his face. There's a bloody wound on his left temple too. His eyes are closed, and his chest rises and falls slowly. But the steady beeping from the heart monitor plays a sick game with my sanity. I can almost believe he's sleeping, and if I walk toward him, he'll wake up. He'll be fine. But the charade is broken as I step closer to the bed, following Maverick's lead. Goosebumps prick along my arms, and a sob claws its way up my throat.

He looks so lifeless. So...*gone*. Like his soul has already left his body, leaving a shell of the boy I grew up with. The boy I call my best friend. The boy I love more than he ever really knew or understood.

My knight.

The same steady beeping from his heart monitor mingles with our sorrow, reaching a feverish pitch, and leaves me raw and aching. Instead of bringing hope—hope he might be okay, that he might wake up—all it does is add salt to the wound, and I can't do anything to change it. He's brain-dead. It's only a matter of time until the beeping stops, and he's gone forever.

It isn't fair.

It isn't. Fucking. Fair!

I want to scream. To rip my hair out and hit the walls until my fists bleed. I want to do something—anything—to take this pain away. Mine. Maverick's. Rory's. Mia's. Henry's.

Why?

Why does it have to be this way?

It isn't fair.

It isn't. Fucking. Fair!

Quiet footsteps sound like stomping as Jaxon appears in the doorway. Without a word, he walks to Rory, and she scrambles to her feet, clinging to him.

"Hey, Squeaks," he murmurs.

Her body wracks with sobs against his chest, but she barely makes a sound. I don't miss the way her fingers fist into his shirt or how Jaxon squeezes his eyes shut as he takes the brunt of her pain, carrying it the only way he knows how.

"I don't want to be here," she cries. "I don't want to—"

"Sh…" he whispers. Turning to Aunt Mia and Uncle Henry, he asks, "Do you want me to take her home? Or to another room? Or—"

"I don't want to be here," she repeats, refusing to lift her head from Jaxon's chest as her agony soaks the fabric of his shirt.

"We'll be…somewhere," Jaxon offers. "I'll keep my phone on me."

"Okay." Mia gives him a watery nod but doesn't let go of Archer's broken hand on the bed.

"Love you, brother," Jaxon adds. I'm not sure if he's talking to Archer or Maverick. Then again, I'm not sure if it matters. We're all family here. And we'll all grieve long after this.

Honestly, I don't know if I'll ever stop.

A throat clears behind us, and we turn around, my heart lodging in my esophagus. When Dr. Scott steps into the room, my brows dip in concern.

His expression is more somber than I've ever seen as he watches us from the doorway.

When none of us say anything, Dr. Scott murmurs, "I'm so sorry."

Mia climbs to her feet, and Henry pulls her back to his front, but neither replies, their faces red and swollen, their breathing staggered and unsteady.

Dr. Scott's eyes are hazy, and he clears his throat again. "Are you aware your son is an organ donor?"

Mia and Henry exchange confused looks. "I, uh," Aunt Mia shakes her head. "Y-yes. I believe he was."

"It's standard procedure to run some tests when someone is officially declared brain-dead if they volunteered to be a donor so we can begin searching for matches."

Henry's hands slide up and down Mia's bare arms soothingly. "Yes, that makes sense. That's, uh, that's good."

"It is," Dr. Scott agrees. His attention shifts to Maverick, and he lets out a soft sigh. "The good news is, we've been able to match him with quite a few people, and he's going to save several lives."

"That's good." Aunt Mia wipes the corner of her eyes, no matter how pointless it is, as the tears continue falling.

"It is," Dr. Scott repeats. He clears his throat again, like the words are caught there as he looks at Maverick again. "I'm so sorry, Maverick."

Mav nods but doesn't say anything else.

"Listen," he continues, "I've never had to do this, but…"

"What is it?" Uncle Henry demands.

Dr. Scott removes his glasses and rubs his eyes, looking exhausted. "Maverick, we, uh, we found a heart for you."

A heart?

They found a heart?

I look back at Archer's lifeless body. The truth slams into me, and I cover my mouth with my hand.

No.

No, no, no, no.

The blood drains from Maverick's expression, and he shakes his head, voicing my thoughts aloud. "No."

"Maverick, he's a perfect match," Dr. Scott explains.

"No," Mav repeats. "No fucking way. Not a chance."

"I know this is hard, but—"

"I'm not taking it," he spits. "I don't want it. I don't—"

"Archer signed up to be a donor long before your diagnosis, Maverick," Dr. Scott clarifies. "He wanted to help—"

"No," Maverick booms. He lets my hand go and takes a step back, shoving his hands through his hair. "No. Not fucking possible."

"He's your identical twin," Dr. Scott rasps. "But even then, it's a miracle—"

"Don't talk to me about fucking miracles." Mav glares at him. His eyes are rimmed with red, and he looks absolutely wrecked. "My brother's dead, and I'm supposed to what? Take his heart so I can live? No, I can't."

"If you don't take it, his heart will go to the next person on the list," Dr. Scott warns.

"Fine," Maverick snaps, waving his hand around the hospital room like the last thread of his sanity has just been cut. "Do that."

Aunt Mia scrambles to her feet. "Maverick—"

Dr. Scott lifts his hand and stops her from continuing. "I

know you don't want to hear this, but there's a good possibility you won't have another chance at this, Maverick. Your brother's gone, but you'd be a fool to not accept his last gift."

"Stop," Maverick snaps. "Stop it. I don't—" He rakes his hands through his hair, tugging at the roots as his face twists with despair. "I don't want to hear this."

Slipping his glasses back into place, Dr. Scott says, "Whether or not you want to hear this, your brother's body is shutting down, and we will be harvesting the viable organs within the next hour. If you refuse to accept his heart, it will go to someone else, and I need to inform the next person on the list so they can prepare for their transplant."

"Maverick," Aunt Mia squeaks. She steps toward him and cradles his cheeks. "Your brother loves you more than anyone else on this earth."

"Mom, don't," he begs. His eyes are wild. Like a cornered beast. One who can't decide if he should lash out or run in the opposite direction and never stop. And I hate it. The look in his eyes. The fear. The repulsion. The raw vulnerability and absolute disgust shining through them.

"He loves you," Mia repeats. "He'd want you to have it."

Maverick shakes his head. "I can't—"

"You have to, Maverick," she begs. "You have to take it. I know this is difficult for you, but I can't lose another son. I won't survive it, do you hear me? I *won't*."

His defeat, his anguish, his fucking heart shattering…it's all palpable. Swirling in the air and making me sick to my stomach as I watch one of the strongest men I've ever met break. Maverick closes his eyes and leans into her touch. "Mom." His voice cracks, and my heart shatters with it.

Wrapping his arms around her waist, he cries into his mom's shoulder, and Henry steps closer, enveloping them in his warmth. I cover my mouth, attempting to contain the sobs shredding my throat while witnessing the man I love crumble into a million unfixable pieces.

The doctor stands beside me, looking as helpless as I feel. After a few moments, he murmurs, "I'll come back for an answer shortly, but we need to make a decision as soon as possible."

55
MAVERICK

I'm not sure how long my parents held me until everyone stepped outside so I could have a minute alone with Arch.

Honestly, it's a minute I'm not sure I want to have. If I do, it'll make this real. All of it. And I've never wanted to erase a situation more in my entire life.

My movements are almost mechanical as I force myself to move closer to the bed. It feels like a dream. All of this does. Hazy. Muddled. Unreal.

Why'd he have to get in the fucking car? Why'd he have to leave? Why'd he have to be on that road? Why'd it have to rain? Why'd the vehicle have to lose control? Why does he have to be a fucking match and make me feel like it's him or me? Like fate had to choose. Like only one of us could be left breathing. And why is it *me*?

"Fuck you, brother," I grit out, kneeling beside the edge of the bed. I grab his lifeless hand in mine and press my forehead to our entwined fingers like a prayer. "Fuck you for leaving me. For doing this." My chest heaves. "Fuck you for dying on me."

The reality crashes into me, stealing my breath and sitting on my sternum until my lungs threaten to give out, just like my heart.

"We've been through everything together," I whisper. "Since birth, man. What am I gonna do? What about our birthday? What about Rory? And Lia? She fucking needs you, bro. I need you. Don't do this," I beg. "Come back. Don't die on me. I'm fucking begging you, bro. Don't die on me."

My tears fall freely as I squeeze my eyes shut, praying to whatever god might be listening to bring him back. To let me take his place. To fix this. Fuck, I'd give anything to fix this. It isn't fair. He deserves the life he's built. The life he's worked so hard for. The one he's cultivated with his blood, sweat, and tears, while I've been throwing my own away, welcoming my impending expiration date.

"I know you see the irony here," I choke out. "How we spent our entire lives bitching about being interchangeable, and now here we are. My body. My mind. Your fucking heart." My voice breaks. "I don't want it. I don't want your heart, man." I take my opposite hand and set it on his chest, feeling the steady *thump-thump* against my palm through the thin, white, hospital sheets. "It was supposed to be me, Archer. I'm supposed to be the one in this hospital bed. The one dying. The one in the fucking casket." I wipe beneath my nose with the back of my hand. "You're the good brother. The one who has his shit together. The one with his head on straight. The one with a plan. A fucking future. I can't...I can't do this without you." My shoulders heave. "I can't take this. I can't take your heart, man."

Fuck!

I want to yell. I want to scream. I want to say it isn't fair. Because it isn't. No one with a heart would say this was fair. That my own twin's life would have to end so I could have mine.

"I can't do this, Arch. You were the one who was supposed to be here. Who was supposed to help Mom and Dad through losing their son. You were the one who promised to take care of Ophelia after I'm gone. You promised. You fucking promised, man." Blood explodes in my mouth as I dig my teeth into the inside of my cheek, desperate to wake up from this fucked-up nightmare and the fallout looming ahead of me no matter what I do.

"I know you," I add. "I know you're laughing at me some-where, finding way too much fucking humor in this, but it isn't funny, man. None of it is. Mom and Dad need you. Rory needs you. Lia needs you. Fuck, I need you. I need you, brother." I sob harder, clinging to his limp hand like it's my only lifeline.

Its my lifeline.

Not *he's* my lifeline.

Because he's gone.

Archer's gone.

My brother's gone.

And I can't even grieve for him properly because the fucking clock on the wall keeps fucking ticking, mingling with the fucking heart monitor, reminding me of the fucking choice I have to make while knowing there isn't one in the first place. If there's an afterlife. If there's a single fucking chance I'll see him again and have to look him in the eye and say I rejected his heart out of grief and guilt, he'll never forgive me.

But the idea of this gift. This fucking bitter gift. Of me accepting it and everything that comes with it. It's more than my weary soul can bear. More than it should ever have to.

I'm tired. So fucking tired.

"I love you," I rasp. "I love you so much, brother, and I'm so sorry. I'm so sorry the roles can't be reversed. Sorry I can't take this from you and won't be the one in the coffin." My forehead falls to the bed, and I shake my head back and forth, letting the itchy material rub against my skin. "Fuck, I can't even say thank you, Arch. Do you have any idea how pissed I am at you right now?" A strangled laugh slips out of me. "I'm so fucking pissed." I press his knuckles against my eyes, letting him feel my pain. My agony. "You know Ophelia's gonna keep you on a pedestal forever now, right? Probably gonna wanna name her firstborn after you."

My chest squeezes even tighter as the words fall out of me, and the realization hits me. He's never gonna be an uncle. Or a dad. He's never gonna get married. Never gonna rule the world like I knew he could. He's never gonna do anything, but because of him, I get to. My body wracks with another sob, and I grip his hand even tighter. "Fuck, man. I wanna beat the shit out of you right now." Another lump catches in my throat, but I force it back. "And I wanna hug you again. One last time." My voice cracks, and I weep even harder. "Thank you, brother. Thank you."

56

OPHELIA

Maverick was wheeled into the operating room four hours ago. Dr. Scott said the surgery could take anywhere from six to twelve hours, and I've been counting down the minutes.

I've never been more terrified in my life. Everyone's in the waiting room. Maverick's family. Mine. Aunt Kate and Uncle Mack. Everyone except Tatum. When I asked my mom where she was, she shook her head and said we all grieve differently.

I didn't push it.

A heavy somberness is in the air. It swallows conversation. Hell, even small talk ended within minutes of everyone arriving. Red-rimmed eyes surround the space. I'm not sure if it's because of lack of sleep, Maverick's unstable future, or Archer's...

I grab another tissue from the box in front of me and wipe beneath my eyes. My mom pulls me against her, rubbing her hand up and down my arm while my dad sits on my opposite side. As soon as they heard the news, they brought me a change of clothes and a sandwich. Both are sitting untouched on the coffee table beside the almost empty box of tissues.

"It's gonna be okay," my mom whispers, but I only shake my head.

I can't believe he's gone. I can't believe Maverick's in surgery. I can't believe my entire world—everyone's entire world—was flipped upside down and torn to pieces, leaving nothing but chaos in its wake. A chaos I can't wrap my head around. A new normal I don't want to embrace. An agonizing hope I refuse to take for granted.

Please make it through this, Maverick.

Pressing the tissue against my swollen eyes, I remind myself to breathe. Dylan and Finley sit on my mom's opposite side. Both are as silent as the rest of us while the clock on the wall mocks me with the minute hand. I swear it's moving backward. Like I'm frozen in time. Frozen in this hell. Not knowing if or when or who will make it out of this hospital by the end of the day. Twisting the shredded tissue in my lap, I glance at the heavy double doors Maverick disappeared through. Where the doctor promised to keep us updated. They're still closed.

Reeves offers me a cup of coffee, but I shake my head, refusing to take it. I should. My exhaustion has morphed into something deeper since we got the phone call about Archer. It's heavier. More consuming. More convincing. Like if I close my eyes, I'll be able to slip into oblivion. I'll be able to escape. I'll be able to believe none of this is real, and I didn't just lose my best friend and potentially my boyfriend within twenty-four hours of each other.

"Caffeine's good for the soul," Reeves murmurs.

I shake my head again. "I'm okay, thanks."

"Oo, I'll take it." Finley grabs the offered cup and brings it to her lips.

Without missing a beat, Reeves rolls his eyes and nudges

the outside of my thigh with his knee. "How are you holding up?"

My eyes water, and I lift a shoulder. "I'm supposed to be holding up?"

He snatches another tissue from the box on the glass coffee table behind him and offers it to me. When I take it, he asks, "You wanna take a walk?"

Dabbing at the corner of my eye, my skin raw and chafed from my tears, I let a pathetic laugh slip out of me. "Not really."

"Yeah, me neither." He collapses onto the chair across from mine and kicks his legs out on the table.

Rory is crying in the corner of the room, her tiny hiccups echoing off the walls as Jaxon holds her. He brought her back to the hospital after Henry called and told him about the match. Before Maverick was prepped, Rory had a chance to wish him luck and potentially say goodbye to her last living sibling as he was wheeled away.

She retreated right back to Jaxon's embrace.

At least she has someone to hold onto.

Me?

I mean, I have my parents, but...I'm a fucking shell. Hollow. Like I've been carved out with a dull spoon and am too numb to really understand the repercussions or how long it'll take to heal from them.

Who am I kidding?

There's no healing from this.

And there never will be.

But so help me, if Maverick is ripped away from me too, I'll...

Fuck!

I don't know what I'll do.

Wadding up the used tissue in my hand, I close my eyes

and focus on my breathing, sending another prayer into the universe.

Please keep him safe.

Please don't take him from me too.

Please make everything okay.

"Hey," a familiar voice murmurs.

I open my eyes and sit up a little straighter in my seat. "Hey, Aunt Mia."

"Hey," she repeats. "Mind if we…"—she sniffs—"Mind if we chat for a minute?"

Dylan, Finley, Reeves, and my dad all stand without a word, and my mom smiles at her friend while doing the same.

Aunt Mia takes her spot while the clock continues ticking away on the wall, leaving me anxious and queasy. We haven't talked since brunch. Since she found out I was hooking up with Maverick after breaking Archer's heart. Then Maverick passed out, and his health took precedence over everything else, as it should. But it never really gave me a chance to apologize to Aunt Mia for the fallout. She was nothing but loving and welcoming when Archer told her about our relationship. And what did I do in return? I screwed his brother.

God, It feels like a lifetime ago. The reminder brings more tears to my eyes. It's funny. I've cried so much, I thought they'd be all dried up by now, but my body keeps producing more, and there's nothing I can do to stop it.

"How are you holding up?" Aunt Mia prods.

With a pathetic laugh, I roll my watery eyes and answer, "Reeves asked me the same thing two minutes ago."

"And what was your answer?"

I blink away the moisture from my eyes. "I'm supposed to be holding up?"

Her sad laugh warms me as she squeezes my knee. "Ditto." Letting me go, she reaches for the last tissue in the box and dabs beneath her eyes. "Life has dealt me a lot of shit over the past few decades, Lia, but the past little while takes the cake."

My heart clenches as I peek at her. "I'm really sorry I hurt your son. I know so much has happened since then that it probably doesn't even feel like it matters, but—" I hiccup. "I'm really sorry."

"Oh, Ophelia." Her smile is sad as she reaches for my knee again. "We all make mistakes. And trust me, I made plenty when I was your age."

"That doesn't make me feel better."

"I know," she whispers. "But our sweet Archer, he..." her bottom lip trembles. "He wasn't one to hold grudges, and neither am I. He loved you, Lia. And I know it hurts right now, but he'd want you to be happy and to live your life to the fullest. I know it with every fiber of my being."

She's right. I know it too. But it doesn't make this easier to accept. He should be here. He should be sitting by me, comforting me, promising me Maverick will be okay. And in a way, I feel like Archer *is* promising Maverick will be okay. Because without him, Maverick *wouldn't* be. The realization only makes me feel worse. Like I'm betraying my best friend all over again for thinking of his brother when we just started to mend things between us.

"I feel guilty," I whisper. "That I want Maverick to be okay when Archer is...when he's..." Moisture floods my eyes, and I cradle my head in my hands, unable to say the words aloud. It's like my body's rejecting it. The reality that Archer's gone. That I'll never see him again, and because of him, his brother's in surgery and has a chance of surviving. Of living a full life.

"I know, Lia." She rubs her hand up and down my back. "I know."

"I feel so broken, Aunt Mia," I cry.

She sniffs quietly. "We all do."

She's right about this, too. We're all broken. Archer? He was a piece of us. All of us. And with him gone...we're all missing a vital part of ourselves. A part that can never be replaced.

Why'd you have to die, Archer?

"And what if Mav—" My words break with a quiet whimper. "What if he—"

"He's going to be fine," she promises. "I know it."

"How do you know?"

Unwavering, she stares at the closed hospital doors where her son is currently fighting for his life. "Because he has to be." She wipes beneath her nose with her tissue and lets out a slow, shaky breath. "Bad things happen to good people all the time. But good things can happen, too, and I think that's what we need to focus on. The odds of Archer being a match is...it's a miracle, Ophelia. A very heart-breaking miracle. We can't dismiss it."

"I know," I whisper.

She's right about this too. We can't. It wouldn't be fair to Archer or Maverick. For everything they went through to get here.

"Listen to me, Ophelia." Aunt Mia grabs my hand and pulls it into her lap. "When my son wakes up with his brother's heart, he will need you." My tears roll down my cheeks and drip off my chin as I hold her stare. "He will need all of us, but especially you. I'm not going to lie. When I found out about you dating both my boys, I was kind of pissed."

I let out a pathetic whimper, and she continues. "Especially because they're twins. I thought, who would do that? Who would act like they could exchange one boyfriend with another identical one?"

"I didn't—"

"I know, Ophelia," she murmurs. "That's the thing. You

didn't look at them that way. You never did. They weren't one and the same to you. Ever. You were connected to both of my boys *individually*, seeing the best of them and recognizing their differences. Their strengths and their weaknesses. I can't thank you enough for that. For proving to them they're their own beings. Proving they're different and unique. Proving they never needed to live up to each other or compete with each other to still hold value. You cared about each of them individually. Loving them individually."

My lips part on a sob, but I swallow it back, holding onto Mia's hand for dear life.

"I think Maverick will need the reminder now more than ever, Ophelia," she whispers. "Please don't fail him."

Closing my eyes, I take a deep, cleansing breath and nod. "I won't. I promise."

5 7
MAVERICK

My nose itches.

I wrinkle it and reach to scratch the thing but stop trying when I realize my arm feels like it weighs a thousand pounds. My eyelids are heavy, too, as I slowly pry them open. The bright light burns like a bitch, causing my dry eyes to water. I blink the moisture away and take in my surroundings.

My family. They surround the bed. Their smiles are a sharp contrast to the white walls and fluorescent lights. I try to sit up but wince. The wind feels like it's knocked from my lungs and my chest? My chest feels almost numb, but there's an ache there too. It's deeper.

The surgery.

Right.

My thoughts feel sluggish, but slowly, everything that happened over the last—shit, I have no idea how long I've been out—rises to the surface. Archer. My surgery. Everything. I lay my head back on the pillow and close my eyes, the pain from earlier catching up to me, making it hard to breathe.

"Hey," my mom murmurs.

I wiggle my nose again. "My nose itches."

With a quiet laugh, she fiddles with the oxygen tube and shrugs. "Any better?"

It isn't, but I nod anyway.

"Good," she replies. "I'm glad to see you awake."

"Where's Opie?" I rasp. My throat feels like I've gargled razor blades, and my expression sours.

"I'm right here," a soft voice whispers. She's sitting on my left, nibbling the edge of her nail. Her eyes are swollen and red as she watches me carefully.

"I'll get the doctor," my dad tells me. He stands from one of the chairs, smooths his T-shirt, and heads into the hallway. When we were kids, Archer and I gave him shit for his obsession with suits. He's never in a T-shirt unless he's sleeping. It's the same one from before the surgery. After he received the phone call about Archer, he rushed straight here. Apparently, he hasn't left since. My mom doesn't follow him. She squeezes my hand tighter like she's afraid I'll slip through her fingers at any second.

So that's why it felt like I couldn't move my arm.

"I assume it went all right since I'm alive," I mutter around the razor blades coating my throat.

"The doctor said everything went perfectly. You won't be able to play hockey or anything, but..." Her bottom lip trembles. "We're so happy you're okay, baby."

"Thanks, Mom." I rub my thumb against the back of her hand. "Do you mind if...if I talk with Opie for a minute?"

She forces a smile, kissing my knuckles. "Of course, Mav. I'll be right outside the door. Lia, holler if you need anything, all right?"

Lia nods.

Once we're relatively alone, she lets out a shaky breath. "I'm so glad you're okay."

"Me too. How's my family doing?"

"Exhausted," she says with a smile. "But I think they're clinging to the good things right now, you know?" Her bottom lip trembles like my mom's, and Ophelia sucks it into her mouth, biting hard on the plump flesh.

"And how are you?" I prod.

Careful not to jostle me, she fusses with a few of the tubes connected to my body and sits on the edge of the hospital bed. Her touch is gentle as she brushes her fingers through the hair on my forehead, pushing it away from my face. "Also clinging to the good things." She gives me a watery smile. "How are you holding up?"

It's a good question. So much has happened I don't even know where to start.

"I, uh…" I clear my throat. "I think I'm still in the processing phase."

"I think all of us are," she agrees.

"I feel guilty."

Her expression falls, and she sniffs quietly. "I said the same thing to your mom when you were in surgery."

"Great minds think alike."

She smiles softly, but it doesn't erase the turmoil in her glassy eyes. "He wouldn't want you to feel guilty, Mav."

He.

My eyes close with the weight of her words, making it hard for me to breathe.

"And he wouldn't want you to feel sad, either," she whispers.

I know she's right. He'd probably give me a dead arm if he saw me wallowing after my successful transplant. He'd tell me to stop acting like a bitch and be happy. Be grateful. A lump grows in my throat as the weight of my gratitude sits heavy on my shoulders.

"I think he'd want you to live your life to the fullest," she adds.

I open my eyes and stare at our clasped hands. "I know."

"So, I think the real question is…how do we live life to the fullest?" she asks.

My gaze meets hers, and my pulse skips as I take in her beauty. Her sadness. Her strength. Her love. For me and my brother.

"I told Archer we're gonna name our firstborn after him," I mutter.

Her mouth lifts. "*Our?*"

"Technically, I said yours, but toe-may-toe, toe-mah-toe."

She laughs. "I think he'd like that."

"Me too." I lick my parched lips. "I really miss him, Opie."

With a sad smile, she reaches for a cup of ice and spoons some into my mouth. "He's easy to miss."

"Yeah, he really is." Chewing on the ice, I let the moisture soothe my aching throat. "I love you, Ophelia."

"I love you too." She sets the spoon in the cup. Her hands shake as she threads our fingers together and brings my hand to her lips, kissing me softly. "I'm so glad you're okay."

I nod. "Me too. I've been thinking a lot about Arch and you and…everything."

She sniffs. "Same."

"I'm not gonna take this for granted. I'm not gonna take a single thing for granted," I clarify. "This life? Fuck me, it's fragile, Goose. It can be taken from me—from anyone—in an instant. Throwing away my second chance by being sad when I'm lucky enough to be alive feels…" I swallow thickly. "It feels like I'm not grateful or some shit. I'm not gonna do that to him. It feels wrong in here." I press my hand to my chest, and she covers it with her palm, the steady beat making her eyes water.

Slowly, she lowers her head to my chest and listens to Archer's heart.

My pulse quickens again, surprising me and causing a strange zing to roll through me. It doesn't hurt, so I don't mention it. I simply thread my fingers through her hair, holding her close.

"Pretty sure this is my favorite sound in the world," she whispers. Her breath slips through the thin sheets and into my skin, warming me. "I love you," she adds.

I'm not sure if the words are meant for me or for Archer, but I know my brother well enough to reply without hesitation. "This heart will always beat for you, Ophelia Grace."

And I know it will.

5 8

MAVERICK

I was released from the hospital a few weeks ago. The funeral sucked, but it felt good to talk about Archer. To reminisce with family and friends, and fuck, the place was packed with plenty of both. After the funeral, my Uncle Jake gave me Archer's laptop from his internship. I guessed his password on the third try. I never asked what he worked on while interning at B-Tech, and that's on me. But as soon as I found Archer's last PowerPoint presentation, I understood why they were chomping at the bit to hire him. In true Archer fashion, he found a way to use B-Tech's technology to store power in unstable countries so they have less downtime on their grid. He also called in a favor from our grandfather, who's now working on a bill to help subsidize the cost for low-income households, making state-of-the-art batteries more affordable than ever for those who really need them during natural disasters and other shitstorms they find themselves in.

My brother's still managing to save the world, even in death.

Why am I not surprised?

After giving it a lot of thought, I decided the only thing to do was keep the ball rolling. I'm not afraid to tap into our family's connections and figure out how to distribute the technology to other countries in need. As soon as Dr. Scott approves it *and* Ophelia's season with the Lady Hawks ends, I'm hoping we can travel wherever fate leads us to help roll out the first phase.

My advisor switched my classes from in-person to online, and my parents moved me back to my childhood home so they can keep an eye on me while I heal. It feels weird being away from campus. The worst part is being away from my friends...my *other* brothers. They each take turns visiting me, but going from living together to weekly visits is a bitch.

Tatum hasn't spoken to me since the night on the roof. She's said a few words to her sister here and there, but we're not the only ones who've noticed her not-so-subtle changes. Her long, auburn hair is now a sharp bob, her favorite color is black, and she's already failing all her classes. Any chance of being accepted into Harvard will be long gone if she keeps this up, and I'll be surprised if she winds up at LAU when she graduates in the spring.

No, the girl is spiraling and has no interest in anyone saving her, let alone herself.

I wonder if Ophelia knows her little sister was in love with Archer, but I doubt it. I also haven't brought it up, and I'm not going to.

As for Ophelia? Well, she rearranged her entire school schedule, too, and she might not officially be living here, but she has a guest bedroom she stays in at least half the week. It was a little rocky at first, but once all the details about our relationship were ironed out, my mom, dad, and little sister accepted it with open arms. Then again, she's always been part of the family. I just get to kiss the shit out of her now without caring who sees.

They say the first six weeks after a transplant are the hardest, but I feel pretty good. Dr. Scott tells us Archer's heart is holding strong so far. I knew it would. Archer never half-assed anything, let alone a miracle. I've been seeing a therapist twice a week since the accident, and we're working through survivor's guilt. I'm not sure if I'll ever really accept how everything played out, but I'm trying, and he's assured me it's all that matters. Ophelia usually comes along with me to my sessions. Therapy has been really good for both of us, but even so, I miss feeling happy. Feeling normal. And so, today, I'm taking a step toward exactly this. Normalcy. Just a taste of it. Even if it's only for one night. Even if I have to fabricate it myself.

The garage door sounds as I grab the bouquet of daisies from the counter and tug at the top button on my dress shirt.

Seriously, I don't know how Archer survived in these things.

The door opens a second later, and Opie steps into the house, freezing almost instantly when she sees me standing in front of her.

"What are you...?" Her curious gaze darts over me, taking in the suit, my freshly shaven jaw, and the flowers. When her attention finally lands on my face, she tilts her head. "Uh, why do I suddenly feel severely underdressed?" She smoothes out her LAU hoodie and wipes her palms on her jeans.

"You look beautiful," I tell her.

"And you look..." She hesitates. "Well, gorgeous as always, but..." Her voice trails off, and she laughs. "Okay, seriously. Why are you standing in the middle of your mom and dad's kitchen dressed in a suit?"

"I want to ask you something."

Her breath stalls, and she slowly lowers her backpack to the ground. "Mav, I'm only eighteen—"

"I'm not asking you to marry me," I clarify. "*Yet*." With a wink, I stretch out my hand, urging her to come closer to me.

A quiet, relieved laugh slips past her lips as she strides closer, tangling our fingers together. "Yeah, thanks for the heart attack." Eyes bulging, she rushes out, "Uh, no pun intended."

With a laugh, I tug her closer to me. "That was a good one."

"It was something," she mutters.

Some might think it's too early to joke about my transplant, but when we can either laugh or cry, it's easier to do the first of the two. Easier to focus on the light instead of drowning in the darkness. And trust me, the darkness is thick as mud.

"So," she starts. "If you're not proposing, which don't get me wrong, I'd probably say yes even though it would make me look like a crazy person, as long as we had like a ten-year engagement, but..." She drags out the last word, waiting for me to finally fill her in as she wraps her arms around my waist and gives me a look telling me I better start talking.

"Will you go to Homecoming with me?" I murmur.

She leans a little further away from me and tilts her head. "Seriously?"

"Yeah."

"You want to take me to Homecoming?"

"If you'll have me."

"I just said I'd marry you," she reminds me. "Pretty sure I'll have you any way I can. But are you sure you want to go to a school dance? Especially after everything that's happened?"

"I just asked you, didn't I?"

"I know, but"—she licks her lips—"the last time you asked me to a dance…"

"I fucked up," I finish for her. "Yeah, I think I remember."

A sad smile hovers at the edge of her mouth as if she's replaying the last time I asked her to a dance and the fallout that followed.

I cup her cheek and run my thumb along the corner of her lips, willing the sadness tainting them to go away. "I'm glad Archer took you." I push past the hurt accompanying his name as it rolls off my tongue. "That you have those memories with him."

Leaning into my touch, she whispers, "So am I."

"And even though he bailed me out that time, too…" I lean closer and kiss her forehead. "He has a habit of doing that, by the way. Giving me opportunities for second chances after I screw up the first time." I kiss her again and gently pull away. "But I've been thinking. If I'm not gonna squander this heart, I won't squander the opportunity to take you to another dance, either. Not when I have the chance." I push her hair over her shoulders, commanding her full attention. "So, what do you say? Will you go to Homecoming with me?"

Considering my question, she smooths out my suit and rests her hand over my heart. As it thumps against her palm, she tells me, "If I say yes, you'll have to pretend you're a grown-up and wear a suit. You hate suits."

"That's why I'm wearing a suit right now," I argue. "To prove I'm capable of acting like a real-life grown-up."

"Classy," she notes.

"Right?" My chest puffs up with pride. "Don't get me wrong, I'm aware I don't have quite the suave energy as Archer did when he was wearing one."

"It's true. Archer was the king of suits."

"Hey! You're not supposed to agree with me!"

Her amusement fills my ears as she points out, "To be fair, you're the one who brought it up."

"Yeah, but still…"

"Don't worry, Mav." She pats my chest, being careful of my healing incision. "You're still the Buchanan of my heart… kind of." Stealing a move from my own playbook, she gives me a wink. "But you know," she muses, "if I say yes, I'll have to buy another dress."

"Exactly." I start swaying us back and forth. "Maybe this time, you'll let me into the dressing room so I can help you pick—"

"Not a chance, mister."

"Fine," I concede, but only because I know Finley and Dylan will insist on going with her to pick out their dresses. "Does this mean you'll let me do it right this time? You'll let me take you to Homecoming?"

Her eyes glaze with an almost crippling concoction of mirth and sadness, but it's less than yesterday, and it's all that matters.

Sobering slightly, she says, "Of course I'll let you take me."

"That's my girl." I brush my nose against hers in an Eskimo kiss, and she sniffs, smiling up at me.

"Thank you," she whispers.

"Are you kidding me?" I squeeze her tighter. "I'm the luckiest bastard alive, Goose." The same tinge of weight carries through the air with my words, leaving me heavy but grateful. Grateful I'm alive. Grateful I'm holding Ophelia in my arms when I was so close to being ripped away from her. Grateful I get to take her to a dance. That my brother watched over her when I couldn't. That I get to call her mine and live out the rest of my life with her.

Without Archer, I wouldn't have any of this. My life. My second chance. Every fucking breath and beat of my heart. It's all thanks to him.

Thank you, brother.

"You and me, Goose," I rasp. "It's always you and me."

"I love you, Maverick."

My eyes close, and I let her words wash over me, easing the sharp ache in my chest like a soothing balm only she can administer.

I love this girl.

I fucking love this girl.

Every. Damn. Thing. About her.

"I love you too, Opie."

We both do.

HIJACKED EPILOGUE

REEVES

L et's back up a bit, shall we?

Funerals are a bitch. I've been to more than I can count. Okay, I could technically count if I wanted to pull up a spreadsheet, but who has time for that shit? You'd be surprised by how many single women are willing to pay for an escort to be their plus-one instead of showing up to a funeral alone. With fake tears and a fake boyfriend half their age on their arm, the combination has only amplified my apathy for the whole thing. When I die, they can donate my body to science and throw a kick-ass party with alcohol and ladies and food.

Good food.

And no one's allowed to wear black, either. I hate black. Black is like a virus. It spreads. It devours. It swallows every other color and transforms it into more of the same. Black. Black. Black. I hate black.

The service was nice, I guess. Maverick and his family spoke. They shared some pretty funny stories and had the guests laughing, which is no easy feat considering the circumstances. At least they weren't fake. To be fair, I've known the Buchanans for a while now. None of them are fake. Ever. I appreciate it about them. The food's decent too. Not my style. I'd take a big juicy burger or a slice of chocolate cake over a chicken salad sandwich and fruit any day of the week, but I'm not complaining.

We just gotta make it through today.

Don't get me wrong. Accepting Archer's absence is gonna be a bitch for all of us, but they're gonna be okay. They're gonna get through this. I should know. I'm a pro. Been getting over family deaths since before I could walk. Fuck, I had family dying before my first breath. My mom passed while giving birth to me, and my dad? Well, let's just say he won't let me forget it.

Yeah. Everyone moves on. Everyone has to. Disney had it right. It's the circle of life, even when we don't want to accept it.

I snatch a grape from the banquet table and pop it into my mouth, scanning the large room for entertainment. I like watching people. Seeing how they interact. How they handle their grief when no one's looking. And even if they catch me watching them, it's not like they care. I'm Reeves. The shallow asshole with his head up his ass. It's not like I'm paying attention anyway, right?

I watch Mav and Lia talk to their parents with their hands interlocked. He just got out of the hospital after a two-week stay. Apparently, recovering from a heart transplant isn't for the faint of heart.

Ha! No pun intended.

Maverick's parents are forcing him to move in with them while he continues recovering for the next few months, and he'll be taking online classes this semester, so he doesn't fall behind. As for Ophelia? Well, she can't exactly take the

semester off, thanks to her commitment with the Lady
Hawks, but I overheard her requesting to move the majority
of her classes online, so she can spend as much time with
Mav as possible when she isn't on the ice. I doubt I'll be
seeing her much until Mav moves back in with us. It's a
shame. I kind of like her. I wonder if it'll make her roommates just as scarce. I doubt it. Finley's a social butterfly and
isn't afraid to force Dylan into being her wingwoman.

Good.

Dylan needs someone who's pushing her.

I tear my attention from Mav and Ophelia, browsing the
room like I would Netflix.

Griffin, Everett, and Jaxon are throwing back a few beers
with some of Archer's internship buddies. I bet a hundred
bucks they're replaying some of Archer's finest moments on
the ice since they all huddle around Everett's phone. I might
be wrong, but I doubt it. And Rory's in the corner, her eyes
swollen and puffy, as she stares at Jaxon from across the
room. Fuck, the longing in those baby blues is gonna land
her in trouble one day.

It's a good thing Jax is oblivious, or I'd break his hand for
touching someone underage. To be fair, he wouldn't cross
the line even if he did know the girl's in love with him. Jax
doesn't have an unhonorable bone in his body. It's one of the
main reasons I respect the bastard. But as soon as Rory turns
eighteen, I have a hunch all bets will be off, and she'll get sick
of waiting for him to see her as anyone other than a little kid.

And when the day comes, I'll pop some popcorn because
that shit will be entertaining as fuck.

With a smirk, I steal another grape and continue perusing
today's crowd.

Aaaand, there it is.

Finley, Finley, Finley, I tsk.

She curses at someone on her phone. I bet it's her

boyfriend. I heard they've been having problems in spite of Finley's insistence it's all rainbows and butterflies between her and Drew. Two hundred bucks says he's already sleeping with some sorority girl in one of his classes. Finley's smart, though. She'll figure it out. She might have to take off her rose-colored glasses and overcompensating optimism to get there, but I have faith in her.

And then there's Dylan.

My gaze falls on the little wallflower despite myself. Black glasses are perched on her button nose, and I tilt my head in surprise. I've never seen her wear glasses.

I wasn't kidding when I said she reminded me of Daenerys Targaryen. Not the seventh-season badass, but the baby deer from season one with wide eyes and a hint of naivety that's hot as fuck.

Pretty sure her brothers would kill me if I started messing with her. Pretty sure Everett would too. I can't figure out if his fascination with her is due to her being a family friend or if his feelings run any deeper.

I'm not sure if I want to find out, either.

Or maybe I do.

I've always been a sucker for poking the bear, especially when the stick up his ass is practically welded there.

Snatching another grape from the banquet table, I toss it into my mouth, stride toward Dylan, and tuck my hands into the front pockets of my slacks.

When she catches me approaching, she shrinks in on herself and folds her arms.

"You know," I start, "I heard a rumor that if a dude takes Viagra and dies, his dick stays hard indefinitely."

She covers her snort with her hand and shakes her head. "Tell me you're joking."

"Definitely joking. You really think I'm gonna Google that shit?" I shiver. "I might look like an idiot and have even convinced Maverick to Google a thing or two, but I learned my lesson in sixth grade when I had to write a book report on *Harry Potter*." I drop my voice a little lower. "Fell down the rabbit hole of Dramione, and let me tell you, there is some fanfic art you cannot unsee, my dear Dylan."

"What's Dramione?"

Brows raised, I explain, "Draco and Hermione? Dramione?"

She frowns. "Doesn't she end up with Ron?"

With a scoff, I throw my arm over her shoulders. "Aw, my sweet, innocent little Dylan. She might end up with Ron in the real books, but everyone's a sucker for a good opposites-attract, enemies-to-lovers story, don't you think?"

"I, uh," she hesitates. "I've never really thought about it, so…I'm not sure?"

"Is that a question?" The edge of my mouth curves up.

She lifts a shoulder, and her blue-green eyes fall to the ground. Even with her glasses shielding her, I notice how puffy they are. And damp and free of makeup. Like she didn't give a shit about getting ready for the outside world today. No. This is Dylan Thorne. The original girl next door.

She's a pretty little wallflower. I'll give her that much.

"Since when do you wear glasses?" I prod.

She touches the edge of her black frames. "Oh. I uh… always, I guess?"

"I've never seen you in them."

"Usually I wear contacts, but sometimes they give me a headache, especially when I've been crying a lot and—"

"Dylan," Everett snaps from across the room. "Come over here."

Peeking up at me, Dylan slips from beneath my arm and scoots her glasses along the bridge of her nose. "Nice chatting with you, Reeves. I'll, uh, see you around."

She darts across the funeral home and into Everett's waiting arms like the baby deer I'd pegged her for.

Yeah, I fucking called it.

Everett wants in Dylan's pants.

The question is, does she want him there?

There's only one way to find out.

EPILOGUE TWO

OPHELIA

A few years later...

With my hand resting on my swollen belly, I soak up the sunshine in the yard while Maverick wrestles with our three-year-old, Archer. Even though he isn't technically a junior, Mav started calling him AJ for short by the time he turned one, and the nickname has stuck ever since.

"Get him, AJ! Get him!" I cheer as my little boy runs across the lawn for the kiddie pool full of water balloons his dad filled earlier today. AJ's swimsuit rides low and shows half of his cute little bum, so I make a mental note to tighten the drawstring, hiding my amusement behind my hand as I stand near the backdoor of our home. Seriously, he's the cutest thing ever. After picking a green water balloon from the rainbow of colors in the tub, AJ throws it toward his daddy, but it slips through his tiny hands. With a pop, it hits the grass in front of him and explodes, pulling the most pathetic pout I've ever seen from his cute little lips as he turns to me helplessly.

472

"It's okay!" I call. "Get another one! You can do it!"

He grabs a blue water balloon from the kiddie pool, and, this time, he races closer to his dad. Mav is on his hands and knees, making growly monster sounds as he slowly stalks closer to our little boy. Once AJ is close enough, he flings the balloon at Mav, hitting him straight in the chest and drenching Maverick instantly.

His scar has faded over the years, but the silvery strip from the top of his sternum to the bottom of his ribs shines in the sun. It's a stark contrast to his tan skin and the dark ink he collected over the years. I don't mind it, and neither does Mav. The scar's a reminder of how precious life is, and I wouldn't trade it for the world. Even if he didn't wear it like a badge of honor, Mav wears his brother's name above his heart and right next to the little goose I spotted all those years ago. It's Archer's handwriting. We got it from his driver's license, knowing his signature was made the day he decided to become a donor. The same day he decided to self-lessly and unknowingly save his brother's life along with countless others.

It's already AJ's favorite tattoo in spite of me pointing out the small goose beside it. We've told him about his uncle, the knight who saved his daddy. It's his favorite bedtime story, especially the part where he takes his mommy to the ball.

We miss him every day. But the memories are sweeter now. Less painful. I still feel him. In the rays of the early morning light. In the smell after a rainstorm. In the gentle rhythm against my cheek when I snuggle with Maverick at night.

He's still here.

He never left.

Pushing to his feet, Maverick chases AJ in retaliation, picks him up, and throws him in the air. AJ's giggles ring throughout the yard, and I catch myself smiling in wonder.

At the life I was gifted with. At the pieces and how perfectly they fell into place to get me here.

When Mav leans closer and whispers something in his ear, AJ stops wiggling, looks at me, and nods.

I know this look. It's sneaky. And mischievous. And *so* Maverick, it's not even funny.

"Boys," I warn.

"We're not doing anything. Right, AJ?" Maverick asks him.

"We not doing anything, Mommy," he agrees, but those big baby blues are gleaming with mischief.

With a grin, Mav swings him over his shoulder, grabbing a couple of water balloons and handing them to our son, casually walking over to me. I give him a pointed look before looking up at our little boy. Most people say he looks like his daddy, but I know better. He has Archer's eyes. His sweetness. His thoughtfulness.

"Archer," I warn.

AJ's smile widens. He lifts his ammunition above his head and pops the balloon on his daddy's head.

"Hey!" Maverick yells. His voice is full of laughter as he yanks AJ off his shoulders and starts tickling him. "You were supposed to throw it at Mommy, not me!"

"I her knight, Daddy!" he argues, attempting to squirm away from his daddy's punishment while his boisterous laughter pierces the air. "You her clown!"

I laugh even harder. He meant jester, but clown? Yeah, it's even more perfect.

"See?" AJ giggles. "Mommy smiling."

Mav stops his assault on our son, rests him on his hip, and wraps his arm around my waist, tugging me into him. "You find this funny, huh?" He shakes the water clinging to his hair like a dog, letting it rain on my face and hair.

"Hey!" I smack his chest and try to pull away from him until he stops teasing me.

With a quick kiss to my forehead, he murmurs, "Love you, Goose."

"Love you too."

"Love you, Mommy," AJ chimes in.

I rise onto my tiptoes and kiss his cheek. "Love you, baby."

Maverick's hand envelops my stomach. "Love you, little girl."

The End

ALSO BY KELSIE RAE

Kelsie Rae tries to keep her books formatted with an updated list of her releases, but every once in a while she falls behind.

If you'd like to check out a complete list of her up-to-date published books, visit her website at www.authorkelsierae.com/books

Or you can join her newsletter to hear about her latest releases, get exclusive content, and participate in fun giveaways.

Interested in reading more by Kelsie Rae?

The Little Things Series

(Steamy Don't Let Me Next Generation Series)

(Steamy Contemporary Romance Standalone Series)

A Little Complicated

Don't Let Me Series

(Steamy Contemporary Romance Standalone Series)

Don't Let Me Fall - Colt and Ashlyn's Story

Don't Let Me Go - Blakely and Theo's Story

Don't Let Me Break - Kate and Macklin's Story

Let Me Love You - A Don't Let Me Sequel

Don't Let Me Down - Mia and Henry's Story

Wrecked Roommates Series

(Steamy Contemporary Romance Standalone Series)

Model Behavior - River and Reese's Story

Forbidden Lyrics - Gibson and Dove's Story

Messy Strokes - Milo and Maddie's Story

<u>Black Jack</u>

<u>Royal Flush</u> - Download now for FREE

Stand Alones

<u>Fifty-Fifty</u>

Sign up for Kelsie's <u>newsletter</u> to receive exclusive content, including the first two chapters of every new book two weeks before its release date!

Dear Reader,

I want to thank you from the bottom of my heart for taking a chance on *A Little Complicated*, and for giving me the opportunity to share their story with you.

I know I probably ripped your heart out throughout this book, and I wish I could climb through these pages and give you a big bear hug. I shed a lot of tears while writing *A Little Complicated*, and I want you to know that I love Archer just as much as you do, so I can only imagine how much this story left you feeling raw.

I'm not going to lie, I've been wanting to write Ophelia's, Archer's, and Maverick's story for years, but I was TERRIFIED of what my readers (YOU) would think. I was terrified of hurting you. Of losing your trust in providing the happily-ever-afters you've come to expect from my stories. Of making you second-guess picking up a Kelsie Rae book ever again. (Please say this isn't true!)

But this story...I couldn't *not* write it. I don't know how to explain it, but it's true. I could've made this story a thousand pages, starting with the beginning of Maverick's secret relationship with Ophelia, and ending with a sweet proposal I can't wait to write one day. But for now, you get the good, the bad, and the ugly center, along with a glimmer of hope. Of acceptance. Of learning to appreciate the little things. The stolen moments. The bittersweet miracles this life has to offer.

I want you to know that the rest of this series will be much more lighthearted (like my previous books) and I'll do my best to mend your broken hearts as well as Maverick's and Ophelia's, though I have a feeling my work is cut out for me. :)

As always, I would be very grateful if you could take the time to leave a review. It's amazing how such a little thing like a review can be such a huge help to an author!

Thank you so much!!!

I seriously couldn't do this "author gig" without you.

-Kelsie

ABOUT THE AUTHOR

Kelsie is a sucker for a love story with all the feels. When she's not chasing words for her next book, you will probably find her reading or, more likely, hanging out with her husband and playing with her three kiddos who love to drive her crazy.

She adores photography, baking, her two pups, and her cat who thinks she's a dog. Now that she's actively pursuing her writing dreams, she's set her sights on someday finding the self-discipline to not binge-watch an entire series on Netflix in one sitting.

If you'd like to connect with Kelsie, subscribe to her Patreon. Patrons receive a wide range of goodies including:

- Exclusive sneak peeks of works-in-progress
- ebook releases one week early
- Special edition signed paperbacks on all new releases
- So much more

You can also sign up for her newsletter, or join Kelsie Rae's Reader Group to stay up to date on new releases and her crazy publishing journey.

Printed in Great Britain
by Amazon